"LOOSE ME! YOU WOULD NOT BE SO CRUEL—"

He laughed. "Does this feel cruel, Shalyn?" he whispered against her ear as his hands began a sensuous caress down the small of her slender back.

She gasped at the sudden hot fire it caused, a rush of warmth through her loins, tingling up through her chest. It confused her as nothing else could, her startled eyes lifting to his face with a demand that he explain it.

"Shalyn." He said her name in a sudden husky whisper of his former voice. "Here Shalyn, I am going to kiss you."

He kissed her once, then again, his warm, firm lips as gentle and light as a feather's tease. Then he kissed her once more, a kiss that showed her the inspiration of the poetry she loved.

"Do we like that, Shalyn? Do we?"

*If You've Enjoyed This Book,
Be Sure to Read These Other*
AVON ROMANTIC TREASURES

COMANCHE WIND *by Genell Dellin*
FORTUNE'S MISTRESS *by Judith E. French*
HIS MAGIC TOUCH *by Stella Cameron*
A ROSE AT MIDNIGHT *by Anne Stuart*
THEN CAME YOU *by Lisa Kleypas*

Coming Soon

MASTER OF MOONSPELL *by Deborah Camp*

VIRGIN STAR

JENNIFER HORSMAN

An Avon Romantic Treasure

AVON BOOKS ◆ NEW YORK

VIRGIN STAR is an original publication of Avon Books. This work has never before appeared in book form. This work is a novel. Any similarity to actual persons or events is purely coincidental.

AVON BOOKS
A division of
The Hearst Corporation
1350 Avenue of the Americas
New York, New York 10019

Copyright © 1993 by Jennifer Horsman
Published by arrangement with the author
Library of Congress Catalog Card Number: 92-97454
ISBN: 0-380-76702-3

First Avon Books Printing: July 1993

AVON TRADEMARK REG. U.S. PAT. OFF. AND IN OTHER COUNTRIES, MARCA REGISTRADA, HECHO EN U.S.A.

Printed in the U.S.A.

RA 10 9 8 7 6 5 4 3 2 1

For better or worse, this book is dedicated to Marjorie Braman, who sensed I held back humor, then innocently suggested otherwise.

And to Pesha Rubinstein, my agent, with loads of appreciation for all the many years of support and encouragement she has given me.

Chapter 1

London, England,
The year of our Lord, Eighteen twenty-three

The naked girl felt heavy in Jack Cracker's arms, a surprise, what with her eye-poppin' beauty and figure as slim and firm as a lad's, all wrapped up in a potato sack—the only cloth they could find. Despite the steady drizzle from gray skies, Jack felt sweat on his brow, but if truth be told, it owed itself to arms that rarely lifted anything heavier than the ale cups at the Fire Fox down on Port Street. "Wait up, Redman," he called in a whisper. "Wait."

The tall redheaded fellow stopped on command. Holding the girl's legs, he turned to see his friend drop the rest of the girl in the mud and stand bent over, hands braced on knees and breathing heavily.

Jack's breath came in small puffs, disappearing in the thick London mist. "I got to catch me breath."

Lowering the girl's legs, Redman looked up and down the long tree-lined, cobbled highway, darkening now at twilight. Not a soul about. Blue-blood streets be as empty as a graveyard.

Jack's grubby gloves, minus the fingers, wiped the rain from his face. "Lord, wh't I woodn't do for an edge off me thirst now." Muck oozed into his worn

1

boots, between his toes. He wondered if he'd get enough coin from the cap'n to buy a new pair.

A carriage raced past. A stream of mud splattered across their legs and the girl. "Curse ye to 'ell," Jack muttered, yet noticeably without enthusiasm. Too darn weary, he was.

"Eh, Jack!" Redman pointed. "Look up at that! Number four."

Jack looked over to see a large bronze number four hanging on the wall—he knew 'is numbers, 'e did, and so he figured 'twas only four or five more buildings. The slip o' paper said number nine, at least that's what the man said. He glanced at her hand, where they had returned the paper, tightly closing her bone cold fingers around it before lifting her up. He peered down the long street as if to see the ninth house. Not that he had to see it, for he knew about it. Everyone in all o' London knew 'bout Number Nine King's Highway. The Hanover House.

'Twas famous on account of its master, Cap'n Seanessy. Cap'n Seanessy ran the Far West fleet from London, ships that nearly supplied as much tea as the honorable East India Company itself, and ships that made the cap'n as rich as the King of Egypt. Lord, the stories told about the cap'n: fighting and blue-blood relations and all the women—'twas said there weren't a wench between thirteen and rocking chairs that didn't sizzle to hot butter at the sound of his name. Oh, the man be famous all right. Half the merchants of Fleet Street owed their livelihoods to him. Even the King owed him. For 'twas the cap'n who paid for six of his ships to be outfitted for war and speed, and then he sent them to join the King's navy in the royal effort to finally rid the Arabian waters of lecherous pirates, which they did. That was why the King's men never did nothin' when half the town watched the cap'n ride up on the great beige steed and shoot the executioner dead to save the three worthless young pickpockets from a hangin', or when he and his "boys," as they was called—the meanest men on the dock—took out some or another whole crew and for no more reason than they found offense with the way the blokes conducted business.

The cap'n was the law on the streets, he was.

For all of it though, the cap'n was said to be as generous as a bride's father on his youngest daughter's weddin' day. 'Twas this they be countin' on. For the beautiful girl belonged to the cap'n. They had showed the note to five people before one of 'em was able to read the letters. *Nine King's Highway*, it said. *Captain Seanessy.*

Redman wiped his face with a wet sleeve. Jack said the cap'n would be thankin' them with gold but—"I dunno, I dunno." He shook his head. "Jack, wh't if th' cap'n don't believe us? Wh't if 'e takes it to mind we be the bloody sons of sods who beat the poor lass or worse?" Slowly, in a frightened whisper: "Wh't if 'e thinks we took 'er rags off?"

Jack narrowed his eyes as if Redman had gone daft. "Do we look like blokes who'd strip an' beat a poor lass senseless? Where's yer 'ead, Redman?" He rubbed his fingerless gloved hands together. " 'Twill be rainin' silver, 'twill! Wh't I could do with a couple o' more bob in me pocket! Come on."

"I dunno," Redman shook his wet curls and wiped his face again. "I dunno . . ."

Yet Redman obediently leaned over and picked up the bundle of the girl's legs, while Jack bent and, with a heave, lifted the girl's shoulders. Sinking ankle-deep in mud, they made slow progress down the street of London's finest townhouses until at last they came to the tall iron gates of Hanover House.

For a long moment the two men stood at the gates opening to a wide gravel road, which led to the en-

trance hall. They stared with awe at the splendor of
the fine old house. Even in the impending darkness
the colossal structure looked as reputable as the
house next door, a house that belonged to the Duke
of Windsor, cousin of the King.

Hanover House had once belonged to the Fourth
Earl of Hanover and was large enough for that great
man's frequent entertaining of the entire English
court. The house rose up four stories—not including
the cellar or the attic where many of the twenty-
seven servants lived—and it reached half as wide as
a proper cricket field, all surrounded by parklike gardens and sky-high, ancient trees. Wild ivy covered
both sides of the house, its long green arms reaching
around the front as well. Four neat rows of shuttered
windows filled the high whitewashed frontage.

"Come on," Jack whispered. "Get on with it."

Worn boots crunched over the wet gravel of the
road. Jack noticed the garden grew wild and un-
tamed here—as if the gardeners had gone on a long
holiday. Bushes, hedges, and trees burst with rugged
green fecundity, though the neatly manicured lawn
stretched out like a smooth green blanket. A longshore boat sat beneath a silver maple tree. Jack stared
with incomprehension at the boat, parked like a carriage under the tree, wondering how in blazes it got
there. Many of the windows were open, despite the
steady drizzle against the thick brocaded curtains. A
cat watched their movement from one sill.

Jack's gaze fell on a discarded sword sticking up
out of the grass for no reason a mortal could figure.
A number of lawn sculptures represented queer animal shapes, ominous in the darkening light: a great
bird of prey with outstretched wings, a lion with an
open mouth of gleaming sculpted-marble teeth, a
huge monstrosity of a stag, its two-foot horns gar-
landed with blooming bloodred flowers.

Jack swallowed while Redman tried to pretend he did not see these terrors. They passed an abandoned carriage, one fine enough for a queen, left like a velvet-lined corpse in the rain. Jack's gaze arched up and over the ivy-covered exterior as, with a heave, they lifted the girl up the short flight of steps to the porch.

The two men eased their burden onto the wide portico. Jack removed his cap, slicked back his hair, and set the cap back, noticing the pagan figures carved into the broad, wooden double doors. Redman's gaze widened. "Jack, look." He pointed to a man's shirt pinned to the wall by a dagger.

Jack paused at the arresting sight. He waved a hand in dismissal as he tried hard to keep in mind the pocket of moneys and what that would be like. Taking a deep breath, he stepped up to lift the knocker shaped like a brass demon on the door. He glanced down at the tall barrel directly beneath the knocker. A cry rose in his throat as he realized first what the slithering creatures were, then that they were alive. He stepped away and turned. "Oh, God . . ."

Neither man looked back as he ran.

Lust, pure and powerful lust . . .

Seanessy felt it in force, and as he pushed one large foot into his tall black boots, he silently cursed the burning ache in his loins. A primitive call to the wild, he knew, and it always came with a vision of his ghostly lover, an imaginary woman he ridiculously compared all others to: with long dark hair that shrouded a larger-than-life, plump, voluptuous form; hair that framed dark blue bedroom eyes. He always imagined her lying in his bed like an invitation, beneath a transparent sheet that revealed round, full breasts and sumptuous curves a man could sink his hands into.

He abruptly groaned, "I need a woman."

A preposterous statement, and Kyler's bright dark eyes filled with a blend of outrage and humor as, with a practiced movement, he pushed the metal spike down the barrel of his pistole. He knew Seanessy well, knew that about the last thing Sean needed was another woman. "Like a dog needs another flea, you do."

For women, all women, from the King's niece, Lady Margaret de Bois, to the comely barmaids in Port Street's inns and taverns, swooned as Seanessy passed. It was not just his handsome good looks: his shoulder-length blond hair that framed a unusually long thin face, the dark brows arching dramatically over widely spaced hazel eyes, his strong fine nose, and wide sensuous lips. Rather, his success with women owed itself also to the bounty of his wit and the wealth of his humor, a recklessness and excitement that bordered precariously on danger.

Seanessy owned a notorious and much-deserved reputation with the ladies, and while he loved the fair sex a good deal more than most men, or at least a good deal more often, he rarely, if ever, entertained any lady in an upright position. Despite many subtle and not so subtle invitations otherwise, Sean valiantly steered away from any entanglements, exercising a trenchant preference for the working wenches, relationships that started and ended quickly, "unambiguous liaisons that I can neatly, happily, and conveniently sever with a pound note."

Seanessy liked his women fast and loose.

Kyler rose to go to the window. In boots he stood a half-inch shorter than Seanessy, a good half-foot taller than most tall men, wide of shoulder and wider of girth, his formidable size crowned by a head as bald as a robin's egg. He peered at the drizzle falling over the front gardens, looking for Butcher and the horses. "Isn't Doreen upstairs? And I thought I saw Molly last night."

"Ah! Well, the lovely ladies had to depart. Molly had to interview two new girls. And Doreen has a performance at the theater tonight, didn't you know?"

"You won't have to feel bad when you miss it, Sean."

Merriment, as it oft did, danced in Seanessy's eyes as he stood to his full height and reached for his well-worn shoulder harness. "Why's that?"

"Bess and I saw Doreen's Desdemona Tuesday night. In case you had any doubts, the lovely Doreen did not land the role for her acting talents."

Seanessy harbored no illusions about Doreen's illustrious talents. "Fortunately," he said, smiling as he deftly began working the leather straps, "she has all those other talents to fall back on."

"Fall back on. Right." Kyler nodded, amused despite himself, as Seanessy called out for his new butler.

Sean's voice sounded through the old house, and more than one servant gave a start. He moved through the reading room, one of the three drawing rooms that looked onto the black-and-white-checkered marble squares of the entrance hall, and called out again at the open double doors. "Charles, you rascal, where the devil are you?"

The spacious, two-story foyer was at the front of the tall building, rising above the neat manicured lawns, and no doubt its architect had intended the grand space as a greeting area for distinguished soirees, parties, and balls. Seanessy had never held a soiree, much less hosted a ball. He had bought the house for its sheer size and convenient location to the port, and then only after the owner of the distinguished Connaught Hotel politely and obsequiously objected not to Captain Seanessy—heavens no!—but to his insistence on housing his lively and ribald officers within the Connaught's plush apartments.

The objection came after one of Sean's officers bought the favors of Madam Bushard's entire whorehouse for the Connaught guests. Patrons of the Connaught still talked about that night, remembering it with outraged curses or fond amusement, depending wholly upon the gentleman's inclinations and whether he had received the favors of one of the ladies. Yet the commotion brought by Slyers's singular generosity forced Seanessy to concede that private housing might be best suited for "the boys."

So he bought the historic Hanover House.

The most conventional use ever made of the grand entrance hall was the time Seanessy and one of his ladies played out an engaging game of chess on its checkered marble floor. The housemaids stood in for the lady's white pieces, while the gardeners and grooms stood in for his black. Seanessy was a master chess player, iconoclastic and nearly unbeatable, and he would have won if the treacherous maids had not cheated for the lady every time he turned his back.

Cursing silently, Sean gave up calling for the butler, cursing Tilly for having hired him—" 'cause 'e goes to my church, ye see"—and he turned to Kyler.

"Sir?" A proper accent sounded at his back.

Sean swung around to confront the older man. "Curse you, Charles! You move like a ghost through walls, but only after I give up calling your Christian name and start cursing your mother."

"Completely unnecessary, I'm sure. She has after all been dead all these long years; one could hardly expect the good woman to answer your summons. Perhaps, though"—he grinned widely—"I might be of help?"

A contrived smile and all farce, which Seanessy noticed. "Charles, you are full of more pretenses than an aging and fat whore. Now where's my cloak? It's still raining out there. I do have a cloak?"

"I'm sure I have no idea," the butler answered.

"Well, I'm making it your life's extraordinary mission to find out. And if I do have a cloak, I know you will be good enough to bring it to me."

"Indeed." Charles quickly withdrew, as silently as he had come.

Seanessy picked up one of his pistoles from the polished mahogany table, a table, Tilly kept reminding him, that was meant to hold gold-engraved cards and a jeweled glove box, "not a man's armaments." He checked the fuse, a routine procedure ever since his last butler—not really a butler but rather a crew member filling in until Tilly could hire a properly trained manservant—fired one of his pistoles at a large white rat. The bullet hit the rat, then ricocheted off the decorative knight's armor nearby to blow a hole in the portrait of sober-eyed Thomas More. The seaman set the pistole back down on the mahogany foyer and forgot the incident.

The next day as Seanessy rode through Covent Garden on his way out of town, he had come upon five brutes beating a young woman to the ground. Needless to say, the empty round he fired did little to deter the beasts. He had had to dismount and do the business by hand, which he would not have minded so much if not for the two daggers, a cracked bottle, and a rusty pipe they used. For his trouble he had received a neat slice across his arm and a ripped shirt, and he had almost missed the fourth birthday party for his nephew, little Sean.

He slipped the pistole into his shoulder harness. The night promised better than even odds of seeing it fired. They were first meeting with Keegan O'Connell, the leader of the Irish rebels, then they were to meet with none other than Robert Banks Jenkinson, Second Earl of Liverpool and Prime Minister of these merry ole shores. O'Connell no doubt wanted guns and money, while Earl—Seanessy's affectionate nickname for the man, one that never failed to irritate him—no doubt wanted guns as well, the larger kind that came attached to a fast and sleek clipper or frigate. The earl would get a flat no, while O'Connell—bless his Irish heart—would receive, as he always did, the full benefit of Sean's generosity.

For Seanessy was many things, but all flew beneath the green and white banner of Ireland. As the unlikely product of an illicit mating between an Irish peasant woman and Patrick Shaw, a rebel priest, Seanessy, like all his countrymen, owned a deeply felt love and passion for the Emerald Isle, despite the many fine trappings bought by his numerous relationships among the English aristocracy. One of these relationships was that of half brother to Lord Ramsy Barrington, for while Ram claimed the Barrington title, the identity of his real father was Patrick Shaw as well.

If O'Connell knew any one thing, it was how to exploit an Irishman to the cause of a free Ireland. Exploit them he did. All O'Connell, indeed all any Irishman wanted was a free Ireland. The first step was parliamentary representation in the English Parliament, with the fervent hope that someday this would lead to reinstitution of an Irish parliament and a separate country at last.

Sean wanted it as much as any Irishman living.

Watching the captain don the long cloak Charles finally brought, Kyler mused, "I doubt you'll convince Keegan of the wisdom of patience."

"You are no doubt right," Seanessy said. "The man's as stubborn as a mule looking uphill."

"Like yourself Sean—'tis the Irish curse." Through the window Kyler caught sight of Butcher—one of Sean's first mates—and a groom bringing around their mounts. "Here's Butcher now."

"Dear Lord, is there a personage in our midst with the unconventional name of"—Charles forced himself to pronounce it, and did so with an incredulous lift of brow—"Butcher?"

"Don't look so alarmed, Charles." Sean slapped the old gent's back as he opened one side of the wide doors. "I'm sure the good man earned the name by a conventional use of the knife."

"Oh, aye." Kyler chuckled behind Sean. "A regular meat monger, he was."

"Meat monger?" Seanessy pretended surprise. "I was sure he told me he had been a tree pruner."

"A tree pruner, of course," Charles said, as if this were very likely. Though nothing in this house was very likely; indeed everything fell into one of three categories: fantastic, inconceivable, and absolutely unbelievable. Like the sheer volume of unattached females. Or the numerous oddities like the barrel of live snakes at the door, put there amid much humor the last time a group of religious zealots got past soft-hearted Tilly to interrupt the captain's supper hour. Of course the most outrageous aspect of this house was the wild men who apparently made up Captain Seanessy's crew, men Seanessy affectionately called "the boys," an ill-fitting title for the dozens of barbarians who roamed this grand old house.

Men like Butcher, Charles saw as he stepped out behind Seanessy and Kyler. His gaze focused on the unlikely form of this meat monger or tree pruner.

Raven-black hair and a thick beard, a man as large as any person's worst nightmare. His face appeared badly scarred too, no doubt the result of his illustrious career hashing about with sharp objects. A number of archaic sabers hung from his wide black belt, this last fitted around animal pelts that only a savage could consider high fashion.

Charles pretended to look impassive, turning from Butcher to the captain himself. The unconventionally tall man had a startling, frightening, and yet somehow utterly imperial appearance; to see him once was to remember him always. Today he wore gray riding pants, tall black boots sporting gold spurs, a loose-fitting white cotton shirt, a loose neck cloth and a wide belt, covered in the long black cape that billowed out behind him. A wide-brimmed black hat topped his shoulder-length blond hair like a crown.

Charles placed his white-gloved hands behind his back, watching as Seanessy took hold of the reins of the enormous beige stallion. The wild steed turned in fast hard circles until Seanessy managed to pull him up. Yet Seanessy's hazel eyes abruptly focused hard on Charles, who straightened instinctively. "Charles, what the devil's that?"

Charles turned to see it. Despite his certainty that not a thing more could shock him, his face paled as he realized what it was. "Why, it appears to be a dead person." A brow raised, he looked rather dispassionately back at Seanessy. "Shall I send for the gravedigger's cart?"

Alarming words. Seanessy dismounted, handing his reins to the waiting groom before rushing up the steps to kneel at the side of the body. Butcher and Kyler followed.

Seanessy gently turned it toward him. Strong hands pulled the sackcloth apart to reveal a thick long stream of wet gold hair over a face. "My God, it's a child!"

He swept aside a good foot-long rope of hair. The hair was as thick with curls as a Negro's hair but colored dark gold, matted and bloodied about her head. Thin black brows arched over her closed eyes. Mud covered the deathly pallor of her pale skin.

Butcher took one look before swearing, "Good Lord! Seanessy, you are the only man I know who when he gets a bedraggled and beaten lass dropped on the doorstep, she turns out as comely as a queen's jewel box. A little frail and too young, I see, and look at that bump!" He shook his head sadly. "May God damn the villain who did it."

Kyler asked, "Is she still alive?"

Sean laid a gentle finger against her mouth. He could not tell. He lowered his head to her chest, catching the faintest trace of a musky perfume, so incongruent with the battered, seemingly lifeless form. The faintest beat of her life remained. "Aye."

"Who the hell could she be?"

A powerful feeling washed over Seanessy as he stared down at the comely child, and this premonition was neatly summed up in the one phrase: "Trouble, that's who," he answered, irritated now, wondering just how much trouble she would be and if he could possibly avoid it. "Curse the blasted luck. Well, maybe I can give her back. Kyler, round up some boys and try to find the whoresons who dropped her off—they can't be far. Butcher, go and fetch Toothless. She looks like she needs more than a bit of patching up. He should be at the Bear's Inn and if not there, try Lord Huntington's. And meet us over there." Because of Charles's presence, he did not say the name of the tavern where they were to meet O'Connell and his rebel outlaws. O'Connell was wanted by each and every redcoat, and if ever caught, he would no doubt be executed on the spot. Although Charles was probably no more than what he appeared to be—an aging manservant with absolutely no political interest or persuasion—Sean still did not know yet if he could trust him. "We're already late."

"Aye, aye."

The two mates stepped quickly out in the misty rain, mounted, and kicked gold spurs to their horses—all Sean's men wore the ancient symbol of chivalry. Sean swept the girl up into his arms, and knowing Charles would be absolutely useless in this situation, he called out to Tilly, his favorite and so often his salvation. For Tilly, bless her grating, sensitive soul, loved nothing more than caring for and tending the multitudes of stray waifs and cats and beggars littering the streets of London.

Carrying two bowls of goat's milk for her cats, Tilly stepped into the hall from the kitchen when she heard the rich timbre of the master's voice. "Oh, no, trouble; I can always tell," she said in a whispered rush as she set the bowls down in the hall. With a sweep of her long black skirts, she ran into the spacious lower gallery, appearing in the entrance hall just as Sean and Charles entered.

"There you are," Sean greeted his head housekeeper. He knew the good woman's penchant for charity was nearly as bad as Butcher's; the girl would be fussed over and nursed like a babe. As if he offered a present, Seanessy said, "Tilly dear, look what I found for you!"

The plump, middle-aged woman took one look and gasped. "My Lord! What is it—"

"Your new pet, Tilly," he explained, stopping as Tilly came close to see. "I found her on the portico."

"Good 'eavens! What 'appened to 'er?"

"I don't know. I don't want to know—that's where

you come in." Seanessy moved toward the staircase.
"Butcher left to fetch Toothless. He'll patch her up,
and it will be your duty to nurse her back to health
and good spirits, give her a bag of coins and some
motherly advice about the company she's been keeping, and send her home."

"Oh, Lord, the poor thing, the poor, poor thing."
Tilly rushed after him, stopping to tell Charles and
two maids to fetch hot water bottles and bandages.

Seanessy waited impatiently through Tilly's quick
orders. "Now," he said, looking down the long gallery, "where should I put her? What room is farthest
from my apartments?"

Seanessy headed up the east staircase.

"Well, we just had the east wing waxed today—
quite a chore 'twas too—"

Seanessy turned from the east wing rooms.

"And the upper gallery rooms be nearly all taken
with th' boys this week, and la!" She imagined the
crewmen mistaking the girl for one of the "others"—
the numerous women who frequented the house and
still made her blush. The horror of the men making
that kind of mistake made her grab her heart.
"Wouldn't do to set her among yer men now, would
it?"

Seanessy stopped at the staircase and in a pretense
of patience said, "Tilly, what room should I put her
in?"

"Well, if ye ask me and I believe ye did, then I
would say the green room, 'tis lovely in the fall light,
an if'n I were an poor invalid tryin' to recover my
'ealth and spirits—"

"That's too close, Tilly—"

"Mercy, cap'n, mercy. Does th' poor, poor girl look
like she's goin' to be a bother to ye now? And
'twould be convenient for me as well, for I wouldn't

have to climb three flights to wait on 'er and I can sleep right next door—"

Listening no more to the good woman's unnatural verbosity, and against his better judgment, he ascended the opposite staircase and quickly swept down the hall past his apartments to the door of the green room. He crossed the carpeted space to the four-poster canopied bed against the far wall. Gently he laid the girl on its soft luxuriousness. Then he removed his hat and cloak and tossed them on a nearby chair.

Two servants rushed through the doors. Instantly Sean silenced their excited exclamations. They started a fire in the hearth and lit the lamps, flooding the room with golden light. Another two maids came in with bandages, washcloths, and a brass bowl filled with hot water.

Tilly dismissed the other servants to their tasks before coming to stand by Sean. Her chubby hands covered her face in a habitual gesture of shock. Though God knew this was not the first time a poor or lost soul had found the way to Hanover House for the captain's help and generosity in these dark days, it was, she realized with consternation, the first time anyone had been practically naked and unconscious. "I'm afraid to see the rest of 'er, I am. Do ye know the girl?"

Seanessy shook his head. He parted the wet potato-sack cloth, only to discover it was wrapped around the slender form many times over. Tilly turned to get scissors before she saw Seanessy had withdrawn a jeweled dagger. This was put to the cloth and he deftly cut a neat line down the length of it. With one hand lifting her limp form, and with Tilly's help, he pulled the wet cloth out from under her.

The young girl wore only a tattered and muddied chemise, the old-fashioned French kind. This, too, he

cut from her cold skin, but as Sean felt just how cold
she was, he whispered, "Tilly dear, we need those
hot water bottles."

"Aye, at once."

He parted the cloth to reveal the startling nudity.
His hand touched the vibrant silken skin along the
delicate lines of neck and well-formed slender shoulders, skin astonishingly tender and utterly feminine,
and his interested eyes widened as he took in the
round, flattened mounds of her breasts, the unexpected enticement of large coral-pink tips.

Not quite a child after all.

Yet there was ample evidence of a bad beating: a
bruise on her arm, and one purplish bruise on her rib
cage. She was as thin as a reed and as pale as porcelain, appearing, he thought, to stand on death's por-
tal.

Toothless might not be enough after all.

He leaned closer. His hand ran over the pink lines
just above one of the tempting peaks of her breast,
thinking them faint blood spots or perhaps a scar.
Why, how odd—

Sean's brows drew together as he saw his mistake.
A pink tattoo? On a woman? He looked closer still,
seeing the tiny diamond with a point inside, and an
odd-shaped face with two dots for eyes, one for a
nose, and a straight line for a mouth, all of it less
than thumb-sized.

Branded like a sheep. The child was marked!

Marked and beaten and all of her wet, dropped on
a stranger's doorstep to be used some more. She was
just a child too—no more than ten and six. His gaze
traveled down the length of her: over the slender
waist as tight and narrow as a boy's, past the feminine flare of her hips and down the lines of slim, impossibly long legs. She looked half-starved; he could
practically count her ribs. Thank God none of his

boys went for young innocents, even when they were not so innocent. "A good woman's like a fine bottle of port," Kyler once said to a crewman who took up with a fifteen-year-old. "You need a goodly few years to make the juices sweet."

Kyler entered with Tilly, who was holding three hot water bottles wrapped in cloth. "I got five men out searching for the bastards that dropped her off. How is she doing?"

Sean brought a luxurious pale green satin comforter over the girl as Tilly carefully positioned the hot water bottles around the cold form. Then she began wrapping the long wet hair in a towel, very careful not to touch the bloodied part. "La! That bump be th' size of a goose egg!"

"Aye," Sean said, "and look at her arms." He withdrew an arm from beneath the comforter, revealing the purple bruise. Kyler whistled, a sound of equal parts disdain and dismay at the scoundrel who had caused them. The whistle stopped midway as he abruptly spotted her tightly closed fist. He gently lifted her hand and pried her cold fingers open to see a tiny slip of paper. He focused on the name and address there.

"Take a look."

In neat letters was a name and address: *Seanessy. Nine King's Highway.* "A dramatic way of droppin' by for tea, she has."

"That is not the only oddity." Sean brought the comforter from her shoulder, leaving just enough for the girl's modesty, assuming she had some, of course, a rather generous assumption considering her circumstances.

"La! She be marked like a Dorset cow!"

Kyler almost laughed when he saw the tattoo. "Not the convent-bred, churchgoing type. Unless current ladies' fashions have changed recently to include tattooing bosoms."

"Oh no, Mister Kyler." Tilly shook her head. "Do not be so quick to judge now. She looks so lost and helpless—"

"And like a lot of trouble," Seanessy finished for her as he turned to retrieve his cloak and hat. "And, Tilly dear, when the child wakes and tells you a woeful tale of kidnappers or cruel fathers—or whatever!—what are you to do?"

"Why, I'll come right in and tell ye—"

The look on the captain's handsome face stopped her cold. She knew that look, a look somehow as powerful as a hard box to the ears. She turned hopeful eyes to Kyler.

Kyler was already moving through the door, disappearing in what he hoped was a prophecy of his future relationship with the girl. Now they were late for the meeting with O'Connell. There was no telling what the Irishman might do because of it.

Tilly had turned back to Seanessy. She thought of Mr. Butcher and the great bounty of his compassion. "Mister Butcher, mayhap?"

"Good!" Sean smiled approvingly and leaned over to kiss Tilly's cheek affectionately before withdrawing from the room. He swept down the well-lit hall, his cape billowing behind him as he took the stairs two at a time. He saw the lights were out in the entrance hall.

His left hand slipped into a pocket, emerging with brass knuckles, but otherwise not a muscle twitched in recognition of the would-be ambush waiting at the bottom of the stairs. As he came down, he saw the man stood to his right. Whistling a tune, he took one step into the entrance hall and swung around, hitting the man with a metal fist and enough force to knock down a fortified brick wall. A grunt sounded and the man fell to the marble squares. Seanessy heard the cocking of a pistole just as he felt the cold press of metal through the wool cloth in the dead center of his back.

O'Connell chuckled from a few feet away, hidden in the darkness near the place where two men held an irritated Kyler at gunpoint as well.

Seanessy's curses filled the space, loud and viciously; he swore at the outrageous Irishman as he extended an arm to help the poor fallen brute to his feet.

Keegan O'Connell just kept laughing. For a minute, maybe two, it seemed the more vicious Sean's curses sang, the louder Keegan laughed. The man loved nothing more than catching Seanessy off-guard, if only for a moment. "I told Carlin ye always led with the sinister paw but he did not see how ye kin after watchin' that fight last spring with yer left hand tied. Remember that, lad?"

Seanessy always fought in the ring with his left hand tied so as to prevent a death blow, and there had been many match fights in the ring. Yet he knew well which fight Keegan spoke of: a well-publicized fight between the Dublin champion and himself, with half of Ireland and a good portion of England to watch it. Neither of the two men was aware that Keegan had had the center of the ring greased beforehand, though God knew they discovered it quick enough. That fight was still talked about, and always with wild hoots and knee-slapping amusement.

"Blast ye, Keegan O'Connell!" Seanessy bit his lip to stop the sound of his amusement, as Keegan needed no encouragement. "My idea of heaven is a piece of green Irish field and nothing and no one between us—" In the same breath he demanded, "Why the hell are you sneaking in here covered by darkness?"

"Ah! I was just checkin' to see if you can still land on your feet, lad," O'Connell said by way of explanation, motioning to the men holding pistoles to back away. Lowering the metal weight in their hands, the men did. "You see, Sean boy, I was gettin' a little worried when you didn't show up. Now the Earl— bless his black tin heart!—knows full well your sterling reputation for keeping appointments with the bloody redcoats." The famous redheaded man laughed. "And you see dear ole' Earl be more anxious than a fair virgin on her wedding night to pass words with you before the boys ship out to the jeweled coast of Malacca. I reasoned Earl'll give up waiting within the next bell and arrive here with a dozen soldiers and a bloody gold-engraved card. I wanted to be first."

Sean chuckled as he crossed the short space to embrace his friend. "I wouldn't be surprised if you knew the exact time and day Wilson swives the upstairs maid."

" 'Tis a scullery wench, lad!" Keegan appeared to be quite shocked that Seanessy didn't know this as he reached up to slap Sean's back. "Aye, the ole man takes his John Thomas to the ace Tuesday evenings when the good wife is at Bishop Westminster's charity seminar. And get this, lad—the man likes it the Irish way!"

The men laughed uproariously, all but Kyler, who was not Irish and had no idea what the Irish way was. Keegan settled down and waved his hand in dismissal. "Ah, lad, information and sacks of cold Irish potatoes, 'tis all an Irishman has these dog days. How fare thee, Seanessy?"

Sean exchanged ribald greetings with the other men. Kyler sighed, wondering when he would get used to the Irishman's calling card as he glanced out the dark windows. If Wilson and men headed to Hanover House—and Kyler had learned never to doubt any of Keegan's information—the last thing they needed was for Wilson to find the Irish rebel here. He opened the door to the study and said, "Step inside and away from the open windows."

Sean slapped the short heavyset man on his back again as the group of seven men filed into the study. The door shut. Sean reached into a nearby drawer and withdrew a bottle of the finest Irish whiskey to be had and the glasses to hold it, glasses made of Irish crystal—cut with the same precision and craftsmanship as a king-sized diamond. He tossed one glass hard and fast. O'Connell caught it and set it on the table with a clink. As Sean filled his glass with the liquid gold, Keegan asked, "You heard about the trouble, have you?"

"Aye," Sean said as he poured his own and handed the bottle to Kyler to pass around. "Jaime and his clan are giving you a lot of noise."

"More than just noise, lad. Two of Jaime's lads pulled guns on the steps of Saint Michael's last week." He shook his head. "Four dead, Sean."

Seanessy stared into Keegan's fine eyes, grief and regret exchanging without words. Ireland was being torn in two: on one side was O'Connell, the great and moderate barrister who sat before him, a man who wanted to work toward a free Ireland within the English Parliament—and on the other side, a new breed of Irishmen who would wait peacefully no more, a faction of men who just wanted to wash the land in blood.

" 'Tis bad enough spilling the blood of the goddamn redcoats, but I'll be damned to Hades if it goes down Irish against Irish. The whole isle will be awash in enough blood to change the color of the

North Sea. 'Tis come to this: I've got to give them something. I've got to have something to show them we are gaining ground. So it all comes back to you, Seanessy. I need you. I need you like never before."

"Aye," Sean said, and every man in the room knew how much he meant it.

"I need ye to get one seat in Parliament by next term."

Sean stared as if he hadn't heard right. "You what?"

The outraged aristocratic breeding in Seanessy's tone was enough to scare half the entire English serving class, a tone that utterly defied his modest origins and spoke instead of Oxford, a blood relationship with Barrington Hall, the very boots on his feet that were worth more than most Irishmen's annum. "Why not just ask me for the King's crown? Keegan, you fool—I may play chess with Jenkinson on occasion, or even wager on the polo field with the King's brother, but I doubt—"

"You know who's coming with Jenkinson tonight, don't you?"

Seanessy almost lost the mouthful of whiskey. "And you do? I haven't a clue. I rather thought Jenkinson just wanted to borrow a ship or two, is all. Who is it?"

"Lord Robert Clives."

Surprise lifted on the handsome features of Seanessy's face. "Robert Clives?" The man was none other than the chief of the honorable East India Company itself, a title that might as well be Sole Proprietor of India. Sean knew him well, knew everything about him, except what the man might want from him. "And I suppose you can also tell me why."

"The why." Keegan took a long draught of the hot Irish liquid. "The why of it is the little problem he be havin' with the devil's trade."

"The opium trade?"

"Aye, lad. Opium. India opium or 'post' is the only thing that poor bloody country has. Worse off than our own rocky west coast, 'tis. Our dear Mister Clives made his fortune by forcin' the Indian seed into the Chinaman's blood and then—if this is not proof of justice in the world!—he lost his own soul to the addiction. Even an Irish bob like me feels sorry for the wretch."

After years in India running the East India Company, whose main business consisted of trading India's opium for China Black—the tea preferred by most Englishmen—Robert Clives developed a monstrous addiction to the potent rot himself. Though God knew Clives wasn't the only one in the upper ranks of the English caste system to suffer an addiction, despite the fact that it was once thought of as the scourge of the faceless multitudes.

Despite very vocal protestations from the London press, Seanessy did not see opium addiction as much of a problem. Clives and his kind were a case in point. Opium addiction was less of a concern than the drunks cluttering the alleyways, especially as long as the opium addict had access to a cheap steady supply. True, there was no more pathetic sight than a mother trading her starving children's bread for a dram of laudanum, but there were probably ten times more gin babes than opium infants. For the poor masses he'd pick opium over alcohol hands down.

This was not the issue, however. "So what does our dear friend want?"

"Help, is what," O'Connell said, explaining. "You see, there's a new Frenchman."

"A new Frenchman?"

"They say his name is the Duke de la Armanac." O'Connell pronounced the French with a flawless accent that spoke of his religious training for the priesthood, training that disappeared the day he met a young girl with blue eyes and laughter even quicker than his own—Corey, his wife.

"Armanac . . ." A memory of a conversation with his brother emerged in Sean's mind and he said, "Ram mentioned the man last June when I was in Malay. He owns title to a fair-sized island in the South China Seas, about fifty miles from the Malacca Straits. Ram was having our agents investigate him—"

"Aye, the man has come from nowhere. Your agents won't find much. No one knows anything about him but that his family fled France during the bloody purges of their revolution. He bought up a fair portion of the poppy fields in Turkey."

Sean whistled. "No more potent rot in the world."

"Aye. And the Chinamen prefer it, there's the problem. The man has a fine fleet of ships to move it into his little island out there. They call it the Isle of Blue Caverns. The lads in the know say it's the new Linton Isle."

Linton Island was the very center of the opium trade into China. Opium was illegal in China, which suited the opium traders, men like Clives, just fine, as it kept prices outrageously high and opium shipments untaxed.

"All bad enough, but word has surfaced that the duke's been buyin' up sizable chucks of opium for five bloody years, that his little isle is stockpiled high to God's own heaven, and that he means to dump it all on the market soon."

Seanessy and Kyler exchanged awed stares; Kyler swore softly. This would ruin the honorable company like no apocalypse ever could. The price of opium would drop to the bottom, collapsing the company, and with it, a portion of England's economy.

"Listen to this, lad. The duke keeps a standing army of two thousand there, and I reason Clives wants a favor from you, a favor that has to do with this opium stockpile and you and your boys' well-known reputation for handling fireworks—"

A knock sounded at the door. Four men withdrew pistoles as they backed into cover, but Keegan just laughed. "That will be for me. Time's up."

Seanessy ignored Keegan, and with pistole in hand, he called out from behind the door, "Yes?"

"Sir." Charles's whisper came from behind the door. "Horses outside. Redcoats all around. I believe the Prime Minister of England has arrived."

Seanessy threw open the door. For one brief and fleeting moment he met Charles's impassive gaze with the surprise of his recognition. So Charles worked for Keegan too! Probably half the servants in his house were feeding Keegan information. Little wonder the man not only knew what night Wilson lay with a serving wench but his angle of preference.

The four Irishmen filed out of the room, disappearing down the darkened gallery of the lower hall. Keegan came last. "Keegan," Seanessy demanded. Suppose Earl wants me to blow up this Frenchman's stockpile of opium. Why do they imagine I will do this favor for them?"

"I haven't a single notion lad." Keegan laughed. "I only know 'tis about time you made the bloody sods pay for what they want. Payment in the form of a parliamentary seat for a good Catholic Irishman." He patted Sean's cheek. "And for God's sake, keep yer naggin' toothache from the poor lass upstairs"—toothache being an Irish euphemism for another kind of pain, one very familiar to Seanessy. O'Connell laughed again. "From what I hear, she's in pretty bad shape as she is."

For one brief moment Seanessy did not know

whom Keegan referred to. Then the image of dark gold hair and a comely face rose in his mind's eye, and with surprising clarity. Blast the girl to hell and back! The way things were going, she was going to be not just trouble but bad luck as well.

Somehow he knew it was only the beginning.

Chapter 2

A gray sky melted into a grayer sea. A light breeze blew over the crescent bay of a white sand beach, lifting her long, loosened hair and swirling it around her face. She raised her dressing gown and climbed down the cliff on to the water's edge.

The sand felt cool on her bare feet as she walked along, watching the ceaseless waves crash upon the shore. She loved the ocean. The ocean, with its power and rhythm, infinite and eternal, confronted one with the profound smallness of the personal world, and offered transcendence upon its shore. Transcendence she desperately needed.

An occasional wave washed warm water over her feet, tickling, and she remembered a time when she would have kicked a spray of salt water high overhead and laughed as she felt its cool drops fall upon her. Not now. There was no laughter in her world now.

Something stuck out of the sand ahead. Her heart started pounding. She looked closer. A round object rose from the wet sand. She held her breath as she cautiously approached it. Then suddenly it turned toward her and she screamed.

28

A human skull ...

"Help me ... Please, help me ..."

Dozing in a nearby chair, Tilly jerked awake. Her sleep-filled eyes searched the candlelit room but saw nothing amiss. Grabbing a taper by its brass holder, she rose from the chair and approached the bed where the young lady slept fitfully.

The poor, poor thing. She looked a comely sight in the candlelight, sleeping so soundly! Thank the Good Maker, the doctor could not foresee any permanent damage. A small mercy, that.

Who was she? A princess separated from her kingdom by a band of black pirates? A lost and helpless orphan changeling? "Well, no matter." Tilly smiled. "I'll see ye get back on yer feet in no time."

Tilly looked to the door. Perhaps she'd just catch a few minutes' slumber in the comfort of a bed. Surely she'd hear if the young lady awoke.

With candle in hand, Tilly swept from the room.

Someone was trying to kill her ...

As the dark phantoms chased her again and again, her breathing changed, coming deeper and quicker. Small beads of perspiration lined her brow. She ran for her life—

The girl woke with a start, bolting up in an enormous bed. Bright amber eyes took in her unfamiliar surroundings: the stormy seascape on the wall, rich mahogany furnishings on the smooth white marble squares of the floor, this covered with an elaborately woven carpet. An old marble hearth occupied nearly one whole wall directly in front of her. Dark green brocade and white gossamer drapes hung from the enormous canopy bed, drapes that perfectly matched the window curtains, and accented the paler green of the satin quilt.

Where was she?

Her dream came back to her, and with it, the panic. Someone was trying to kill her!

Her gaze flew to the night table at her side. A glass of warm milk and cheese, a fruit tray, and a candle. A man's shirt covered her naked form.

Where was she?

She tried to make sense of the unfamiliar splendor of the room. A tingling alarm raced through her in a dizzying wave of pure sensation.

Something was terribly wrong . . .

For a minute or an hour, she never knew, she searched for a clue or for understanding, not in the room but in her memory. She drew deep, even breaths, willing her heart to ease its frantic pace and forcing the tension from her body. She closed her eyes to the external reality of strange surroundings. She waited for the cloak of memory that guides one's consciousness.

She stared into a black velvet night, as she hoped for the illuminating light of recollection; she waited first with a deeply ingrained patience, then with increasing alarm as the darkness neither changed nor altered. Her mind's eye saw nothing but a void.

She opened her eyes. Nothing changed. She raised a hand slowly to her head, where she felt a large bump. This too was a void of sensation. No pain defined the apparent accident, and her ribs . . . She felt a slight soreness there, but it was slight indeed.

An instinctive brake pushed her panic back. She slipped from the bed, crossed the room with quiet steps, and opened the smaller of two doors to discover the wonder of an inside privy, which she used.

Where was she?

She emerged soundlessly, her every movement cloaked in an unnatural stillness as she crossed the room to the other door. The girl's silence and grace

spoke of a miracle, a miracle so complete, not even the
air seemed displaced by her movement. Her pale hand
gently pushed open the door leading from the room.

She stared into the grandeur and magnificence of a
house she had never before seen. She stood in the
middle of a long hall ending in a richly carpeted,
curved staircase that led down to the foyer at the end
of an entrance hall. Another hall, a row of rooms,
and a staircase were directly opposite, like a mirror
image. Nothing and no one stirred.

A palm went to her forehead, rubbing hard, as if to
stir her thoughts or memory. Where was this grand
place? What was going on here? Why was she here,
and what was she doing?

Someone was after her—

She looked down the long hall. She had to flee, to
run far away! Every instinct urged it, and quickly.

She needed clothes and money.

She retreated back into the room. A thorough
search failed to produce any clothes. Where were her
clothes? What were her clothes?

She did not panic, but stood poised, ready for fight
or flight. First get clothes, a pair of trousers and a
shirt, this large shirt if she could find no other. Then
escape. She had to escape, before it was too late.

Quietly she stepped into the hall again.

Voices floated up from below. She slipped back in
the doorway, listening and waiting.

"So what did Jenkinson and Clives want?"

" 'Twasn't the prime minister or Clives but Ram.
Ram sent a letter with Clives, if ye kin believe that.
Seanessy be explainin' it. There be trouble in Ma-
lacca."

"What kind of trouble?"

The voices drifted off. The prime minister? Clives,
she knew that name. Could he be referring to the
English Prime Minister? And Clives—Robert Clives

of the East India Company? Was this London? And if so, what in merciful heaven was she doing here?

Her heart began pounding as panic threatened to submerge her again.

She had to get out of here.

She slowly made her way down to the next door. It was unlocked. She slipped through and found herself in a drawing room. She surveyed the surroundings, looking for something familiar, but she found nothing in the spacious room. Not quite true, she realized, coming to stand before a Jean Auguste Ingres masterpiece, *Odalisque*. She knew that artist.

Where? Who had been with her? When?

She rubbed her forehead in distress as no answers emerged. She silently made her way to the other door. This too was unlocked. It opened into an enormous bedchamber. A breeze lifted the dark blue velvet curtains and the white gossamer gauze lining at the tall windows, and drew her gaze to the oversized canopy bed where a man lay. She moved closer to see the handsome blond giant sound asleep there. She did not know him.

Who was he? Was he the source of her danger?

Her gaze swung around the spacious room, past the enormous marble hearth, the rich carpet, and three chests of drawers. She looked up at the magnificent oil *Brittania* on the wall. The depiction of China and India kneeling to an Imperial Britannia pricked a spark of anger.

So like the English! Puffed-up cocks in a chicken coop, the British were, preening, full of self-importance and grandiose notions and utterly blind to the sly Oriental fox that sat waiting on its haunches, watching, ready to pounce . . .

She turned away. She spotted the dark blue chair. A pair of trousers, a thick black belt, and a shirt were draped over it. Boots had been placed neatly beneath. Her eyes darted to the nightstand nearby. A fruit bowl, pitcher, and goblet, and a folded letter alongside a jeweled dagger.

She did not need a dagger but no one would know that. She picked the knife up, then took the letter. She unfolded it and read past the formal preamble, names that meant nothing to her, except that apparently this man held a family relationship to an English lordship. She began reading:

August tenth, the year of our Lord, Eighteen twenty-three
My dear brother:
I try to imagine your surprise at finding Lord Clives in your house delivering this carefully penned and sealed letter from me. I can only say desperate times call for desperate measures. These are suddenly desperate times. By the time you receive these words we will be somewhere mid-Atlantic, sailing to Boston, and from there to Washington, where I will at last assume the position of ambassador. Seanessy, suddenly the quaint provincial society and bucolic setting of Washington seem a welcome and much-needed respite from the hot sun, the tangled web of intrigues of the tea and opium wars.

For Joy is threatened and I will not have that.
Two of our house servants were found dead, throats slit, the bodies placed in a queer kneeling position on the garden path where Joy is in the habit of walking. I do not have to describe the effect of this on Joy; you can easily imagine, knowing Joy's mindless dismissal of the conventions of her class and the intimacy she inspires from all people, especially her servants. She not only knew the man and woman well, but she

knew their families and gave language lessons to
their children in the mornings. At first I assumed
the murders the result of some secret family
feud: the kind of incomprehensible Oriental barbarism we British cannot hope to fathom. I put
my men on it of course and alerted the British
counsel, but not wanting to take the chance, I
made immediate plans to take Joy and our children away, a full two months sooner than we
had planned.

The day we were to hoist sail, even as our
trunks were being packed, the *North Star* was
blown up by Chinese dynamite, killing two of
our men and injuring another five. No warning.
No threat. Sean, the explosions occurred only
minutes after Joy, holding little Sean's and Joshua's hands, stepped down the plank.

I cannot say who is responsible for this, or
those persons would be lying in a pool of their
own blood this very minute. As you will quickly
deduce, the threat could be from literally any
one of a hundred different players in the opium
and tea trade: any one of the major tea merchants in China, any of the "post" dealers between India and China, any one of the ten Ho
Cong families. Sean, it could be the Emperor of
China himself for all I know. As I am certain
Clives is raving at this very moment, it might
also be one French Duke de la Armanac.

The Duke de la Armanac. She read the name twice,
then again. This name meant nothing to her, though
she knew both Lord Clives and many of the Ho
Cong families. All of China and the China Seas knew
the Ho Cong families. Chang Ki Pien might be Emperor of China, but only because the Ho Cong families did not want the ancient title. The ten families

ran every aspect of China; one could not so much as pass a passel of cold dirt without their approval, which came with a pretty price.

Searching for another clue, she continued reading:

Of this last possibility, I can only relate the details of our brief connection with the man and his island. As you might remember, I discussed with you that rumors had begun circulating last February regarding a shift in the opium trade to a man of French aristocracy: the Duke de la Armanac. Over the last five years the duke has bought huge quantities of Indian opium, then the Turkish opium fields, bit by bit, finally securing the largest acreage in Erzurum Hills and importing the potent seed to an island called the Isle of Blue Caverns. Rumors began claiming he was undercutting the company's choice opium again and again, and that the Ho Cong families, who feed the precious rot into the Chinamen's blood, preferred to deal with this French duke.

Rumors also claim he now has enough opium in reserve to dump it onto the market until the price drops out. If true, he can continue long enough to cause the collapse of the opium market and our very own honorable company. The company, as I'm sure Lord Clives will be telling you, claims the duke convinced the Ho Cong families to deal with him by playing their own games of ruthless, murderous intimidation. I never believed it. I was imagining our dear friend Clives dreamed these wild schemes and rumors while under the influence himself, desperate as he was for anything to maintain the company's opium monopolies in this region.

Of course, when these rumors first surfaced I had made our own discreet inquiries into the family name. Our agents discovered nothing of interest to me: de la Armanac is an old titled name of France, referring to an area near the Italian and Swiss borders before Napoleon. Apparently the family lost most of their vast lands in the Napoleonic purges. (I discovered this land is currently being considered for restoration, including the family title—they have high connections to the scoundrels of France's Chamber of Deputies, and a familial relationship to none other than Louis XVIII.) And it was during the bloody purges of the revolution that the family had purchased the Isle of Blue Caverns as a refuge from the blade of the guillotine, while initiating the Turkey opium production.

So when I received an invitation to the Isle of Blue Caverns, I accepted, naively thinking it was no more than a request for civilized society so wanting in this region. Last month we sailed into the isle's small port. It is an island of haunting natural beauty: calm bays on the leeward, a mountainous range covered in lush tropical foliage and violent seas on the windward. Inexplicably, much of the windward side of the island has been destroyed by fire and cutting, which the duke dismissed as malaria control—destroying "stagnant ponds, no more." Of course, this explanation is ridiculous; we learned the man uses his slave population in a quixotic quest for treasure—a long-ago lost Chinese pirate treasure rumored to be buried on his island. You are no doubt laughing at this, pleased as it is an indication of the kind of intelligence we are dealing with here.

I can not relate all of our strange impressions of this man, his lovely wife, and their island. The important facts are that he maintains a standing army of two thousand men, a slave population of at least a thousand. Nor can I attempt to describe all that happened during our short visit. The duke was cordial, urbane, and, like so many others of his kind, grandiose with the absurd pretensions of a dying aristocracy. We finally reached a point in our conversations—conversations already a bit strained by the duke's conventional response to my wife's well-exercised intelligence and its articulation—where he began inquiring into our Malacca trade operations, the number of our ships, agents, and merchants, and the outrageous tariffs we endure, a conversation that traveled to our increasingly potent attack in the China Black tea war in England, how the Chinese were beginning to reap rather severe repercussions of the new competition for the rich prize of the insatiable English tea palate.

I didn't see where the pointed conversation was leading until he at last made an offer—a shockingly blunt offer to buy us out. At first I imagined it was a poor attempt at humor but then actual numbers fell from his mouth. Five hundred thousand pounds for our Malacca shipping trade and routes. Of course I laughed rather too long and hard at his arrogance. He gave no sign whatsoever of any hostility when, still amused and wishing like hell you were with me to enjoy this spectacle, I declined. I put the whole matter down to poor breeding and the endless delusions of French aristocracy.

Until the murders and the explosion.

While I do not have proof that they were the ruthless conceit of one Duke de la Armanac, he is well-known for employing these persuasive tactics. Joy and I discussed certain impressions and encounters that left us—and indeed all my crew—with the idea that the island hides a dark secret. I know you, Sean: you will want to shoot him first and wonder about his guilt later. If you do manage to discover some small measure of prudence and determine his guilt—an enormous if, I know—I leave it to you to demonstrate the consequences of threatening us. We can take no chances with Joy's life.

If, indeed, the duke is responsible for the murders and explosion, the next task will neatly complement Clives's and the Earl's request for assistance, assistance only you can provide. The Earl has offered us four years' shipping free of British tariffs in return for destroying the opium stockpile on the island—one good explosion should do the job. Conveniently the duke intends on spending the fall season in London, and he will be there by the time you read this. A small amount of ingenuity should land an invitation to the island. Our dear friend Clives will be able to tell you more.

In consideration of the wealth of your love for Joy and our children: as you will need to be assured, the girl who loves freedom has lost hers; she does not leave the reach of my arms, and as her enthusiastic guard, I will not leave her side, or place her in a position of danger until the matter is completely, wholly resolved.

To the tradition of our toss, you win the pleasure.

Yours,
Ram

She set down the disquieting letter. The South China Seas. Malacca. Malay. Penang, where the Brit-

ish fought the Dutch for control of the ports, while
the Orientals quietly went about their lives and business. Tea plantations. Aye, she knew these places. She
knew of the opium trade. She knew Malacca. She
knew the English outpost there, the Tampin River,
the dangers and beauty of the jungle, washed for
months in a deluge brought by the monsoons. 'Twas
where she was from—so maybe there was a reason
for her being in this house. She had lived there, but—

When? What was she doing here in London?

Malacca. In her mind's eye she saw the mountain
range rising from the crystal-blue lagoons, crescent
bays and swamps, the island covered by an impenetrable jungle populated by deadly snakes, screaming
monkeys, and spiders the size of fists. She knew the
beautiful English settlement made of sun- and rainwashed white stucco buildings and mansions, and
the native township of Tunku Hamzah alongside.
'Twas where she had to return. Somehow she knew
she had to get back to Malacca.

She felt the swift racing of her heart; she must get
on with it. She examined the clothes over the chair.
Too large. Curse it! She stepped quietly into the room-
sized clothes closet. Boots lined the floor. The man had
enormous feet! She searched through the finely tailored clothes: cotton and silk shirts, a number of coats,
short sack and formal, a riding cape, and dozens of
trousers, all of them huge. Nothing she might wear
without drawing more attention than if she were bare-
skinned.

Had the degenerate undressed her, then hid her
clothes?

Her hands went clammy, her legs went numb.
Panic stole her breath. She closed her eyes, feeling feverish with confusion. For the love of God, what was
happening to her?

She steadied her pulse and breathing. She needed

answers even more than she needed clothes. With no choice, she abandoned the clothes closet and returned to the bed. She climbed atop. Light as a whisper, not touching him at all, she straddled the sleeping giant. She held her small weight poised as the razor-sharp edge of the blade rested a hairline from his jugular vein. She knew the exact point to cut and with how much force.

She knew it from experience.

The same hard-earned experience guided a keen intelligent assessment of her victim. Unusually tall for a man—he would be awkward and slow. Sleeping on his back with his hands behind his head as if he had not a care in the world. As if he might wake whistling. He had impressive biceps, as thick as many men's thighs, and the telling display of athletic veins beneath sun-washed skin said these muscles were well exercised. The uncommon strength could only be got by simple hard labor. No doubt he was dull-witted to boot.

No matter. The numerous scars on his upper arms and shoulders suggested that while he might be a veteran fighter, he had been frequently wounded. Long blond hair as straight as straw seemed to indicate he was indolent and slatternly. The stranger's rugged features were handsome and striking: a broad forehead, a long face, thick bushy brows, and high cheekbones, prominent large nose, strong square-cut jaw, and generous mouth. This was of no import. Only his answers mattered.

Seanessy's dreams filled with images of the girl he treasured, Ram, his much-loved brother, and his nephews, little Sean and Joshua. They swam in the sea as Chinese junks filled with dark-skinned people surrounded them, shooting poisoned pellets from blowguns while laughing at their frantic struggle. The laughter sounded louder than a wailing wind.

In this dream he watched from his ship's bow, tossing coins in the air, as Keegan, Clives, and Wilson shouted from his side. He couldn't understand what they were saying. He only knew the desperation to save Joy and Ram and their two boys more precious than any other life, and a mounting terror as the coins kept landing facedown.

"Kill first! Wonder later!"

The amber gaze watching him narrowed, before she realized the man was dreaming.

A dream that changed, altered, grew, with the sudden feel of a slight weight riding him. Hot and always filled with lust in the mornings, Seanessy felt his dream fade, change with images of Molly's red hair, her plump figure riding him as his hands curved around her heavy voluptuous breasts.

He opened his eyes.

Only to see this was not Molly. His disappointment felt swift and powerful as he woke to see thick and crinkled gold hair tumbling over a nightshirt, framing a flushed face and brilliant amber eyes. Absolutely dazzling eyes, he saw. Paper-thin, raven-black brows arched over the shining pools, the color startling against the gold-blond hair. He felt the slim thighs a hair's breadth from his skin. Heat grew in that mercilessly thin space where they almost touched.

"Child, I like my women wanting, but comely as you are, you look too young and definitely too frail." He sighed and relaxed into the pillows, closing his eyes again, trying to remember who she was. "I'd likely rip you in two."

This made no sense to her, and her brow creased with confusion. Seanessy's mind was coming fully awake, but he still could not remember where he had seen the girl before. He opened his eyes again and demanded, "Who the devil are you anyway?"

"Your worst nightmare, blackguard," she responded, pressing the dagger to his skin. "Do not move. I will happily slit your throat."

He could barely see the blade but he felt its cold sting. The girl's voice held a curious blend of accents, English and some unidentifiable lilt. He abruptly placed her in memory. "Why it's you!" He looked at her angrily. "I knew you would be trouble." He wondered out loud as he looked about the room again, "Where is Tilly?"

This made no sense. "Tilly?"

"You have at least met her? Well, curse the good woman to hell and back—"

The knife pierced his skin. "I am not interested in this Tilly. I do not think you grasp my eagerness to use your weapon. Shall I show you, blackguard?"

His hazel eyes narrowed with annoyance. "So you want to play with danger, do you?" Seanessy seized the offending hand in a hard grip. "Well, listen up, child: you have mounted me naked as I slept and though, normally," he said as his gaze dropped to a tempting peak of breast beneath the thin cotton of his shirt, "I wouldn't be interested in sinking my flesh into a battered bag of thin bones, you're a bit more than passing fair, child; I suspect you'd do in a pinch."

She first was confused, a confusion quickly overcome by shock. Why, he talked of rutting! With her!

Color shot to her cheeks and all of it evidence of fury. More when he added, "And the pinch of it is, child, this waking heat in my loins and an otherwise empty bed."

"You dare threaten me with rutting!"

"Rutting?" He almost laughed. "Pigs rut, child, I—"

She never let him finish, for she never warned twice. A swift jerk of her arm between his thumb and forefinger freed her wrist in an instant as her other clenched fist shot straight and swift and strong, landing a goodly blow at his throat. His neck collapsed painfully and he choked, sitting up to cough.

"What the blazes!"

The girl was trained in the Oriental art.

Seanessy's face changed with his astonishment. More as she leaned over to calmly set the dagger down on the bed. She did not need a knife to kill him. Had she wanted to, the blow at his throat could have been his end; he too knew the move well.

"I do not need a weapon, I need some answers and you will give—"

He never let her finish. He snapped his arm up to his side. Instantly her hand shot out with a quick slice that, had he not anticipated it, would have cracked bone. As it was, a slight jerk made her hit air, while a twist brought her arm behind her back with force, and before she could adjust to his speed, his free hand had struck her at the elbow. She gasped as her arm bent back. His strength knocked her forward to lay on his chest with her arms trapped and held tightly behind her, and knowing the impossibly long legs were far more deadly than her arms, he wrapped his legs around them, pinning them firmly to the bed, her body to his.

Never had Seanessy enjoyed anyone's surprise more.

She could not breathe, then she was breathing too fast. She tried to control it, but this was not possible with the shocking sensation of being held so tightly against his strong body. Hot waves of shock emanated from every place their bodies touched, pulsating most from the vulnerable apex between her legs where she felt his hardness. Her breasts pressed against his chest. A hot congestion grew there, and breathlessly she lifted her head to meet his laughing hazel eyes, realizing their mouths were but inches apart.

"Your Oriental masters should have told you that as pretty as these tricks are, they are no match for a good London streetfighter. Though really, child, my mind is as anxious as my body to learn what you will do now."

Her stomach turned queer somersaults as she felt his hard throbbing heat between her legs, somersaults that melted into an alarming hot gush.

A deep husky groan rose up, and to her innocent ears, it sounded like the growl of a wild beast. She tried to hide her fear, her training demanded this, but it appeared in the color flaming her cheeks.

Color he mistook for passion. "Aye, there's the pince of it again." His tone changed completely. "Actually, it's rather surprising to me, too. I'd never suspect you could incite much more than my aggravation. You're really too young ... And he could feel, How slim you are!" Regaining his composure, he added, "But being a generous sort, if you just lift up about an inch, I might be kind enough to return the pleasure." He watched as something strange entered her eyes. Suddenly he realized it was fear. "Of course, the alternative is begging for my mercy. And put some sincerity into it."

A neat row of small gritted teeth concealed a fierce and swift panic as she spat, "I beg for no man's mercy!"

With her arms and legs trapped, and with a small pained cry, she threw her head back and smashed her forehead into his nose. An abrupt, deep grunt sounded as he released her arms and legs. Instantly she rolled in a circle off the bed, landing catlike on the floor.

Breathless and dizzy, she listened to original and very colorful curses, mixed with warm amusement, ending at last in "I deserve no better, I suppose, for not throttling you from the start." He chuckled again and reached out to pick up an apple from the fruit bowl. Looking her over he asked, "Really, I'm curious. I never heard of any woman being accepted for the training. Where did you learn it?"

She made no response. Her eyes widened as he pulled himself up, easing his back against the headboard before returning his gaze to her. Large white teeth bit into the succulent fruit. All the while she waited, poised and tense and ready to defend her life against his next attack.

"I was in the Japan Isles," he said, thinking to ease her distress first, before he hung Tilly over a pit of snapping gators for allowing this. What time was it anyway? He looked past her to the mechanical clock on the hearth. Kyler already had ten men watching the bastard at the Connaught. Cherry Joe and Knolls would have gotten the dynamite by the tenth bell. They'd set the explosion on the duke's ship, the *White Pearl*, for the twelfth bell, so as to leave no doubt of timing. They'd give his French duke the rest of the afternoon to think about it. He'd exchange introductions later this evening.

His trigger finger already trembled with eagerness. Kill first, wonder later, and curse the bloody consciousness that sparked doubt! If he didn't shoot the duke, then according to Wilson, in order to get O'Connell his seat in Parliament and four years of shipping free of all British tariffs, he'd have to spend the next several months in the South China Seas until he somehow managed to blow up this mountainhigh supply of opium.

Odds were he'd probably kill the duke first. Never mind the precious parliamentary seat, 'twill be for you, Joy, for you. He still had trouble imagining a man so stupid, so utterly mad as to threaten the life of Joy. Joy! Of all the women in the world! He knew maybe a thousand men who would kill anybody for looking sideways at the girl, himself and Ram included.

There were still many hours to wait. He forced his thoughts back to the immediate circumstances, trying to keep in mind the girl's fear.

"A number of years ago the boys and I—my crew," he explained casually as if they now sat chatting over tea and cakes, motioning with the apple as he spoke, "were sailing the Orient, the Japans specifically, exploring possible trade opportunities and routes. We sailed into a tiny port at a remote fishing village for some repairs and whatnot. On one of its sandy beaches we saw a group of men preforming a strange dance, each man synchronized with the next and the whole thing remarkable for how very slowly it transpired. As if time itself had ceased. Always curious, I inquired as to the nature of the queer dance form. I was told the men were monks of an old temple housed nearby, that they practiced t'ai chi, the ancient Oriental art of defense.

"Needless to say, the boys and I found considerable humor in the very idea of a defense relating to the strange slow dance. Against the protests of my interpreter, I approached the man leading the dance. A man named Hiroko. I asked for a demonstration of its application to fighting. He refused. He said the ancient art had no application to fighting; it was used only for defense, and besides, he rather doubted an Englishman, any Englishman, being a lowly uncivilized barbarian who did not own the sense or consideration to bathe, could benefit from a demonstration of the ancient art. At length we agreed on a payment and Hiroko, half my size and weight, gave me a demonstration of the strange dance's rather startling application to fighting. I returned to consciousness the next day.

"Again Hiroko refused my request for instruction.

Not for all the jewels in the Kyoto, he said, as productive a use of his time 'as tossing cups of water into the ocean.' The ancient art was taught from boyhood, the training had far more to do with the mind than the body, and I, being a barbarian, could certainly never benefit. Finally a price was set. I stayed six months with that man, and teach me he did." With feeling he added, "I think I learned more in that six months than many men learn in the whole of their lifetime. For instance, child: I know you did not learn the Oriental tricks in an English seminary for girls."

Her eyes held his for a long moment before looking away, surveying the surroundings for something, anything familiar. A mind-numbing weariness washed over her; she fought it back. She felt so confused and she didn't know anything but that she had to escape.

She had to run.

He studied the girl: bare feet spread and arms slightly raised, looking more ridiculous than Blackbeard in a nightshirt and cap. She rubbed the palm of her hand against her forehead, a gesture of distress. Rather extreme distress. He saw her fear now, and the sight of its magnitude brought an awareness of the herculean effort she put to hiding it. Perhaps they should ring for breakfast. The brat could certainly use a decent meal.

"So where were you in the Orient?"

She did not understand the question, yet alone his changed manner. Where was she in the Orient? Malacca, but—

She shook her head, hesitantly as if trying to clear the confusion in her mind. All she knew was that someone was trying to kill her.

There was only one person with her and he could do it.

She turned to flee.

"Oh, for God's sake," he swore softly as he came off the bed and pretended to lunge for her. Anticipating the strike of the hard sole of her raised foot, he was not disappointed. He caught the small foot, aiding its flight into the air. She dropped backside to the ground, but used the defeat to roll backward, legs over head until she was upright again, though crouched, her toes holding her weight, her hands lightly touching the cold floor.

"You're very good, child. I am impressed."

She took one look, her eyes widened dramatically to accommodate the magnificence and wonder of his unclad state, the erect and engorged manhood—he was quite naked!—far more threatening than the bit of amusement and much larger flash of irritation in his hazel eyes. For a long moment she was utterly transfixed by him, it, that part, the novelty of its transformation, a previously unimagined horror.

"You suffer a deformity!" A grotesque deformity, she saw, swallowing her fear with effort. "Like a demon, you are!"

He followed her wide-eyed gaze to discover the genesis of her words. His eyes narrowed as he chuckled meanly at this, probably the last thing he expected from the wench. "I might have known that on top of a battered and beaten bag of bones, the foulest and most ungrateful disposition, you'd be a virgin to boot. Listen, child: where did you come from? I'll pay a handsome sum to send you back—"

She did not wait for him to finish. She sprung high in the air, the first leg lifting her, the second leg kicking up to his stomach. Ever quick, he leaped back just in time; catching her foot in two hands and using brute force, he blocked the thrust of her practiced kick.

Yet she had even more reason to fight now. The

giant's amusement, a sound as deep as the ocean and yet as light and carefree as a mockingbird, still sang through the room when her clenched fist shot up to his throat again. He ducked, so her fist hit the hard corner of his chin. The strong grip eased from her foot, which raised in a quick hard punch to his midsection. She heard his satisfactory grunt as she swung around, meaning to follow through with a series of hard, rapid kicks until the giant dropped. His arm shot out and curved around her waist. He flung her bodily through the air to the bed. Facedown and on her stomach, she started to roll out of it only to feel his full weight come over her, his huge hands and legs pinning hers.

She felt the great heat of his body, the hideous stiffness of his enlarged loins pressed against her buttocks. She knew fear. Breathing fast and furious, her heart pounding savagely, she held perfectly still, waiting for his next move. It took her by surprise.

She felt the tension in his great muscles, and he held still as if collecting his senses. Then she heard a great husky groan. To her utter shock he lifted partially from her, separating their bodies by half a pace and releasing her hands but for the briefest moment. She started to roll out from under him but already it was too late, for he tossed her up higher on the bed, spun her around, and neatly, quickly pinned her arms and legs with his, holding her trapped and immobile.

Fear and disbelief mixed as his hard-muscled thighs nudged hers apart and wider still, so that his thighs crossed over hers and his thick shins held hers hard to the bed. Again.

The intimacy of the position felt so queerly, inexplicably embarrassing! Every strained nerve of her body leaped where he touched her, which seemed to be everywhere and all at once. His hard staff burned through the cloth of the nightshirt on her abdomen and stomach, she felt it, while his rib cage brushed against her breasts. That strange tingling congestion rose there again, gathering and growing as she forced herself to met his bright, wild eyes.

"So, my audacious chit, will you answer the question?"

She shook her head, the movement making her aware he had a good portion of her hair caught in his hands.

"You won't say? Why not?"

"I don't know! I am so confused! Who are you?"

"Please call me Seanessy." The hazel eyes made a brief study of her lips: wide, sensuous, colored like late summer strawberries, and he groaned, glancing away of necessity. What the devil was the matter with him? Comely, aye, but the rest of her a battered bag of virgin bones. "Dear Lord, where did you come from?" In an apparent shift of subject, "What do you mean, you don't know?"

She shook her head, squirming to escape the unbearable sensations brought by his weight and heat, only to realize this was not a good thing to do. Hot shivers raced down her spine. "I do not know," she cried breathlessly. "I do not know!"

Seanessy focused long enough to grasp what she meant. He would swear she lied, but her own confusion and desperation gave him pause. "Do you mean you truly do not know where you learned the Oriental art?"

She shook her head.

"And how did you land on my doorstep?"

"Your doorstep? I don't know what you mean! Please," she pleaded, "I am confused. I do not know you or what I am doing here; this situation is so strange to me. Like a nightmare ... I woke in a strange room—there is something wrong ... Some-

one is after—" She did not trust him to finish. "I
found you sleeping here. I thought I could get answers from you—"

"By putting a dagger to my throat?" He almost
laughed. "You have a lot of pluck, girl."

"I don't know who you are or what I am doing
here. You took my clothes—"

"What? I? Take your clothes?" He looked as if the
mere idea offended him, and it did. "I saw what you
had to offer, and believe me, it was hardly enough
enticement. Besides, nefarious as my reputation is
with women, I at least like to know their names before I part them from their clothing. What is your
name?"

The awful truth overcame her at last. A truth infinitely more terrifying than everything that was happening to her: the giant's weight or heat, the ease of
his humor, or even the oddity of his deformity. The
horror seized her, like a jolt into a nightmare played
in the light of day.

She did not know her name.

Seanessy saw the alarm in her face and said after
a sigh, "I knew you'd be trouble."

He drew a sharp, almost painful breath. He needed
to get a grip on the desire her slim form not only incited but somehow kept inflaming. Men were such
beasts really, separated from their animal natures by
the thinnest of lines—this unlikely brat was very
nearly pushing him over it. He forgave his apparent
weakness but only after deciding he'd better send for
Molly before seeing his agents.

Returning to the less immediate problem, he offered, "I found you yesterday, apparently badly used:
beaten and half-naked, dropped like a parcel on my
doorstep. In your hand was a slip of paper that had
my name and address on it."

He watched as she took this in, her expression revealing her shock. "I don't believe you!"

"Its validity does not depend on your belief. Of course I've heard a hard blow to the head can result in memory loss, and you have had a mean whack. Though I've never known anyone so unlucky as to actually have it happen to them."

The short speech did not seem to eliminate her terror, and assuming the magnitude of this discovery had subdued her as well, he lifted his weight to touch the visible bump on her head. A mistake, for instantly her elbow shot up to land a hard blow to his chin. He suffered the briefest moment of surprise, which she used to try to scramble out from under his weight, but the beast's speed utterly defied his size. His weight came back solidly, his long forearm pinning the undersides of her arms entirely.

"This has got to stop," and now he meant it.

"I cannot breathe," she lied, desperate to be free. Her body seemed completely untroubled by his deformity, his huge staff pressed hot on her abdomen. A curious tingling tension pulsated from the spot, she felt an almost irresistible urge to writhe and twist beneath him, and it scared her. "I beg you!"

"We've gone from battering to begging me in the space of a moment. Really, I have more fun under cannon fire. Considering how frisky you are in the morning, I'm sure you'll be surprised to know I like a strong cup of tea before I take a beating. Look, I want to let you up, I do. But you will have to promise to behave."

She absorbed part of this speech as he spoke but it required effort. The man's language flew in the same amazing speed with which he moved, all of it dancing, spinning, flying with remarkable agility. She understood only that she'd kill the monster if he let her up, and this time she would not underestimate him. She nodded.

The cool air brushed against her skin as Seanessy raised off her, sitting back on the bed, needing a good long minute to recover and trying to ease the ache and the inexplicable race of his pulse.

"So which was it: you do not know or you will not—"

A rock-hard heel landed in the vulnerable spot beneath his ribs. Then another and another. Seanessy grunted again, the last grunts expelled with a soft curse. His hand snaked out to catch her foot, but too late. She leaped from the bed and stood poised, obviously ready to fight.

He came off the bed so quick and fast, she had not time to take a single step back. Mercilessly strong arms seized her weight and stopped her scream as he tossed her back to the bed and hard, knocking the wind from her lungs. Before she could even think to roll out, his weight returned. "Another forfeit," he said, piqued and irritated.

"Now listen," he said in the tone of an exasperated parent. "I am going to let you up. But if I have to chase you around the room or tackle you again, I'll know that—virgin or no—you enjoy it, that what you really want is the consequences of romping half-naked with a man with a good deal of heat in his loins. Understood?"

She realized he awaited her nod. She gave it, buying time and trying to guess his next move. To her surprise, he lifted his weight and eased his back against the headboard again. After a moment's incomprehension, she came quickly off the bed and backed away.

"I give up," he said as he returned to the half-eaten apple and bit into it. "Perhaps you can tell me why you are so bent on mistrust? Is there a reason, or is this a routine you go through with all the lucky men in your life?"

"I do not know who you are! You say your name but it means nothing to me." The palm of her hand went to her forehead again, and she rubbed as if trying to stir life back into a stiff limb. She whispered, "I don't know what I am doing here. I don't even know my name."

Her fear softened the worst of his annoyance and exasperation. "You really don't, do you? Well, you must remember something." Hoping to hear some place he could send her off to, he asked, "How about where you're from?"

She realized she did not know where she had been born, who her parents were, if she even had parents, a brother or a sister or a pet, a dog or a bird. "I don't know! It's as if there is a black empty space in my mind and I try to look through it . . ." She paused, struggling, expecting her memory to return any moment, certain it would return and this, the man and this house, the whole upside-down world would make sense to her.

In the void that followed, the questions ignited a panic.

Dear Lord, who were her parents? Where had she been born? Did she have a brother or sister, two or ten or none?

She had known loneliness, at least she thought so, but even in the seclusion of the darkest isolation one always had the company and comfort of memory. Of self. This loneliness was awesome in its reach, and nothing existed besides the fear, the certainty that someone chased her! That being caught meant her death!

She felt dizzy, and a feverish wave of heat washed over her—

She tried to fight the swoon and the brief struggle

saved her, for it gave Seanessy—ever quick—enough time to jump from the bed to her side. He caught her up in his arms, grateful to spare the girl another head injury, the last thing she needed.

He set her gently on the bed. "Easy," he said as she watched him through a gray fog that dissipated slowly as she drew deep breaths. "No more acrobatics today. Are you thirsty?"

She nodded, realizing it as he asked.

He poured her a glass of water at the table and returned to the bedside, where he indulgently held it to her lips. Small pale hands circled the glass, and for a moment he studied them. Delicate hands, unaccustomed to labor.

"Are you able to breakfast, do you think?"

He did not wait for a response as, still impervious to his nakedness, he moved to the marble fireplace and rang a long gold rope to summon a servant. She studied the blond hair brushing his broad muscular shoulders and back, tapering to a lean waist and firm buttocks before her gaze traveled down the long length of his legs.

He was a danger! Like a great Nordic god, he was!

The idea made her blush hot and she tried to look away, but a queer fascination kept her eyes on him. She swallowed, watching as he went to the dressing table and began to bathe. She half expected to hear the deep timbre of his voice raised in song, his manner seemed so carefree—as if he had not a trouble in the world!

Seanessy disappeared into the huge clothes closet, and she forced herself to drink the rest of the water. The effort she put to the simple task told her she had been through much. Not that she needed any more evidence.

What had happened to her?

She felt her bruised ribs and saw the smaller bruise

on her thigh. Bruised by blows. He said she had been
brought to his doorstep naked, beaten, and unconscious. Could that be true? Who had brought her?
Why?

What was her name? Her name . . .

He returned with black trousers, the kind that
strapped to feet, and a loose white riding shirt. He
sat on the bed to pull on his boots. Her lids lowered
as she felt a quickening of heart brought by his nearness. How strangely he affected her!

"We know you speak English."

One of the Chinese tongues too, but she did not
feel inclined to tell him that, tell him anything for
that matter. Yet somehow she knew Malacca too, a
province on Malay. She remembered the letter, the
words about his brother's wife being threatened.
Had she lived there in Malacca? With whom? When?
Why did she feel she had to return to Malacca?

Because she would be safe there. But safe from
what? From whom?

"How old you are? Do you know that?"

She looked up to see his interested stare. He
watched her closely, his hands clasped around a knee
as he leaned back, guessing. He'd never had a talent
for guessing a woman's age with any degree of accu-
racy. He could only call the parameters; she did not
look much past ten and six, if that. Yet the question
seemed to surprise her, and she appeared to think of
it. Not a good sign.

The most basic of all personal questions. At least
she knew that! "One and twenty, but—"

"One and twenty?" He shook his head, buttoning
his shirt, then standing to tuck this beneath his trousers. "As likely as a dry Irish wake—"

A knock sounded at the door. "Yes?" Seanessy
asked.

Charles swept in and announced breakfast in the

garden room. The older man showed absolutely no surprise that somehow, some time in the dark middle of the night, the beaten and unconscious girl had made her way to this room. Most women did, it seemed. "The morning post has arrived—"

"Bring it into the breakfast room, Charles."

"Your secretary is here as well. He's waiting downstairs."

"Barton? What does he want?"

"I'm sure I have no idea."

"Well, not today. If there's anything pressing, tell him to write it down and leave it with the post. Jackson and Cherry Joe?"

"Not yet, sir."

"Let me know the moment—"

"Yes, of course. Also a Madam, ah, Molly"—a raised brow revealed his discomfort—"has made an appearance, but finding you presently or otherwise engaged, she too has withdrawn—"

"When?"

"Just now, sir."

"Catch her. Send her up—"

"Up, sir?"

Charles looked pointedly at the young woman, and Seanessy was surprised by his meaning, more surprised that Charles would condescend to concern himself over the girl. Charles, though, was full of surprises. "Well, send her somewhere for now. I don't care where. Tell Molly it could be a broom closet this morning—she'll catch my meaning. And where the devil is Tilly? No—please spare me your speculations. Just find her. And send up a breakfast tray for our young lady—she is half-starved.

"At once, sir." Charles withdrew.

Seanessy returned his attention to her. "Here, what about this?" The question was asked as his finger gently teased the spot above her breast marked by the strange form. "Do you know how or why you got this?"

The look in his eyes made her breath stop, and for an interminable race of seconds, she stared questioningly into the compelling gaze. The burning memory of his hard masculine torso pressed so intimately against hers flooded her mind. She forced herself to look down where his finger gently rested. Confusion joined a rush of heady sensation brought by his nearness: fear and something else she could not name. A slight shake of her head told him she did not know what he meant.

Seanessy stood up and withdrew, and she watched with keen interest as he retrieved a hand glass from the dressing table. Returning to the bed, he held it up and very gently drew the shirt from the spot. "That, child. Do you not remember that?"

In the mirror's reflection she saw the thin pink and blue lines on her skin. A mark. Like a scar. The lines formed a diamond, a point, and a face.

She was tattooed. Someone had marked her like a beast.

A trembling hand reached to the spot, brushing over and over the queer lines. She tried to wipe them from her skin, but to no avail. An ink mark, done with needles and conscious purpose; she would wear it to the grave.

She drew her shirt over the mark with a tightly clenched fist and raised her searching eyes to his.

"So what I have is a battered young girl dropped on my doorstep whose memory was stolen by a hard blow to her head. Toothless saw you last night—"

"Toothless?"

"My ship's surgeon. But he's only a bones man. I'll have Tilly send for a neurologist at the academy. She'll watch over you until—"

"Do you, you have a seaworthy ship?"

"Any number of them, child."

She suddenly reached for his arm, needing more of his attention. "This must be why I sought you. I need passage on a ship! I must escape—"

"Escape what?"

The question came in the demanding lilt of English aristocracy, yet the intimidating tone did not in the least threaten her as she braved the confession, "I don't know, but I am in danger. I must get away as far as possible before it is too late."

Seanessy stood over her, hands on hips, staring down. He wondered if on top of everything else she might be quite mad. Where did one send mad people these days? Wasn't there a proper Quaker institution in Yorkshire he had read about?

He did not hide his suspicions as he asked, "And just what is this danger, child?"

Her gaze swept the room as she cried, "I don't know! I mean, I can't remember. Yet I . . . I know I am in danger." She lifted up to her knees, pleading, "Please! If I could just have passage on your ship before 'tis too late. Passage to Malacca or even India—"

"My ships are not passenger ships—"

"I could work. I am strong—"

"Strong? Are you daft, girl? Think you strong enough to fight off the determined advances of seventy-five hardened seamen bent on a little female raping? Pretty as your tricks are, they are no match for a man with loaded guns and a living target. And while you might not be particularly appealing to my tastes, I daresay on an empty blue sea, they'd have to shoot you to stave off the riot you'd cause."

Fury and indignation flashed in her eyes. She decided she hated him and all his haughty posturing. He was so maddening and arrogant, as if he ruled the world with the gods. Pretty tricks indeed! She could have killed him had she wanted to.

Slowly, with venom, she repeated, "I must escape. I must do it now. If you are such a weak-handed captain that you could not assure me safe passage from the lawlessness of your crew, then I would ask you make arrangements on a worthier ship."

"Why, you ill-mannered, impudent little brat! You are more irritating than a rock in a boot. Anyone with half a simpleton's wit would know—"

Listening outside, Tilly chose that moment to interrupt the arresting tête-à-tête before Seanessy resorted to throttling the girl. She opened the door, only to watch the young lady roll off the bed and stand with hands raised and feet spread, ready to fight.

Seanessy took one look and laughed.

Seeing it was only a servant, relief, powerful and heady, washed over her where she stood. She almost collapsed. Dear Lord, she was so frightened!

Tilly looked surprised, no doubt owing to the fact that in all her forty-eight years this was the first time she had ever frightened anyone. "What's wrong?"

"I trust you know the answer to that, Tilly," Seanessy said as he moved to the door.

Tilly rushed into an explanation. "Cap'n! Cap'n! I'm so sorry. I must have fallen asleep—"

Seanessy had never been in the habit of listening to excuses, and he interrupted to say, "Tilly dear, do you know what I woke to this morning?"

Tilly shook her head, bracing.

"I woke to find the brat straddled over me with my dagger at my throat."

"Mercy!" Tilly took this in. "Wh't in 'eaven's name did ye do that for?"

"She's frightened. It's a long story that I hope I never have to hear. Basically it appears that she's lost her memory. She can't even tell me her name. Do with her"—he waved his hand in dismissal, realizing he had no idea what to do with her—"whatever you

think is best, Tilly. And oh." He stopped in front of
the woman as he moved toward the door.

From the other side of the bed, she saw she had
lost his attention and worse, his interest, and somehow it was so maddening. She might not be able to
remember all the men she had met in her life, but
she'd wager a roomful of tea he was worst of them!

"Send someone out for a neurologist at the academy to check her over. Not that irascible quack who
tried to help me with my headaches." That doctor
had told him his headaches were the result of "nerve
irritation and acidic air," and he had prescribed a
half-year in a Swiss sanitarium to relax his "humors."
The mendacious man pretended to be outraged when
he had demanded to know how much of a kickback
he got from this Swiss sanitarium. "Get the best. I believe there is more than one thing wrong with that
pretty head."

He chuckled when he saw her angry glare, chuckled because, happily, he could shut the door on it,
her, the whole unpleasant incident.

He had a killing to arrange. Right after Molly . . .

Chapter 3

Molly gasped as Seanessy's greedy hands deftly untied the laces of her new cherry-red corset, the color perfectly matching the lip paint she wore. Faint red smudges of it appeared around his handsome mouth. He let his lips tease the sensitive area just under her ear. She hoped he got a good whiff of the French perfume there—cost a whole friggin' pound, it did, and just to make sure, she asked, "Do you like my new perfume, Seanessy?"

Seanessy managed a husky aye, though his mind strayed far from any thought of perfume. Especially as he freed her heavy breasts and cupped their impressive weight in his hands. He closed his eyes and breathed deeply, savoring the sweet mercy of her presence.

Thank heaven for Molly. Especially after what he had just been put through. No. Do not think of that.

Molly giggled girlishly, in a way only Seanessy inspired. She sometimes wondered if she might actually love him—a ridiculous thought for the most successful madam in London—but there it was nonetheless. As she'd told her girls: after three marriages and hundreds of men, Seanessy was the only man she'd bed for no better reason than the fun of it.

He lifted his head from her neck, and as he aligned

her body tightly against his length, the image of
bright amber eyes against dark gold hair rushed
through his mind. His pulse leaped as he remembered the coral-pink tease of her breasts and the feel
of her slim form beneath him—

He was suddenly kissing Molly as if he were a
man dying of thirst. It made Molly dizzy. When his
lips finally left hers, she released a trembling sigh, almost embarrassed by how shaky she felt—like a
schoolgirl again—and with a nervous laugh, she said,
"Well, aren't we all fired up . . ."

He whispered sweet things about what was inspiring the fire, all of them lies. He only knew he needed
a release—that was all he knew or cared about. He
effortlessly lifted her impressive weight against the
door. Neither the location nor the position had been
randomly chosen. Very few people knocked in this
house, and the lock on this door had long ago disappeared.

A rap sounded, affirming Sean's wisdom. Holding
Molly's weight against him with one arm, he used
his free hand to stifle her amusement. "Go away,
Tilly—"

"I would, master, I truly would if I just knew what
to do. Ye see, the young lady refuses to put on the
proper dress—"

"Tilly." He pronounced her name loudly and with
a warning that sounded through the door. "What
leap of imagination makes you think I am in any
way interested in the young lady's state of dress?"

"Oh, but she insists on donnin' a pair of trousers,
sir!"

"What?"

"Trousers, sir. She wants to wear trousers!"

He collapsed with a frustrated sigh. "Why doesn't
that surprise me?" Molly used the distraction to
drive him mad, with some degree of success. "Look,

Tilly, I suggest you indulge the girl's fancies. I wouldn't want you to suffer her blows—they can be quite deadly." Returning to Molly's expert ministrations, he said, "Off with you, Tilly."

Tilly's hand grasped at her heart as she bobbed a curtsy to the closed door and left. She had never known of a woman wearing a man's clothes. Oh, the things that went on in this house! She'd have to go see her vicar again to get the assurance that being a good light in a house filled with sin, but charged with more charity and human goodness than Westminster Abbey, would not be a detriment on Judgment Day . . .

Seanessy always took his time, and he was just getting warmed up when another knock sounded.

"Seanessy, are you in there?" Kyler asked.

"Not quite, Kyler."

"What the devil are you doing in there?"

"I wouldn't want to shock you, my friend."

A woman's laughter sounded, and Kyler, recognizing Molly's gaiety, did not stifle his chuckle. "It seems Harding and boys caught the two bastards that dropped the package off last night. I'll keep them waiting until you feel up to seeing them."

Seanessy buried his laughter in Molly's perfumed shoulder. "Save me, Molly . . . save me."

"Master." Tilly's excited voice came next from the other side. "Should I give the young lady a pound note or two? She says you promised her a note before she goes on her way, and there 'tis, sir—" Tilly whispered as if it were a royal intrigue with global consequences. "Methinks she's meanin' to leave before the doctor gets here. She says she refuses to see a doctor, and, well, if ye ask me, she's a little touched from the terrible things that have been happenin' to 'er and I think ye should make her wait—"

"Tilly, as God is my witness," Seanessy almost cried from behind the door, "I'm going to kill you."

The words gave Tilly pause. She waited for more to be said. No more words were forthcoming and she asked, "Does that mean aye or nay?"

The young lady without a name waited a few moments after the kind serving woman left. She cautiously opened the door and peered outside. No one moved in the hallway. She quietly headed for the entrance hall at the bottom of the long curving stairs.

Seanessy at last emerged from the green room, having finally managed to send Molly into a pleasant slumber. He was smiling as he shut the door, but the smile disappeared in the instant as he issued the single word: "You!"

A delicate hand flew to her heart as it leaped in fright. Startled eyes turned to see her nemesis, thankfully fully dressed, including a well-worn shoulder harness and two expensive silver-handled pistoles—fifty calibers if one. Against her will she thought of all the hideous sounds coming from the next room, and when she imagined the scene he had just quit, a blush went from the roots of her hair to the tips of her toes.

He kept his concubines here. Even without the assurance of memory, she felt certain that she had never been subjected to this odious form of her sex's subjugation before. As soon as she left, she could be reasonably sure she would never be subjected to it again.

He was just such a beast!

His sharp hazel eyes looked her over. Tilly had pulled the thick blond hair back and worked it into a single braid that fell down to the small of her back. That hair would be a vanity to any other woman, it was so beautiful. His own sweet mother always wore

her hair in plaits. He loved old-fashioned braids—
and, Lord, the rope of her hair was as thick as a
man's fist. Aye, the girl was a pretty thing with her
hair away from those eyes, but the rest! She wore a
man's large dark vest over a clean white shirt and
black cotton trousers rolled up over her ankles to ex-
pose her bare feet. He laughed as if it was a bad joke.
"Well, don't we look ridiculous!"

Wide eyes considered him, as if he spoke in an incomprehensible language. He might have been, for
all his comment mattered to her. She might look ridiculous, but she hardly cared. She could never defend herself wearing a woman's gown. She felt
certain she would be defending herself.

He watched her glance swiftly down the stairs,
and with hands on hips he demanded, "What the
devil are you sneaking around for now?"

"I have to get out of here before—"

"On no, you don't. I have plans for you."

She looked at him with mistrust and loathing both.
"Am I your prisoner?"

"I haven't decided yet," he replied. "I'm going
down to meet with the sorry fools who dropped you
off on my doorstep." He saw her take this in with
surprise, then fear. "Perhaps the wretches will trigger
your missing memory, hmm? And Tilly has sent for
another doctor to examine you."

She hesitated still, and he felt at last a moment a
pity. The image of a normal young lady's life rose
unbidden in his mind: morning French and music
lessons followed by a pleasant stroll, luncheons and
afternoon teas, perhaps a visit to the dressmaker, the
park, or the botanical gardens, the whole uneventful
day ending with a fireside Bible reading. This "normal life" contrasted so sharply with the poor child's
circumstances: how she awoke in a strange man's
house with no memory whatsoever, past the terrify-

ing certainty that someone was trying to harm her, while her "education" consisted of how most expediently to kill a man. He watched the fear tremble ever so slightly on the soft curve of her upper lip, and as the silence of his scrutiny stretched a moment too long, the palm of her hand went to the furrow of her brow.

He abruptly wanted to ease her terror, if only for a moment. "I suppose I should first give you a name. You need one, you know."

"A name?" The lovely eyes registered surprise.

"Until you remember your real name. You need something more than 'hey you' for addresses put to you, do you not? Well now, let's see. How about . . ." He appeared to be considering names. A smile lifted on the handsome face as he suggested, "Cordelia?"

She gasped with obvious horror.

Seanessy discovered she was quite unused to being teased. "Agnes?"

She shook her head slightly, worried he might start calling her that.

A dark brow rose with the inquiry, "Bertha? No? Wilhelmina? Matilda?"

Why, he was teasing her! As if she were a silly schoolgirl with nothing more on her mind than a ridiculous flirtation. The idea fueled her growing frustration. "Captain Seanessy," she said through pressed lips and narrowed eyes, "I don't care what you call me. It's of no importance whatsoever." The only thing that mattered was getting out of here and on her way to Malacca before it was too late. If this arrogant, overbearing man would not let her go by way of the front doors, then she would simply use the bedsheets and slip down the window.

She dismissed him by presenting her back as she stepped into the bedroom. But Seanessy was never so easily dismissed. Strong hands gently touched her shoulders, turning her around. Surprised, she instinctively raised her arms to fling the hands off but caught herself just in time. She had learned that much about him at least. She looked up from the large and callused hands holding her shoulders to the bright hazel eyes, eyes that seemed to dare her with their humor.

Somehow her consciousness riveted to his light touch and how close he stood to her now, the maddening idea of how she had to look up and up to meet the laughing gaze. Her heart started a slow hard thud again. Heat rose in her cheeks, part anger and part something else, as she remembered the feel of his hard body pressed against hers.

Seanessy pretended not to notice these emotions. "I've got it," he said with a knowing smile that completely ignored the fury flashing in her eyes. "Shalyn."

"Shalyn?"

"Aye." He nodded, pleased with his ingenuity. "Shalyn," he repeated in a thick Irish brogue. "The wind fairies that fly through the green hills of Ireland and the name given to a young shepherd's true love. From an old Irish folk tale sung by all good Irish women to their bairns on cold winter nights. In this tale a series of startling, admittedly unlikely circumstances, remarkably similar to yours, befell a young and beautiful lady—"

"Oh, call me what you will! I truly don't care. And I especially do not care to stand here and listen to a foolish children's story. If you will—" She looked at his hands, the look a demand.

Forever undaunted, Seanessy smiled as one hand fell away but only returned to the delicate flesh of her pretty neck. She froze with the strange sensation this caused, an exquisite half-pain, half-tickle as his strong fingers gently applied pressure at either side.

"I really do need you to meet the two luckless devils who delivered you to me. Just in case it provides me with the happy information of where to give you back. Hmm? Shall we, child?"

"I should have killed you when I had the chance!"

"Delusional still, are we?" he commented as he led her down the hall to the stairway. "If I had nothing better to do, or if I possibly imagined I could get it up after the dubious pleasure of knowing your engaging character, I'd give you another little bedside romp to prove just what these irritating and vacuous threats could lead to."

The hot sting of color shot to her cheeks as the words brought back the shocking image of his hideously enlarged staff again. Was that normal? Dear Lord, it—he—was monstrous! How flagrant and crass he was! Like an animal! All the English bluntness—

What could possibly be her connection to this man? It had to be a mistake, the idea that she might have been seeking him out before she lost her memory. She felt certain she would never have sought a man of his barbarous character. Ever. For any reason. Why, oh why had she held his name and address in her hand?

What did it have to do with the people who were trying to kill her?

Mercy, she must remember . . .

Until then, she decided the best offense was simply to pretend he wasn't there, difficult if not impossible with his height towering over her and the heat of his hand on the small of her back as he led her down the stairs through the long hall of the lower gallery. She imagined a death blow to his throat, despite his warning, praying the pleasant fantasy would allow her to suffer his company until she could escape.

She pretended not to notice the wonder of the pictures in his house as they passed through the gallery, but she owned a selfish gaze. Greedily her eyes focused, then lingered on the treasures here, which to her dismay, he noticed. "So we like pictures, do we?"

She gave up the pretense with a shrug, unable to deny it. Especially as Seanessy stopped to let her stare up at an El Greco masterpiece. The strange elongated arms reaching in desperation to the heavens for God's grace gave her a moment's pause. She knew that desperation, and seeing its very image brought a flood of emotion. Dear Lord, how had she known the despair of that hopelessness?

"Perhaps it is not such a bad thing that you lost your memory after all."

His surprising sensitivity caused a moment's bewilderment, while the gentleness in his tone brought her hesitant eyes to his, to discover his stare. The complexity and depth hidden in his character came as a surprise.

All of it disappearing as he said, "Come along, child. I have a lot to do today, including arrangements for murder."

Murder? Was this in reference to the disturbing letter she had read? Or something else?

Seanessy laughed at her alarm. "Do not look so shocked, child. If you behave yourself, you just might escape my wrath."

That he could count on!

Contempt charged her increasingly adversarial feelings for the man, but Seanessy didn't notice as he led her into the garden room in the back of the house. For a large man he moved with impressive grace and ease—as if he owned the world! Without even realizing it she made a brief note of the weapons he wore, from his boots up: gold spurs on metal-tipped boots, a metal-studded belt, the jeweled dagger—and what was that?

She stared at the thick bulge in his trouser pocket. A billfold. A thick wad of money. She needed that money to buy passage on a ship. How could she get it?

She remembered a story she had once read, a story describing the amusing exploits of a pickpocket. When the victim was distracted, apparently it was an easy chore . . .

The delicious scent of sweet jasmine filled the air, mingling with the aroma of freshly baked breads and roasted pork. The sound of raised masculine voices reached them, voices shouting about Wilson and Clives, Parliament, and a seat for Irishmen. Sean guided her reluctant steps through the tall, broad wooden doors. She looked up, not expecting it.

She froze in her tracks. The large doors opened onto the two-story, sky-lit space of the garden room. A musky fecund scent filled the air: the scent of rich moist earth, a profusion of ferns and plants, ivy and jasmine that spilled from every conceivable space. Mature juniper and cherry blossom trees grew wild beneath the skylights, crowding against the high roof. The air warmed beneath the glass of the ceiling, sending streams of enchanting light filtering through green leaves to a floor made of large broken stones, each stone step surrounded by a carpet of bright green moss.

Yet she hardly noticed the wonders of the garden room. She stared at the long carved wood table set near a waterfall and fishpond at the far corner of the room where a number of ships' officers enjoyed a hearty breakfast. The noise and bustle of the men sounded like a great roar in her mind. Her eyes darted from one unfamiliar face to the next—the most frightening group of men she had ever seen!— any one of them might be her enemy, the men sent to chase her down!

Seanessy allowed her the reaction, waiting patiently behind her. A backward step put her against the iron wall that was his length, and he felt the tension in the small lithe body pressed against him. His arms came around her front in what in another circumstance might have been an intimate embrace, but given the girl's terror, it was more like the indomitable bars of a closing gate.

The surprise was his as his body greeted the relatively chaste alignment with a sharp jolt of heat. Again! He didn't understand, especially after the tumble or two with Molly, and it incited a small sense of wonder, then perplexity, both of which disappeared in irritation. "Listen, child," he said, drawing in her scent with his next breath, the faintest trace of a perfume put to a hair soap by Tilly. "Granted my men look like hell, but they generally refrain from devouring innocents like you. They will not hurt you, child." Terror stayed in her eyes and he sighed. "Look, get it through that pretty head, I am the only man here who is likely to abuse you. And the worst of my abuse will be little more than a hard swift box to the ears."

She found no comfort in his words. All she knew was the danger surrounding her, penetrating and dominating each and every sense. Someone was after her. And if she had to imagine a face to go with the phantom who chased her, it might have been any one of these men.

With her heart pounding and filled with dread, she prepared to run for her life. Ignoring the obvious fear and tension stealing into her delicate form, Seanessy greeted his men from his ship the *Wind Muse*. Fear shimmered in her eyes as he exchanged words in a whispered conference with an enormous bald-headed man in the seat near the head of the table.

He still held her thin upper arm, and tightly too, as

she braced for the moment of their recognition. One by one the men looked over to see her. "Well, I'll be a son of—be this the poor beaten lass we found on the doorstep last night?" Butcher marveled at the startling dark eyes. "She's a sight prettier than Venus on the rise!"

"If men looked that good in their trousers, I'd be wearin' skirts and wavin' a weak wrist."

The comments grew more ribald but she hardly heard them, except that apparently she reminded them of someone, which caught Seanessy's attention and seemed to amuse him as nodded to Kyler. Then he came to stand behind her and held up a hand to his men to silence them, that was all.

"Gentlemen." Sean smiled, and said by way of explanation, "The girl has just taken her first terrifying look at your less than charming appearances. Give her a moment to muster her herculean strength to overcome any maid's natural terror. Now," he added in a businesslike tone, "did Cherry Joe come through with the dynamite?"

"He came all right, but not with the dynamite."

"We had to literally pound on the bedroom door—"

"That man's as randy a tomcat before shipping out."

"And how he does it with that wife of his—shrewish, ugly as all sin, a figure like a mountain, wide end down, and there he is going at her like it's Judgment Day."

"Well, I am beginning to grasp the inexplicable power of this thing we call chemistry," Seanessy said as he gently pressed down on the girl's shoulders, forcing her into the seat next to the head of the table. With that, she lost their interest, a relief of sorts.

The butler approached Seanessy with the post. Butcher and Kyler discussed how Wilson was likely to pass the legislation that would allow a Catholic to take a parliamentary seat. They mentioned the Lady Barrington, whose Christian name, she gathered, was Joy. The girl watched a colorful blue and yellow parrot land on Butcher's shoulder as he held up an open palm of bread crumbs. There was something about this man. Long dark hair and a thick beard surrounded his red ruddy cheeks and bright blue eyes. "Cannot take a chance with that lady's precious life. Maybe we should just shoot the man," he said thoughtfully. "No kin blood lost and then we have an easier time blowin' up his island."

Unobserved, she kept glancing toward Seanessy's billfold, hidden in his trouser pocket, then up to the huge bald-headed man directly across the table from her. When he caught her stare, he winked. She looked shyly away, certain the man, like Seanessy himself, could kill ten dukes with his bare hands.

She glanced over to the next man, a tall, dark-skinned mulatto, a startling sight as he not only sat at the table as an equal but had folded a newspaper in front of him. As if he had finished reading it. As if he could read. A white servant stood at his side, pouring him tea.

A white person served a Negro. Her mind repeated the fact three times before she absorbed the wonder of it.

"Hamilton?" Seanessy questioned. "What say you?"

A smile displayed the Negro's white teeth, bright against his dark skin. "For Lady Barrington?" he asked with a deep British accent, an accent like Seanessy's: no dropped consonants or rolling slurs but rather the rare flawless English enunciation, and it startled her. "The man might very well be innocent, Captain, but God Himself would not want us to take the chance with that lady's precious life. The only question for me is whether the bullet should go to the head or his heart."

Startled eyes darted from one face to the next, her head reeling as the sentiment was heartily ayed around the room. White men listened with respect to a Negro!

Next to Hamilton sat a handsome younger man named Richards who wore the fashionable dress of a dandy, foppish down to the long lace ruffles demurely poking from a blue velvet jacket. He looked like a gay Adonis: startlingly incongruent with the rest of the men here. Especially the man he sat next to.

She stared at the largest man she had ever seen. He looked as mean as a bulldog and as big as a bull. Short dark hair covered Slops's huge head like a tight-fitting cloth, small dark eyes were set in the round face. An unwavering look of pained discontent sat on his face as he ate what appeared to be a whole side of ham, this gargantuan breakfast smothered in maple syrup.

The *Wind Muse*'s galley chef, Slops was not known for his emotional verbosity, much less a sympathetic nature, but when he caught the girl's stare, he tried to force a smile. It came out as a halfhearted sneer.

She almost screamed. She looked quickly away and swallowed. She had to get out of here.

"Speaking of the day's murders . . ." Seanessy felt up to it now as he finished a plate of soft eggs, pork, and cottage pie with jellied toast. "Let's have a look at those men who brought me my trouble here. I want to meet them."

"Do not get excited, Sean," Kyler cautioned. "Believe me when I say it was hardly worth the effort." Kyler looked over to one of the servants. "Gordon, go fetch those two foul-smellin' shirkers from the basement oven room and bring them out." He withdrew a pistole and handed this to the much smaller man. "Here, you might need this."

As if it were no more than a dust rag, the young man took the weapon and left.

She watched with alarm, startled when the man named Butcher suddenly addressed her, brushing the two birds from his shoulder. "How are ye, lass? Did Toothless patch you up?"

She looked at Seanessy as if uncertain whether she should speak.

Noticing her empty plate, Seanessy motioned to a servant to serve the girl, either forgetting or not caring that she had already eaten. "Only too well," he answered for her, and with an amused grin, he offered the brief explanation: "This morning I woke to find the brat straddled on top of me—"

"They all end up there," Butcher interrupted with shocking disinterest, and a wrong assumption. "As long as I live I'll never understand how you do it. Me, I have to pay a lady five quid for the same pleasure."

Her lashes lowered in pain and her cheeks colored sharply. As if she was not enduring enough humiliation, Seanessy chuckled and added, "Well, this one did not come with an invitation. She might be a pretty thing but certain telling exclamations left an unmistakable idea that she's quite unused to the saddle. And no sooner had I awoken than I felt the sharp point of a dagger—my dagger!—at my throat and heard the child's melodic voice tell me . . ." He turned to her. "What was it, child? 'Do not move. I will happily slit your throat.'"

The last caught everyone's attention before they roared with laughter. Even Kyler appeared amused, though his gaze found her to measure her reaction. If looks could kill, Sean would be quite dead. Butcher had almost lost a sip of tea and spent several seconds clearing his throat before finally saying, "Surely you jest?"

"No, but here's the best part: when I grabbed her hand with the dagger, one twist and she's free. Then I felt a good swift punch at my throat—you know, one of those Oriental moves, and then the impudent chit tells me, 'As you can see, I do not need a dagger to kill you.'" Seanessy laughed at his men's surprised faces. "The girl, if you can believe it, is trained to the Oriental art."

"What?" Butcher cried, and after a good three minutes of expressed disbelief, most of it accompanied by curses, even Seanessy's apparent sincerity could not convince any of the men it was true. Which Seanessy had anticipated, and he knew she'd have to give them a demonstration. "Well, where the devil did ye learn it, lass?"

This could not be borne! Speaking of her as if she did not now sit here, and in such crass terms! She could not answer if her life depended on it.

I'm going to kill him ...

"She doesn't know," Seanessy answered for her again, his hand already reaching for a knife. "The blow to her head—she can't remember a thing."

"Nothing?"

"She doesn't even remember her name. And she has the idea someone's chasing her." A number of the men looked to Sean's eyes as if to ascertain the truth of this; the idea that she was probably mad exchanged without words.

"Now, lass." Kyler tried to ease the tension. "You'll find half the masculine race willing to chase you to the end of the earth."

"Me for one, darling," Butcher smiled, and seeing her extreme discomfort, added, "You know you're as safe as the crown jewels here, lass, don't you?"

She made no answer of course, and Seanessy

added, "In my kindness I've provided her with the perfect name. Would you like to hear it—"

That was it. She never thought; she only acted. With her heart pounding furiously, she leaped away from the table and to her feet, swinging around to flee. And for a girl she was quick. She reached the other end of the table when Sean winked at his men and called her name, "Shalyn!"

She swung back around in the same moment Sean raised his arm and sent the knife spinning through the air. Any other female in the world would have a stinging slice of the blade through her right arm but Shalyn's fist shot out. The dagger spun to the floor with a clamor.

The incident did more than impress Sean's men. The drama pressed the name Shalyn into their collective consciousness as they applauded. Butcher smiled, remembering his wife, Kenzie, as she told the shepherd's tale to little Brenna and young Kenyon by the firelight one winter night. "The beautiful Irish wind fairies and the lady a shepherd loved ..."

Seanessy chuckled at her fine show. "Remarkable, isn't it? Now let's entertain guesses at why anyone would train a girl to the fighting art. And, Shalyn darling, sit down, will you?"

The girl was apparently as unused to taking orders as she was to being teased. A murderous rage filled her and had no vent but the wind of a sudden flight. Seanessy swore under his breath as he rose to give chase. "I've spent half the morning chasing her."

"You might be askin' yourself why, Seanessy," Butcher said, and the men all laughed. Yet Seanessy had already shot after the girl, catching her just at the door. The strong arms came around her, only to find she melted like water, sliding right under. A clever trick, and before he could rectify it, with a sudden jerk she twisted free and turned to face him.

"Shalyn," he warned, "if you make me lay hands on you again, so help me God I'll make it cost."

She replied with all her strength put to a punishing blow to the beast. Sean laughed as his arm, even quicker, deflected the blow with a circular motion that threw her back. She used the motion like a skilled warrior and bounced back, putting all her lithe body into a swift kick to his groin, but too late. His arm shot the kick up and back to land her finally on her bottom.

The fall jarred her from her head down her spine; it took a full minute to recover. The men chuckled with amusement from the table, and nearly everyone watched as Sean bent over and whispered something in her ear. Flushed from the exertion, she went suddenly pale. Seanessy took her arm and pulled her back up to her bare feet, a movement that allowed her a sweet revenge of brushing against his side.

"Ah." Kyler pointed. "Here they come, Sean."

Holding her arm, he turned to see the two misfits, and at the same moment, he felt the sudden fear and tension steal into her form again. She just stared at the two men who had brought her there, waiting for recognition. Without realizing it, she was suddenly leaning against Seanessy's strength.

Trying to ignore this, Sean immediately saw what Kyler meant. Anxiety worked into the two men's tired, unshaven faces. Dull eyes swept the magnificent surroundings before they exchanged frightened glances. The large, heavyset one first removed his blue cap, combed back his hair—as if to rectify his disheveled appearance—then replaced it. The other man stood tall and lean, too lean, the kind got by not enough victuals and too much hard drinking.

Butcher briefly considered the men. "Working stiffs, Sean. When the blokes is lucky." He dismissed them with a wave of his knife. "Nothing worse than liftin' a coin or two and spendin' the cold nights bent over cups."

"Aye," Seanessy said. "Shalyn," he questioned, his voice filled with a surprising gentleness, "have you seen them before? Do you remember them at all?"

Stricken, feeling relief and disappointment, she shook her head. She had no memory of either man; they might be strangers on a street. These were the men who had found her and brought her to Seanessy's house?

"No." She found her voice. "I have no memory of their faces. I have no memory of anything!"

Disappointed, Sean looked back at the two misfits. "For God's sake, rest easy," he swore as he returned Shalyn to her seat at the table. "You are not even on the list of people to kill today—much as you deserve to be. I want some information on the pretty package here that you dropped off last night."

"They said they found her on Hyde Street," Kyler prodded.

"Is that right?" Seanessy said.

"Aye, aye, cap'n!" Jack Cracker nodded eagerly, too eagerly. "See wh't 'appen be this: we comes across th' girl as we be leavin' the Silver Cup. She looks done for and we be meanin' to call in the gravediggers, we did, when we sees she's still breathin'. Why, she be as wick as Old Mad George during his hey day, I say to Redman here." He pointed. The other man nodded vigorously. "Then we saw the paper in 'er 'ands. Redman 'ere"—he pointed—"brings the paper 'round cause ye know we don't know letters or nothin' and finally some bloke says 'tis ye, Cap'n Seanessy. Nine King's Highway. So we know where to take 'er."

The other man nodded, a hopeful look in his eyes. "Indeed." Seanessy settled unkind bright eyes on the two unlikely do-gooders. "Where do you suppose she came from?"

"Don't know, Cap'n." Jack shrugged. "She be just layin' there in th' alley. Nothin' but closed windows of a tenement all around and not th' kind o' place you would expect to find a woman so . . . so comely and all—"

"So! Was there anything nearby this place where you found her? Anything at all?"

"Piles of rubbish, is all. Oh, well, there be a brick by her foot. We thought she might of tripped on it, runnin' from somethin'. A lead pipe by 'er 'ead too."

"A lead pipe?"

"Aye, like th' kind used for the new plumbin' and such."

"How long?"

"Two paces. Maybe less."

She listened with pointed interest. A lead pipe? Someone must have knocked her on the head with a lead pipe. Her hand reached up to the mysterious bump on her head and she asked, "There was no one else in this alley?"

"Nothin' but a passel of mice."

Seanessy rubbed his chin, realizing distantly he needed a shave. If this was true, and he did not see why they might lie about it, then either she tripped on a brick or someone hit her with a lead pipe or both. Or neither. He sighed. The pipe and brick could all be coincidence.

"So when you brought her here, was that before or after you went to the pawnshop?"

It was as if they at first didn't hear the question. The man Jack swallowed, exchanging alarmed glances with his friend before attempting to deny it. "Oh no, 'tweren't like that! We never—"

He stopped, swallowed as Kyler stepped to Sean's chair and leaned over it for a whispered conference.

"No, no," Sean said. "Too bloody. Tilly and my other servants would never forgive me."

Kyler made another suggestion.

"Not that one either. Too much noise. I hate hearing grown men scream like cats in an alley—"

Kyler then said, "Well, not the—"

"Why not?" Sean asked indifferently.

"Half the time they go mad first—"

"Well, there's two of them. Better odds—"

"We daren't mean no harm by it," Jack blurted, wiping his sleeve across a perspiring brow. "We seen it as our due, we did, not 'urtin' the lass or nothin' and takin' 'er all the way 'ere—"

"What was it that you removed from the young lady's possession?"

They exchanged glances. " 'Twas a queer piece of brass and glass. 'Tweren't worth more than five bob at th' thrift shop over borderin' Park Street. Mister Rowe Eaten's place. 'Twas clasped in 'er 'and wit the paper that 'ad yer name on it."

Seanessy motioned to one of the men as Charles appeared with his post. "Check out the other pawnshops in the area as well. She must have had something else with her, even if only some clothes.

"Yes, right away."

"One last question," Seanessy asked. "Why did you bring her here? Why didn't you just leave her to fate?"

Jack and Redman exchanged glances before Jack looked down, finding a sudden fascination with the large hole at the tip of his boots as he said, "I could not leave 'er there."

"We wanted to, we did," Redman spoke up. "But . . . well—" He stopped, swallowed, and shook his head. "She was too comely by far . . ."

"I kept thinkin' of me own girl. I know we were the first blokes to find 'er but we weren't goin' to be the last, and 'er bein' so pretty, 'twas plain a lot o' blokes would not care that she canna open 'er eyes. 'Twas clear she was in trouble too, and, well, we thought there might be a bit of reward and we were goin' to knock on th' door . . ."

"Ah, fear set you back, did it? The snakepit, was it?" And when they nodded, Seanessy laughed as Kyler shook his head. Missionaries were as rife as beggars in London streets and the barrel of live snakes proved an excellent deterrent to the endless proselytizing of the zealots. "Well, gentlemen, the only devil I know is fear and it's a mean one at that. All quite unnecessary after all." Seanessy said, "I hear you've both been after work on the docks?" They looked startled, more surprised as Sean turned to Butcher. "Give them something rich to hold them over and then set them up on the *Sovereign Wind*; she's due in by Friday, am I right?"

"Ah, Sean," Butcher protested. "A man needs a whip to get a day's labor out of sods like this—"

"Then find a whip, dear man."

"Curse all, Sean." Butcher looked cross. "For all you know, these are the worthless sons of bitches that knocked the poor lass on her head!"

"Don't be ridiculous. First of all, Shalyn would not let either of these two close enough to land a blow, would you, darling? Second"—he never waited for an answer—"would they by miracle knock her senseless, strip her, and then extend the kindness necessary to carry her nearly a mile to my house to keep her safe from a raping? I think not. Now off with you two. Gordon—"

Gordon led the two away.

Seanessy finished his breakfast. The men asked questions about her lost memory, but she felt tense and nervous, and not just from the masculine attention. She reached for the necessary composure to escape.

"You might be English but you didn't learn those tricks here. You must have been in the Orient?"

"She remembers Malacca," Seanessy said.

The men exchanged glances. Their Far East shipping enterprise operated from Malacca. "What do you remember about Malacca?"

She remembered in picture-perfect clarity the port at the English settlement of Malacca, the sun-washed white stucco buildings, the church steeple rising above the governor's mansion and Tunku Hamzah nearby: the small village where the natives lived. She knew the lush jungle-covered mountains, the road that circled the bay of crystal-blue water and eventually wound around to the Tampin River.

"I know I have lived there, I feel quite certain of that, but I can only remember the place, its tropical geography, the mountain range and blue of its ocean. I remember the Tampin, its flooding during the monsoons, but when I try to place myself in these pictures or remember who was with me ... nothing. I don't remember."

A silence followed, as if they half expected her memory to return as they waited but saw only her growing distress.

"Well," Butcher finally offered, "there's your connection with Sean—Malacca's our port. We ship from there. Mostly tea now but some tin and silk."

"But what connection is it?" Seanessy asked. "Why was she given the Oriental training?"

The men explored reasons why someone might have a white girl trained to the arts, and all of them struck her as wild and farfetched. She only half listened. Urgency mounted. She needed to get out of here. She had to escape.

"Pardon me," she interrupted Butcher midsentence

and looked at Seanessy. "I must be excused of necessity from your company. The water closet?"

Seanessy considered her for a brief moment before he set his tea on the table with a light chuckle of amusement. "You're too polite—it's a dead giveaway, Shalyn. Gordon." He motioned the young man over. "Escort our sweet mystery lady to the guardlope." He had the habit of using the old-fashioned word for the privy. "Keep her at a distance and by all means shoot to maim if she so much as looks at you wrong. And, Shalyn darling, keep in mind the medals young Gordon has won for his marksmanship."

"Indeed? A celebrated marksman?" She pretended surprise.

"As a matter of fact, there are only two better shots at this table, and not one man here couldn't hit a rabbit's ear at two hundred paces."

Shalyn rose. "I see at last I am your prisoner."

"For you own good."

"Come along then," Gordon said, as he picked up Sean's pistole. He led the beautiful girl through the doors, careful to keep the cocked pistole raised.

Seanessy was not the only man who watched the long gold braid swing to and fro across her back with each light and poised step. He had never felt such a damnable lure from a woman's backside . . .

He shook his head, as if to rid himself of a spell. "I knew she'd be trouble!"

Yet he hadn't anticipated just how much.

Within minutes a scream sounded as Tilly discovered young Gordon unconscious in the lower gallery. Seanessy was already cursing as they rose and raced into the hall.

Once free of her guard Shalyn had dashed through the front doors. She might have lost her memory and with it her past, but she had not lost her wits. Anticipating exactly what would happen, she did not make a run to the street and freedom, not now. She would wait until after they went through the gate looking for her. The one place they'd never find her was behind a search.

Shalyn tore down the stairs and around the house. Breathing hard and fast, she ducked into the tall shrubbery and crouched down. She did not wait long.

Within a minute came the sound of running boots through the open front doors. Seanessy's curses made her smile, the first she ever remembered, and it was sweet indeed. Butcher laughed, "Never thought I'd see the day when one of 'em runs from your greedy hands, Sean."

"So much for gratitude." Seanessy sighed, and with hands on hips said, "She'll be headed for the docks. Give it your best shot, Butcher. That girl won't survive the day there. I daresay, I'll have little pleasure in collecting the shattered pieces. I'll be down at the ship within the hour myself to see our good fireworks—"

He abruptly realized his billfold was missing.

"Why, that little termagant lifted my billfold!"

The deep sound of his laughter gave her a moment's pause before she heard a threat that raised the hairs on her neck and made her blush. A threat that involved baring a portion of her anatomy to the hot sting of his hand. She'd never see him again, she began telling herself over and over as she waited long minutes after the last of the men departed. Keeping to the cover of trees and shrubs, she rather calmly put herself through the iron gate and stepped onto the London street.

Dark eyes searched the tall masts resting in the harbor, then traveled up to the gold sun sinking over the ubiquitous rooftops characterizing the decidedly ugly city of London. Only two ships remained. His gaze traveled up the long straight lines of the tall mast, the tallest in the harbor, and the only clipper. He read the name in large gold and black flowing letters: *Wind Muse*. Scorn marked his clean-shaven face as he thought that only an Englishman's flight of fancy could create that wholly imaginative name.

Neither the man nor his two darker-skinned bodyguards noticed the magnificence of the proud oceangoing vessel. The great Dutch seven-hundred-tonner measured one hundred and sixty feet along her main deck and thirty-four feet at the beam, with not three but four towering masts. It might have been a fishing boat for all his admiration. He thought the ornate bulkhead and gilded stern ridiculously extravagant, rather than elegant. The tremendous power packed in the neat row of over twenty cannon was observed with more interest, then dismissed as inadequate to defend its enormous cargo hulls—he understood these oversized ships were relatively easy prey to pirates.

A breeze blew across the crowded docks, scattering a few fat raindrops. He turned up the fur-lined, tailored redingote, and with his gold-handled cane out front, he moved toward the ship. The two men followed him obediently. Boxes were piled up three high around the wide wood plank, yet no men guarded it or the cargo crowding the dock. A brow rose at the curiosity. No one was in sight.

The three men started up the plank.

A low vicious growl stopped them before the second step. They all looked up. Standing at the top of the plank was a creature as large and wide as a carnival bear. The black and white fur lifted on its thick coat and it stood poised, looking a split second from a decision to attack. The enormous animal barked, low and mean, then its lips curled over large white teeth in a snarl.

The man held up his hand to the two behind him before rather calmly opening his coat. He grasped his waist pistole and slowly drew it out. The dog barked again, then howled for help, alarmed by this. He aimed the barrel to the right first, judging how quickly he could get in the two shots, not willing to take any chances. The barking sounded viciously. A strong forefinger edged the trigger—

"You shoot and you're as good as gutted."

The three men's anxious gazes flew around the immediate surroundings, but there was nothing and no one. Light footsteps approached the place where the dog stood on deck above the plank. "All right, all right. Let's see what you caught this time."

A face appeared above the dog. A red scarf covered dark curly hair falling to a wide arch of shoulders. The man leaned over slightly as if one with the creature, and he did not smile. "What's your business, man?"

The Frenchman kept his uncertain gaze on the dog, still snarling. "Monsieur, the creature?"

Edward raised a tattooed forearm. The dog sat. He lowered his hand. The dog lay down, watching with keen animal interest, but showing no sign of a threat.

"May I ascend, monsieur?"

"That all depends on your business. I've got no time for peddlers today," he said, then noticing the expensive tailored clothes—a gent's garb—and the two dark-skinned Arabs, men who looked so strangely similar to each other, he added, "especially the religious kind."

"I am on a mission of inquiry, monsieur, no more. I need but a moment or two to ask my questions."

The Frenchman's English was flawless. "Come along then," Edward said, watching as the finely dressed gentleman climbed aboard, the two men behind him. "You can leave the baggage."

The Frenchman hesitated, then passed quick words in an Arab tongue. The two men fell back to assume two straight-backed positions on either side of the plank. Trained like old Oly here, Edward thought.

The Frenchman proceeded up the plank. As he came to the deck, he looked briefly around the main deck: the tall masts over galley lofts and carpenter's room, the main cabins. His gaze swept the well-scrubbed decks, neat coils of rope, and stacked crates of goods.

Observing with a judgment shrewder than most, Edward asked pointedly and with no humor, "Is it all fine enough for you now?"

The dark eyes settled on Edward's tall frame at last, naked to the waist. The man's well-muscled physique gleamed with a faint sheen of perspiration, despite the cool, fair breeze of the day. A tattoo in carefully penned Latin beneath a magnificent picture of a ship spread across an impressive biceps. Sean always claimed the Latin words explained the unnatural courage of his crew. Presently the Frenchman translated the words in his mind: "Only one death to fear."

"I will speak to the captain, monsieur."

"Not likely."

The Frenchman's eyes narrowed just slightly. The great dog sensed Edward's mistrust and rose to sit by him, staring up with small animal eyes. "The . . ." He searched for the English word but produced, "The number one officer?"

"Slightly more likely but still in the realm of absolute fantasy." He spotted a small puddle of mud or soup spilled outside the galley stairs and shouted to a nearby seaman, "Sexton, get deck mop on those steps there!"

" 'Tis just a small bit of—"

"I don't care if it's a drop of spittle. Get on it!"

"Aye, aye!"

It took the Frenchman a moment to catch up with so many English words, and when he did, cool arrogance entered his tone. "Monsieur, I ask you to direct me to a person of authority."

"You're looking at him."

The English bluntness always irritated him, a thing Edward was counting on. He was surprised, though, as Edward surprised many people. The crew certainly knew their quartermaster; each man was intimately acquainted with his authority, despite the look of a common deckhand.

"Very well," he said with a slight bow of acknowledgment. "I understand this ship shall be sailing to the South China Seas in a week's time, no?"

"Aye."

"I want to know if a young lady has recently inquired as to purchasing passage."

"This is not a passenger ship. You, Isaac!"

"Aye."

"Start hauling these crates to the galley before Slops comes topside with an ax!"

"Aye, aye!"

The Frenchman waited impatiently for Edward's attention to return. "Perhaps not, but still my master would be interested if you knew of a young lady making an inquiry?"

A strange question. Someone had lost a woman, and it was Edward's considerable experience that a man lost a woman when he didn't deserve her in the first place. And if this gentleman was any reflection of the "master," he did not blame the woman for her unconventional flight. "And who's this, ah, 'master'?" The last word was drawled, accented to underline the man's relative status.

He seemed not to notice. "My master is a private gentleman, one who is seeking this woman." From his vest pocket he withdrew a piece of paper. He carefully unfolded it and presented it to Edward.

Edward took the paper and stared at the drawing of a young woman. And stared. She was beautiful, one of the loveliest women it was his misfortune not to have ever seen before: long hair was pulled back over a delicate face as comely as a slow-rising dawn at sea. The artist had drawn coal-black thin brows over dark haunting eyes. Tragic eyes.

"I have never seen her." He handed the picture back.

The man looked disappointed, carefully folding the paper again and slipping it in his vest pocket. He said only, "We have reason to believe she will be seeking passage to India, the Straits of Malacca. Any information concerning the young lady will be rewarded with fifty of your English pounds—"

"Fifty pounds?" Edward whistled, his arms crossed over his chest. "Either your master's mighty desperate or the lady's mighty determined not to be found." He met the Frenchman's eyes and decided, "Or both, I see. What did he do to her to make her want to put thousands of miles of deep blue sea between them?"

Edward smiled slightly as he saw the question pricked the man's temper. There was nothing on God's green earth more irritating than a Frenchman who still didn't know they had lost the war. For a long moment the Frenchman seemed to have been rendered speechless. Then: "I do not believe that is any of your concern, monsieur!"

"It sure as hell is if you want to hear if she ever does wander up this plank."

"The young woman has lost her mind. She is insane. My master is frantic with worry, imagining, certain, the worst has happened to her." He had found only one ship leaving soon for the Far East and he had offered that captain a hundred-pound reward, rather than the fifty-pound note. "Please, if you have any news of her ..."

He turned away, and thereby missed the changed face of Seanessy's quartermaster. "Wait! You never said where I could reach you."

Too late. The Frenchman quickly raced down the plank, cursing the Englishman, then all Englishmen, under his breath. Barbarians! All of them!

Chapter 4

Her anxious eyes kept glancing to the side and to the crowded street beyond where she stood at the port master's window. A smooth sheet of gray clouds hung low on the horizon; the muted color permeated everything. Dull London gray. The Thames stretched in each direction like a ribbon of murky green, while in the distance dozens and dozens of ship's masts looked like ravished stalks in a forest consumed by fire. Smaller fishing vessels sat alongside proud oceangoing vessels. Sailors and other people—maids, errand boys, peddlers, apprentices, shoppers, travelers—bustled about, maneuvering between carriages, horses, vendor carts, and carefully watched crates. Three scroungy dogs cornered a bawling chicken, barking wildly and adding to the noise. Two beggars sat outside the door of a tavern, cups and bored pleas aimed at the indifferent passersby.

London was new, exotic, wondrous! She felt certain she was seeing it for the first time. Hidden within her caution and weariness, she greeted every sight and sound with wide-eyed fascination—it seemed at once foreign, strange, and extraordinary. So many people speaking English!

The man and woman behind her kept exchanging

contemptuous glances until the woman's gaze fell to the young woman's bare muddied feet. She almost screamed. "How indecent! This is too much! The streets are becoming rife with scoundrels and foreigners! Something must be done ..."

When she heard this, her back stiffened. She looked down at her muddied feet and bit her lip. She felt quite unaccustomed to presenting herself in public, she was certain of that. She tried her best to ignore the couple, grateful when at last the two gentlemen in front of her stepped aside.

The port master, an older gent, marked off the two passengers proceeding to board the *Georgian* which sailed within the hour to Amsterdam, then turned to the girl: "Name, please?"

The simple question took her by surprise. A name, she needed a name. "Shalyn."

The older man looked irritated, though he barely glanced up from the large leather-bound books that he wrote in. "Your surname, miss—" From the edge of his gaze he caught the oddity of the shirt and vest, imagining the rest. His gaze lifted to the lovely face.

The girl that Frenchman had been looking for just this morning! Lord, oh Lord! Fifty-pound reward— twice his annum! He swallowed as his heart started racing. All right, all right, just slow down ...

He realized immediately that he must stall her long enough to get the word to the unpleasant Frenchman. But how? He glanced to the sides just as she said, "Seanessy."

"Seanessy?" The name gave him pause. What did Captain Seanessy have to do with it? What did the captain have to do with her?

He gambled she had drawn the famous name in her own desperation to escape the unpleasant Frenchman, a slip he could use to intimate her. "There is no Seanessy booked on the *Georgian*, I can tell you that. But I'm wonderin' if the cap'n knows you're running around using his name?"

Surprised he would address her so familiarly, she lifted a dark brow with indignation. "I do not believe I gave you leave to question me or my particular circumstances. Furthermore, I am not interested in the *Georgian*, unless it is bound for the Far East. Now, I want passage aboard the next ship leaving for South China Seas. Especially one that would go to the Straits of Malacca."

The man and woman behind her sighed with impatience, rolling their eyes. Foreigners acting like the Queen of Sheba!

The woman tilted her purple silk hat to hide her contempt.

"China Seas?" the port master questioned as if she had asked for passage to the moon. Was the girl green! This was perfect. "Well, passage to the South China Seas be difficult to book, miss. I don't have anything at the moment. Ah, if you could step aside a moment, I'll send someone round to check the docks for the first ship sailing today."

"Oh?" The man's sudden kindness took her by surprise. "Well . . . yes. If you can be quick about it."

Shalyn moved aside while the man ignored the vigorous protestations of the couple waiting behind her and stepped outside his window, disappearing down the docks. A strong finger tapped her shoulder. She turned to see the man who had been next in line. "What is the meaning of this? Where did the clerk run off to?"

"He will be back shortly." She dismissed the man as she turned away. "He just went to discover which ships are sailing today to the South China Seas."

"The South China Seas? Where on earth did you come from?" The man appeared outraged at her ignorance. "There are no passenger ships that sail the horn at this time of year, there never have been and there never will. I daresay we have enough ship-wrecks as it is without sending passengers around the horn so close to winter. Good Lord, miss, don't you know anything?"

Alarming words. She turned back to the man, whose wife had glanced away as she muttered, "There ought to be a law against unescorted women . . ."

"But the clerk said he was going to—"

She stopped, her mind rushing ahead. If what the irate man said was true, where had the port master run off to?

She never waited to find out. Her bare feet were moving. "Good riddance," the man said as the beautiful girl disgracefully dressed in men's trousers vanished into the crowded street.

She ran down the street as if chased by demons.

Nearly a mile away she ducked into the alley to catch her breath and hold her throbbing head. Her legs burned, her heart raced as the narrow and deserted alley began spinning.

Think! What was the worst possibility? The port master had left to alert someone! Why else would he disappear like that? They were searching here for her! Who? Who?

She had to remember! She had to!

Had the people pursuing her put everyone on notice: port master, ship captains, the English redcoats? Had they described her physical features or had they shown a miniature of her face? How had the port master recognized her?

Breathing deep and fast, she abruptly realized such sweeping effort was too farfetched. There must be another explanation. There must . . .

The dark eyes focused on her attire. Clothes she had taken from his house. The abominable Captain

Seanessy! Had his men reached the port master's office first to alert him to a girl wearing trousers and looking to book passage to Malacca? And she, like a fool, had even used his name!

She wondered which was worse: the dark phantoms of her missing memory or Captain Seanessy. It hardly mattered; she had no intention of falling victim to either of them. If no passenger ships sailed until spring, she'd have to get passage on a merchantman heading for India or Malay or Singapore, braving the wind and storms and terrors of the cape. Somehow she'd have to do it. Beg, bribe, or threaten, she had to have passage on the next ship that sailed.

First she had to find the ship . . .

She tossed her head back to look up at the gray sky, her heart slowing at last as she told herself over and over that she would be safe once she sailed. The nightmare would be over.

Not that she had any idea what she would find once in Malacca. Perhaps nothing. Or perhaps she would find the very thing that would trigger her memory and unlock the mystery of her life. And if she never found it, at least she would be safer there. Somehow she knew that.

As she collected the scattered fragments of her senses, the image of a small wood house perched on the levee of the mouth of a river, all surrounded by the verdant green of the jungle's edge, emerged in her mind's eye. Her heart leaped; she tried to seize the picture.

The image faded like a dream upon waking, then disappeared altogether. Who was with her in that house? Dear Lord, would her memory start returning like that? With fleeting glimpses and small bits and pieces of a much larger puzzle? That would take years! Time was the one thing she felt certain she didn't have, at least not here in London. In London her life was but a sand glass turned upside-down.

She stepped out of the alley. The street here was still crowded, but in the crush she felt anonymous. A few passersby stared, but not many, and those few turned away after an amused smile or a shake of their heads. She spotted a group of sailors congregating atop various-sized crates nearby. Puffs of tobacco smoke rose from the group. Dice rolled at their feet. Laughter sounded with the outcome.

Now or never.

She approached the men. Three feet away, she beckoned, "Good day, sirs." The gazes of four hardened seamen found her. "I am searching for a merchantman leaving for the South China Seas or even India. Could you—"

"Will ye lookit that! 'Tis a little lassie playin' at being a man—"

Another man withdrew his pipe in a cloud of smoke and laughed. "This here's a first for me—"

"Ain't the goddamn Brits got laws 'bout that—"

"You a lawbreaker, little girl?"

The question sounded as a larger man rose on unsteady feet and the others laughed. Drunk, she saw, knowing danger when she encountered it. Not that any or all of these men could give her any problem, but she could easily imagine the attention she'd draw with her fighting skills.

"Sir," she said sweetly, "if you are interested in a demonstration of my unusual talents, I would beg for a place of privacy."

The others burst into encouraging hoots and obscene curses. Surprised by the easy piece of luck and excited, the man wiped his lips on his sleeve, before a wide smile broke over his bearded face, revealing a cork-filled grin. The sight startled her and she stared a moment too long. Poor people used cork to replace lost teeth, squeezing it between the remaining ones.

Her tongue raced over her neat row of small white teeth in reassurance.

The man completely misunderstood the gesture. He wiped his mouth on his sleeve, grinning as he swept his arm toward the ship with an invitation. As he followed Shalyn up the plank, the other men roared with excitement. The dice were put into play to determine the lucky dog who would go next.

Shalyn's bare feet touched topside when she felt his large hands on her. She caught a strong whiff of his foul scent and nearly retched. She ducked out from under his reach, not willing to let his filthy hands touch her again. The man laughed, thinking this a game. He lunged for her. She ducked again and he stumbled, falling flat on his stomach. Shalyn positioned her bare foot on his spine, applying a painful pressure. The man cried out with the sharp pain. Confused, he tried to get up. She applied slightly more pressure. He grimaced in acute agony.

"I'll let you up only after you provide me with the name and whereabouts of a ship that will be debarking soon for the Straits of Malacca or India. Do you know such a ship?"

Breathing hard and fast, he could not speak to save his life. The she-witch was a demon risen from the bowels of hell—

She applied a bit more pressure, knowing the exact point at which the fragile spine would snap and careful not to come that close. The pain was enough—the last thing the world needed was another cripple. "Do not tax my patience."

"The *Wind Muse*." He gasped, feeling suddenly nauseated. "The *Black Comet* too, take yer pick—"

The *Wind Muse*. A fanciful name. One would have

to be fair and good to call a ship the *Wind Muse*. The *Black Comet* was an ominous name.

She discovered she was superstitious. Still, it mattered which left first. "Do you know which one sails soonest?"

He grunted in agony. "Probably the *Wind Muse*."

"Where?" she asked.

"Dead end of the fourth pier."

She withdrew her foot and turned away. The pain disappeared as if it never was. He stumbled to his feet, and with the sole idea of a raping and a killing, he lunged for the girl. She swung around with a hard kick to his kneecap. With a scream, he felt his consciousness splinter into a blinding white light of shocking pain. He stumbled and fell, hitting his skull on the hard wood deck, blackness exploding in his mind.

Shalyn walked down the plank. The other men waited with excited, rancorous laughter. "Excuse me," she interrupted, pointing to the deck. "Your compatriot has badly injured himself. I believe he needs your attention."

Laughter stopped and grins vanished as they turned their gazes toward the deck. The girl slipped silently past them and onto the crowded Port Street. A large cart filled with squealing pigs and hay and pulled by two mules moved slowly along the street, and she fell in step alongside it, glancing behind her to make sure none of those bumbling drunken sailors gave chase.

"Hey you thar!"

Shalyn spun around and looked up to see a woman calling down from an upper apartment window. Relief washed over her in force as she saw a maid beating a rug outside the open window, calling to someone else. She looked over to see a vendor who hawked a cart stacked with iron pots and pans.

"'Ow much for that small pan?'"

A man standing outside a tavern pointed her out to his friends as she passed, and the small group burst into laughter. Another man smiled at her and tipped his hat, while his wife stared with astonishment, then burst into smothered giggles. Finely dressed merchants gathered around the plank of a newly docked ship. Another raggedy vendor passed, hawking hot potatoes for sale.

By far most people appeared too bent on their individual missions to notice her. She caught sight of a young apple vendor approaching in the opposite direction. "One apple please," she said. "And if you could kindly direct me to the fourth pier?"

"Fourth pier be right on the way. This here be the ninth pier, so just keep the numbers in yer head. And take yer pick of me apples."

She selected a shiny large one from the top, then withdrew the billfold to pay for the apple. The dark-haired teenager looked confused by this.

"A pound note for an apple, miss? Ah." He chuckled. "A poor bloke like me don' see enough coin inside a year to change a pound note for an apple farthing."

She looked at the crisp bill, realizing she hadn't a clue about English money. She suddenly wondered how much she had stolen from the captain. She returned the apple. "I'm sorry. I haven't any coins."

The young man looked at the lovely girl, his good mum's complaints sounding in his mind, *"Jack lad, ye be supplyin' 'alf of London's beggars with fresh apples! La! I'll see the day when we be sittin' outside flowershops and bakeries with our own tin cups."* To which he always replied, *"Ye should have raised me with a cold hard heart, mum ..."* And then they'd laugh.

Softhearted he was. He could hardly bear the disappointment in the lovely girl's dark eyes. He

couldn't resist. "Ah well, I guess 'tis yer lucky day."
He handed her back the apple. "Compliments of
Jack, portside apple vendor." He bowed. "At yer ser-
vice, my lady."

Shalyn smiled at the gift until her eyes came to the
boy's own muddied bootless feet. A poor apple vendor with a kind enough heart to give apples away.
On impulse she stuffed the bill into his worn vest
pocket. The boy's face changed with wide-eyed disbelief, and she laughed. "Perhaps 'tis your lucky day
as well!"

The boy looked at the pound note and leaped into
the air with his excitement. Shalyn slipped back into
the throng. By the time Jack recovered enough to
want to give thanks, she was gone. Disappearing like
any good fairy. He carefully folded the pound note
and returned it to his pocket. "Mum." He laughed.
"Ye won't believe it when I tell . . ." Here was one
person who would not escape his thanks, and he
dashed toward the fourth pier.

The port master nervously counted the man's
money, forgot what he was counting, and started
anew. He had sent a young boy with the message.
Any minute now. The only trouble was that the girl
had disappeared—

"Sir." The waiting man stamped his cane on the
wood deck. "Just how long does it take you to count
a flat four pounds from an even ten?"

The port master looked at his hand that held only
four notes, realizing he had counted all the way up
to fourteen. He checked again, then marked the sum
and the change in his ledger. He removed a pound
note to hand back just as someone rushed up to the
window with a sudden burst of motion.

"Yes?" The Frenchman shoved a startled Englishman from the window, ignoring the outraged excla-

mations of the rest of the people in the line.
"Monsieur, you sent word that you found the young
lady?"

"She was just here! She disappeared that way." The
port master leaned out to point north, though this
was a guess. He had no idea which way the girl had
gone. He noticed the five dark heathens waiting in
the street, each man wearing the same fine black
trousers, boots, coat, and stiff-neck collared shirts as
if it were a uniform. Foreigners all. Arabs by the
looks of 'em. The Frenchmen snapped his fingers at
these men, barked an order in rapid French, and the
men dispensed like rats in the crowd. "Wait," he
called. "What about the fifty pounds?"

"When we catch her, monsieur, when we catch
her," and the foreigner quickly stepped into the
street.

"All hands to the quarterdeck!"

Twenty minutes to the fireworks, but it had been
unanimously decided that they should all enjoy a
cup before the countdown. All thirty-three crew
members working on board the *Wind Muse* emerged
up the gangway from the galley and hull, onto topside. Arriving in twos and threes, the men of the
Wind Muse climbed the ladder onto the quarterdeck
where Edward and few other officers already waited.
Sensing the crew's excitement, Oliver, their much-
loved mascot, barked excitedly from below. He stood
on two paws, yelping to be lifted up.

Walking behind Hamilton and Tucker, Butcher
climbed the plank. They would just stay long enough
to see it, then he would return to the search for the
girl. As the search progressed he had kept hearing
Seanessy's parting words: "She won't last a day in
port . . ."

He kept thinking of the girl's long braid.

The persistent thought sprang from an unpleasant memory of a Caribbean port. A couple of years ago they had sailed into a pleasant seaside village near Port au Prince, one that supported many trading ships' layovers. They were getting their land legs when he caught sight of first one, then two men with a woman's plaits hanging from their belts. He had smiled, pointing it out to Seanessy. "The half-witted sods are cuttin' their wenches' hair for mementos on lonely blue nights."

Seanessy had smiled too, but then another man passed with a two-foot-long rope of dark hair and another short light-colored one swinging like scarves from his belt. Sean stopped suddenly. "Butcher, have you ever known a man foolish enough to part a woman from her hair?"

He made a brief inquiry. Turned out the savages wore the braids as trophies from rapings. Sean hoped he had stopped the barbaric practice when he offered fifty pounds for every braid that came with its owner's ballocks. From that time on the sorry example served to remind Butcher of his sex's cruel barbarism to the fairer.

He kept thinking of that girl's lovely braid.

Butcher knelt down to pet Oliver, a big lug of a dog, before hastening up the ladder and greeting the mates. He interrupted Hamilton's explanation of their search to Edward, asking, "Is Seanessy arrived yet?"

"Not yet," Edward said, cup already in hand. With a smile he added, "And the man's got less than a quarter-hour to get here too. The fireworks are probably the only bloody thing on earth that won't be waitin' on him."

"That will be a rude awakening for the captain." Tucker laughed.

"Who's out there to warn the luckless bystanders?"

Butcher asked as he grabbed a tin cup and marched to the rum cask.

Edward had not considered the necessity of this measure but did so now. Cherry Joe and young Greyman had laid enough dynamite to blow the duke's ship sky-high; it would light up the dock for miles in each direction. Cherry Joe crouched hidden in a water barrel at the very moment, waiting to light the fuses before running for his life. No one ran faster than Cherry Joe. The explosion would send fiery pieces of the *White Pearl* sailing into the air. It would be raining fire for a hundred paces in all directions.

Someone should clear the way of innocent bystanders.

"How do ye think we should go about it?"

"Set someone outside the nearest tavern, acting drunk and mad like, and then have him start randomly firin' shots minutes before. That should open a clean path for a distance."

"Who wants the duty?" Edward asked the men. "You'll be gettin' a bird's-eye view of the fireworks."

Tucker had the highest rank of the volunteers, but he had no watch to mark the time. Hamilton produced an expensive gold pocket watch. Tucker cocked and readied his pistole and left to encouraging cheers.

Butcher's gaze traveled up the long mast to the lookout step and saw Prescott. In the olden days ships had a proper lookout, a small basket with a side railing a man could grab a hand to. Nowadays the lookout was no more than a rat line melded into the tallest mast, so only the most surefooted men got the duty. Prescott was not only as surefooted as an alley cat, but after surviving four different drops into the deep blue sea, he still had no fear of heights.

Butcher called up, "What's it look like up there, ole man?"

With an arm around the mast, Prescott put the glass to his eye, surveying the doomed ship. The *White Pearl* sat less than four hundred paces away, a sleek modern clipper that was registered to one Duke de la Armanac. "Cherry Joe keeps peepin' like a tom from the water barrel." He shouted, "Methinks his fingers be itchin' to strike a light and run like the devil for his randy life."

The man laughed below, and Butcher asked, "How many hands on deck?"

"Four hands on deck that I can see. Two more in the hold. Skeleton docking crew."

"What say you?" Butcher asked the men. "Will Tuck's pistole fire call them out? Or are the poor bloody bastards doomed? Given six on board, I say ten pounds four mates go up and two come out—"

Bets were placed and Cummings, whose mind for numbers was as sharp as Seanessy's, began accepting terms for the popular wager.

Prescott surveyed the stretch of street before the doomed ship, looking for Tuck. Within minutes he caught sight of him and watched as the man casually assumed a position against the wall of a nearby tavern and then took out Ham's watch, studying it.

The street grew more crowded near the noon hour. Prescott raised the glass higher to view the street beyond, trying to anticipate who would be near Tucker when he started shooting. A group of redcoats moved too fast. An old man with a music grinder and a little squirrel monkey strolled in front of two young apple vendors. Young Jack was one's name, he knew that lad . . .

Appearing from nowhere, two large men fell in step behind the two boys. Suddenly Jack collapsed. The other lad turned to him in alarm, while the two men grabbed that one's arms, pulling them hard and high behind his back before landing a blow to his neck. "Sir!" Prescott's voice sounded alarmed and the men gathering beneath fell silent as their gazes lifted. "Looks like some kind of commotion going on down the street. A circle's forming around two lads, an apple vendor and another fellow who's bein' beat by two men—" His voice rose, "Mother Mary! 'Tisn't a lad at all! 'Tis a young wench dressed in breeches! And, my God, the bastards are taking fists to her—"

"The girl Shalyn!" Hamilton called out as he dropped the cup and flew toward the ladder. With a curse, Butcher rushed to the side and leaped the twelve feet to the deck, racing down the plank after him. Oliver followed.

"What the hell is Shalyn?"

"The captain's new pet, I hear."

"That be worth a fight!" Knolls said, the popular sentiment revealed in a loud cheer as all the men clambered for the ladder.

Edward suffered a fleeting moment's indecision, but thinking they'd all be blown to hell in the explosion, he called out, "Hold your steps, mates!"

The men all stopped and turned to him. He glanced at where Butcher and Ham ran through the crowd, and thinking of the imminent disaster, he shouted, "An army couldn't pass between Butcher and Hamilton—they don't need any help." The men mumbled complaints and he added, "At post for the fireworks."

A surprise attack, a rush of motion; Shalyn cried out as the man threw a fist into poor Jack's stomach, doubling him over, only to send him crashing to the ground with a rock-hard hit on his neck. Her hands were trapped behind her back in a tight thumb clasp, while the other man grabbed her at her waist, squeezing the wind from her. Dizziness exploded in her head just as she heard a deep and familiar voice shout, "Hold it!"

The two men looked up to see the enormous Negro with a cocked pistole pointing at them. The man holding Shalyn froze for a split second as Ham warned, "Easy mate . . ."

Ham stopped as the man charged in a blur of motion. Hamilton saw a leap led by a raised foot and he fired. The foot hit Hamilton hard in the chest at the same instant the bullet exploded in the dead center of the man's torso. Hamilton went down with a jarring thud, falling hard on the cobblestone street. The villain lay in a pool of blood.

A huge dog leaped on the man holding Shalyn and she screamed as the man fell back. The sickening crack of his skull sounded against the cobblestone. With a desperate push she rolled over. Face to the cobblestone, she screamed again as she felt the dog's paws on her back. Hands behind her, she curled up and sprung to her feet.

Riding up on mounts, Seanessy and Kyler had just reached the ship when the streets exploded in a sudden confusion of shots and screams and cries for help. Seanessy had one leg over his horse when pistole fire turned his head down the street, and he heard Edward shout from the quarterdeck, "The lass named Shalyn! Butcher and Ham went to the rescue!" The two stallions leaped into a gallop. Edward shouted to their backs, "And mind the goddamn explosion!"

Oliver kept his large jaw on the fallen man's neck, waiting for the order to retreat. Breathing deeply, Shalyn stood up. A thundering crash of horses' hooves roared down the street. Butcher yelled, "Duck, Shalyn!"

She ducked as she saw another man poised with a bronze hand cannon raised toward Butcher, a pistole in his other hand for Hamilton. Too slow, the man screamed as a knife pierced one hand almost at the exact instant four different pistoles fired simultaneously. The bullets' deadly impact lifted the villain off his feet, hurling him to the ground with ungodly force. As the smoke cleared, Hamilton, still lying on the ground, dropped his weapon with relief. Butcher rushed to where the well-trained animal held the man, the dog unaware that man was quite dead.

Shalyn turned toward the horses. Kyler swung off his mount, slapped its back to return it to the stables, and rushed over to Hamilton. But all she saw was Seanessy. The moment would live in her consciousness forever: Seanessy sitting tall and handsome in the saddle, putting his agitated horse through paces as he swung his smoking pistole back into the shoulder harness, no more alarmed or worried by the fatal fight than if he had just returned from a good fox hunt. Then he swung off.

She started to run for her life.

Only to find her knees unwilling or unable to support her, and she dropped. The street resounded with renewed pistole fire. Seanessy held two cocked pistols in hand, ready to fire when he saw it was Tucker.

"Curse it, Tucker!"

"Back off, Oliver! Home, boy! Home!" Butcher cried to the dog and then shouted, "The fireworks!"

Sean was already flying. Shalyn felt his arms come around her and sweep her up into the air. She screamed, half-protest and half-terror as, holding her tight against his chest, Seanessy ran for cover. Tucker's shots continued to fire indiscriminately in the air as he started dashing through the streets like a madman.

Then the world exploded. First one crash, then another and another in a deafening blast of heat and light and fire. There was a brief moment of soundless quiet lit by a magnificent gold and red blaze before the sky rained burning bits and pieces of wood. Seanessy dropped to the ground, careful to shield Shalyn's small form and hold her head tight against his chest. A hot piece of wood hit Oliver. Seanessy heard the painful yelp just as he felt a sudden hard stab on his back, cutting right through the thin cotton shirt. The searing pain made him swear. He stole a glance behind him to the empty dock where the *White Pearl* had once sat, seeing nothing but a blazing, burning piece of timber. Butcher was leaning over the poor apple vendor to shield the unconscious lad.

The world suddenly went quiet. Quiet save for the frantic pounding of Shalyn's heart, and with some small surprise, she realized she was still alive. She felt the huge body lift partially from her to turn and view the utter chaos around them.

Seanessy watched as Hamilton and Kyler stood up to survey the three dead bodies. Smaller fragments of red-hot wood still fell from the sky like an afterthought. Various-sized pieces of smoldering timber surrounded the area, everywhere; the entire street looked like a battlefield from hell. He looked back into her terrified dark eyes and sighed with a disparaging shake of his head. "I knew you'd be trouble."

Shalyn felt her heart racing still and her trapped fingers trembling with the vibrations of an aftershock from the mighty explosion. She drew deep uneven breaths and kept her face buried in Seanessy's chest as he carried her up the plank of the *Wind Muse*. A deafening cheer of Seanessy's men rose as he stepped up the plank. Backslapping men and hearty exclamations of congratulations surrounded him, but she hardly heard.

They had found her. Somehow the dangerous people knew where she was. How? Where else were they looking? Had they sent more men already? They probably had seen Seanessy carrying her to his ship—

She had to escape London! Before they located her once more, she had to be gone. Yet she could not venture on the docks. Anywhere. They were everywhere!

She stole a brief glance up and behind, half expecting to see the dead rise up to chase her. Seeing no phantoms in pursuit, she returned her face to his chest, forced the background noise away, and concentrated on the soothing sound of his swift and steady heartbeat. She breathed in the strangely compelling masculine scent of soaped and hard-worked leather, the faintest trace of gunsmoke . . .

"The purpose of fear," an ancient voice said in her mind, *"is to drive us to save our lives. We have no fear, for we have no interest in preserving our lives . . ."*

A smaller voice questioned this wisdom. *"But, master, why then do we go on? If life is not precious to us, why do we cling to it so?"*

"You must accept death as the inevitable conclusion . . ."

She did not want to die!

Seanessy set the girl to her feet to accept a rum cup, still bantering and laughing with his men as if this was the happiest day of his life. She spent several moments struggling to free her hands from the thumb clasp, but she stopped, realizing that the more she struggled, the tighter it felt. "Sir," she interrupted Butcher, "please, if you would unlock this thumb clasp?"

Still talking to a group of men, Butcher knelt behind the lass to see the clasp. "Shalyn darlin', 'twill need a metal saw taken to it." And rising, he returned to his conversation.

She would not suffer the indignity long. "Please," she began, stepping in front of Butcher to catch his fleeting attention. "If you would be so kind as to get this saw—"

She stopped, froze as the enormous dog lumbered up the plank. She watched as he seemed to circle Seanessy's legs, tail wagging, small gaze lifted to Sean with adoration as if Sean might be the very reason for his existence.

Laughing, exchanging congratulations still, Sean reached his hand down to pet Oly's head as someone asked, "So what the devil was all the commotion before the blast?"

One of the men asked, "Was it this pretty piece?"

Seanessy laughed as his hands came to Shalyn's slender shoulders. "Ah, let me introduce you to young Shalyn."

Shalyn looked up to realize she had the keen interest of over twenty men. Without her realizing it, the sudden masculine interest made her lean into the security of Seanessy's tall frame. "Now as everyone can plainly see"—Seanessy chuckled—"I grant the girl's beauty, though—now mind these words—it is a potentially fatal lure. For no female since Eve herself has brought the world more trouble."

The men accepted the words with warm chuckles, but more than one man failed to match the words with her face. Samuel said, "Pretty, aye, but ye look harmless enough!"

"More beautiful than Botticelli's Venus, even in trousers—"

"She looks as fragile as porcelain—"

"It is but a clever ruse," Seanessy assured them. "Believe me, slight as she is, if trouble is flies, this comely maid here is a day-old corpse. Our luckless child was strolling down the street when a group of Arab sods happened to be searching for live game to bring to the block."

"Oh no! You are wrong!" She swung around to face him. "Those men were searching for me! They're the ones I can't remember—"

"Shalyn darlin'." Butcher patted her back in reassurance. "Those dark-skinned barbarians be Arab infidels—we checked them out." He waved his hand, a gesture of disgust and dismissal as he explained, "For three hundred years these foul lechers have been sailin' into London to snatch up our fair-haired girls. And there you were: an unattended beautiful young lady—theirs for the picking. If'n Prescott here hadn't seen you, you would be on your way to some heathen's harem—"

"Ha!" Sean laughed and said with scorn, "Shalyn and a sheik! That paints a pleasant picture. I can just imagine some lard-ass prince lying down the total of his stolen wealth for this pretty piece, only to find the first time his greedy hands come upon her, the girl's got his ballocks in her hand and she squeezing!" He shook his head with apparent regret and drained his cup. "I should have let the wretched pimps have her."

Arab sheiks? She couldn't believe this, she just couldn't! "They spoke French! I heard them—"

"Half the dark sons of Mohammed speak that silver tongue, lass," Butcher said. "Doesn't mean anything—"

"They were looking for me! They're the ones I fear!" Urgency filled her voice; she felt desperate to make them believe her. "They knew me! I know they were looking for me—"

"Shalyn," Seanessy chuckled. "Why would any

man in his right mind look for you after even a moment of your less than rewarding society?"

With a dismissive grin, Seanessy headed toward his quarters beneath the quarterdeck. Shalyn scrambled through the crowd, pushing past idle, drinking crew members to leap in his path. "Please, Seanessy—"

He looked down to see her upturned face, the turbulent emotions in her lovely eyes. Truly beautiful eyes, he noticed again, distracted suddenly. Catlike dark eyes, so heavily fringed with dark lashes and accented with thin brows of the same color. Where had she come from?

The thick mass of hair had loosened from the plait and he reached up, brushing stray wisps of it back to the gold halo it made around her face.

He abruptly realized she was speaking. "What?"

"Please, you must see. They were after me!"

"Were, and now dead, two key words that might serve you well as clues—"

"You're wrong. I know you are wrong. There will be more. And," she added with wide-eyed alarm, "they won't stop until they find me! Oh, please, I need passage back to Malacca! You must be made to see this."

She was far too distraught to notice his sympathy as he considered her. "My poor little catamount," he said, a look of pity mixed with amusement in his eyes, "just your bad luck to have a couple of pimping slavedrivers pick you off the street. Now I'll never get the idea out of that pretty little head. Look, child." He leaned close to emphasize the point. "Think of it this way: even if someone was chasing you, searching for you, I have over seventy men on this ship alone. You are perfectly safe! Now we'll see . . ."

Breathing hard and fast, she could hardly listen.

For he stood so close! His mouth was so close! Her mind teeter-tottered, she could not think of what he was saying. She felt his warm breath tease her skin, a pleasant taste of apples and ale—

"Apples!" She drew back, so he saw the sudden worry in the lovely eyes.

The exclamation brought his scrutiny. Apples? What the devil did apples have to do with anything? "Apples?"

"Apples! The poor apple vendor. The boy who was with me when they attacked and the ship blew up. He is injured."

For a too long moment he just stared down at her, wondering. He finally turned and surveyed the crowded deck until he spotted Butcher. "Butcher, was there a boy at the explosion?"

"Aye, Sean," Butcher called back. "Toothless has him in the sickroom, patchin' him up. A good-hearted lad; I've seen him around. Sells apples or something. He was all a-fret about the lass there."

Relief swept through her. The boy had enough trouble with his mother's consumption and no means or job—

Seanessy started forward, only to find the girl at his feet again.

"Please, I beg—"

"Begging, are we?" He appeared genuinely surprised, then: "And to think I haven't even started."

Any woman of experience would have grasped the innuendo, but if she did have any experience, it was no help now. She decided it was best to ignore the nonsense. "Captain Seanessy," she began again, confused by his smile. "You see, Jack has a poor mother, an invalid with the consumption, and he tries to support her by apple vending, hoping he can soon remedy their poverty by finding work on a ship. Well! I was thinking, you have so many men here"—she motioned with her head—"that you might be good enough to extend your charity to him?"

He just stared at her. She tried to read his expression, but it was regrettably indecipherable. Then without taking his eyes from her, he shouted out, "Tucker?"

"Aye, Captain?"

"Tell the injured lad he can stay on as deckhand. Not this one. Send him to the *Merry Luny* when she docks. Put him to the gunwales. See what the lad's made of before giving him a class."

"Aye, aye, Captain."

Seanessy started for his quarters again, but Shalyn quickly stepped in front of him, her fervor to make him see renewed by the unanticipated success in gaining a place for Jack. "If I could have your ear for but a moment more?"

Any pretense of patience disappeared as he stood there waiting. Keenly aware of this, she rushed on, "Just consider this: what if you're wrong?"

"Look, child, if I'm wrong I will know about it soon enough. There are a half-dozen men trying to uncover your past as we speak. Meanwhile you are safe." His gaze narrowed, his voice rose. "Until the sharks swimming beneath this ship are hungry enough and I toss you over."

He turned away, abruptly noticing the number of stares they had solicited, more when Shalyn stomped her bare feet in abject frustration and fury. "You mean, bullheaded monster of conceit and arrogance!"

Seanessy turned to see the fury shining bright in her eyes and coloring her cheeks, her hapless ferocity inspiring a frantic struggle to free her hands. He threw back his head and laughed.

He was just so maddening! So infuriating! She wanted to—

She abruptly noticed the way he stared at her.

For all his amusement vanished beneath sudden ire as he remembered, "Why, I had forgotten!"

Like a rabbit with the scent of fox, she froze. She cast a quick glance to the sides, searching for the best escape as she started to back away. He advanced, and indeed he bore the unwavering, amused look of a predator catching a trapped and helpless animal. She bumped into the side of carpenter's room. Trapped. "Why are you looking at me like—"

"It just occurred to me," he said slowly as he stepped in front of her, "that I should be taking advantage of these thumb constraints."

She cried out in protest and tried to duck, but too late. Seanessy swept her up in his arms again and, escaping the interested gazes of a number of men, he carried her swiftly to his quarters. Someone leaped forward and opened the door just as he reached it. He quickly stepped through. The door shut.

She searched the spacious room in confusion. The elegant but spartan furnishings ran a faintly familiar tune, as if she had been here before, but the thought, indeed any thought, disappeared as her startled eyes came to rest on the obscenely enormous bed in one corner.

They were alone . . .

Sean removed his shoulder harness and hung it on a peg near the door. He faced her again just in time to see her turn from the bed. She looked confused, then frightened, neither of which made sense to him until the moment she uttered the only idea in her mind: "You would use my helplessness to molest me?!"

"Molest you?" he questioned, then, with irritation, "Don't get your hopes up, brat."

Yet he stepped toward her. She held perfectly still, not knowing at all what he was about and certain it was worse than no good. She slowly shook her head and, unconvinced of his intentions, frantically tugged at her trapped thumbs. A warm and lively amusement shone in his eyes as he came to stand in front of her, his tall frame less than an inch away. She was acutely conscious of this, more when he said slowly, "On the other hand ... perhaps it's unwise to limit the possibilities."

She did not dare an answer as she felt the effect of his nearness immediately and powerfully. Her heart pounded hard and slow, uncertain of the exact nature of the emergency. She shook her head in negation as he leaned over, his large warm hand curving around her neck as if to hold her in place. "And you know, Shalyn, there is something about you. Something very provoking about this small slim form of yours ... Something I want, and I want it badly."

She tried to take a step back. "Don't," was all he said as his arms came around her and not only stopped her flight but aligned her slender hips tightly against his. "I like this part."

Alarm and fear sprang into her eyes as her head went back at a sharp angle to meet his laughing eyes. Her stomach somersaulted, her next breath flooded her senses with a warm rush of heady sensation. She could scarcely breathe, let alone reason how best to respond to this inexplicable attack.

"Loose me!" The demand sounded in a queerly breathless voice. "You would not be so cruel—"

He only laughed at the mistaken idea. "Does this feel cruel, Shalyn?" The words were whispered against her ear. Shivers raced from the spot. "Does it?" he asked as his hands began a sensuous caress down the small of her slender back. "A torment of some kind?"

She didn't understand what was happening; she just didn't. She gasped with a strange rush of shivers like tiny pinpoints of fire as the clever hands slowly caressed the curves of her waist and hips, all of the strange sensations disappearing as at last he said, "The truth of the matter is that I don't normally deal pickpockets a cruel hand. But then again"—his tone changed—"I've never had my pocket picked before you."

"What? Oh, please—"

His hand found the slight bulge over the small of her back at last. With malice he reached his large bare hand over and around the tight curve of her buttock until she gasped.

Gasped with the sudden hot slap of fire it caused, a rush of warmth through her loins, tingling up through her chest. It confused her, confused her as nothing else could, and she squirmed as if to stop it. Only to send another hot slap of excited shivers through her. She gasped in a half-cry, her startled eyes lifting to his face with a demand that he explain it.

It took him by surprise. He wasn't expecting it. All he knew was that there was suddenly enough heat between them to light Salisbury Cathedral. His other hand found her belt, flicked it apart, and then reached around, so both large hands cupped her bare buttocks before he lifted her small weight over his length. She gasped again, a hot tingling pleasure making her squirm—

"Shalyn." He said her name in a sudden husky whisper of his usual voice. "No . . . no," he tried to caution her. "Don't move. It will only make it worse."

She waited, scared, but despite the words he made no move to release her or even remove his hands from the embarrassing and shocking position. A small cry sounded as she felt the caress of his hands, somehow soothing and stirring both, and then a husky voice asked, as if curious, "Worse? Did I say worse?" The question was posed with a husky chuckle. "I didn't mean it. Here, Shalyn, I am going to kiss you . . ."

"Kiss me? Oh no." She shook her head. Get the idea out of his mind! Kisses were associated with love and passion, and most all of Shakespeare's sonnets, which she adored. Kisses had nothing to do with Captain Seanessy!

Seanessy meant to change her mind. He kissed her once, then again, his warm firm lips as gentle and light as a feather's tease. She froze with the shock of it, tingling shivers making her gasp for breath.

He smiled at this before kissing her again.

A kiss that showed her the inspiration of the poetry she loved. "Do we like that, Shalyn? Do we?"

She could not answer. A warm flood of sensation rushed through her, and her back arched instinctively. The tips of her breasts brushed against his chest and she gasped, confused and frightened as tiny aftershocks of heat resonated through her loins. He felt each one, with a husky groan; he could almost see the coral-pink buds tighten beneath the cotton shirt. "Dear Lord." He might have lost any semblance of control if he had not abruptly become aware of her bare feet kicking frantically against his shins, showing her to be a most unwilling victim.

"Stop this! Oh, please! What do you mean to do to me?"

He tried to focus on the fear of the unknown in her eyes, managing with some hard-bought effort. He slowly lowered her until her toes touched the floor. "Not," he said, "what I want to do with you."

He remembered the billfold and unceremoniously removed it and pocketed it where it belonged. His hands tightened and fastened her belt. She was breathing too hard as her head spun with the lingering tumult of her scattered senses. Queer tremulous tingles still resounded through her. Her knees felt weak.

Mother in heaven, how did he do that to her?

He brushed his lips against her ear, but only to whisper, "If this little exercise teaches you anything, let it be that I am a danger to you. I don't have a clue as to how you do it to me, child, but you do. You would do well to remember it." Then he turned her around and bent down on a knee to examine the locks on her thumbs. "Well, I suppose we should get you a metal saw, hmm? That way at least if—when—I start molesting you again, I can be assured of receiving at least a few sobering blows."

Seanessy laughed when she added in a voice trembling with feeling, "You can count on that!"

He still didn't believe her.

Shalyn tried to pretend it didn't matter as she sat on a hard wooden chair in the captain's quarters, but it did matter. She had tried to explain how suspiciously the port master had acted, seeing her there, then leaving, but Seanessy dismissed this without thought. He was just so . . . so maddening!

The fact remained that she could not risk appearing on the streets again, subjecting herself to the very real phantoms of her missing memory again. She truly did not want to die. They meant to kill her. Why? What had she done?

She must find her memory . . .

Butcher sat behind her with a metal saw, trying to cut open the thumb lock that kept her hands behind her back. Seanessy moved about the room as he passed quick instructions to two men who were apparently not crew members but agents of his. They were discussing the Duke de la Armanac and the number of men he had in London. She tried not to stare at him, but somehow his every movement demanded and received her full attention as he laughed at something Toothless, the ship surgeon, said, then ran long fingers through his hair. Feet apart, he drained a large goblet of water. After setting it on the table, he began unbuttoning his shirt.

Just as gay as you please!

Toothless knelt at the low table mixing a concoction. Pouring this and stirring that, the haggard old man finally brought the cup to his nose to smell. Despite his appearance, he probably knew more about the medicinal arts than the best-trained surgeons at London's finest academies. First of all he had received the full benefit of physiological studies at Virginia's William and Mary College, and though that was over two score years ago now, human bodies, he oft thought, had not changed all that much. He had spent the next best twenty years of his life married to a beautiful Shawnee woman, living with her people far west of the Colonies. The savages taught him more about healing and medicine than any bookish scholar of medical and physiology texts in the world. When his wife died, he had returned to the "civilized" white world, only to find that it seemed a good deal less civilized and more barbaric, that his heart, mind, and soul had been forever altered by his Indian past. He hadn't drawn an easy breath until the day he signed up with the iconoclastic Captain Seanessy and sailed out into the wide blue sea.

Seanessy had been stuck with Toothless ever since.

Sean saw his agents to the door and turned to see the doctor hiding a smile behind an old hand as he said, "Aye, this will take the sting out of yer burn and dry it up like an old hag's—" Toothless glanced over at Shalyn and changed his mind. "Ah, hair."

"Well, if it's anything like your other ministrations, that potion will bring a howl of pain and no doubt paint my skin green with infection."

The old man chuckled like a hyena, his frail bent form shaking like a bowl of jelly. "I'll just let it cool for a bit."

The spacious apartment sat beneath the quarterdeck. Sure fast footsteps continuously sounded from overhead, but somehow the sound was muted and soothing, like the patter of rainfall. An expensive dark tapestry hung on the polished wood wall, depicting mythological creatures of the sea. Shalyn stared at this, then at other things: the hand-carved Oriental trunks, matching bedposts, colorful bedclothes, and a low table, thick brocaded pillows around it instead of chairs. She tried to reconcile his obvious fine taste with his character, but found it impossible—she would swear the captain would be happy in the hay of a foul-smelling barn.

There were many other strange adornments in this room, things drawn from the Orient and Arabia. It was odd, but the curious choice of furnishings seemed reassuringly familiar. They were in no way European. The beechwood walls and flooring had recently been polished, and a faint lemony scent mixed with a wine aroma of the doctor's secret concoction for burns. She studied the tapestry on the far wall in front of her. Beautiful sirens bathed in the sun on jagged rocks rising from blue waters. A lush green island rose in the background ...

An island ... She closed her eyes as a white sandy beach appeared in her mind. Footprints. The scene suddenly came at her in a rush as if she were running after the footprints, and how strange—

It disappeared, vanishing the moment she opened her eyes. She looked up to see Seanessy taking off his shirt, only to find it stuck like glue where he was burned. With wide-eyed fascination, she watched as he tugged once and ripped the burned skin from his back. The tightly corded muscles of his back tensed with what must be an excruciating pain and yet all the while he was insisting that some or another ship would be late, as if he didn't feel it.

She turned to watch as Seanessy stretched out on the indecently large bed set upon rollers to absorb the motion of the sea. The movement sent the thick long rope of her hair over Butcher's hands, and he lifted the whole thing over her shoulder. " 'Tis this hair of yours, lass." Butcher shook his head. "These Arab heathens are willin' to part with a whole chest full of gold for a pretty young wench with hair like yours. Why, I know of a man whose fair-haired daughter was snatched from a bench in bright daylight right in the middle of Hyde Park."

"They didn't care about the color my hair, except, perhaps, as it identified me."

She waited for Seanessy's response, but he appeared suddenly subdued. She lost his attention again, though Butcher was telling her not to worry about it, that Seanessy had sent men out to try to find her relations, and where she had come from.

"I don't have much time," she replied. "You don't believe me, but it is true." And somehow I must make you believe me ... "I must get away from here before 'tis too late!"

Butcher looked over at Seanessy, his concern obvious without words.

"You're not going anywhere, child."

"You have no right!"

"Perhaps not," Seanessy agreed evenly, easily, this having little meaning for him, as his gaze filled with a strange sad light and he stared at Butcher. "Once I was riding past Saint Paul's Cathedral when I came across a crowd shouting and staring up at a man standing on the edge of his death. In the moment I saw he was trying to gather the courage to leap. In the same way I suppose I had no right to race up the four flights of steps to that upper landing and yank the man back to a safe spot. So mind my words, Shalyn: I really don't care about these, ah, rights; if I have to lock you in a basement room to keep you from courting disaster, I will."

Silence came over the room for several long moments. Even Toothless seemed suddenly subdued by the reminder of life's sanctity and tenacious humanity that tried always to save it.

Shalyn stared, for a long moment she stared, unaware of the emotion shimmering in her eyes as she did. She half wished he could keep her safe; she wondered if it were possible. They were so close to finding her. They might even know she was here on board this ship!

True, the captain was a great fighter and he did have a number of men working for him, all of them fighting men. How many men could be after her, anyway? Perhaps it was best that Captain Seanessy was mean enough to extend his protection. At least for now. Until her memory returned or she somehow convinced him to grant her passage to Malacca.

Stripped to his waist, Seanessy stretched out on his bed at her side. The angry burn sat in the dead center of his back, but he was not thinking of this, not as his gaze suddenly discovered the arresting view.

After the explosion, he had attempted to help the girl up, only to watch her roll from his grasp and right into a burning piece of wood. She had sounded a brief shocked cry, that was all, and somehow that sound had struck his gut like a jagged piece of ice. She had taken it in the arm. Toothless had ripped her shirt all the way to the collar; the rest had practically fallen off her slender form and now sat in a heap at her small waist. The long gold braid hung in front of one shoulder, curving delicately over her front. She wore only the loose-fitting vest, and as she leaned slightly forward, the vest gaped slightly, offering him a side view of the rounded lift of her breast. Against his will, he imagined opening the vest completely before cupping the full softness of those tempting peaks as he laid her on the bed and then parted the slender thighs—

Toothless never warned of pain. He sneaked up behind and slabbed the ointment on Sean's bare back. The searing unexpected sting brought a loud animal cry, a sound only slightly louder than the curses that followed. The other men chuckled, but a wild fear sprang in her dark eyes as she waited for Seanessy to leap up and kill the poor old man.

Apparently unaware of the danger, Toothless laughed like a madman, one effeminate hand held over his toothless mouth as his small body shook with his high-pitched laughter.

"You cod-sucking sadistic son of a bitch—"

Seanessy stopped suddenly. Still tense with anticipation of violence, she watched as the huge giant seemed to collapse and lose wind, turning his head away as his curses changed with the warm deep sound of laughter.

Laughter because, God knew, he deserved it, lascivious bastard that he was. She might think she was twenty-one but she had a piss-ant poor memory, and she looked closer to ten and six. That might be plenty old enough for some men, but it felt like robbing the cradle to him. And the vixen, for all her worldly abilities, was a white-clothed virgin. She was also irritating, foul-tempered, shrewish, and most certainly mad.

He turned around to find her interested stare. She seemed to want to say something, but then hesitated with sudden uncertainty. He swung his long legs over the bed and got up to retrieve a fresh shirt from his trunk. Toothless stepped to her. "Lass, this will hurt," he said, holding a freshly dipped cloth. "Would ye like a drab of laudanum before I touch ye?"

"Oh, heavens." She shook her head. "I am strong enough for that."

Toothless gently brought the cloth to the girl's arm. She stiffened with the stinging sensation but briefly, and made not a sound. More than one man watched with admiration. "Look at that." Toothless chuckled, his free hand covering his mouth as he exclaimed, "The young lass has more pluck than the captain!"

Seanessy was the first to admit it.

Chapter 5

Mr. Rowe Eaten walked into a fantastic dream. After thirty-one miserable years of suffering in the dusty cramped space of his father's pawnshop, hour after hour, week after week, month after month. Thirty-one years of staring at shelves filled with every imaginable possession abandoned by poor masses: hair combs, brushes, hand mirrors, shawls, fichus, all kinds and sizes of coats, hats, even corsets, fibulas for boots, saddles, all kinds of jeweled boxes, reticules—most of these had been stolen— cheap glass jewels of all kinds, ribbons, festoons of lace and of silk flowers, hairpins, an entire store filled with the abandoned hope and tragedies of the truly bereft.

His whole life he had had to listen to their sad tales, tales that always ended with him offering a coin worth one-twentieth of the value of their last treasure. Of course they always argued over his price; they had to, and he had to listen to their pathetic haggling impassively, shaking his head. "Not a charity," he'd say as his heart twisted and he felt like dying.

The worst were boots. He had nightmares filled with nothing but boots. Boots in all sizes. Boots as small as a four-year-old's tiny foot. Boots caked in sewage from the mudlarks—mudlarks was the name given to boys and girls who searched through the sewers for anything of value. The last trade of the mudlarks and the gin girls and boys—the children abandoned to alcohol and its terrible gin streets—was always their boots. When they gave up their boots against the winter cold for a cup of gin, they would be dead soon. Everyone knew it. Lately his hands would shake as badly as theirs when he reached to take them, for he was handing back a death sentence.

Then he would go home to eat his wife's miserly meals and listen to her complaints, her hateful complaints that never changed or stopped as she chided and berated him for every penny that left the shop. "Two pence for a 'air comb? La! Ye are a fool, a fool! Oh, ye think ye are so fine wi' yer soft 'eart but 'tis yer 'ead that's soft! Canna sell it for four pence, and if ye . . ." and, how strange, lately he had begun to wonder if maybe he hadn't died and was serving a sentence in hell with his nagging hateful wife and a pawnshop filled with children's boots.

So today after it had happened, and after his heart stopped slamming in his chest and his hands stopped shaking, and after a long hour or so staring at it, he thought that maybe it was a message from God. The message was redemption for his long suffering! His fortune made for five bob. No more nagging hateful wife. No more pawnshop. No more boots! Here was a billet to heaven!

Taggart would be here in the hour . . .

Rowe Eaten reached trembling hands to the bottom shelf of the counter. He clutched the carved wooden box, and though no solicitors or customers were in the small shop, he bent down behind the counter, just to make sure no one saw. He carefully unfolded the plain lace handkerchief to stare at it again.

"Why, ye ole fools," he had told them, "this be a bit of brass and glass!"

"Brass and glass? Looks like gold plate to me!"

Forcing his eyes away from the miracle, he had placed his hands palm side down on the counter to hide their sudden trembling. With a pretense of contempt for the men, he said the boldest words of his life: "Take it next door then. Ye won't get more'n five bob from me."

The two oafs grumbled and fidgeted before the fat one asked, " 'Tis a done deal if ye throw in a couple of farthin's to warm me and my bloke here with a round of gin cups."

"I am not a charity."

"Ah, ye'd cheat yer own mum from 'er last bowl o' porridge, ye would!"

He withdrew five bob from the cash box. The stout man snatched it up, and without a backward glance they left the store. Five bob had got them out of the store.

He stared at the fortune.

Intricate gold lattice work formed a five-point star, its centerpiece a twenty-five-carat uncut ruby stone, more valuable than a diamond and three times larger than any he had ever seen before, even in books. The gem would be worth five times as much once it was cut. Seven other uncut bloodred rubies sat on the solid gold star, each at least five carats.

Fit for the crown jewels.

Master Taggart would start at two thousand pounds; he would hold out for four. Then he'd pay Giles to tell that miserly shrew of a wife—the fat nag who had given him twenty-two years of suffering— that he had died, that he had leaped off the London Bridge to his death just to escape another day with her. Oh, how she'd cry then! She'd be so sorry! He'd purchase a quiet cottage in Yorkshire or Stratford or maybe even faraway Dover. It would have a proper dining room, it would, and a drawing room, and a pretty garden, and a houseman and maid. He'd eat roast mutton, cottage stew, rarebit every night—

The door opened. His heart leaped in his chest as he placed the ruby star back in the box, closed the lid, and shoved it deep into the cupboard. He stood up, and his gaze settled on the two men. They appeared tall and strong-looking, healthy, well-fed brutes, dangerous-looking somehow, not the type of men to while away hours shopping for a bargain on boots.

He knew, part of him knew, even before he heard the tall one say, "We understand you purchased a little ruby and gold piece from a couple of blokes?"

"Ruby and gold piece? Me?" He forced a laugh, but it sounded strange to him. A moment later he realized the sound came from the dark edge of his hysteria. "Do I look like I ever handled a ruby and gold piece? Look around—"

A pistol manifested itself in the man's hand. He did not smile. "And I wager a bullet in your head that you did."

She stood at the side window, staring out at the fog drifting quietly through the front lawns and waiting.

The men who meant to kill her waited outside. She was sure they had watched Seanessy carry her to his ship, then later followed Seanessy and Butcher here to the house. They were waiting for an opportunity.

Sean's men sat at a serving table behind her playing a queer dice and card game as they watched over her. They quietly discussed the upcoming parliamentary elections, relating it to Aristotle's *Politics*—not the common type of men.

She had read Aristotle's *Politics*.

She rubbed her forehead. She remembered a library. Images, scenes, and pieces of her missing life began to surface in the quiet. Another image of a house in the English countryside rose in her mind. A large Tudor-style house with a meadow in the back and rolling green countryside in the front.

A profound quietness surrounded her. Tucker kept glancing up as if to make sure she still stood there, and it was odd how she seemed to blend in with the background like a chameleon. He smiled. Like a hungry cat watching a grassy field at night, she was.

Indeed she used a hunter's trick: she had cleared her mind of all thoughts and feelings, so that her body melded to its surroundings and consciousness emerged as a blank state. Each and every slight movement and sound received her full attention: an owl's mesmerizing hoot, a slight rustle of a squirrel in the branches of a tree, a noisy carriage racing past on the street, and all of these sounds interspersed with the house noises: a maid's melody as she went from room to room lighting the lamps, the crackle of the fire in the nearby study, the distant sounds from the kitchen, all the backdrop for a few of Captain Seanessy's officers eating a late dinner in the garden room down the hall.

Seanessy. She did not like him: his grand arrogance and conceits, the relentless sting of his formidable wit and insults—he treated her as if she were little better than an indolent scullery maid! And the incessant humor with which he viewed the world, as if all of God's creation were one giant jest for his amusement! Oh, he was maddening all right! And a mere glance from those hazel eyes could change her fear and apprehension to bright shining fury in the space of a second.

She glanced at the men watching her. They thought she wanted to escape. They had no idea of her state of terror. The more she thought about it, the more she came to see that Seanessy was her only hope; it was the reason she had had his name and address in her hand. The only place she was going was with Seanessy, on board the *Wind Muse* as it sailed to the China Seas. Somehow she had to convince him . . .

She tensed with the sound of horses' hooves. Through the fog she made out the two grooms coming past the front gate, leading two horses. The sound of their laughter stopped her, her keen gaze riveting on the servants' easy gait and manner, the plain common clothes. She relaxed a bit as they led the horses up to the door.

Then she recognized Seanessy's horse.

Was he leaving? Where would he go at this hour?

Anxiety changed her features as she watched. "Tucker, is Seanessy leaving now?"

"Aye, lass, that he is."

The information brought a panic. Just what they would be waiting for! Merciful Madonna, she was doomed!

Boots against marble, raised masculine voices, laughter sounded down the hall. How could she make him take her? How? If she degraded herself to beg? Could she do that? Did she have any other choice?

Seanessy did not notice the girl as he pushed a pistole into his shoulder harness, calling out to his butler, "Charles! Charles! Where are you, you rascal? I need my cloak—"

Shalyn stepped from the shadows of the room, unclasping the cloak from her shoulders and swinging it off. She handed it to him. "Here. I have your cloak."

A boyish grin greeted her as he took the cloak. "So! You're worth something more than trouble after all." He swung it over his shoulders, and realized for the first time that he had missed the girl at dinner. "You skipped dinner, child! A bad idea. If anything could possibly redeem you in my eyes, 'twould be an extra bit of flesh on that pretty form—"

"Where are you going?"

"Where am I going?" he repeated, surprised she would ask. "Out."

"Out," Butcher said as he checked the barrel of his pistole too. "To lay down the law to a trespasser."

"I want to go with—"

"Nay, child. You can believe this is not a place one takes a young woman to."

"I am dressed like a man. If I had a hat—"

A mild kind of amusement reached his eyes as his hand touched the lever of the front door. "A blind man would recognize the femininity in your package at a distance. No." He raised a hand to silence her. "You can't come, Shalyn. Even odds I exchange gunfire tonight, and the last thing I want to think about is what the return fire is aimed at."

The door opened and he disappeared. Butcher saw the alarm in her eyes and said, "Shalyn, look—Tucker and Sammy will be stayin' with ye. No one could get past them. If someone does, invite them to stay on—I want to meet them." The man grinned, his eyes crinkling, and with his beard and long hair, he looked like a dark-haired version of Saint Nicholas, though she was too distraught to take comfort in the thought. Butcher patted her shoulders, bid farewell to Tucker and Samuel, and followed Seanessy out.

The door shut.

She stared at the closed door as her heart began a

slow escalation. If they had seen him carry her on board his ship, they would know she was at his house. They would be waiting for just this opportunity! She needed a place to hide. Dear Lord—

She raced to the door and opened it, darting through just as Seanessy swung up on his mount. "Seanessy!"

Tucker followed her outside.

She ran up to Seanessy's horse, reaching for the bridle as if to hold him there until he told her. "Where can I hide? In case they have discovered where I am?" In a whispered rush: "Is there a place in this house, a secret place? I remember reading that many old houses have hidden rooms or cupboards."

For a long moment nothing happened as Seanessy took in her words, accented dramatically by the emotion in her eyes. He used every ounce of his great will to steel himself from the effect of those eyes filled with fear. He drew a deep breath, as if he needed to concentrate. To no effect.

He looked to Butcher for help.

"Well now," Butcher said in a subdued voice, "the lass does know how to handle herself, and she could sit out of the way—no harm there, past the foul language of the sorry losers." Then, "Hey, Raul, lend me your hat, will you?"

The groom tossed his hat to Butcher, who in turn tossed it to Shalyn, who caught it. Seanessy watched as a fair and delicate hand quickly knotted the long gold plait before she crowned her head with the groom's black hat.

The girl looked all eyes now. This hardly aided his ability to resist her. He knew when to give up. He leaned over. She felt his large gloved hands come around her waist, lifting her off her feet to a position in front of him. Butcher saw Seanessy's disgruntled face, guessed the problem, and chuckled as they rode out to the street.

Seanessy looked down as Shalyn pressed against his chest. They passed through the gate and into the street. He pulled the folds of his cloak completely around her, but he did so for her rather than any imagined men watching outside.

If it weren't a mercifully short ride to the Connaught, Seanessy would have swung off the mount or turned the girl around to face an accounting of what she was doing to him. He had given up trying to make sense of what about the girl sparked the incessant and irritating wealth of his lust—the minute she drew close, he felt as if he were thirteen and in sight of the maid's bathing tub.

He'd send a note to Doreen . . .

The new oil lanterns threw a gold light into the thick mist. Set back from expansive front gardens sat London's finest townhouses. An occasional carriage passed, and Shalyn watched as the footmen inevitably tipped their hats to Captain Seanessy and called friendly greetings. As if he was famous or revered. Towering colonnades marked the entrance to Hyde Park.

She too was acutely aware of every place their bodies touched: she felt his chest behind her neck and head, his hard stomach against her spine—he sat so straight in the saddle!—his arms around hers. She drew a small sharp breath. The sensual warmth of his body ignited a tumult inside her—her heart, pulse, every nerve strained to greet him. The effect drew her bit by bit against him; without any real awareness, she eased more and more of her weight into him.

A soft voice asked, "You think I am mad, don't you?"

He stopped the horse suddenly. The great beast

threw its head back and danced a bit in the middle of the cobblestone street. Thick moist fog enveloped them, billowing slowly through the street as Seanessy stared down at the dark mystery of her eyes. "You know, Shalyn, this persistent thought that men are pursuing you, it is the stuff of mad minds."

She surprised him with a whispered rush of words. "I know, Seanessy, I know. You can't imagine what it's like though—to wake up in a stranger's house with no memory of how you got there or who you are. With no memory of any yesterday, but knowing that I must remember. I must, before 'tis too late." She grabbed her head, careful where the bump protruded slightly. "My head hurts from thinking and trying to remember something, anything, the endless circle made of my thoughts, a nightmare that won't end."

The horse danced restlessly, and Seanessy let it start forward again as she shook her head. "You'll see, Seanessy. You'll see. They're searching for me, and when they find me—"

"Yes?" The hazel eyes narrowed in the darkness, showing his interest. "What happens when they find you?"

On the heels of a contemplative pause he heard the whisper of her terror: "They will kill me."

"Oh, for heaven's sake! What rot! Shalyn, your loving and kind family is probably out searching for you as I speak, mad with worry—"

Seanessy stopped, drawing his horse up, shielding her head with one hand as he searched the darkness, only because Butcher had suddenly stopped. A baby cried out nearby, the cry growing louder against the distant calls and sounds of the city's nightlife. As they rode into the park, she searched the darkness for the source of the cry, spotting a beggar woman on a bench beneath the golden light of the lantern.

Butcher had stopped his horse in front of bench.

Seanessy swore softly as he stopped his mount too. "Curse his ripped heart."

Shalyn leaned far to the side to watch, interested in this. That afternoon when Butcher had taken her back to the house, he had related a fascinating and utterly unbelievable tale of how Seanessy was related by blood to one of the great titled houses of England. She had been listening intently to each and every word when Butcher had tossed a bag of coins to a beggar on the street. He had never stopped. He had never said a word—he had simply lifted the bag from his coat and dropped it onto the woman's lap.

"Are ye mindin' yer babe, woman?" Butcher was asking now, a queer kind of gentleness in his tone. "That's a hell of a wail he's got goin'."

Dull eyes greeted the frightening sight of any maid's worse nightmare: the man sitting atop a black stallion, his long black hair and beard, piercing blue eyes, buckskin breeches and boots, a belt decked with carved knifes and two ivory-handled pistoles. She seemed to struggle briefly to focus. A trembling hand brushed matted hair from her face before she tightened the ragged shawl about her shoulders.

Gently Butcher asked, "Are ye sucklin' the babe on a gin cloth?"

She weakly waved him away, barely making sense. "Be the only thin' stop 'is fits, 'tis . . ."

"The babe needs 'is mother's milk, woman. He be cryin' out for food, for a mother's milk—"

A weak bitter laugh echoed into the darkness. " 'E don't need milk to make 'is sufferin' longer, mister. 'E don't got long for this world, 'e don't. All o' mine be buried afore they cut a tooth."

Butcher searched through his pockets but came up empty, as if, Shalyn thought, watching this, he didn't remember giving his entire money bag to another beggar just that afternoon. "Sean, ye got five quid?"

Seanessy knew not to argue with Butcher; he never did anymore. He simply withdrew his billfold, pulled out a five-pound note, and then gathered up the reins and pressed his horse to Butcher's side.

Sean handed the money to Butcher. "I need you tonight, you know."

"Aye." Butcher nodded.

The horse started off again. Shalyn looked back to where Butcher stood on his horse talking to the woman. "What will he do to her?"

"He will pay her for the child."

Astonishment changed her face as she watched Butcher and the beggar woman disappear through the dark trees. "I don't understand. She'll take his money for her child?"

"Aye. A drunkard, Shalyn. All she knows is hell's own unquenched and endless thirst for a cup."

The thought brought a sudden memory of an opium den hidden down narrow alleys where pitiful addicts drowned their sorrows in the sweet mercy of opium smoke: the image of a woman crouched in one of those narrow alleys outside, wearing only a ragged transparent kimono, worse than naked as every ounce of worn flesh lay bare for the indifferent inspection of the passersby. She could still see the hopelessness written in dull eyes that no longer saw the world around her.

"What will he do with the child?"

"He will bring it to my sister-in-law's poorhouse, Chester House, where a dozen hardworking women will fuss over and care for and pray for the little orphan unto death. Which will—pitifully—be a mercy. Those precious few children who do survive their mothers' drunkenness inevitably are cursed to a life of dullness and apathy, and all the great misery that brings."

"Why does he do it? If it is so hopeless?"

"Why?" Seanessy repeated. They passed under another gold lantern, and she looked up to see a profound sadness in his hazel eyes. "Because of a young woman named Kenzie, the black rift she tore in his soul, and his desperate attempt to mend it."

She twisted around so that she might stare up at Seanessy's face, her eyes searching as she consulted her intuition. Without even realizing it, he drew back on the reins to stop his horse again and meet the intimate probe of these dark and mysterious eyes. Like a brush against his soul that let him feel the startling depth of her own heart. So he was not surprised when she whispered, "'Twas Butcher whom you saved from the church ledge."

"Aye . . ."

A soft light filled his eyes as he looked down at the lovely upturned face. He could not comprehend how it was that she had no idea of her effect on him; an innocence and utter guilelessness surrounded her every movement and gesture and word. As if she had been isolated from the compliments, flattery, and attention her beauty would have gotten from men. The spirit of a gutsy boy packaged in the most unlikely feminine form . . . He studied the mystery in her eyes for a moment, then her slightly parted mouth, wide and more sensual than he knew wise to contemplate. He traced a line over the paper-thin velvet of her black brows, feeling the irresistible pull brought by the softness so intimately pressed against him, all the girl's trouble vanishing in his mind as he thought of kissing those lips.

She turned back around, the spell breaking as he pressed the horse forward again. Another memory surfaced of the dark pleading eyes of hungry children, a hundred or more, all desperate with want of food. She stared out at the sea of faces from a rickshaw and, how strange! A young voice, her voice, said, *"God save them!"*

"These do not deserve the mercy."

"Oh, but it is so sad, the suffering of children—"

"They are paying the price in this life for their wickedness in another. See them not as starving children but as prisoners of their own foolishness, vulgarity, and greed."

She could not; she did not even try. *"My mother's master was said to love the hungry and the poor more than all others; He said the meek shall inherit the kingdom of heaven—"*

"The Lord Christ? He was a foolish wise man ..."

She shook her head, trying without success to put a face to that strange Chinese voice in her mind. Her palm rubbed her forehead as she struggled. Yet no name or face emerged. The voice without a name ...

She had to remember, she had to!

The quick clip of hooves sounded loud against the cobblestone as Seanessy stared down at her. The lovely dark eyes were hidden in shadows but he knew her distress by the hand on her forehead beneath the ridiculous hat. "Are you remembering something?"

She shook her head. "There is a strange voice in my mind ... Chinese, someone I know, but—"

Seanessy hid his alarm. "And what does this voice say, Shalyn?"

"Just now? Things about the Buddhist belief in karmic retribution, things I don't believe—the idea that the poor woman Butcher seeks to help is not deserving, as her suffering now is punishment for long-ago sins from another life."

The answer startled him, hinting at the surprising inclination of her mind. "Aye," he said in response, "the minds of our miserly species are full of such rubbish. Recently a number of prominent members of British society have been courting so-call spiritualists and mediums who propose these absurd notions." The horse fought the bit again, and Seanessy sighed. "Here, I am tired of fighting this beast. We can walk the rest of the way."

He swung off, brushed his pants before turning around to help her down. Only to find she had leaped agilely down as he had and now stood poised, apparently waiting for him. "So you think they are false beliefs as well?"

"Indeed," he said, holding the reins and moving to the side as a carriage raced toward them. "The idea is too fanciful and more self-serving than a murderer's plea of innocence. People use it to justify all manner of atrocities, especially the present injustice of the world."

"Then is it a Christian death that you believe in?"

"A Christian death is just as self-serving. With the indifference of happiness and the contempt of bliss, heaven is just as blind to the miseries of earth—"

"Seanessy!"

A feminine voice called from inside the carriage as it stopped at their side. Seanessy greeted the driver as a comely lady leaned out the window, two others waving and smiling behind her. He laughed. "Melissa!"

A jeweled band held back rich dark curls from a pretty round pale face. The woman leaned halfway out the carriage window, her bare breast pressing against the pale green fabric of her gown. She did not seem to know that the rounded edge of a nipple escaped the skimpy confines of her gown as, laughing, she reached her chubby arms out to Seanessy.

Seanessy stepped to the window and kissed her mouth.

Shalyn's eyes widened with shock. This was scandalous! Her mouth opened as if to protest, but no sound came out. Two other women appeared on either side of Melissa, each vying for a spot in the small carriage window.

"Can you meet us at the Fitzroy for a late supper tonight?" the wanton creature asked. "Everyone is going—"

Seanessy leaned forward with a grin and asked a question about the menu. With girlish giggles the women raved about an appetizer, a main course, and a dessert; a furious debate ensued about which course Seanessy would enjoy the most; Seanessy enthusiastically expressed a desire to devour each one, especially making a point of "a fondly remembered English tart."

The women laughed as if it were wildly amusing, and with promises and adieux, the carriage took off. Shalyn felt her heartbeat escalate as her breaths came quick and shallow. She was suddenly remembering his large hands on her, the feel of their bodies pressed together, the heat of it, and then, then his kiss.

She felt her face grow hot.

"You're blushing, child. Is something wrong?"

"Who was that woman?"

"Melissa? An old acquaintance."

"Do you kiss all acquaintances you meet on the street?"

"Well, no!" He appeared quite shocked by the idea. "Only those that I've bedded or intend to bed."

The look on her face made him laugh. "Oh, Lord," Seanessy said. "I might have guessed you were prudish to boot."

"Me? Prudish? Why, you ... you—"

"Unless ... why, Shalyn." He stopped to stare down at her, and in a pretense of alarm, said, "If I didn't know any better I'd say you were jealous!"

"Jealous? Me?" She pointed as if he might need a visual aid. "Of, of her?"

"You are right," he admitted easily, "an absurd idea. Why on earth would you be jealous of her?"

Shalyn nodded, though she still felt quite peeved. The whole conversation annoyed her no end; worse when she heard his laugh and the words, "You were jealous of the kiss."

Her eyes widened as if to encompass the outrage. "You want me to kiss you again."

"I what?!" For a moment her throat constricted with horror, which had the unfortunate effect of delaying her protest. The emotional intensity of her objection grew when she saw the absolutely wicked amusement in his gaze as he stared down at her. "Oh no." She shook her head adamantly. "Oh no, Seanessy!" She all but pointed at him. "You get the idea out of your mind! I would remind you my arms are free. I would not be the victim of your mauling again."

"Mauling?" Seanessy tossed his head back and laughed like a werewolf at the moon. "You are as ripe as late summer fruit! And methinks the lady doth protest too much."

"You haven't even begun to see my protest!"

Seanessy let go of the reins. The horse took off, but he didn't care. He laughed meanly. "You are full to bursting with false bravado, child." He leaned over, his cape tossed about his shoulders. "I say I'll have your backside to the wet ground for my mauling inside of three minutes."

Her gaze narrowed menacingly, but this was a trick, a stall. Because he could, she knew he could. Why did he have to be so tall and strong and quick?

Oh, he loved this! He relished it! She bit her lip, wondering if she could outrun him. Probably not.

She glanced into the surrounding darkness, and noticed, "The grass does look very wet ..."

"Beggar's luck," he said and announced, "for I intend to be on top."

Stifling the nervous rush of sensation, she tried to look cross instead. "If I forfeit, will you at least put your cape under me? I truly do not want to be against the wet grass."

"Oh, very well," he relented. "I'll even do the business standing up if you hold still."

"You will be quick about it?"

"I might want to, but if experience has taught me any one thing, it's that it's best if one takes one's sweet time."

"Not too slow," she said hopefully, then added crossly, "oh, very well. Get on with it."

She stood very still. He approached. Her heart began a slow escalation as he came to stand in front of her. She desperately tried not to think of the taste of apples and spice and what it was like to be kissed by him. He first brushed stray wisps of her hair over and around her ear. She gasped as tiny shivers darted from the spot.

Warm amusement filled his gaze as he stared down at her, his large hands gently circling her wrists as he brought them behind her back, the movement arching her toward him. Her hat fluttered to the ground.

She searched his face and saw the mad pleasure of an ogre tormenting his vassal. "Just because I forfeit doesn't mean I really want you to," she said, trying to give it conviction, sounding so queerly breathless again. How did he do this to her? She felt certain he should be boxing her ears instead of kissing her. "I'd really rather not suffer your kisses again!"

"Shalyn, has anyone ever mentioned that your

eyes darken dramatically every time you tell a false-hood? And they are so dark now ..."

She was shaking her head and he was laughing, his amusement a tickle against her ear. She felt large warm fingers on the back of her neck beneath the weight of her hair, his other hand gently pressing into her back, gently aligning her against his body. She gasped with the strange rush of heady sensations. "Oh, I think I made a terrible mistake!"

He laughed. "Let me rectify it, child."

The black cloak surrounding them, she felt the enticing heat of his body growing. She went very still, mesmerized by his darkening gaze as he leaned even closer. "You know, Shalyn," he began obliquely, his mouth so close, his voice sounding rich and deep and distracted as if he was now thinking of something far, far away, "I don't understand why I want to kiss you, but I do. There's a part of me that is quite certain it is the very last thing I want to do too, that I would be much happier hanging myself, and yet ... yet ..."

The sentence was never finished. Panic tumbled into confusion as his hand gently reached around to her chin and he leaned over. Trembling slightly, she forgot to breathe. He first kissed her closed lids before letting his mouth lightly graze her forehead where he drank the lingering trace of a sweet lavender scent—the soap Tilly had used on her hair. She felt another rush of tiny shivers, a feverish trail where his moist lips touched her skin before the curve of his fingers gently parted her lips for his kiss.

A warm firm mouth covered hers. He pulled back slightly. "Open up, Shalyn," he whispered huskily as he gently bit her lower lip. "The business works best with two people participating."

She gasped with a sudden deep breath, her lips parting with an invitation. Seanessy did not waste the gesture. A cry sounded in her throat as she felt the gentle molding of his mouth on hers, the warm intrusion of his tongue. The slight tremble of her lips, like an uncertain cry, told him she was indeed a novice at this, and with effort he called upon all the gentleness he knew.

So tenderly did he first kiss her, she felt a strange sense of wonder, mixed potently with some small distress, which he answered with the sensual press of mouth, deepening, fueling a tingling warmth surging from far inside, growing, spreading, until—

The pleasure magnified as his tongue teased with a beguiling eroticism that sent her into a soft swoon, melting and helpless. He broke the kiss but did not release her. "Dear Lord," he said, brushing his lips against hers, "you taste like warmth and sunshine. Shalyn," he said her name. "Shalyn . . ."

He kissed her again, deeply and yet gently, and somewhere in the space and wonder of this kiss, he had lifted her up, while pressing her tighter to him. Quite suddenly it changed.

Her consciousness riveted to the heat there, to the press of his hand on the small of her back as he forced her against him there—

She panicked, braced for the rutting, the terrifying rutting—

Seanessy felt the exact moment he lost her. A bucket of ice water might have just fallen over her head. He lifted partially from her to stare into the dark pools of her eyes.

"What's this, Shalyn?"

She bit her lip, anxiety changing her face. He peered through the darkness to see the unexpected emotion. "What were you thinking to make you suddenly afraid?"

"I . . . I thought you would . . . you know . . ." She couldn't finish. She suddenly remembered a surge of dread, a feeling of helplessness as hands came to her person . . .

"I'm afraid I don't."

She searched his face. "I can't say it."

"Why not?"

"It shames me."

"Just give 'it' a name—" He abruptly recalled, "Oh wait. I remember. You called it 'rutting,' am I right?"

"I don't mind when you kiss me," she whispered, her hand touching her lips where she felt the lingering sensations.

A bemused smile changed his face as he wondered at an honesty as beguiling as her innocence.

"But I don't like the rest."

He considered her for a moment. "More than that, it seems. The rest frightens you, a bit more than a virgin's fear too, I'd wager. Do you remember an unpleasant experience?"

As he asked the question, he watched her hand wrap around her wrist, rubbing. "I don't remember, Seanessy! I remember feeling . . . helpless, and I don't know! It's all so vague, I don't really know."

With his own alarm he took her delicate wrists in his hands, studying them, as if he could see marks left from ropes. Someone had tied her up. Strong warm fingers gently soothed and stroked the trembling limbs as he forced himself to remain calm, marveling that he could. "So tell me, Shalyn: just what is it you know about the physical play between a man and a woman?"

She felt so curiously, disastrously close to tears. She squeezed her eyes shut for a moment and shook her head.

"Shalyn, I need to know. I want to know what has happened to you."

"I don't know, Seanessy!"

"Tell me this then: what is it you imagine happens after kissing?"

She held herself against a chill. "Mating."

"Mating, another fine euphemism. Shalyn," he began, his voice gentle, his tone quite frank. "You can believe there is nothing you can say to me I haven't already heard before. Look at me, child: they are just words. Words have no potency unless matched by action. I'm trying to figure out what happened to you. Tell me what you imagine, ah, mating is." He hid his fear of her answer, if there was an answer. "Do you even know?"

"Mating is ... well, when a man tries to fit, fit that part of his body into the woman. It doesn't usually work, I know. It doesn't work, when somehow ... I don't know! I know people who have children have made it work somehow but I ..."

"You suffer a deformity!"

Seanessy's brows crossed as his mind raced over this, placing her words alongside the exclamation and creating a telling picture. Some man must have tied her up—no doubt to avoid the girl's remarkable ability to defend herself, only to find himself unable to perform. "Dear Lord." He tried to temper the violence of his emotion, and it was hard. "You know, I can hardly wait to meet your past, Shalyn. I believe it will be a singular pleasure." He bent over and retrieved her hat. "Here, Shalyn. Can you walk still? Good. We are already quite late. Now let me attempt to explain a few facts to you—"

"Facts?" she questioned as they resumed walking, her mind settling uneasily on the subject. "You mean about ... mating?"

"Why not?" He grinned as he gently placed a protective arm around her shoulder. "I've always been quite certain that knowledge is both liberating and enlightening. Every young woman should be fully informed on the subject of physical intimacies between men and women, if only to save her the shock of her wedding night. So let's see . . ."

Shalyn listened intently as he began his explanation, not realizing how the arresting conversation eased her from the terror of an experience she somehow couldn't remember but nonetheless still felt its lingering effects. Of course she knew most of what he told her, except for the disconcerting parts where apparently her experience had led her astray, despite her maddening failure to remember what that experience was. That was a surprise. To her credit, she only started blushing when he finally got to explaining certain variations, and she realized she was imagining these things with Seanessy. Her heartbeat grew more rapid, and she swallowed as she turned the startling images around in her mind. "Does everyone do that?"

"Aye." He chuckled at her surprise. "Adam and Eve were only the first. Now I see an enlightened—very!—expression on your face. I suppose I can rest assured the remaining parts of your education will come the old-fashioned way."

They came out of the park and onto the street, and Seanessy began pointing out the sights as they walked into the London night. She forgot all about their conversation, and only because the London night was a marvel to her. London! Carriages and riders made their way along the street even at this late hour. People congregated outside taverns and eating establishments. The faint scent of roasting pork reached the street, mingling with the pungent odor of chimney smoke. A boy standing on the corner hawked newspapers. Another man stood on a crate and with Bible in hand, shouted verses at the indifferent passersby. A group of young boys taunted the poor man, and he turned his ferocious passion on them. A couple strolled arm in arm nearby, laughing at some shared amusement, and she studied the woman's slow unhurried gait, her fine and pretty clothes: a pale rose-velvet cloak and matching hat, a fetching parasol used in the night as a walking stick. She caught sight of a white-clothed chef standing in the alley for a breath of cool air as they passed—everything and everyone was a source of fascination to her.

Which Seanessy noticed. "So you don't remember ever being in London before, Shalyn?"

She shook her head. Seeing this brief glimpse of its famous nightlife and hearing the raised English voices still felt exciting, foreign, and new to her. She had the strangest sense that she had been here once long ago. She must have been here as a child. The image of the lovely Tudor-style house rose in her mind's eye again and she was about to tell him this, but they turned down the gravel road leading to the famous hotel, the Connaught.

The Connaught rose six stories, one of the tallest buildings in London, its ornate carved-stone facade a tribute to modern architecture. Golden light came from any number of the windows. Seanessy greeted the grooms pleasantly before turning to warn her.

"Shalyn," he whispered as they started up the stairs, "show me some mercy here from your, ah, warring countenance. Grant me a truce, if only temporary. Mind everything I say, without exception, no matter if you don't understand. For your own safety. Will you, Shalyn?"

Cautioned by the rare seriousness of his tone, she nodded. "Aye." The last thing she wanted was someone's—anyone's!—attention. He swung his cape off his shoulders and placed it about hers, watched how it enveloped her shoulder to toes. The wide-brimmed hat covered her head and shielded her face.

She looked as if she were masquerading and was pleased with the effect. He pulled the hat down a bit. Butcher already waited with Kyler. Seanessy took Shalyn by the arm and escorted her up the wide steps to the front doors.

The moment they swept into the brightly lit space of the entrance hall, everything became a blur of movement. The doorman greeted Seanessy, who dismissed the necessity of the doorman leading him to the waiting tables in the game room.

Shalyn's gaze swept the rich place, its dark polished furnishings, the magnificent chandeliers with the new modern gas lights ingeniously shaped like candles. Men she recognized from Seanessy's ship approached and surrounded him as they moved down the hall.

"The place is swarming with 'em, Cap'n. A head count of fifty-five."

"His apartment number?"

"The entire second and third floor—the duke is residing in twenty-seven, -eight, and -nine, ye know— the north suite. Two men posted at the door—"

"Only two?"

"Dogs inside, Sean—trained killers by the looks of 'em."

"Dogs? Well, Butcher, take a turn through the kitchen. Now." Sean stopped and turned to the men as they approached the crowded hall where music and raised masculine voices drifted to them. "I want humiliation made worse with no bloodshed—"

"No bloodshed? And so how do we get Butcher through the door?"

"Which lovely ladies are working the house tonight?"

"Oh, I've seen Kelly, Teresa, and Mary—"

"Fetch Mary, will you. That lady's ample charms can take out the men without a shot fired—'tis the oldest trick in the book. She lures the beggar down the hall where you wait, then her scream draws out the other."

Butcher nodded. "Let me do the rest, Sean. I'll need the master key."

"Tell our dear concierge it's for a charitable cause and hand him a donation," Sean said. "Oh yes, and for the little beasts, those dogs of his: send someone to the ship for those miniature barrels—you know, Oly's mugs—and set these around their scruffy necks." The other men laughed, interrupting him midsentence, and Sean chuckled too. "And a bouquet of flowers with my card should be just the thing to draw him out for an introduction."

"Aye, aye." The men rushed off.

Shalyn didn't understand a word they said, but then she wasn't thinking of it as they turned a corner and Seanessy's arm swept her into a wide open space. Tables crowded the hall. Men gathered at the white-linen-covered tables with cards and dice and chess sets; drinks of ale, port, and whiskey; decorated bowls of fruit and cheese; and plates of bread. An enormous counter ran along the opposite wall, where four men rushed to fill drink orders. The greatest novelty was the wall behind the counter. Shalyn stared into the longest looking glass she had ever seen, the mirror running the entire length of the bar, reflecting the room. Musicians serenaded the patrons from the corner, the gay melody drowned in the boisterous noise of the men.

She realized with some astonishment that a good portion of the men here were Seanessy's, from his ship. Greetings were called and exchanged. Slight movements brought Shalyn's keen gaze to the far corner where, oblivious to the plotting and seemingly in deep commune, Frenchmen gathered at four of the tables. Seanessy conferred in whispers with a group of men, some familiar, and just when she imagined he had quite forgotten her presence, one of the men appeared at her side. "Shalyn! Our beautiful young troublemaker!"

Her amber eyes greeted the handsome young man. Richards. Bright blue, blue eyes danced with excitement and merriment. He sported two ivory-handled pistoles as well. "May I escort you out of the way. The captain wants you seated around the corner. If you will." He motioned with a sweep of his hands.

A swift pang of disappointment surged through her. She hesitated briefly. She wanted to watch Seanessy and see what was going to happen. She was surprised by the power of the desire. Richards gently took her arm, leading her around the corner. He obsequiously fetched her a chair and set it against the wall.

Shalyn sat down reluctantly only to realize she stared straight ahead into the long mirror. She had the best seat in the house, a front row seat for the theatrics in the room. She bit her lip as her interested gaze peeked from behind the hat, only to see Seanessy laughing as he sat at a table with Kyler, Ham, two well-dressed men, and the three men wearing the dark blue uniforms of British naval officers. One of these men was no less than "an admiral!" she said in a whisper, noting the round face, heavy jowls, long sideburns, and graying sides to neatly cropped hair. "Richards, is that not the gold braid and uniform of a British admiral?"

"Aye. Kingston," Richards told her, standing guard at her side. "One of England's finest and the captain's good friend."

"I am surprised," she confessed, watching as the boisterous table erupted in friendly laughter. "And the other gentlemen?"

"Ham is our navigator, don't you know? Kyler is captain of the—"

"No. The men clad in a gentleman's dark velvet."

"Don't let that fool you, miss! Lord Marshmaine may look the dandy, but the man is regent magistrate of London's constables, and probably possesses the only fortune larger than ole George's. And then the young Lord Winifield Scott there is William's son-in-law."

"William?" She did not know who that was.

"The king's brother, miss. You see," he bothered to explain, "the company was not randomly chosen for an evening's amusement."

Men of authority and position. She watched with heightened interest. Dark-clothed waiters bustled about the table. Several minutes passed as everyone seemed to be talking at once. She watched three women approach from across the room and surround the table. "Who are they?"

"The ladies? Ah, Molly's girls."

She tried not to be scandalized by the idea of women serving strangers in bars. She knew this happened: that all unworthy women abandoned by men were shred of dignity and forced of necessity to serve men to whom they had no familial relationship. It was a Western way. It was not the Oriental way: no woman, servant, or lady would ever serve men that were not members or honored guests of the house where she belonged. "They are serving women of this bar room?"

The question at first confused young Richards, and he brushed an errant curl from his forehead. Either Shalyn was greener than a rainwashed field in sunlight or she had landed here from a foreign country or both.

"Aye." He smiled. "Like barmaids, they are."

Shalyn had not heard. Her attention was riveted

on those beautiful women: their indecently loosened hair and rich gowns with shockingly low-cut bodices over the ample swells of their bosoms. Laughter erupted from the table as the wanton women swarmed around Seanessy like bees to a blossom, bending over as if purposely to display their charms to his gaze. Even when they were not, she felt a twinge of embarrassment for their humiliation. To sacrifice one's dignity for want of coin . . .

Laughing at something, Seanessy lifted Mary onto his lap. With no small horror, Shalyn watched as he kissed the woman.

Color rose in her cheeks as she turned it over in her mind. True, he had just pressed a kiss on her own lips, but at least he had not done it in public view. Why would he do this to a woman? Did he have no feelings? It was the cruelest denunciation of a woman's chastity and dignity. Making her little better than a prostitute—

A prostitute? She looked back up. In the mirror she saw the woman's rosy cheeks as she laughed. She certainly did not seem to mind. The admiral fitted his hands around her friend's derriere, laughing as well.

Dear Lord, they were prostitutes; the concubines who visited his home were not enough. The captain, indeed all the men at the table, cavorted with prostitutes . . .

Something in her nature prevented from her judging these women and the men who gave them coins, for the desperateness of her own circumstances made her realize how far one might trespass to survive and be safe.

Butcher and two other men appeared and approached the table. Words were exchanged before Butcher took one woman's arm and led her out of the room, disappearing with a number of others. For several long minutes and more Shalyn watched with fascination and awe the lively scene at the captain's table. She was struck by the novelty of Englishmen's boisterous recreation. The English were so loud, so crass, so blunt! No hidden depths or secrets behind the surface facade, and this seemed so strange—that one would put one's whole person up for public display and scrutiny.

The idea seemed at once foolish and barbaric and yet—

Yet it was also deliciously compelling . . .

After nearly an hour Butcher reappeared with the prostitute. She couldn't hear what he was saying but he seemed pleased—very. Seanessy laughed and raised a crystal glass for a toast. She could not make out the words but the table erupted in laughter. Seanessy grabbed the pretty woman's arm and pulled her down for another public kiss as he swept a bill into her bodice.

Merciful mother in heaven . . .

For a long while nothing interrupted the riotous amusement of the party. A dull ache began to throb in her head from her injury. She ignored this, sitting perfectly composed in her chair. Laughter erupted every few seconds from various tables. The noise seemed to rise; the musicians gave up trying to compete. It was hot.

"May I trouble you for some water?"

Richards quickly flagged down a waiter who served her at once. She finished the water and felt relieved. She was certain she was unaccustomed to so much noise and commotion. She needed to transcend it. A religious chant emerged in her mind. The noise became a backdrop in her head as the chant grew louder in her consciousness. With it she relaxed, easing the tension from her body—

Suddenly like a great burst of arctic wind, the Duke de la Armanac swept into the room. Shalyn stared straight ahead into the mirror and a tingle of alarm shot up her spine, alarm owing to a magnificent and imperial presence that seemed to absorb the space around him, as if in fact he were larger than life. With hands on hips, he surveyed the crowded room with his dark gaze. In those first few seconds she noticed everything and all at once: that he was handsome and devastatingly so came as a surprise; she had not expected it. He wore fine traveling clothes: black boots and pants, a white silk and lace shirt, and a black, red-silk-lined cape, tossed carelessly over one shoulder.

Yet nearly everyone was drawn to the unnatural fury in his dark eyes. Raven-black hair, brushed with gray, was combed back above sharply chiseled features, accented by a pointed goatee. He had dark brows and eyes, a large fine nose, and a perfect mouth, except for the hard lines around it—lines that suggested a conceit and arrogance more monstrous than Seanessy's, and until she saw it, she wouldn't have believed this was possible in a mere mortal being.

Twelve armed men rushed in behind him, fanning out in a practiced line of defense. Shalyn's keen expertise spotted five warriors from this group who had been trained to the Oriental arts, as Seanessy had called it. That there were so many used by a French duke was a surprise until she recalled the connection to the Chinese opium trade.

Silence rushed like a wind through the crowded hall, disappearing in the whispered amusement of the Englishmen. Seated at the four tables, other members of the duke's guard were not amused, but alarmed, as they quickly stood at attention. Richards stood at alert, not the only man present to suddenly withdraw a pistole. This silence escaped the captain's table, where Admiral Kingston finished an amusing anecdote about the publisher Taylor and his newest mistress, and the table burst into laughter, profane against the new stillness and silence that was the room.

She didn't realize she held her breath until it was released in a rush. Even in those first few moments she could not stop the comparison of the two main players here, for Seanessy had that same unnatural arrogance. Yet Seanessy's arrogance was and always would be altered by an ever-present devil-may-care amusement, and an unmistakable greed and lust for life.

One by one the men at the captain's table quieted and turned to see who stood there. Shalyn gasped as she caught sight of the reckless sedition in Seanessy's gaze, half expecting that the Duke de la Armanac would shoot Seanessy for the impertinence suggested by his careless manner: the amused grin as he turned, the hands brushing back his long hair, then holding his head from behind, and the worst, his long booted feet on the table.

"Well." The rich timbre of Seanessy's voice called out. "If it isn't the great Duke de la Armanac himself!"

The duke removed his expensive white gloves and snapped his fingers. A man leaped forward and nodded toward the blond captain. "And you, sir, are Captain Seanessy, I presume?" the duke said.

His voice matched perfectly his appearance: regal, authoritative, and unmistakably taxed as he folded his gloves in his belt before returning his hands to his hips. Shalyn could hardly believe Seanessy's response, though, the very light of amusement in his eyes, as if this were all great fun. He merely nodded to Butcher, who rose and crossed the room to where Shalyn sat transfixed.

"At your service, Your Grace," Seanessy said with

a great show of obsequiousness. Without bothering to rise or indeed even drop his large booted feet from the table, Seanessy named the other men seated around him, "Please allow me the pleasure of introducing the gentlemen here: Lord Marshmaine, Constable General of London, Lord Winifield Scott, Admiral Kingston, his officers Crowely and Billings, my captain Kyler, and my first officer Hamilton."

The duke first said nothing as his dark eyes traveled over each of the men at the table, understanding at once the message in the presence of the constable, the admiral, and the King's own brother's son-in-law. A show of British brutality and power, which neither alarmed him nor interested him except as it meant he would have to absorb the loss of his finest ship without due compensation.

The fine dark eyes stopped but briefly on the oddity of Hamilton—a Negro man seated as an equal with whites, who then dared to raise a cup to his honor—but he made no response, past the slightest narrowing of his gaze. He drew back slightly as if cushioning the affront. The English were so barbaric and crass with their liberal abolitionist sentiments!

"Your Grace," Seanessy continued in the same outrageous manner, "allow me to offer our sincerest expression of sympathy upon hearing about your terrible misfortune today. You did receive my condolences, did you not?"

Condolences that came the way of three trained guard dogs wearing ridiculous red ribbons and Swiss mugs around their necks as they devoured a leg of lamb each, then the most enraging part: a bouquet of flowers on his bed, a blunt warning that there was no one and no place, either private or public, this outrageous rogue would not try to reach. The two large men at his side stepped forward, but the duke held them back with but a slight lift of his hand and shake of his head.

"A terrible crime," the admiral was saying. "A fine seafaring clipper like that—blown sky-high! Marshmaine," he asked loudly and pointedly, "I do hope you are trying to find the culprits?"

Marshmaine replied, "Oh, I assure you I am doing my British best, Admiral."

The Duke de la Armanac held himself quite still; all his fury was unleashed in tightening lips and the quiet thrust of a demand: "What is the meaning of this?"

"The meaning?" Seanessy questioned. "Why, I'm not sure I know, Your Grace. I have no idea what the meaning is of fine seafaring ships being blown to hell. It is alarming how it seems to be going around these days; my own dear brother suffered the same not long ago."

The duke absorbed this with a quizzical look. "Your brother?"

"Oh, you know him, Your Grace. Lord Barrington. I believe you recently entertained the Lord and Lady Barrington at your island estate. Apparently you rather boldly, if not rudely, made him an offer for our Malacca shipping enterprise?"

It was an Irish grin Seanessy gave him; full of mischief and the devil's own humor. Shalyn slowly rose from her seat, to stand between Butcher and Richards. She could see the strange effect of Seanessy's words as they turned over in the duke's mind, resulting in an expression of skeptical disbelief. "You?" He seemed torn between laughter and outrage. "You—claiming a familial relationship with Lord Barrington?"

"I see you are surprised, Your Grace. The truth is we were brothers in heart—long before we learned it in fact. Suffice to say, we are half-brothers. It is a well-known secret that Lord Barrington maintains the land and wealth of the Barrington title, while drawing his actual blood from an illicit mating between a rebel priest and his good mother, Lady Alicia Barrington, the same as my dear mother, Mary Seanessy—"

"Good God, man!" The dark eyes widened with obvious shock that anyone, even this outrageous captain, would trespass so far from the conventions of society as to publicly announce such a vulgar piece of family genealogy. "If you will kindly spare me these details of your sordid paternity."

"As you wish, Your Grace," Seanessy relented easily. "The part of our admittedly notorious past that I hope interests you is simple and it is this: there are no persons living I love more than Lord and Lady Barrington. Nor is there a limit to my unqualified and unparalleled affection. I might put it in trite sentimental banalities: I would be happy to die a thousand deaths for them. Which is why I hope you can be coerced to exercise your own efforts in preventing any more of these, ah, explosions."

Antipathy shimmered in the duke's dark gaze. Very slowly, he said, "This is an outrage."

"Aye," Seanessy completely agreed. "And so are the deaths of two dearly loved servants, so carefully positioned in Joy's garden walk, and then the explosion on her husband's ship as she passed down the plank with my young nephews in arm. Mind my words: an intolerable outrage."

The duke's jeweled fingers clenched at his sides. The men behind him, even those who could not comprehend English, understood the nature of the insults. They stepped forward to answer them. By this point every man in the hall not only held a pistole but aimed it at someone. The tall dark man closest to the duke said, *"Damme comme un Anglais!"*

The duke snapped an order in rapid French and Shalyn gasped as she heard the warning: "Easy! This is not the place." The admiral, acting for Seanessy, motioned with his hand. The pistoles were lowered reluctantly. Butcher kept two queerly curved daggers positioned in his hand.

The duke turned back to Seanessy, who watched with what seemed like mild interest.

Slowly, with mounting fury, the duke demanded, "How is it you are so certain I had something to do with an explosion—"

"Quite the contrary, Your Grace," Seanessy interrupted him. "You misunderstood me. I assure you I am not at all certain. For if I were certain," he said with sudden soft viciousness that reached across the space to act like a hard slap on the face, "my hands would be dripping in a French duke's hot blood as I hung his head, like those of so many French noblemen before him, from the very Tower of London."

Whispered gasps of shock raced through the French side and Shalyn alone spotted the movement: "Third behind!"

Butcher's eyes whipped to the raised dagger a split second before it flew at Seanessy's neck. With a flick of his wrist, his own blade sailed through the air. Across the room the man's startled scream sounded loud and unnatural. All eyes turned to the arresting sight of the man's hand pinned to the wall by Butcher's knife. The man's dagger dropped to the carpeted floor, followed by a bright stream of red blood. Shalyn instantly ducked out of sight as all gazes returned to Butcher.

Two men rushed to aid the injured man, while simultaneously the duke halted all motions of retribution before a bloodbath started. Admiration rose in her amber eyes as she peeked from behind her hat to see this. The courage necessary to stop the waiting violence in this roomful of fury and warring factions seemed both noble and grand, every bit as large as Seanessy's reckless boldness.

Once the men seemed to settle, the duke turned back to Seanessy, and in a voice made strong with control, he said, "This impressive little charade, Captain Seanessy, would be amusing if it were not so terribly deadly. And because of the deadly nature of this outrageous game you play with me, I will condescend to protest my innocence. I assure you I had nothing to do with any explosion on board any of Lord Barrington's ships."

"Indeed," Seanessy said, noticeably without interest or conviction, unwilling to give the man any quarter. "I am so glad to hear this, Your Grace. Now that I can count on your prayers for Lord and Lady Barrington's continued good health, I am left with the awesome task of trying to discover the real culprit to cast in my little drama. You wouldn't have any educated guesses, now would you?"

The duke laughed as if the affair was now becoming a bad joke. "I care to aid you on this difficult task only insofar as it also aids me and mine. But I find this situation"—he looked at the men and the table—"your company in particular, increasingly taxing; I must take leave. If you could temper your impertinence and these outlandish insults, I might be willing to entertain a notion of another, perhaps more fruitful discussion of your perplexing difficulties. Until then, Captain Seanessy . . ." Without further word, he turned and left the room.

The twelve men followed him out. The remaining French guards slowly returned to their seats.

The men at the captain's table watched in silence. Admiral Kingston sighed and asked, "What say you, Seanessy: guilty or no?"

Seanessy considered the question. "I wish I knew.

For I've never met anyone I would like to think deserving of my animosity more than that grand bag of hot pretensions. Like a self-declared king, he is. My hands are trembling with their restraint."

"A self-declared king indeed! Reminds me of someone," the admiral said, and the laughter dissipated the tension. "And, Seanessy, I have never known you to exercise restraint." Nodding at the remaining tables of Frenchmen, he ventured, "I wager fifty pounds sterling it takes less than a quarter of an hour to clear the room of those foul smelling frogs."

Sean laughed, but Richards had approached and now leaned over the table, whispering something to him. "What? The duke is—!?"

Richards nodded, grinning.

A dark brow rose over Seanessy's laughing eyes.

"Kingston," he said, "you have a bet. Double if my boys do the dirty business in less than ten minutes."

Butcher sighed and took Shalyn's arm to lead her away.

Wagers were made even as Admiral Kingston's fine loud voice crossed the short distance separating the French from the English: "Well, I say! French dukes are like their farts: always making a lot of noise and raising stink and never wanting to go back where they came from!"

The insult was quickly translated for those who did not speak the English tongue. An outraged Frenchman tossed a drink; the toss was answered by the nearest Englishman's fist. The fight was on . . .

Chapter 6

"Shalyn, Shalyn."
"My name is Shalyn."
"There is an Irish myth . . ."
"Is it a happy story?"

A haunting sadness sprang in his hazel eyes.

She needed to find the treasure to make it a happy story. A gray sky melted into a grayer sea. She felt the warm sea breeze against her hot cheeks as it blew across the crescent bay and lifted her long, loosened hair around her face. She lifted the rich silk of her dressing gown and climbed down the cliff to the water's edge.

The sand felt cool on her bare feet. She walked along the shoreline, watching the gentle swell and waves lick the shore. She began looking for seashells, treasure.

An occasional wave washed warm water over feet, tickling. The treasure was hidden. She searched and searched, but there was nothing but white sand. She turned suddenly to see the pink silk kimono draped across the cliff. She screamed. She started to run. Someone was chasing her. A dark shadow.

She looked behind. The shadow was so close! She ran faster and faster, still searching the white sand for the treasure. The clouds gathered, darkening. The shadow grew and grew. She heard its breathing. She needed that treasure!

The tide was coming in!

Something stuck out of the sand ahead. Her heart pounded harder still. She looked closer. A round object rose from the wet sand at the shoreline. She held her breath as she cautiously approached it. Then suddenly it turned toward her and she screamed again.

A human skull washed in the tide . . .

He was hot and hard and filled with lust for the girl. He was chasing her laughter. Like a siren's song, the musical sound drove him half-crazed as he chased her.

Shalyn, Shalyn!

He caught her. Carefully he cushioned her fall. Her laughter stopped as he came over her slim form. Her eyes darkened as he parted her gown. His hands slid impatiently over the soft rise of her breasts. Oh, Lord. The scent of her. He took her mouth beneath his, a kiss without end. He let his lips travel over the petal-soft skin to finally reach the tempting peak. His hand raised her skirts, parting her slim thighs to feel the welcoming moist sheath. Oh, Lord, he would not last—

Richards pounded on the door.

Seanessy woke to the impatient pounding perfectly matched to his heart. For a long moment he suffered a disorientation, simply because he needed that time to realize the carnal dream was just that—a dream. Not since he was thirteen and had discovered just what chasing that cotter's wench led to. "My God!"

He swung his bare feet to the floor and moved quickly to the door. "It had better be good," he mumbled as he opened it. "What?"

"Shalyn, Sean. You better have a look."

Seanessy followed Richards through the sitting room into the hall. A single lamp lit the space above

Richards's chair, just alongside the green room. Richards's discarded book sat on the floor. The door was open. Seanessy heard the sound before he saw. He stepped quickly through the door. The bed was empty, the bedclothes rumpled.

"In the closet," Richards said behind him.

As long as he lived he would never forget the sight of her. The closet doors were open. Shalyn sat curled up in the farthest corner of the empty closet. Her eyes were closed. Trembling like a leaf caught in an autumn wind, she was shaking her head with a weak choking cry, a doomed child's last plea.

"Shalyn!"

He swept down to lift her out. She woke from her nightmare to feel strong arms around her. She cried weakly against him, her clenched fists hitting his rock-hard chest as he lifted her up. "No, no, Shalyn," he said in an urgent whisper as he brought her feverish form against his strength. "It's me, Seanessy. Seanessy!"

She cried out, her cry stopping as she realized the fact. She collapsed against him all at once. He held her tightly against his body, her arms clinging to his neck as if her life depended on it, and it did, it did. "Seanessy."

His name was a magic powerful enough to pull her from the dark world of night terrors into a safe world of mercy and sunshine. "Seanessy," she kept repeating over and over again, part of the incantation that saved her. All she knew was that she wanted never to let him go. In the dark place of dreams, where truth supersedes all lies, she knew she was safe. Seanessy made the world safe. Seanessy would not hurt her.

The shock of her slender form on his felt like a lightning bolt, the all-too-real answer to his carnal lust. Dear Lord. He closed his eyes, trying to temper the sudden racing of his thick blood, feeling her slim soft curves pressed against his hot skin. Every breath pressed her breasts against his chest and—

He would have her backside to the bed in the next minute. He attempted to ease her feet to the floor.

"No. Please," she whispered, "don't let me go."

She heard his soft vicious curse. He swept her up in his arms. She buried her face in his chest, hardly aware as he carried her through the doors and down the hall into his sitting room, lastly into his bedchamber. He set her on the bed. There was a brief moment of separation. A muted cry sounded in the cool night air before he drew her back against the warmth of his body.

She felt her raw and frightened emotions melting like ice beneath a warm summer sun. She took sweet deep breaths. She closed her eyes, feeling the tender stroke of his hands through her hair.

"You are trembling still," he said as he drew the comforter over them both. Her shuddering form pressed against his hot length. He felt her toes on his shins, her hips against his heat, pounding with feverish desire. His hands combed through the tousled mass of her gold hair. He wondered if he had ever felt anything so tempting as the tease of her warm breaths on his neck. He desperately needed a distraction. "Shalyn mine, a nightmare?"

"Aye . . ."

Lightly, in a whisper, he asked, "Were you chased by phantom shapes?"

"Aye!" She buried her face against his chest, unaware of the effect of this. "I am looking for a treasure, seashells on a beach. I feel like I know this beach. It is so beautiful . . . and I feel as if, as if I have found solace there. Then suddenly I realize someone is chasing me. The dark phantom. I start running and running. And then—"

Her voice choked, her fear palpable.

"Yes?"

"Then suddenly I see skulls, human skulls stuck in the sand. People buried alive! And I, I—"

She could not finish. The terror of the skulls was frightful; she felt as if she had caused the hideous deaths, that it was her fault. Seanessy tightened his arms around her. "Shalyn." He brushed his lips tenderly against her forehead. "Shalyn, my poor, poor waif. There are times when I am as grateful as a rich heir for your lost memory."

Gratitude was the last thing she felt. She had to find her missing memory. Because they were coming for her. She would find this beach in the South China Seas. Somehow she knew it was real. As real as the fear it inspired. When she knew what had happened to her, and who was chasing her, and why, then she would know how to fight them.

She had to convince Seanessy to help her get there.

Seanessy shifted away slightly, desperate to relieve the tension alighting on every nerve, muscle, and piece of flesh in his body. Her each breath came at a cost, an ever-increasing cost as he felt the tips of her breasts brush light as a feather against his chest, an unbearable tease.

Lord, she felt so soft and slim and warm . . .

He chuckled softly as he actually felt his pulse in his groin. She gasped, startled eyes looked up to find him. "Are you laughing at me?"

"Myself, Shalyn, myself."

He looked down to see the amber eyes searching his, and even in the darkness, the faint light of a crescent moon shining through the open window, he saw the question. Her lips—

No, do not think of those lips! Remember she's a virgin!

Moments ticked by, filling with a voluptuous promise.

"Seanessy?"

"Yes . . ."

"My name? Shalyn." Just as in her nightmare she asked him, "Was it a happy Irish tale?"

"What?" He was having a great deal of trouble concentrating. "Oh. Ah, well . . ." His passion-drugged mind caught up to the question. It caught him off-guard. Why had he decided to call her Shalyn? A lovely name, aye, but the story was told to young people to prepare them for the inevitability of their arranged marriage, to warn them of the tragedy brought by the passion of true love.

"Is it?"

"Aye." He returned his hands to her hair and he lied, " 'Tis indeed a happy tale, though admittedly not a very good one."

"I don't care. Would you tell it to me now?"

The words were a soft whisper of desperation—the desperation of a young woman who badly needed a distraction from the tired circle of her thoughts, if only for a moment. Seanessy was many things, and one of them was kind. So it was with kindness that he said, "No doubt you will be surprised that I am not well-known for my ability to spin tales, but for you, Shalyn, I shall try. It goes something like this." His gaze searched the ceiling as if he might see the story printed there. "Once upon a time the Irish people did not believe in true love."

"Oh?" she asked.

He stared at the upturned face. "Do you, Shalyn?"

His voice sounded light and teasing. She rewarded him with a smile and a nod. "Aye, 'tis a heavenly wonder when it comes," he agreed, his voice taking on an animated Irish brogue. "But long ago the Irish were too world-weary to believe in such. The goodly Irish folks worked too blessed hard pullin' potatoes from an unyielding soil, workin' from dawn to sundown to harvest enough to keep the bairns from cryin' out in the dark middle of the night for want of food.

"One day in the midst of a cold hard winter, a lad was born to a lowly cotter woman who etched the barest livin' from a rocky plot of a baron's piece of land. The lad was as bonny and brawny as a knight's by-blow, quick of mind and faster of feet. He grew and thrived. His life, like many an Irish lad's, was a great joy to his mother."

A single lamp lit the spacious room and bathed them in a soft golden light. Almost touching, they faced each other on their sides. Seanessy rhythmically smoothed the long and loosened hair that spread behind her across the crisp white bedclothes. Even as he spoke, he studied the beauty laid before him: the dark and delicate arch of brow over lovely eyes, the flush in her cheeks, the tempting curve of her lips, lifting slightly with childlike anticipation of his story.

"The winter his mother died, the baron gave our deserving orphan to his shepherd to learn the care and keeping of sheep. Learn he did. The flock thrived and multiplied under the boy's care. It was during the spring when rain colored the land its emerald-green and the skies turned corn-flower blue that he first saw her.

"She was the baron's youngest daughter and she was beautiful. A young girl made of joy, gaiety, and laughter. She had hair the color of late summer fields, and eyes that were dark with promises."

Shalyn laughed, catching his trick, and the sweet music of it went through him like a caress. His control was a new kind of marvel to him. Desire burned hot and bright through him; he wondered if he had ever wanted a woman as much.

"A highborn lady she was, and many, many worlds separate from our young shepherd. He could not presume to so much as speak to her, nor could or would she condescend to speak to him. He was as invisible as the air to her. She never noticed him long enough to learn his name. It did not matter. The piercing sting of true love had struck our shepherd's heart; he was forever changed. He told himself it was enough just catching glimpses of his lady as she rode about her father's lands, or sang from the window of the keep, or strolled the flower-filled meadows nearby. It was enough that he heard her laughter each night in his dreams, where she laid in his arms and they whispered the secrets of lovers. It was enough.

"That year, as the nights grew long and the cold north wind began blowing across the lowlands and it was time to leave for the high country, our shepherd knew misery, the unbearable misery of separating from his true love. And yet to not leave meant banishment and eventually starvation. With a breaking heart and a heavy spirit, he forced himself to go."

Shalyn's eyes, like poetry, somehow conveyed every emotion of her heart. Her long lashes briefly brushed the high curve of her cheeks before returning to his face with expectation and hope. She seemed unaware that somewhere in the space of the story he had aligned her slender form against him and how he envied her absorbed attention. His entire consciousness fixed on the press of her slender curves, the faint scent of rosewater in her hair, the growing heat between them. Continuing the story was a struggle that felt as difficult as scaling the cliffs of Dover . . .

"Yet the angels took pity on the young man's sorrow and sought to breathe the girl's spirit before him. They sent the young lady out riding that day. They urged her to take the worn path that leads far up to the high country. Along the way her fine spirited mare felt the prick of a thorn. The mare raced as if chased by demons—and the girl lost control of the reins. Up and up the mare carried our young lady, charging full speed. She never saw the low-hanging branch that hit her head and knocked her from her seat.

"With a pounding heart, our shepherd watched the daring ride and his young woman's fateful fall. He raced to give her aid, finding her unconscious. When finally she woke in his arms, she had no memory of her life, or her station in it. She only knew the kind blue eyes of the shepherd who saved her. He named her—"

"Shalyn." She smiled up at him.

"Aye, he named her Shalyn. Shalyn. The name of the high mountain fairies who watch over the lonely shepherds all the winter long. His dreams had come true. For one long cold winter she belonged to him." The fateful and tragic words were out before he could change them for her. "And," he added quickly, knowing she needed a happy ending, "ah, from that time on they lived happily ever after."

"Did she ever remember her former life?"

"No," he lied. "Never. Blessed with true love, they lived happily ever after."

She looked confused. On the heels of a thoughtful pause, she told him, "That isn't a very good story."

"I did warn you, did I not?"

"Seanessy," she cried in a whisper, "I don't want to end up like the Shalyn of your story. I can't tell you how it feels to have no past memory. It's a loneliness deeper than the river Styx . . ."

His arms came around her, as if to encompass and soothe her desperation. "Shalyn," he whispered, his lips lightly brushing her forehead, "my poor mystery child. Shalyn . . ." Unable to resist, he let his finger trace the contours of her mouth until she gasped. "I want to kiss you again. I want to very much . . ."

In the space of the moment she became aware of all things: he wore only loose-fitting cotton shorts, the kind for sleeping, and she only a nightdress, this thin cloth between their warm skin doing nothing to inhibit the shocking intimacy of his hard warm body aligned to hers as they lay in his bed. She felt that pulsating heat in her loins, a hot gathering in her chest. It frightened her; her next breath came with another small gasp.

"Shalyn." He said her name in a whisper as his lips lightly caressed her neck until she arched back with another gasp. Every nerve was alight with expectancy and fear; she couldn't move and she couldn't think to know if she should.

Seanessy groaned deep in his throat, the sound dying as he buried his face against her neck. His large strong hands fitted around the curve of her buttocks, gripping her tighter and holding her still. "Dear Lord, Shalyn—"

"I . . . I should leave now."

He ran one hand slowly up her back and buried it in her hair.

"Seanessy . . ."

She said his name and then forgot why.

He always gave as good as he got. "Shalyn." He said her name in a husky whisper as if they now played a game, and they did. A game as old as the seasons. He lightly touched the contours of her mouth, his hand sliding along the arch of her jaw to gently take hold of her chin for his kiss; his other hand slid over her backside.

The movement started to scare her, to pull her again to another time with another man, but then no. This was Seanessy. Seanessy. As soon as the name echoed in her mind and she drew a deep breath, her heart started pounding, hard and slow and hard and slow again. She closed her eyes as she felt the brush of his lips on her mouth, so lightly it made her gasp again, the gasp bringing his warm firm lips to hers.

The kiss was hot and tantalizing, fueling her blood

with a slow-burning flame. Her neck arched as if she were offering herself to him. Seanessy accepted. She felt his lips brush over her mouth and her closed eyes, and finally alight along the curve of her neck as his hand drew slow, sensitive circles in the small of her back, over and over. He shifted his weight, always careful to keep the slender form against him as he let his hands lightly stroke the sweep of her side. Hot shivers raced from the place his hands touched her, and she gasped.

She felt rather than saw his smile as he watched her respond. "More, Shalyn?"

She started to shake her head, but the question was rhetorical and whispered lightly against her ear. Tiny sparks shot from the spot. He answered her secret wish by pressing his lips to hers, tilting her head back so he could drink to full measure. And he did. Her entire consciousness centered on the hot pleasure of his tongue and mouth on hers. She was hardly aware of his hand loosening the string of her nightgown, gathered at her collar, and pulling it apart.

He brushed the thin cloth from her shoulder. "I want to see you, Shalyn . . ." He whispered these words against her mouth, lightly kissing, tasting each and every small gasp of her breath. The nightgown gathered at the mercilessly small waist. He lifted from the sweetness of her mouth to view the soft swells of her breasts. "Oh, Lord, Shalyn . . ."

A warm callused palm lightly stroked the side of her breast, his thumb grazing the peak. The incredibly lush pink tips tightened dramatically, and feeling this, he almost lost any last semblance of control as a small cry of pleasure escaped her. He caught the next in his mouth.

The kiss was long and deep, drawing hot serums from her body, and in the most unlikely places. She didn't know what was happening, even that it was happening. She didn't know anything except that he was kissing her and that somehow she needed the kiss more than she needed air. She never wanted his mouth to leave hers. She wanted this kiss to last forever . . .

The strokes deepened, making her twist and arch into the warmth of his palm. He groaned. Dear Lord, her breasts. She felt so soft and slim. He was so hot . . .

She was clinging tightly to his neck, tighter as his lips left her mouth to graze on her arched neck and lower. Slowly. She felt rushes of hot tremors as his mouth came to her breast. She gasped with surprised shock. Her gasps came faster as the slow thud of her heart dropped to her loins. Hot thick pleasure pulsated through her and she said his name in bewilderment as warmth rushed between her legs, making her writhe and twist. With the same innocent bewilderment she said his name again. He answered her with his mouth on hers.

Then suddenly he stopped. He tensed. He pulled away from her. She was breathing hard and fast. "Hold still, Shalyn. Hold still." He leaned over her and seized the pistole lying on the night table. The crack of the barrel sounded as he cocked it, sitting up, his eyes on the door.

A giggle sounded, and it seemed like a hard slap to her face. She sat up. She first felt the cool air brush her bare breasts, then a wave of dizziness and disorientation as if she were waking from a dream. She was aware of hot moisture in a place she never before had reason to think much about.

The assault of a woman's perfume arrived a brief second before its carrier. Shalyn took one look at the darkened outline of a tall, voluptuous woman and knew she was beautiful, though why she bothered to note that, she would never know. She was very glad she was not holding the pistole. She would have shot her where she stood.

"Seanessy, Seanessy . . ." Doreen took a long minute to see there was another woman in the bed with Seanessy, which was not at all unusual. "Couldn't wait for me again, could you," she laughed, seeming genuinely amused. "You lusty beast!"

Shalyn covered her nakedness, rose from the bed, and calmly, so calmly, moved to the door. She never turned back. Seanessy fell back against the covers and closed his eyes, laughing at the worst bit of luck in what otherwise had been an exceptionally lucky life. He wondered at a disappointment so keen as to be painful.

Then he heard only: "If you ever touch me again I will kill you."

Doreen watched the strange creature leave the room. The door shut. "Well, la de da—"

Seanessy held up his hand, and she stopped instantly. "No, don't speak. Not a word. Just listen—"

She awaited his instructions, her eyes sparkling with good-natured anticipation.

"Take off every blessed stitch of clothes."

Excited, she obeyed, piling her clothes into a heap at her feet. He did not look at her when he said, "Lie down on the bed and part your thighs. I believe, I am quite certain, I am coming."

"And he did!" Doreen later told her friends. "Three times without stopping, like he was a dying man and I was his last chance!"

She thought, I want to kill him . . .

Shalyn stared at the stunning star made of gold and studded with rubies. It could not possibly be real; it could not possibly have once been in her hand. Kyler had called her into Seanessy's sitting room, one of the last places she wanted to find herself after last night, but he'd said it was important.

Butcher, Kyler, and Seanessy stood waiting for her response.

She looked into Seanessy's eyes. He stared back steadily, his face expressionless. If he thought at all about the horror of last night, he gave no sign of it.

Perhaps, she thought, slow torture, then a kill.

Holding up the ruby jewel, Seanessy stared, wondering how she could look so tempting in his blue silk dressing robe. Even though it covered her neck to toes. The sleeves were rolled up, and it trailed behind her. She clutched it tight at her neck, staring up with those lovely dark eyes, the delicate lines of her face framed in the crinkled gold hair knotted at the back of her neck. Dear Lord, she was lovely.

After last night. After rutting, as she called it, with ... with ...

For a moment he forgot the woman's name.

Doreen, he remembered. It had taken him three swipes at Doreen to rid himself of the heat this unlikely girl put in his loins. Three times.

What in blazes had he been thinking of last night? Kissing and petting the girl like a lovestruck adolescent with too much heat in his loins and precious few outlets. Good God, she was a virgin.

Shalyn stared at him. The way he looked at her.

A murderous rage filled her. She decided to forgo the torture. She'd go right for the kill ...

Seanessy stared at her eyes, eyes darker than midnight, filled with emotional intensity as she tried to remember these bloodred uncut rubies set in gold. In those eyes was all the evidence of how badly he had hurt her. The last thing he wanted was to hurt her, the very last. Thankfully Doreen had interrupted them just in time ...

He grimaced still. What a bloody rogue he had been! Seducing her when she woke three sheets to the wind with terror. He knew a name for that kind of ruthless seduction. There was just something, something about that slim body of hers! And that something of hers raised his cock to full sail and kept it there with a gale force wind.

What the devil was his problem?

The poor girl! He just was not a man to attach soft sentiments to his bed, but he'd have to explain, as gently as possible. He would make it perfectly clear that he'd never touch her again, that if he did he'd submit to a well-deserved castration . . .

"Well, Shalyn?"

The way he stared. She felt her cheeks grow hot with the memory of last night. Slowly her hands fitted over her cheeks with silent mortification. She shook her head, slowly and then more adamantly.

"You have never seen this before?!"

They stood in his room, Kyler and Butcher behind him. They had hoped the pretty piece would trigger her memory, if she even had a memory to trigger— Sean had begun to wonder.

A delicate palm went to her forehead; she rubbed.

Seanessy took her palm, turned it up, and brusquely slapped the treasure into her hand. "Well, Shalyn mine, 'tis yours. Wear it in good health. And speaking of health." He turned to Kyler. "Send the good Doctor Rush up."

With a sigh of disappointment, knowing how much Sean wanted the girl out of his life, Kyler left the room to pass word to the doctor.

Seanessy just stared at the lass, while Butcher stared at him. He knew that tone of Sean's, irked and irritated, the exact tone he used moments before his fists connected with someone's face. The poor lass had turned her back to them, unable to bear Sean's proximity.

"Sean," Butcher said slowly, meanly, "what the devil did you do to the lass?"

"Nothing that is any of your concern, my friend." The words were a warning. "And nothing I don't regret with every breath I take. Butcher, if you will?"

With a sorry shake of his head, Butcher left the room.

Shalyn tensed, afraid of being alone with him. She did not dare turn to look at him. She clenched tight the folds of the blue silk dressing robe Tilly had given her and wished desperately she were a thousand miles away.

If he touches me, I will kill him. I will! I swear I will . . .

"Shalyn, I am so sorry. About last night. I did not mean to hurt you like that. Needless to say"—he chuckled lightly to diffuse the tension of the moment—"I am hardly in the habit of lying with untried young women! It's inexcusable, leading you through the trifling preliminaries like that." His booted feet stepped quietly behind her. "A goddamn gnat has more sense."

The rage swelled through her.

"And one of the hundred reasons I should have kept you out of my bed and my greedy hands to myself is how much I've hurt you." His hands came to her shoulders and he gently turned her toward him. She flinched under his palms, but faced him, her head high. For a moment he was startled by the emotional depth in her eyes; her vulnerability was his point. "Shalyn, I am so sorry . . ."

Breathing hard and fast, she stared up at those cock-sure hazel eyes and thought, I am going to kill him. I am! I'm going to kill him . . .

Dear Lord, those eyes. He saw that she was about to cry. "Shalyn darling," he said softly, alarmed by her extreme fragility. "It's something you'll understand when you're older. You see I'm not a man who assigns any importance to the act of lovemaking, much less meaning, and I can't—"

"Why, you insufferable oaf!" And she raised a quick open palm and landed a hard slap to his face.

"What the blazes—" Seanessy grabbed his cheek with shock.

"That's what I think of your honeyed words! Words meant for some silly lovestruck schoolgirl! Save them—I care less than you about last night, except as to make certain it never happens again!"

Never in all his life had Seanessy felt his blood boil so hot or so quick. "Why, you vicious ungrateful little termagant—"

And the fight was on.

Dr. Rush stared at one of Diego Velazquez's lesser paintings, *Surrender of Breda*. A hand went to his overstuffed brocaded vest pocket. He withdrew an eyeglass and, holding it to his eye, he stepped closer to the picture.

A lesser piece by the master, but still absolutely brilliant. He stepped back, pleased. Imagine owning a Velazquez! Two Rembrandts, a Rubens masterpiece, and a Van Eyck. He had heard that Captain Seanessy's private collection rivaled any in all England, and still, he had not been prepared for this.

When the captain's man had arrived at the academy and explained the unusual situation—a young lady found on the doorstep, who had apparently lost her memory—he'd leaped at the opportunity to visit this house.

A smile lit the doctor's face, a smile owing in part to the pleasure of his private viewing of the gallery and in part to the captain's explicit demand for secrecy. The captain need not have made the request; a pistole to his head could not drag the information from him. Few people excited society's interest as much as Captain Seanessy, and if it were known that he had come here, especially with the extraordinary circumstances surrounding his new patient, every lady between the ages of fourteen and eighty would be on a singular life mission to get every blessed detail from him.

As the doctor stepped in front of the next picture he chuckled out loud. So it was true after all! Here was the proof!

Vermeer's *The Spinner*!

Some years ago now, a fantastic story had circulated throughout society, but he had never believed it, certain it was spawned by the exaggerated romantic interest in the famous man. Apparently there once was a pirate who sailed the channel through the Mediterranean waters. His name was Benito de Soto, captain of a ship aptly named the *Black Joke*. This beast was known and feared for his savage decapitation not just of the crew of the ships he took, but also of all passengers, including women and children. Hair-raising descriptions of the speed with which he would do the dastardly business had circulated in the *London Times* for years, followed by scathing editorials indicting both Admiral Gaylord and William, brother of the current king and next in line to succeed. William, humiliated by the editorials, had approached Seanessy with the task. After all, the captain had helped the young American navy rid its seas of Giles and his ships. The rumor claimed that Seanessy was not interested, as he had at the time been engaged in some highly profitable East Indian venture. In desperation, William continued to escalate the amount he'd pay for Benito de Soto's death, but got no response until, at last, he offered Seanessy this painting.

It apparently took Captain Seanessy and his men only two months to find the *Black Joke*, capture the crew, and set fire to the ship. Benito de Soto and most of his crew were brought to the admiral, who quickly dispatched justice.

And this marvelous painting was proof!

"Doctor." The captain's butler stepped quietly inside the spacious room. "I believe the patient is ready to receive you."

The patient lay backside on the bed, her arms and legs neatly pinned by his. He did not accomplish the feat unscathed; his triumph came at a cost. The girl had landed three goodly blows before he had managed the trick.

He'd felt each one of them.

She'd give him another as soon as he let her up.

Seanessy felt the full effects of his growing dilemma; the problem was one of potentially catastrophic proportions. He stared into her eyes, eyes full of spite, venom, and fury. She was breathing hard and fast. The tangled mess of her crinkled gold hair spread in a rich fan across the comforter. This was not the problem. He could handle her comeliness, it being little more than a singular pleasure to stare at her, still more excitement with her fury and his need to harness it. On a good day he probably could handle that, it that were all there was to it.

No, most of his problem lay in the fact that somewhere in the space of this brief battle, her robe had parted. She was naked beneath him. It made him lift slightly, a ridiculous act of torture, in order to view the most luscious coral-pink tips of her breasts.

He swore softly, viciously. Red-hot desire swept through him in a near-violent quake. He didn't know whether to laugh or cry; and because his predicament was too pathetic for tears, he started laughing.

"Let me up, you fiend!"

"Fiend? Shalyn darling." He laughed, his chest

bouncing lightly against hers, that curious tingling alighting there, her body knowing this game even when her mind did not. "You really must generate more appropriate endearments if you keep insisting on these intimacies with me. You know what I'm thinking, don't you?"

Actually no. She looked into his eyes, searching the handsome face. Then she realized: "Why, you want to kiss me again!"

Her shock would live forever in his mind; he laughed even harder. "It's only the beginning, too."

"Well, I want to punch you!"

"And, perversely, that only makes me want to kiss you more!"

"And do you know what I think of you? Why, I hate—"

Seanessy stopped her from saying the words.

"No. Do not say that, child! 'Twould be a piercing blow I'd not easily recover from." With sudden inspiration he said, "You love your literature. Do you know your Shakespeare? One of the last sonnets—" To her utter amazement, he recited a sonnet from memory:

> "Those lips that Love's own hand did make,
> Breath'd forth the sound that said 'I hate,'
> To me that languish'd for her sake:
> But when she saw my woeful state,
> Straight in her heart did mercy come,
> Chiding that tongue that ever sweet
> Was us'd in giving gentle doom;
> And taught it thus anew to greet;
> 'I hate,' she alter'd with an end,
> That follow'd it as gentle day
> Doth follow night, who like a fiend,
> From heaven to hell is flown away—"

In a moment of self-discovery Shalyn finished it in a whisper: " 'I hate' from hate away she threw,/ And sav'd my life, saying—'Not you.' "

Shalyn stared up at Seanessy in total awe, bewilderment, and no small amount of discomfort. Awe that he could, would recite Shakespeare, bewilderment that she had the same unlikely talent, and discomfort because this had so altered her view of him as to render her blissfully speechless for a long moment.

Then suddenly: "Number one hundred and forty-five. I remember it. The last lines are so sweet . . ."

Seanessy grinned down at her, pleased, and she returned the look, dazed. Shakespeare had always worked magic for him: during those days as a young man at Oxford when, for a number of years, he had been surrounded by no one but blue-bloods, nothing lifted a lady's silk skirts quite like Shakespeare's sonnets, and while he quickly forgot those generous and accommodating women, he never forgot the sonnets. He loved singing them almost as much as gaining the favors they aroused. Until now. Until Shalyn.

"So," he said, trying hard to concentrate, "Shakespeare heads the long list of favorite works. High-minded stuff. Which is your favorite sonnet?"

The question was asked as his hand brushed over her forehead, stirring something in her and making her uncomfortably aware of his hard body over hers. He kept his weight from her but the brush of his shirt teased her bare skin and his belt buckle pressed against her stomach while a fleeting memory danced through her mind.

A black enamel box filled with treasures: two books, one of them of Shakespeare's sonnets, a seashell, and a ring. She tried to seize the gossamer vision, cling to the fragile glance into the mysteriousness of her missing past, but it vanished.

"Seanessy . . ."

"What?" he asked, forgetting the question, forgetting everything as his gaze caressed her breasts. Oh, Lord. It occurred to him that while she had a maddening innocence about her, a beguiling ignorance of the effect of her comeliness, she did not have a young maid's modesty. Nudity brought her no shame, and there was something so fascinating and alluring and maddening about that . . .

Shalyn closed her eyes and tried to steel herself against the physical havoc he wreaked upon her senses. How did he do this to her? He could turn her insides to a simmering pot of hot stew by nothing more than walking into the same room as she. Toss in a poet's sweet song, and she was not only his willing victim but an eager one. The most disconcerting aspect of the dilemma was: "I still want to kill you."

A knock sounded and Charles announced the doctor from behind the door.

Sean closed his eyes briefly, trying to quiet his sudden laughter and temper the rage of his pulse. He just didn't know what to do with her! There was but one way out: he'd ask Butcher to take him outside and shoot him.

Of course, he could put her picture in the paper.

An excellent idea, the perfect solution. A grin spread over his face. He released her all at once as he bounded off the bed.

Shalyn sat up, drawing the folds of the robe tight about her neck. Flushed, breathless, she felt her galloping heart beneath her hands at her chest. What a beast he was! Except for his Shakespeare, and how she did love his Shakespeare, but except for that, he was an insufferable, maddening—

Seanessy opened the door to Dr. Thomas Rush.

With a polite "Good day" and an obsequious bow, Dr. Rush shook hands briefly with Seanessy. Consumed by his thoughts, Seanessy hardly noticed how the doctor's intelligent gaze traveled quickly from him, past the beautiful young woman who was his patient, to fix eagerly on the *Britannia* hanging on the wall opposite the bed above the marble hearth. A loosened neckcloth hung by a plain gold pin that seemed to be slipping as he nodded, his eyes shining with pleasure while he stared. His dark waistcoat was unbuttoned down the front of his short, stocky frame to show a similarly unbuttoned brocaded vest. He let drop a large black bag.

"I am in absolute awe, Captain," he first said, removing the kerchief. "Your man was kind enough to show me the downstairs gallery. A fine Rembrandt! Two Rubens and more Hogarths than the National Gallery!" He moved closer, wiping the kerchief to his forehead. "And this, this is—"

"A *Britannia*," Seanessy supplied, but watched as Shalyn reached a trembling hand to smooth her disheveled hair.

A neat well-trimmed beard bobbed as the doctor nodded. "In a private collection!" Emotion rose in his face as he stared at the pictorial representation of India offering Britannia plates filled with jewels and strings of pearls, and China waiting to present her porcelain and tea. Mercury and Father Thames looked on the proceedings, while an East Indiaman appeared in the middle, symbolizing the treasure fleet.

"Captain Seanessy," he began, obviously thrilled, "I had heard your private collection rivaled the best. Your house holds some of England's greatest treasures. Yes, yes." He nodded, marveling. "You know I did a year at the National Academy."

"I did not." Seanessy pretended some mild surprise at the information, while watching Shalyn seated stiffly, demurely on the bed. That was until he noticed her eyes. If looks could kill, he wouldn't need Butcher to do him the favor.

The doctor was nodding, quite unable to turn away from the painting. "Yes indeed. One glorious year." He chuckled. "Until my money ran out. My father, may God rest his cruel soul, refused to release my annum until I gave up my harebrained notion of painting and agreed to his course of Oxford and medicine."

Sean smiled at this. "There's no greater tyrant than a determined father."

"Yes, yes, quite so. Well, well, it worked out for the best in the end. It seems I have the necessary passion for painting and yet little of the necessary talent. Now where in heaven's name did you get this?"

"That? The East India Office at Severndrog. Bought for sixty pounds."

Shock marked the doctor's gaze, followed by the humor of it. "No, that cannot be?"

"I'm afraid it is," Sean replied. "The result of two drunken officers who had no idea what they were handing me."

A hand came over the doctor's breast as if he was experiencing sudden heart palpitations, and he was. "That sixty pounds could buy such priceless beauty!"

She looked up to focus on these proceedings. She too had admired the painting, its beauty nearly overcoming her objections. "But it is a fatally flawed beauty after all," she said boldly, staring off at the kneeling forms of India and China. "Only an Englishman would imagine the supplication of China and India to Britannia—two nations as great as, if not much greater than, their mistress Britannia."

Dr. Rush could not hide his surprise; Seanessy did not even try to. "Greater?" The doctor decided to humor the beautiful young woman, who he realized must be his patient. "In what way can you imagine it?"

"In many ways," she said, the need to explain the obvious point interrupting the dark circles of her thoughts for the moment. "China and India are far greater in size and population, and much, much longer and richer in histories. English history only goes back to Arthur and the turn of the millennium. The Emperor of China has fish older than that! Why, there are books written in Chinese that were brought by way of India, and these books are said to date from four thousand years ago!"

A long silence followed the remark.

She first took the surprised silence unkindly, as a bigoted Englishman's response to an enlightened, worldly view, but abruptly a ringing started in her ears and her face flushed as it occurred to her that while she could not recall her name, she knew a good deal about Oriental and Indian history. She knew without a doubt the name of the Emperor of China and the Sultan of Brunei. She knew the Rajah of Sarawak.

Her amber eyes found Seanessy's.

"Are you remembering things?"

"No and yes." Frustration and confusion vied equally on her distressed face. "I can remember history, places, things I know. I remember almost every book I have read. I can name a dozen Indian rajahs and a half-dozen seaports in the Straits of Malacca. Yet 'tis so strange, I cannot picture people in my mind. I cannot say how I know, when or where I lived there, who was with me ..."

Dr. Rush retrieved his large bag and approached the bed where she sat. "I was told you suffer complete memory loss? That you could not say your name? Hmm?"

She closed her eyes, both hands pressing her forehead. "No." She shook her head. "No. I try and I try but it's as if I never knew. Captain Seanessy and his men call me Shalyn."

"Well, that's a pretty name." He set his large black bag on a table and opened it. Gentle hands came to the side of her head, turning it to better see the bump. "Does it hurt, my dear?"

"No. A little sore, but that is all."

He proceeded to examine her. Eyeglass to his eye, he examined her head, neck, and eyes. "So far so good. Yes, yes." He parted her hair to examine her skull, reminiscing out loud in an engaging gentle tone. "My word! You do so remind me of a lady I used to admire—she had your same dark eyes and brows with rich gold hair." His gaze fell over the length of it and he added, "Though not nearly so long."

She looked up and appeared interested.

"Oh my, but Hanna was quite beautiful and so richly talented; I think half of her father's students had debilitating crushes on her."

"Her father's students?"

"You see, her father was Sir Gideon Brackton, the pioneering, and I must say brilliant, just brilliant, surgeon at the academy then. Quite famous." He chuckled with fondness. "Miss Hanna Brackton caused quite a scandal when it was learned she was the artist who drew the diagrams for her father's anatomy class."

Seanessy stood over the doctor like an anxious parent. He realized of course that the doctor chatted for a good cause, to ease her obvious distress, that the trick was working. Seemingly without guile, he managed to draw Shalyn's thoughts from his careful examination.

She never even wondered whether it was proper to inquire as to the nature of the diagrams; it was not in her nature to restrain her curiosity, which the doctor had been counting on. "What kind of diagrams were they?"

"Well, to be quite frank, diagrams of human anatomy, pictures that she could only have made by attending her father's dissections of human corpses. Does that upset you, my dear? No? Well, you are more enlightened than most. Half of society refused her, despite her family's connections. And she didn't seem to care at all. I remember once she laughed at what she called 'those old stuffed corsets!' "

The next sound drew Seanessy's keen interest; her laughter was light, carefree, girlish, as enchanting as a siren's call. He loved her laughter. The doctor chuckled with her, and it was obvious his entire manner was richly, marvelously contrived for the sole purpose of setting his patients at ease.

"What happened to her?"

"Oh, she married one of her father's students. A young man. He came after me. I can't remember his name. Stiler? No, that wasn't it. Well, I heard he had accepted a commission with the King's navy. Hanna moved her young daughter to the countryside as I remember. That's the last I heard. I've often wondered what became of her. Such a free and gay spirit ..."

Withdrawing a magnifying glass, Dr. Rush proceeded to examine Shalyn's eyes, using a magnifying glass and making her look this way and that from the side, talking to her all the while, answering her surprising interest in the subject of dissection, its usefulness, and the legal problems, how the law forbade the taking of any cadavers from consecrated ground, which left the academy only the occasional hanged prisoners to dissect. "And they are always pickled from drink and diseased, the very worst subjects ..."

The doctor went on to explain what constituted a fine stiff, causing Seanessy a bemused smile. He knew no other woman who would be able, much less

willing, to entertain a doctor's discussion of the
worth of cadavers, let alone a woman with an apparent interest in the morbid subject.

"Buddhists," she said, "do not believe in any
inherent value of a corpse; indeed any physical desecration unless it touches the spirit is not a crime.
Once you are dead, the body is physical matter, unworthy of enlightened concern."

"Is that so?" He looked at her queerly and then
with humor. "Would there were more Buddhists on
the boards at the academy ..."

Dr. Rush reached a point in his examination where
his sensibilities made him look at Seanessy pointedly.
"Perhaps it would be wise to protect the lady's modesty? Yes?"

Seanessy did not oblige the doctor, except to turn
around. Before Shalyn, he would have thought the
need ridiculous, that his wealth of jaded experience
had taken him a thousand miles away from titilla-
tion. Now the last thing he wanted to see was that
robe off her shoulders. A clenched fist took hold of
the dresser as if for support, as he began a series of
extremely difficult mathematical calculations in his
mind, stopping only when the humor of his situation
made him grin boyishly.

Once she saw him turn, with little hesitation she
untied her belt and let the silk robe slide from her
shoulders. She sat poised on the edge of the bed with
her eyes lowered.

She wore no corset, chemise or underclothes!

The doctor overcame his surprise. He pretended
nothing was amiss. He examined the faint bruises on
her upper arms, then—

"What is this?"

His eyeglass fell out. He put it back to see the tattoo. "My dear, do you know what this is?"

She shook her head, blushing now.

The doctor looked closer, making out the strange shapes and figures done in pink and blue. "Most extraordinary. Well, yes, yes. We are quite through." He helped her pull up the robe and said, "Well, my dear, you are apparently in good health, despite all. Save for your memory loss." He pulled up a chair to face her. "Now, is there no memory at all. Nothing?"

"No." Sensing a sympathetic ear, she suddenly rushed forward: "Except, except—"

"Yes?"

"I remember places but no people."

"No other memory?"

She nodded slowly, the emotion springing into her eyes as she unconsciously scanned the room for a source of danger. "I feel as if ..."

"Yes?"

"I am in danger, someone—" Distress crossed her brow, her hands tightened on the folds of her robe. "Someone is trying to catch me, they are looking now, as I speak, and if ... if ..."

"Yes? What do you imagine happens when they find you?"

"They will kill me!"

"Oh my. You do not know who this is or could be?"

"No!"

"Easy, my dear, easy. You are safe here. Come now, draw a deep breath. Good. Now tell me, do you hear a voice in your mind?"

"No."

"Are you quite certain?"

After a contemplative pause, "Well, sometimes, twice now, I did hear, I heard a man's voice."

"Did it frighten you?"

"The opposite! It was comforting somehow because, because it was familiar."

"Oh." A brow rose. "What did this voice say?"

"That gratitude was a most valued emotion. Oh, and last night I remember this voice told me that I should not feel sympathy or pity for the suffering of children, that they are suffering now for sins of a past life, the Oriental philosophies again ..."

"Hmm. Well, now." This was not what the doctor expected; he seemed taken aback. "Let's try a little experiment: when I say mother, what comes into your mind?"

Mother, mother ... She closed her eyes and said, "Kindness, gaiety, and tenderness ..." The dark brows crossed and she whispered, "Longing ..."

"Father?"

She heard the Chinese voice say, *Someday he will return with our riches ...*

What could that mean? Where had she heard it? "I do not know." She shook her head. "Nothing really."

The doctor sensed something more. "Anything else?"

She shook her head before asking urgently, "What of my memory?"

"It could come back."

"Yes?"

"It's very difficult to say with any degree of certainty, my dear. 'Tis rare indeed to lose one's total memory. I have known in all my practice only four cases. I must warn you, however: it does not always come back. Many times it is gone for good. I had one case a number of years ago where the patient's memory returned, but only part of it. It seemed he could remember everything up until about the age of ten and four, then"—he snapped his fingers like a magician—"nothing. The rest of his life was a blank. He would not have recognized his wife of fifteen years had he met her on the street."

The information sent a chill through her. Panicked, she cried out, "But I must remember! I must!"

"Now, now, dear," he said, "violent emotions, I can

assure you, do not help. If anything, they shall hinder your progress. You must get rest. Your memory has no chance of recovering if you tax yourself."

"So she should rest," Seanessy repeated, it making perfect sense. He often felt that doctors were little more than distributors of common sense, and if you had your own, you never needed to consult a doctor. No doctor had ever helped his bloody headaches.

She was hardly listening to the kind doctor's continued list of his prescription: bed rest, quiet walks, perhaps some reading, but then as he thought of what books she might find in the captain's library, he added, "Though do be careful not to select any, ah, licentious novels. None of those modern novels they write these days." He shook his head disparagingly at the thought of the risque turn of the newer novels. Mary Shelley's, for instance. Horrifying stuff. "And refrain from indulging in any red meats or cheeses, noted to stimulate the biles . . ."

The long list went on but she hardly heard. She felt suddenly dizzy. She sat on the edge of the bed, holding her head. It was as if a dark, dangerous, and deadly monster didn't just wait in the darkness for her, but was already moving closer. She had to remember, she had to.

It was all his fault. At least since last night, when he was around, all she could think was how much she wanted to kill him, instead of who wanted to kill her. Not that she could confess to actually hating him. No, her sentiments went deeper. She would just very much like to see him tortured and in pain.

Except when he had sung that sweet sonnet . . .

After promising to return in a week's time, Dr. Rush rose and motioned for Seanessy. "Captain Seanessy, if you will."

Seanessy followed the doctor out. He closed the door behind him. "Yes? Is there more, Doctor?"

"This is a very serious condition she is suffering. The prognosis is not good, Captain. Not good at all."

"You mean you do not believe her memory will return?"

"I would be surprised if it did."

"Yet as the blow to her head heals, and if she rests—"

"The blow probably had nothing to do with her memory loss."

Seanessy stared, comprehension dawning. Still he had to have it spelled out. "I'm afraid I do not understand?"

Dr. Rush's keen eyes held a sudden sadness. "Captain Seanessy," he said solemnly, "that poor young lady had been beaten and dropped naked on your doorstep. I refuse—absolutely!—to imagine any of a dozen barbarous situations that might have ended in such a scenario. She is seriously marked, suggesting the abuse has gone on for any number of years, perhaps even the whole of her lifetime in those heathen hovels of the Orient, a place where no Christian woman should ever be. We know this. She has obviously endured unconscionable treatment there and now lives in a state of terror."

With growing alarm, Seanessy asked slowly, "Exactly what are you saying, my good man?"

"That young woman, sir, is insane."

Chapter 7

He was going to kill her.

She made him furious; not since he was ten and three had a woman ever gotten under his skin like Shalyn. He wanted to—

No! Do not think of that!

Yet it seemed all he did think about, all through the meeting with the cagey band of thieves better known as London's premier tea merchants, Bowser and Thackery. Seanessy sighed as he finally managed to see the old goats and their voracious agents through the door. He stood in the hall with Butcher, watching as Tilly ushered out the small dark-haired man who was clutching etching paper and a box of chalk.

"Now who the hell is that?"

"Get a grip, Seanessy." Butcher sighed, setting down the knives he sharpened. "You are losing your mind. That's the artist you just sent Taylor out to find. Had to pay him triple what was already an outrageous price to get him here."

Seanessy stared a moment. "Well, he'd better be good."

"A half-decent picture of Shalyn's comeliness be worth a fortune if you think about it."

Seanessy grunted. The crew waited at the docks for

him. Kyler and Paterson waited in the study with the log books. A horse doctor waited in the stables. The *Wind Muse* would be sailing soon and thank God for that. He needed a thousand miles at least between him and the girl.

He headed to the stables. "Butcher, go out and try to distract her."

"Me? Why me?"

"Well, she likes you."

"Aye! And I care for the lass. She's got more pluck than a Michaelmas goose. She's been hurt enough. I won't help you do anything to hurt her."

"Oh, for heaven's sake, I am not asking you to string up that pretty neck! Just distract her while our very expensive artist sketches that comely face for the papers."

"You're provin' to be the real distraction for the lass. Why don't you go out there?"

"Me?" Sean pointed, incredulous. "Because as soon as I get close enough to that girl I get one of two overwhelming urges. One—especially after this latest stunt of hers!—is to throttle her good, and the other—"

"Ah." Butcher waved his hand as he reluctantly followed the artist out to the garden. "I have no mind to hear about your personal problems."

Butcher found Shalyn in the garden. He hated this. He took one look at the lass and hated it more. He first dismissed Bryce and Tompkins nearby, watching over her as she stood in the shade of the willow near the edge of the pond, cloaked in shadows and pressed against the tree trunk as if for support. The two men left quietly as he moved to her. The artist stood to the right, behind a clump of bushes.

The blue sky filled with billowing gray and white clouds. The air felt rich with moisture and the tantalizing scents of the garden. Her back was to him. The gold hair made a thick braid that was lifted into a crown atop her head, but she still wore the boy's rough breeches, one of the captain's oversized shirts, and a vest.

Get the bloody business over, he thought.

She lost her thoughts to the afternoon stillness of the garden. Not a perfect stillness, with the distant chatter of the monkeys—unbelievably, there was a monkey tree in Seanessy's garden—chirps of robins on a branch above her, and the quiet intermittent whisper of the ambivalent breeze. She thought the garden would be beautiful in any season, but it seemed especially so now, with colorful blooming of fall blossoms and the darkening of tender green leaves. Statuesque trees and pockets of flowers interrupted the smooth carpet of grass: clusters of white lilies stood in proud sheaves, alcoves filled with blue and white lances of tall delphiniums and columbines, and nearby, lovely masses of blue forget-me-nots grew in profusion along the edge of the pond. The branches of the apple trees in the orchard bent, heavy with unpicked fruit, while the cherry trees still held their velvety color. Tall ivy-laden walls enclosed the whole. The shade of the tree felt like a cool hand on her feverish cheek, and she closed her eyes, breathing the scents.

A memory emerged in her solitude. How strange! It was a sunrise. She remembered a magical moment when a pale sky slowly changed and flushed with vibrant color. She stood on a white sand beach, watching this, the pink glow of color spreading across the sky, and in that moment, she remembered her heart stood still with silent awe; she knew transcendence: she knew she would survive.

A moment when she knew she would escape . . .
From what? What was it? Where was she?
Butcher did not try to conceal his approach, his

boots crunching loudly in the crisp grass. He stopped a good six feet from her. "Shalyn darlin'," he said, "Sean sent me out to see if you were all right."

Shalyn had turned with a startled jump, and as she turned, her arms lifted in readiness to fight the phantoms in her mind. A brow rose but Butcher otherwise remained impassive to the demonstration of the depth of her fear that Dr. Rush named as madness.

Shalyn grabbed her heart and felt a sweet relief. Butcher. It was only Butcher.

Dark circles underlined the hot and feverish anxiety in her eyes. "Oh, you poor lass," he whispered, suddenly feeling her pain, its depth and poignancy, as he stepped close to her. "Who the devil did this to you? Sean's right, you know, 'tis probably a bit of mercy that you can't remember what has happened to you.

"The boys were thinkin' to change your name to Marcella, you know." His tone changed with the subject. "The feminine form of Mars. Or perhaps Taima, which Sean says means the crash of thunder. Fitting after the little scene you created, lass: shimmying down knotted bedclothes from the second-story window like the bad beginning of a wretched penny novel. And by the way," he said as he pointed a finger like a schoolmaster, "Reese's arm is not broken after all, but we all wondered why it was necessary to break poor Thayer's nose? 'Tis the third time this year that I know of, and while he swears he's used to no longer breathing through it—"

Through gritted teeth she said, "Then tell Seanessy to let me go."

Butcher just shook his head. "He can't, lass, you know he can't."

A palm went to her forehead, and distress changed her face, somehow making her look much younger. Much younger than twenty and one. The amber eyes could not meet the scrutiny of his; she looked at her bare feet as she whispered with feeling, "He has no right. No right."

Butcher felt no sympathy here. "He's taking it, Shalyn," he replied with masculine simplicity. "And only because he owns, among other things, a ripe imagination. We all do. And so we imagine how ye'd like bein' introduced to the crew members flat on yer back, how they would rid themselves of the pieces by feeding what's left of you to the sharks—"

She covered her ears, her lips pressed into a hard line.

Butcher grabbed her arm like the strike of a snake and said slowly, "You're a fool, girl. Get the notion out of your head: these tricks of yours are pretty and entertaining, no more. They are no match for a man—"

She said heatedly, "Seanessy's own men—"

"The boys were laughing, girl. Laughing at the brave and foolish show you made. Laughing because, for all of it, you did indeed present them with a dilemma: everyone knows of Sean's unusual interest here, and knowing the unpleasant things he would probably do to any man who laid hands on you, how were they then to restrain your flight?" The dark eyes held hers, desperate to make her see. "And then you know how easily I solved the problem."

She tried to deny it but couldn't. She had been desperate. She hadn't known what Seanessy intended to do with her for two days. She had thought he was acting out of kindness until this morning when she heard one of his men return with the report on a hospital where they cared for people who went mad. He meant to put her in a madhouse. She saw it was time to leave. He was not going to give her passage. She'd have to get it herself.

Mounted on his horse when it happened, Butcher

had simply grabbed her plait. That was all. Grabbed the long rope of hair and held it until she relinquished the idea of an exit.

She searched Butcher's worldly face, looking for an argument or rebuttal. There was none past the fear, the terrible fear. She had been so afraid! As his men had stopped and surrounded her, her mind produced the terrorizing idea that these were the phantoms chasing her. She had to escape them; it was all she knew . . .

The amber eyes shimmered with emotion. "I will not go to a madhouse!"

"Look, lass." Butcher sighed. "The one thing I don't know about is when someone's mad and when they're not. 'Tis a line separating the two as thin as a spider's web and just as sticky. If it's any consolation, Sean just sent someone to check it out. This Quaker place. They say it's different. Like going to a chateau on a Swiss mountain lake for the season. Kindness and cleanliness and, well, not really a madhouse at all." He studied her eyes, still full of rage. "Ah, Shalyn, he's desperate, lass. We'll probably be sailin' out by week's end, mayhap less. The boys are preparing the ship now. He does not want to leave you with only Tilly—"

"Then tell him to take me with him!"

The softspoken plea held urgency, the wealth of her desperation. "You can't sail with us, lass, ye can't."

"I swear I would not be a bother, I swear this!"

He shook his head. That was one thing that was out of the question, absolutely out of the question. Too dangerous by far, even if she wouldn't cause Seanessy a single problem. He offered a compromise, the only one he could. "Well, let's see now. What if you do stay here with Tilly for the season. Just until there are a few passenger ships sailing the horn. Maybe then . . ."

By then she would be dead or worse. Yet if it was all she had she would take it. She had no choice. As soon as Seanessy and most of his men sailed, she would walk out of here and never look back—

Or maybe she could sneak onto his ship . . .

"Let me speak to him. How's that?"

She nodded, formulating a plan as she sat. At some point he would have his trunks packed—mercy, the odds of her stowing away in a trunk and remaining undetected until it was too late for Seanessy to turn the ship back were astronomically piled against her. As likely as a bank's charity.

So distracted by this train of thought, Shalyn never noticed Butcher's quick glance toward the bushes. Seeing that the artist needed more time, he sat down on the grass, staring up at the thin green blades on the branches of the willow tree. A pair of noisy robins returned to a noisy brood, fluttering and chirping and blissfully unaware of the stormy silence below.

Butcher watched two maids come out, carrying a picnic basket. Sean was taking no chances now, he saw, and perhaps that was best. The servants quickly, quietly spread the thick quilt beneath the branches of the willow tree.

She observed the two maids smooth the thick sky-blue goosedown quilt, then arrange a large basket and two crystal goblets next to a wine bottle. The very idea of a picnic was so incongruent with her nightmarish reality, she could only stare in a stupor of bewilderment. She drew a shaky uneven breath, the idea penetrating her taut and tired senses slowly: the kindhearted Butcher had arranged a picnic.

The questions rushed at her. How many picnics had she been on? One? Dozens? Did she love them?

Loathe them? Would she ever remember a thing as pretty and fine and commonplace as a picnic?

Yet the picnic had not been arranged by Butcher, but rather by Seanessy. Butcher handed her a note attached to the picnic basket. She carefully unfolded the paper to read: "Shalyn mine: Please indulge yourself. For you will need extra padding on a certain unmentionable portion of your anatomy if you ever try another harebrained stunt like that again. Seanessy."

Butcher dismissed the maids with a motion of his head and vowed not to look again at the artist nearby sketching her portrait. As he watched her cheeks turn crimson, her eyes darken with fury, he heard the unmistakable rumble from her stomach. He had to laugh. "So," he said with a chuckle as he reached to pour the wine and open the basket of food, "how long since you last ate? Or should I even ask?"

She tried to dismiss Seanessy's threat as hot air, and somewhat less successfully forget it as she thought for a moment, then sighed. "I can't remember anything these days. And 'tis becoming a big problem."

Butcher opened the basket and withdrew fresh-baked bread, cheeses, ham, chicken pies, a bowl of sliced fruit—all picnic fare. He poured the wine and handed it to her.

"Oh no." She shook her head. "I'm not permit—"

The curiosity of the words startled both of them. A clue. Their gazes locked, hers confused and his questioning. "Do you remember being forbidden wine?"

"No and yes . . ."

"*. . . no sluttish inebriation in my house!*"

The voice echoed in her mind, like the fading memory of a dream upon waking. Butcher studied her face and said, "Aw, lass what does that matter? Here. Taste and see if you like it."

She took a small sip. The fruity sweetness filled her mouth and a slow smile started. Like heated nectar, the next sip soothed her throat and filled her stomach with its warmth.

"Look behind you, lass."

Dazzling quick reflexes swung her around before the words were finished. For a girl she was quick. Pleasure made her laugh as the clan of monkeys tumbled toward them.

"Meet the bane of Sean's otherwise happy peaceful garden," he said easily, the conversation suddenly as light and airy as the warm fall breeze, perfect for a picnic. He deftly began slicing cheese and bread. The boldest among them leaped back and forth along the edge of the blanket, noisily begging for handouts. "The only thing I've ever met more pesky than these furry fellows are the mosquitoes in the Americas."

Pleasure enhanced her beauty as she delighted in the new company, any last fear dissipated for the moment by a dozen excited, shrieking little monkeys. "May I have a piece of bread to toss?"

He tore off a chunk of bread and handed it to her. She threw it to them. The creatures clamored for the treat like a group of starving waifs. The monkeys were not tame, so he was surprised when one of the little fellows approached on all fours, stopping at her bent knees, moving back, then leaping forward. "You are a greedy fellow!" She handed him a piece. "Will you share with the others, yes? Oh, but not the ducks?"

The ducks were determined not to miss out. With noisy quacks they waddled quickly out of the pond to join the burgeoning number of creatures that surrounded her. She laughed as one insistent monkey climbed on his neighbor's back, leaping ahead to snatch the torn bit of bread. "Oh, look, that one has a baby!"

A tiny baby monkey clung to its mother's back.

Butcher's bearded face broke into a huge grin. For a moment he forgot his deception, the unpleasant circumstances as he saw the girl could charm the blackest of hearts. He watched as she tried to reach the mother and child with a piece of bread, laughing as she finally made a good throw. Using her tiny hands, the mother brought it to her mouth and gobbled it up.

Shalyn turned to beg more from Butcher.

"I see we have another problem." Butcher chuckled. He knew only one way to handle this. He leaped to his feet and with a loud roar, sent the creatures into a scurry of flight.

In a pretense of anger, Shalyn chided him as he returned to stretch out on the blanket. "Butcher, you are a terrible bully!"

"Sean's always tellin' me there's only so many mouths a man can feed, and God knows, sweet Tilly makes sure they are daily gorged on food fit for a king."

She watched the monkeys clamor up their tree in the distance as Butcher sliced more cheese and bread, handing them to her as she asked distractedly, "They are so charming—where did Seanessy get them?"

Butcher laughed. " 'Tis a long tale, lass."

"Yes? Did he buy them in a shop?"

"Nothing so easy. 'Tis hard to believe, but we once came across the little beasts floating in the sea."

"In the sea? How can that be?"

"Well, about two years ago, the American navy offered Sean a pretty sum for use of two of his ships to join two of their warships to nail a certain Captain Gibbs to the cross. This wretched cap'n was a plunderin' merchantman in Caribbean waters—"

"Seanessy took money like a mercenary?"

"He did and 'twas wrong of him, I know," he said, but with absolutely no contriteness as he handed her a crusty cottage pie carefully folded in the blue napkin and still hot from the oven. "Perhaps Sean should have told them he'd do it for naught more than the pleasure of capturing the man, but as 'twas Captain Gibbs was responsible for two dear friends' deaths, and methinks, as I remember, Sean wanted the money for a widow who had kept his shirt wet for a week with all her sorrow and grief."

"How sad . . ."

"Aye, life can be a sad tale indeed, though last year the lady married again, and rather well."

Butcher did not bother to explain Sean's two friends had been captains of merchantmen Gibbs had plundered. Gibbs had set one of the ships to blaze with the captain and crew on board—there were no survivors—while the captain of the other vessel suffered an even worse fate at Gibbs's hands. Indeed Sean would have done it for the pleasure of revenge.

"Anyway, our four ships finally came upon Gibbs's three vessels. Right in the act they were, firin' on three merchantmen. Three merchantmen set ablaze. Ah, lass, 'twas a fierce battle; it always is when the battle is unto death. Our ship did not even catch the worst of it, but Madonna!" He shook his head with a chuckle as he remembered. "We could hardly maneuver her a compass point to the side. The other three ships were worse off. So it was up to us to sail through the wreckage of the three merchantmen to find all the survivors. Suddenly the lookout spotted these crates floating here and there. The noise told us what it was—the monkeys were half-mad at the thunder of cannon fire, the scent of fire and smoke, and the want of water."

"So you saved them!"

"We did, but it was a chore. The waters were swimming with sharks by this point, and without being able to maneuver the ship well, if at all, and with no longshore boats left, the only way we could save the bloody things was to do the business by hand. The task was not popular; Sean's boys, like all sailors, do not relish swimming with man-eating predators—'tis a tricky chore to emerge whole from a shark frenzy. The only way Sean could get someone to go in with him was by making it into a wager, giving more than generous odds ..."

The harrowing climax of the story almost lasted until the end of the well-baked strawberry tarts. She managed to swallow the last delicious bite when she realized that he was quite serious, that this had really happened. "He risked his life for crates full of monkeys?"

"Aye, that he did lass, that he did."

She laughed suddenly, a sweet girlish sound, forgetting the whole upside-down world gone mad. For a long moment she laughed, and he watched, enchanted by the sound. When she finally quieted, her amber eyes met his with gratitude and she said, "I can laugh, Butcher."

"A sweet sound it is, lass."

"I like picnics," she added, and in a relieved moment of self-discovery: "I love monkeys, strawberry tarts, and clear skies. And you know, Butcher, I love Seanessy's life, I really do. I love Seanessy's passion and support of art and artists, I love going to the theaters and dining at night, all his adventures and all his fun, traveling whenever he wants. In these last few days I discovered I want to be just like him."

Butcher didn't know whether to laugh or cry. He started to laugh when she continued, "If, when I am finally safe, when I remember everything and, well, when this is all over, I would like to—" She stopped, abruptly noticing the man hiding in the bushes. "Who's that?" She pointed.

"Who?" Butcher felt his heart leap.

"Butcher, what's that man doing there?"

"Oh, probably just one of the boys strollin' out in the garden. Let's see . . . who is it?"

Shalyn stared for a long moment. The boys were hardened seamen who drank and played cards and wagered on how many men their captain knocked about on any given evening. The boys were not men who took pleasant afternoon strolls in gardens, much less crouched hidden in a bush, obviously eavesdropping. Butcher himself was one of those boys, and as kind and generous as he was, he'd not while away an afternoon on a picnic, telling a scared young woman wild stories drawn from Seanessy's past all in the hopes of hearing a laugh.

"Shalyn! Shalyn!"

Too late. Curse the bloody luck.

She found him in the garden room. Joined by Kyler and Hamilton, Seanessy sat at the head of the great long table covered with maps, papers, large red books opened and stacked on top of one another. He held one of the new French pencils in his hand, stopping to drink from a huge goblet of water. He drained it, setting it down with a clink before he returned to his books.

She quietly approached the table.

Kyler and Hamilton noticed her.

"Sean . . ." Kyler said, motioning.

Sean looked up. The girl stood at his side. For a long moment the shimmering emotion in those eyes held him mesmerized. He glanced at the paper she held up. Slowly he set his pencil down and reached out and took it from her.

The silence was palpable as he studied it.

Worth every pound he had paid—the artist was good. No—much better than good. Good did not describe the rendering of the delicate lines that drew the lovely face, and the richly crinkled silk that made her hair, the perfect depiction of the sensuous fullness of her mouth, the small pointed nose, and those eyes. If one did not know her and saw only this picture, one would realize at a glance, hers was neither a frivolous nor an easy life. The artist had somehow captured the intensity of her eyes, the secret tragedy revealed there.

He meant to unravel the secret.

He set down the smooth sheet of paper.

"It goes in the London paper tomorrow."

She shook her head; she couldn't speak.

For a long moment she was mute. He dismissed her by returning to his books, a gesture that said it would be useless to discuss it or plead, that his mind was made up. Until the moment she fell to her knees before him. He reflexively reached to lift her up but she held his forearms. Desperate to stop him, desperate to make him see, she pleaded, "Seanessy, Seanessy, don't do this to me. I beg you! You don't know what it's like, Seanessy. This nightmare. I've lost my memory and now I'm afraid. I very much fear that the good doctor is right, that I'm losing my mind. Inside me, I have this panic, the terror that they are looking for me, right now, as I speak, that they won't ever give up until they find me, that I have to get away before they do find me. All I know is that if they do catch me, I will die. And I don't want to, Seanessy!"

The magnitude of those words brought a soft vicious curse, and with her kneeling between his outstretched knees, he grabbed her hands, his gaze locked to her and filled with a sudden fierce anger that frightened her to the depths of her soul.

"Listen, Shalyn mine: no one is going to hurt you. No one. For I am not going to let anyone hurt you, much less kill you. Do hear me?"

She shook her head, the movement sending first one plait, then the other dropping to her waist and making her look so young, too young. "Seanessy, please—"

A gentle hand came to her lips. "No, child. I will not entertain notions otherwise. You see, Shalyn, it occurs to me I have two possibilities here. The first possibility is that this whole thing is a colossal mistake, that there are no dark phantoms chasing you down, bent on some kind of unimaginable horror. Shalyn, it is entirely possible that somewhere out there you have a loving family frantically searching for you. Hear me out: it's possible, nay even likely, that you had simply stepped outside for a stroll or tea or shopping, then you were accosted by I don't know who, an ugly band of nefarious mischief-makers who knocked you on your head, stole your jewels and clothes, and left you for dead. And what if what you are remembering is the terror just before you fell?"

Sending the long rope of her hair over her shoulder, she shook her head, frightened, terrified that she could not make him see, that he would do this to her. "If it is true that I am the lost member of this loving family, then why did I have that jewel clutched in my hand, why didn't these other thieves take it, why did I have your name and address in my hand, and Seanessy, why, dear God, why do I have that hideous mark?"

He searched the lovely upturned face for a long moment before he released her with a sigh, leaned back in the chair, and folded his hands neatly behind his head. With masculine simplicity he said, "Then, Shalyn mine, it leaves me with the second possibility.

Someone has abused you. And badly. Someone is indeed searching in hopes of catching you, only to abuse you more. Well, Shalyn," he continued matter-of-factly, "I want to meet this person. Badly. Because, you see, I mean to kill him." This with a grin as if giving her a treat. "For you, Shalyn! So I do not have to see this terror in your lovely eyes ever again."

But Shalyn could not escape the desperate urge to run, run from a frightening past she could not remember. She tried hard to steady her terror at the idea of her picture in the paper, to still her heart long enough to make him see, but she could hardly speak. She shook her head, her eyes large and luminous, washed with tears. "Oh, Seanessy, please . . ."

Seanessy cursed when he felt every muscle tense with the effort to resist drawing her into his arms. He would not touch her now. No matter what.

"Kyler . . ." he said.

"I don't know, Sean. No doubt there needs to be a reckoning of the man who put this fear in such a courageous creature. Yet . . ." The bald man sighed, looked away, and in that moment he saw the obvious solution. "Why not send the girl off next week with Richards to Ram and Joy in Washington? Ram will keep her safe, Joy will surround her with more kindness and care than a host of pious Quakers. And leave the business of vengeance to me after she departs."

Seanessy considered this plan, the only reasonable course available as he willed himself not to stare into her eyes. "I'd really like to do it myself, you know."

"I'll fire an extra bullet or two in your name."

"Very well," he agreed. Then to Shalyn he promised, "No picture in the paper." Until you're gone.

Relief felt heady, overwhelming. She reached for his hand and took it, bringing it against her hot cheek. For a moment her gratitude was so powerful, she could not give it a voice.

Then he said gently, "I am going to send you to America, Shalyn. To stay at my brother's house. Joy will see that you are loved and cared for until you are well enough to be introduced into society."

Shalyn and society. He considered the inevitability of some sniveling bumpkin of a fool—an American no less, and no more ridiculous people existed in the world—courting the girl, the kind of gentleman who would embarrass himself before he got his pants off. Why the idea bothered him, he couldn't say. Except that as he imagined this scene between Shalyn and the American bumpkin, he felt a strange surge of . . . of rage.

Like jealousy. Him? Jealous? Why, how extraordinarily ordinary! Lord, if he didn't get rid of the girl soon he'd probably end up doing something so perfectly droll as wanting to marry her! Commissioning someone to build a little cottage by the seashore where they would live happily ever after. Dear Lord, save me.

He had to get away from her, a thousand miles away.

"What was I saying?"

Kyler shook his head and chuckled.

"Oh yes," he recalled, still bothered by Shalyn's American bumpkin, whoever he would be. "Anyway, Joy will introduce you to society. What precious little society Washington has, that is. Americans are hopelessly provincial and naive, but so very amusing because of it, good-hearted despite it. I'll send Tilly with you too. She loves Joy; I daresay she will welcome the trip. You will need a trunk full of clothes and . . ."

He started making plans. Shalyn's gratitude still kept any words from leaving her mouth. Her heightened sense of survival kept her from telling him she was not going to America to live with his relations, that she had another plan. For somewhere in her dark past she had learned well how to keep a secret, especially a secret meant to keep her alive.

Kyler watched from the window, finally shouting as the carriage pulled through the gates, "He's here." Over an hour late, the Frenchman was. The duke had sent his card, requesting a visit on Tuesday evening. Seanessy had agreed; all they needed was to smooth his ruffled feathers, strike a deal, and get an invitation to the island. They'd blow the opium surplus sky-high.

It was a fine carriage too; Kyler had never seen one of this make. Gold-lined and black-enameled, top of the line. There was nothing like it in London. The man must have had the carriage shipped.

Butcher looked up from the cards. "How many with him?"

Kyler counted ten men riding behind the carriage. "An even dozen." Two footmen rode on the side, leaping down to open the door as the carriage stopped in front of the house. The steps were flung down, a carpet laid.

"Good God." He chuckled at the show, and to the men behind him, he said, "The type of man who requires two servants to take his boots off at night. One to pull them off and the other one to powder and paste his tooth comb."

The men laughed. Butcher motioned to a waiting manservant. "Fetch the cap'n. Tell him Molly's hosted his hot flesh enough to last her lifetime."

Impassioned French swearing sounded as the duke or one of his men discovered the barrel of snakes. Kyler chuckled. The doorbell rang. Charles, ever obsequious, went to open it. Booted feet sounded from the entrance hall as Charles and Tommy took hats and gloves and welcomed the men to Hanover House.

Seanessy shut the door and quietly stepped into the hall. He spotted her as he started down the stairs. Shadows hid her as she apparently stared into the entrance hall, watching something intently.

Shalyn. The very last person he wanted to see.

His foul mood showed in a harsh light in his eyes as he appraised her. This mood owed itself to the last hour or so with Molly, an hour in which he learned just how far his untried desire for this slim one-hundred-or-so-pound package had gone. Molly had appeal only when he closed his eyes and conjured someone else: someone with impossibly long legs, a delicate flare of slender hips to that mercilessly tight and narrow waist, the luscious pink tips of her breasts—

Don't think of that now.

He closed his eyes a moment, trying to rid himself of the annoyingly persistent images. He could not have her, and what's more, he told himself again and again, he did not want her. That was if he thought about it. Which he rarely managed to do. She was far too young. She was a virgin with a previous entanglement that she could not remember, but that was surely characterized by some perversity, an entanglement that left her vulnerable and fragile. Worse—the girl was probably quite mad.

As if he needed even more reason than the little cottage by the sea. A fate that was certainly not for him and one he had always imagined he was invulnerable to. Until Shalyn. Until all her trouble.

"Shalyn," he said as he descended the stairs, "why is it I always find you sneaking about in shadows like a Covent Garden thief?" Covent Garden was the sorry side of London: rat-infested hovels of all manner of thieves, pickpockets, weary prostitutes, and pimps.

She looked up with a gasp. Guilt sprang in her eyes, though for the life of her she could not understand why. She glanced down the stairs again, swallowing, checking to see if he could see ...

Just then Charles led the Duke de la Armanac and his entourage into the gallery drawing room. Seanessy looked from the girl to the duke. Enlightenment dawned in his shrewd gaze, and the moment it did, he didn't know whether to laugh or box her ears. "Smitten, are we?"

The inexplicable anger in his voice put the same in hers. Her chin tilted up. "Don't be ridiculous. I just wanted to hear. I was hoping ..." Her voice trailed off. She swallowed, then asked point-blank, "May I join you?"

"Don't you be ridiculous. Look what you are wearing. Some men might actually enjoy viewing that slim derriere outlined in breeches, but I'll be damned if they do in my house."

"Why, I went all over London with you wearing this! Your friends all loved it; they thought it eccentric and refreshing, and any number of women are starting to wear trousers—"

She stopped because after a angry "Huh!" he continued down the stairs two at a time, disappearing into the lower gallery. Shalyn's mouth pressed into a hard line, her brow crossed with mean thoughts. He was so ... so ... something! Terrible! Incorrigible! Mean!

"There you are!" Tilly said moments later when she found Shalyn sitting on the stairs. With a whoosh of wind she sat down too, easing her considerable weight next to the girl. "Oh, now, did you get to see him, Miss Shalyn? Our French duke?"

"Barely," she said, still cross. "Seanessy caught me

at it. They're in the gallery drawing room now." She didn't know why but: "Oh, I wish I could see him again!"

"I was out back when he came in," Tilly told her. "Charles says his carriage be the finest rig he's ever seen. Velvet-lined, gold-trimmed, and listen to this, Charles swears the gold is as real as Fat George's crown. And Mary says he's more handsome than an Asherella prince and every bit as majestic. The French be like that," she explained, in the event Shalyn didn't know. "The French nobility is to our English lords and ladies as peacocks are to game hens. I cannot help but think it's a shame, a livin' shame. Why, lords and ladies nowadays hardly dress any better than a tea merchant or a country vicar! The only difference be their fine silver tongues. That's one thing that'll not change until the last breath leaves the last English soul. Didn't used to be like that in the old days, you know. Why, I remember my mother once met—"

"Tilly." Shalyn knew to interrupt the kind woman or be still listening when the sun rose. "Is there some way we could eavesdrop?"

The question drew a blank stare, yet the blank stare changed with the realization of where the men convened. "Oh, aye! There be a peepin' hole the size of a goose egg from the other side. Oh la! I'll never forget that night 'twas made. Oh, but the captain—"

"Will never know. I'll never tell him."

Footsteps sounded behind them. They turned to see a woman descending the stairs. Not just any woman, but the most strikingly beautiful woman Shalyn had ever seen. A fine high melody sprang from her lips as she carefully pulled on pink lace gloves up to gold-bangled wrists. She all but beamed with a secret pleasure.

Shalyn's breath caught as she waited for the woman's impossibly tight bodice to give way. English women were so immodest! Tilly nudged Shalyn's elbow conspiratorially. "A good evenin' to you, Mistress Molly."

Fine eyes came to the two women crouched like children in the darkness on the stairs. "Good heavens, Tilly, what are you doing down there? Lord." A gloved hand came over her nearly naked bosom. "You gave me a start!"

"Shall I show you to the door, mistress?"

"I believe I know the way."

The idea made the beautiful woman laugh with a levity and gayness Shalyn envied. She remember the afternoon out in the garden with Butcher, and how his storytelling and the little creatures had made her laugh with abandon. Envy turned to longing . . .

"Evenin' tides to you, Miss Molly," Tilly said.

The two women watched as the creature seemed to float down the stairs, followed by enough silk and lace to cover a dining table for twelve. Tilly giggled like a girl half her age as Molly disappeared. "Did you see that? Done up like a dog's dinner. La, 'tis just my point—"

Shalyn decided it was best not to think about the wanton creatures who patronized the house so frequently. Why they bothered her so much, she swore she'd never understand. "Tilly, about our plan?"

"Shalyn miss, the master would hit the ceilin' if'n he catches the two of us. Oh, come on," Tilly said as she took Shalyn's hand and stood up. "We'll just have to be as quiet as nestin' mice."

This was not a great difficulty for Shalyn.

Tilly led her down the stairs and through the gallery to the room next to the drawing room where Seanessy entertained the duke and his men. No lamps were lit in the adjacent room, as no one was expected to use it. Masculine voices came from the wall. She heard them almost clearly. Seanessy was asking about a Ho Cong family. Tilly quietly fumbled with a matchstick before striking and setting it to a candle. She put a finger to her lips for silence, unnecessary because no one moved as easily and soundlessly as the girl.

Tilly set the candle down on a drawing table. She went to a carefully placed chair and with a heave, she pushed it a foot across the carpeted space. She motioned for Shalyn. In the candlelit room, Shalyn saw the large plaster hole in the wall. "One of the boys threw a heavy vase when he found out he didn't make the cap'n's officer's rank," Tilly said in a low whisper. "The master let him go that night. I've been meanin' to see it repaired ever since."

The plaster and wallpaper had been ripped about a foot by the vase. Light shone straight through a hole about three fingers wide. Just enough.

Tilly leaned over and peered through.

The plump woman rose, grabbing her heart. "La!" she whispered. "He is a fairy-tale duke!"

Shalyn peered through the hole. Tilly was right; he was a devastatingly handsome man, made more so by his extreme aristocratic bearing, a thing that affected his every manner and gesture. Exaggerated gestures, she noticed.

". . . Captain, you must realize you are shipping six, seven percent of the tea market." The duke stood, pausing as he opened a silk knee-length jacket, and withdrew a long cigar from his breast pocket. Her fascinated eyes watched unseen as he held the cigar in the air, waving as he continued. "The point, monsieur, is that it amounts to a formidable threat to the Chinese, to the Taniko family specifically."

She could see only the wide width of Seanessy's back, the neatly tied long blond hair. He wore a charcoal-black vest over a white cotton shirt, his shoulder harness over that. The two heavy pistoles might be an extension of his arms for all the ease with which he wore them.

Seanessy sat at a great rosewood desk, facing his distinguished guest as Charles held a tray of whiskey and crystal goblets, serving the men in the room. The butler did not ask Seanessy. Seanessy only rarely drank, one of the many things Tilly had told her about her master. The fact that two or three times a year a terrible headache knocked Seanessy out, keeping him bedridden in a dark and quiet room, kept him from drinking. He suspected alcohol made the headaches worse when they came, so he rarely indulged. It was hard to believe anything at all could go wrong with his body, let alone a headache.

Shalyn did not have to see Seanessy's face. She knew without thinking about it that his face would remain expressionless in that way he had, a way that gave no clue what he was thinking, but somehow left no doubt that he was. Kyler stood to the side, his intelligent eyes veiled too as he listened.

The duke seemed to study the cigar a moment as if he just realized he had withdrawn it. "One has only to calculate seven percent of the tea market to discover the reason and purpose of the treachery. The pieces fall into place once one views the picture in its entirety."

The silence was overpowering as Seanessy considered the words. He reached for his glass of water, brought it to his lips, drained it, and refilled the glass. "On the other hand, Your Grace, a circus fool using an ounce of imagination could produce your very own reason for such treachery. I personally can generate three good ones."

The duke's smile did not reach his eyes; his chuckle sounded cold. "I am the first to admit financial interests in the region. Nor will I deny interest in the shipping enterprise you and Monsieur, er, Lord Barrington worked into such a formidable profit—"

"Which interests you more," Seanessy interrupted, "the profit or the political threat?"

Again the duke's laughter somehow conveyed the aristocratic contempt he had for the Irish peasant before him. Shalyn's brow rose, and she bit her lip, half expecting Seanessy to tire of this grandiose pretense, stand up with some clever speech, and then shoot the duke dead, ending the whole by calling for a late supper.

"I believe you answered your own question, monsieur. It is no secret that it has been many years since I was last motivated by want of coin."

"Aye." Seanessy leaned back, his hands reaching behind his head, a gesture that seemed casual but that she now associated with his boredom and then impatience. "I am wondering just what your ambitions are."

"Control." The duke paused, staring at Seanessy with a hooded gaze as if measuring the man and the limits of his honesty. Some incomprehensible signal made one of the duke's men leap forward and strike a kindling match, holding it up for the duke's long cigarillo. A sudden cloud of smoke filled the room. "No less than control of the entire Chinese and Indian trade routes."

The warm sound of Seanessy's laughter sang in the still and quiet room as he said simply, "You are dreaming, man. Or mad, or both. You have three great nations and a thousand players to choke or rein in on a mercilessly tight leash."

The aroma of the cigar reached the hole in the wall. Shalyn first felt it as a physical sensation, a tingling that raced up and down her spine before reaching all the way through her fingertips.

She had smelled this before!

She rubbed her head, dizzy with the scent . . .

Memories rushed at her. Of an Oriental man disappearing in a blur of confusion . . .

"Mad? I think not, monsieur." The duke said simply and with humor, "Judging one's sanity is a faulty game at best; I refuse to participate. Especially as I am so close, monsieur, so very close. Surely your, ah, compatriot Lord Clives must have explained the situation to you?"

The disclosure brought a steely silence into the room. Seanessy and Kyler exchanged glances, unable to conceal their surprise. "So he has," Seanessy confessed. "I'm surprised, Your Grace: first that you know, then that you would let me know you know. Of course it has been brought to my attention." He played his card: "Yet not by a compatriot." With feeling: "I am Irish; in other words"—he smiled and drew on the tired cliché—"I bleed green. As do all my countrymen. Clives, indeed all Englishmen are a festering wound, one threatening the life and blood of my kin."

The duke considered Seanessy through a thick cloud of smoke. Finally: "I need the Taniko family out of the game. Like you, monsieur."

"And you want me to do it for you."

The duke chuckled. "Oh no. You misunderstood. I hardly need your help in removing the obstacle made by this perfidious tribe of animals. Quite the contrary, I propose to do you the favor."

Shalyn could tell that the words surprised Seanessy, that he hadn't expected this. She knew too the effect of those words; she could feel Seanessy's sudden escalating tension, released in his reply: "Do me no favors; you can believe I am not a man who needs help with my killing. Now, I find this game is tiring, to say nothing of irritating; get to the point, man. What is it you want?"

The duke was the only human she could imagine who would remain undaunted, and undaunted he was. "I believe I made that clear. I want your shipping enterprise."

"And I believe my dear brother made the reply clear."

"Monsieur, I am not asking Lord Barrington."

"You might as well be," Seanessy said. "The answer's the same. It's not for sale."

"At half a million pounds sterling?"

Half a million pounds. The outrageous sum hung in the tense silence as Seanessy and Kyler exchanged surprised, nay, shocked glances. "What?" This came from Kyler, who shook his head in disbelief.

"This is a surprise." Seanessy almost laughed. "Why, that's four times its value, perhaps more!" He swore. "You could buy half of London for half a million pounds."

"I have no interest in London," the duke replied with but the barest hint of humor, and in the moment Shalyn studied him, she saw he had rehearsed this whole thing. "So you will consider it," the duke said simply. "And do take into consideration the sheer volume of difficulties and costs incurred by keeping that little piece of worked-over swampland, the terrible headaches involved?"

Headaches? How queer! Shalyn waited anxiously through the silence, wondering if he could possibly know about Seanessy's headaches and purposely prick him with the knowledge, or was this just a coincidence?

The duke continued, "Trust me to know the impossibility of overseeing one's interests from abroad as you and Lord Barrington are more and more forced to do, the increasing difficulties and escalating espionage from the Oriental heathens and the rest.

And"—he drew on his cigarillo—"I believe you will discover—"

A man rushed in unannounced. The duke stiffened dramatically as the man bowed quickly before stepping over to the duke. He leaned over to whisper a rush of excited French words.

The Duke de la Armanac demanded as he rose: "This man is alive? He saw her?"

More whispered words passed between the duke and his agent. "Yes, yes at once." Strain, even anxiety crossed the duke's face as he rose to address Seanessy. "I'm afraid I am called away. My business is finished." For a moment he held the bridge of his nose in consternation, overwhelmed by the news just brought to him. He looked up again, his dark gaze empty of any expression or sentiment. "You will need to consider it, and exchange correspondence with Lord Barrington—"

"Our correspondence has been exchanged." Seanessy said smoothly, and even Kyler, who knew the speed of Sean's wits so well, was absolutely shocked by how quickly Seanessy turned this whole predicament to their advantage. "Lord Barrington has left the matter to me."

"Indeed?" This was the first time the duke appeared surprised.

"Aye." Seanessy smiled, "Naturally he told me about your previous offer. We both were considering it when, ah, our consideration was interrupted by the untimely threats. The situation has changed; my doubts have vanished. You have named a price that, frankly, I find irresistible."

Now it appeared as if Seanessy had arranged this whole charade to extrapolate the highest price possible, as if he had been a dickering haggler at a village market, manipulating the price by the time-honored pretense of reluctance. The duke appeared stunned.

Seanessy continued, "I'll be happy to join you on your little island to arrange the details and work out an amicable transition. As it is, I was planning on journeying to Malacca, hoping to conclude my business there before the monsoon season. I understand your island sits north of the Straits of Malacca?"

"Now you will be telling me your navigator has already worked out a course."

With a grin Seanessy named the exact coordinates of the island and added, "I was planning on debarking before the week's end . . ."

Kyler's quick mind grasped Seanessy's purpose and he braced, waiting. Seanessy always pressed his luck. He saw that Sean wanted to be on the island before the duke returned to it. That way they'd have plenty of time to find the opium hidden there . . .

"I am impressed, monsieur—"

"And appalled," Seanessy said frankly. "You see, Your Grace, unlike you and yours, Irish peasants are not burdened with the aristocracy's contempt for money and the sweet things it buys. Of course I knew you would be making another offer and of course I hedged my words to squeeze a better price from you. And I got it. So when do you plan to leave London?"

The duke's face remained impassive, save for his eyes. "My departure is uncertain," he answered finally, flatly. "I will forward to you a letter of introduction. You may pass it on to Monsieur du Luc, my overseer there, though in all honesty I do not know when I will arrive, how long you may wait."

Seanessy rose. "Until the monsoon season, Your Grace."

"Good—"

Seanessy looked to the duke's waiting agent and did not hide his curiosity. "Is there anything I might help you with?"

"No, I'm afraid not." He forced a smile. "It is only a minor domestic problem. To our mutually beneficial future, monsieur."

He bowed. Charles led the duke and his party out. Seanessy remained standing until the door shut. He swung back into the chair and lifted his booted feet to the tabletop. A very pleased grin spread across the handsome face, widening when Kyler laughed and said, "There's the Irish luck for you, Seanessy!" as he sat down and poured himself a healthy shot of the Irish whiskey.

"Indeed."

All Seanessy had needed was that invitation to the island, then once there, an excuse to prolong it enough to discover and destroy the opium supply before this man ruined England, and with it Ireland. Sean and his boys would find the warehouse full of this precious white powder, blow it sky-high, and— somehow!—manage to escape before the man's two-thousand-man army became engaged. Prime Minister Wilson would be his bloody best friend. He and Ram would get four years' shipping free of British tariffs. Ireland would at last get the all-important place in Parliament.

All in all, a winter well spent.

"Charles," he called out. The man practically leaped through the door. "Charles, I trust you will save me a trip to speak with O'Connell."

An irritated smile spread across the old man's face. "Indeed. And Mister O'Connell asked me to ask you if you know of a Mary Brackton. Apparently the duke is making inquiries into this lady's whereabouts."

"Brackton, Brackton. I have heard the name. Now where was it?"

The name sounded familiar somehow to Shalyn as

well. She sighed, wondering how she could possibly be surprised that she couldn't remember it.

"Oh, well, can't think of it now. Keep the messages flowing, old man. And see my trunks packed. We sail tomorrow for Malacca."

Shalyn withdrew from the hole, her thoughts spinning. She hardly noticed the pained look on Tilly's face as she motioned for silence still, then pushed the chair back across the floor. She was thinking of his last instructions. Trunks.

Trunks. It would be her only hope. She closed her eyes and crossed her fingers like a schoolgirl, praying this slim hope saw her onto his ship sailing first to a duke's South Sea island and then to Malacca.

Malacca—where she knew at last she'd remember.

Chapter 8

He had to say goodbye.

He knocked on the door quietly, then opened it and entered. The drawn curtains muted a bright morning sun. The huge green feather quilt buried her in the bed. Beneath the covers Shalyn panicked.

She moaned softly.

Booted feet came to the bed. Concerned hazel eyes looked down. "Shalyn, Tilly says you are, ah, indisposed. I suppose that means you have your monthly, am I right?"

His bluntness irked her, more when she felt color warm her cheeks. Of course he'd know all about the unmentionable subject. Of course he'd come right out and mention it! He was so . . . so blunt!

"Poor, poor Shalyn . . ."

Poor Shalyn plans on going to Malacca with you.

She pushed her hair off her face as if in distress. With her flushed cheeks, she did in fact look ill.

"Does it hurt that bad?"

She said nothing.

Somehow he could not help touching the girl. A cool hand came to her forehead. The soft skin felt vibrant and warm. She looked incredibly lovely too, despite everything, with the long rope of gold hair trailing off the side of the bed, and the warm invitation of slightly parted lips. He saw she wore her shirt and trousers beneath the covers, and he imagined parting the shirt and slipping his hands over—

He put his head down between his large hands, chuckling at the absurdity. There he went again. Lord! How she stole his mind! What a relief to be done with her!

"Well, Shalyn mine, I suppose this is goodbye."

Not if I have anything to do with it!

He sat on the edge of the bed. The scent of his shaving soap reached her. She breathed deeply, her dark eyes staring up at him. How handsome he looked! He wore white cotton breeches, black boots, a wide black belt, and a loose white canvas vest; that was all. His hair was tied back and his skin shone with that dark golden touch of the sun against the white. His bare arms appeared nothing but muscles—

She thought of his kiss . . .

Realizing he awaited her reply, she tried to make her voice sound weak. "Aye."

"Now you know Kyler will be seeing to everything—"

She nodded, thinking of his trunks. Again. All night she had thought of his trunks. She had examined them last night. Two trunks sat in his bedchamber now, one of clothes, the other of books. She heard him call to someone, a man named Edward, to send a man for his trunks. They were coming. She had only to remove most of the books, stuff them under the bed or in the closet, and climb in. She could easily fit inside, but it would mean bent knees. She reasoned she could go perhaps five, maybe six hours before suffering cramps from the position. Of course she needed a good deal more time undetected than that; she had to remain hidden at least three or four days before she let him discover her intrigue, maybe longer. Otherwise he would simply turn the ship around to return her to London.

That was after he killed her . . .

This was all secondary, though. The first part of her plan called for getting inside the trunk undetected, then praying no one opened the trunks to inspect them before they set sail. Then she would start worrying about how to hide on a ship for four or more days.

The problem had kept her up all last night. It seemed everything hinged on it; yet there seemed little or no hope of succeeding. She had hardly closed her eyes when Tilly arrived with morning tea, and this last day in London—she prayed!—had begun.

Seanessy mistook the worry in her eyes for pain. "You're not afraid anymore?"

"No." She forced a smile. "Not with Mister Kyler."

"That's my girl!" He looked pleased. He had not expected her to be so congenial at their parting. He supposed it was owing to her ailment; she just had nothing left with which to fight him. A bit of luck there. For the fiftieth time he said, "You will love my brother and sister-in-law."

"If they're anything like you . . ."

He grinned at her teasing.

"And I have always wanted to see America." She forced a smile, looking as if it had taxed her to do so. Magnanimously she added, "One hears so many stories about America . . ."

"Few of which are true," he said, adding with boyish ease and levity, "The Indians almost never eat the Christians, unless of course they are of the Protestant flavor, and contrary to popular belief, there are more religious fanatics than criminals. By twelve."

The sweet girlish sound of her laughter made him realize again how much he loved the pleasure. He smiled down at her. Despite all, the parting and her monthly, what a fine humor she was in! He had never seen her so ... so agreeable.

Partings were sweet indeed.

He should have parted that first morning!

Shalyn realized she appeared too well and needed to be more ... indisposed. As if struck by a sudden pain, she closed her eyes and moaned again.

With concern: "Should I ask Tilly to fetch you a dram or—"

She shook her head and reached her hand out to touch his, and wanting this over before her excitement burst out, she squeezed it. "I don't know what to say Seanessy. I suppose I should thank you—"

"You? Thank me? You *are* ill! I was rather looking forward to a well-placed kick or punch—"

"I would if I thought it would do any good."

She smiled, a smile so endearing it made him want to take her into his arms. No, he realized, that was the last thing he should do.

"Well, goodbye, Shalyn." He suddenly stood, wanting away from the maddening appetite he had to fight constantly when he was near her. "I will no doubt see you again sometime." Not too soon, he prayed. Five years ought to do it. That would surely mean she would indeed be married to a Mr. American Bumpkin. No, don't think of that either—

"Goodbye, Seanessy. Be careful."

He leaned over and lightly, chastely kissed her forehead, catching a faint taste of the perfume of her skin. What was it? That sweet scent drove him mad, more when he imagined taking those soft lips beneath his as he felt the full softness of her breasts and—

He checked the impulse. "Here, this is for you."

He draped a gold chain over her head. The ruby star slid over the bedclothes. Shalyn stared at the piece. She had forgotten all about it.

"You left it on my bed," he said by way of explanation.

He watched her inspect the spectacular jewel, saw the mistrustful look in the lovely eyes as she did so. He could hardly wait to be sailing beneath a blue sky with no more of her trouble. No more daily—nay hourly—battles against his worst nature, against lying the girl backside to the bed and taking those sweet lips—

Shalyn wanted to conclude the interview just as much but for entirely different reasons. She grimaced as if struck with pain.

Not needing any more reason to leave, Seanessy leaned over to kiss her goodbye once again, whispering his last goodbye for five years. His lips lightly pressed hers, intending the kind of kiss one might give one's mother. Yet his lips lingered and lingered, and in the long space of those moments, his heart and pulse leaped as he stiffened with the irresistible pull of her untried sensuality.

"Shalyn." He closed his eyes and said her name.

He caught her gasped breath in his mouth. He swore softly as his hands came under her arms and lifted her out of the bed. She was suddenly kneeling on the bed as he held her, her back arched dramatically, her arms braced against his for support. Which she needed desperately as his mouth came over hers, and he was kissing her.

Warm, firm lips molded her mouth to his as he swept his tongue into the moist softness. It was like an avalanche breaking, this unexpected, unintended, madly ill-advised kiss. He only thought he would die, that he wanted her as he wanted his next breath, more; he wanted her more than anything past or present.

She felt a moment's utter surprise before all knowledge left her. All knowledge but the warm firm lips on hers and the oh-so-erotic probe of his tongue as he molded her against the hard outline of his body. The long tail of her hair swung back and forth in midair, a near-violent motion that mimicked perfectly the sudden rush of her heart and pulse. She didn't know her eyes were closed, and her arms lifted around his neck as she was suddenly clinging to him as if her life depended on it.

"Good heavens!"

Seanessy stopped the kiss but did not look to where Tilly stood in the doorway; she quickly turned around and left. He stared instead at Shalyn's lovely upturned face, flushed cheeks, and still-closed eyes, amazed by his body's reckless enthusiasm as it greeted the small form against him.

He never said anything. A thousand words could not express what that one kiss and her response said. He gently brought her arms away and lowered her to the bed. Confused dark eyes opened to him with a question, only to see his back.

He shut the door on the unspoken sentiment of that kiss. For nearly five minutes Shalyn stared at the door as her heart slowly spiraled back to normal. She shook her head as if to rid herself of its spell, at least its effect. She tried to tell herself it didn't mean anything; he didn't mean anything by it, the kiss changed nothing.

She knew this was a lie, one of the lies she needed to embrace and believe in order to stay alive. She abruptly realized she was wasting precious time. Time that might separate her from her precious life. She leaped up. She fluffed the bedclothes to look like a person slept there before she tiptoed to the door.

The sound of Seanessy's boots rang down the hall, then the stairs. She had no time to waste. Men were coming for his trunks. The ship was leaving before noon. Quietly she opened the door, slipped through, and shut it. She rushed to his door and closed it behind her. She padded silently through the sitting room and into his bedchamber where two trunks sat on the floor.

A push told her which one was filled with books. She opened the lid. Three by three she shoved the books under his bed. She looked down to see more than a dozen rolled-up parchments. What were they? She decided to leave them, as they might provide some cushioning effect.

Breathing hard from the swiftness of her exertions, within ten minutes she had cleared over three-quarters of the space. It was just enough room.

She stepped back to make certain no books might be seen under the bed from the doorway. Then she climbed inside. She lay on her back, knees up. She could last inside perhaps five hours before getting cramps. Merciful heaven help me . . . Tilly had promised to leave her alone all day as she had told the kindly woman she needed one day of rest to recover.

She had less than a half-hour . . .

She carefully set the trunk lid down. Darkness engulfed her. The long journey to Malacca had begun. Begun with a fervent prayer that no one would bother to check the cargo.

A thunderous clamor moved down King's Highway; more than one interested servant peeked out stately windows to see hardened and terrifying-looking men racing horses down the cobblestone street. Like the Red Sea for Moses, the billowing fog seemed to part for them. The devil was full of tricks like that. For most all the servants guessed what house these men headed to.

Nine King's Highway.

O'Connell and his band of Irish knights turned horses onto the gravel drive of Hanover House. Stallions felt the sudden cutting bits in their mouth and reared angrily in the air. All seven men kept their seats. O'Connell, wild to the core, withdrew a pistole and fired three shots into the air with an angry urgent curse.

Kyler and Richards sat in the garden room with supper, enjoying the new peace and quiet of the great old house. The sound of pistole fire outside reached them. Kyler set his paper down and looked across to Richards. "What the blazes?"

They rose, removing cocked pistoles from shoulder harnesses. The two men rushed through the halls into the entryway, heading for the windows when the enormous front doors opened. There stood O'Connell, his men falling behind him—more guns than a well-equipped platoon.

"Seanessy? Pray tell the man has not left yet?"

"He's long gone, O'Connell." Kyler returned his pistole to its nesting place, folding his thick arms across his chest, bracing for this newest catastrophe, whatever it was. "The *Wind Muse* sailed out for the straits today."

Soft curses sounded. The Irishmen, all of them, looked alarmed. Then in a whisper of what sounded like fear, O'Connell asked, "And the pretty lass? Where is she now? With Sean?"

Kyler tensed. He almost did not want to hear what was coming. "Upstairs." A steely gaze riveted to the Irishman. "I gather you are about to tell me who she belongs to?"

"You won't believe it when I tell, my good man. For the who is a good deal worse than Pandora's own box . . ."

First she dreamed of beautiful picture books. Page after page of enchanting forests of green dancing elves and their charming little forest cottages . . .

The enchanting pictures turned to nightmarish images of heads in sand and terrifyingly cruel hands coming to hurt her—

The nightmare disappeared as she opened her eyes. Opened her eyes to complete, inexplicable darkness. She caught her scream in a loud gasp.

The trunk! She still sat in the trunk. She stiffened, afraid to breathe as she listened for a clue as to the situation. The last thing she remembered was the trunk being lifted onto a carriage, the men's curses at the weight, grumblings that the captain's "high-minded books would weigh the 'ole bloody ship down to a snail's pace . . ."

Distant sounds of shouting men reached her. She felt a strange rocking and abruptly realized what it was.

The ocean lifting the ship.

Dear Lord, she'd made it, she'd made it! She was sailing on board his ship to the Straits of Malacca! Hallelujah!

She felt an aching stiffness in her legs. She tried to stretch but there was no room. Yet that discomfort was nothing compared to the urgency with which she had to relieve herself.

She had to get out.

Where was she? On board, surely, but where? Probably right in the captain's quarters. The room sounded very quiet. She would risk a peek. Gently she pushed on the roof of her cage. Nothing gave, and she pushed harder. Still nothing gave. Her heart kicked in and she used all her strength.

Locked! Someone had locked it!

If someone found her now, she knew Seanessy would turn the ship back. It would be just like him! He would be mad too, fire-spitting mad—

Yet she had to relieve herself.

She squirmed in discomfort. There was just no way around it.

The door opened, and Seanessy and Butcher stepped inside.

"I am starved!" Seanessy combed long fingers through his wind-tousled hair. "What's our dear Mister Slops's poison?"

The chef was rather unaffectionately called Slops, the name deriving from the huge man's malicious torment, a torment that many crew members, including Seanessy, felt increased as the voyage stretched and supplies dwindled. Toward the end of every voyage Seanessy would ritualistically begin threatening to let Slops off at the very next deserted island they sailed past, while Slops replied with serious threats of more potent poisonings.

"Slops's stew," Butcher said, straight-faced.

"Very funny. Let me know when you tire of amusing me and decide to work—"

"Those be his words, Sean. I have nothin' to do with it."

"The maps are in my trunk."

The words were like an ice pack to her heart. She froze, just froze. 'Twas too soon! They probably had not yet said goodbye to the last green sliver of merry ole England. It could not have been more than an hour or two out to sea! He would turn the ship around. Why, he might even drop her off at the nearest land somewhere with a pocket of money—

She held her breath as Butcher fumbled with the lock.

Fate was indeed a fickle but an obliging lady that day. For just as Butcher began to lift up the lid, and sudden light poured into her world, a crew member burst inside to announce the emergency: "Cap'n, our wake just tipped a boat o' fishermen!"

"Oh, really!"

This came from Seanessy. Butcher dropped the lid with a curse. "Well, be they floatin', man?"

"Not one of them. Edward dropped over the side to rescue the bloke."

"Curse all! That's the best way to get drowned! If I lose my quartermaster—"

The three men went through the door.

A hot wave of relief washed over her. Now or never. They would be back soon, heading for the maps. She lifted the lid, climbed out. As soon as her unsteady legs felt her weight, her knees collapsed. Dizziness engulfed her. An enormous thirst burned in her throat and her stomach grumbled unpleasantly. Slops's stew sounded appetizing.

One thing at a time.

She looked around for a better hiding place.

The amber eyes swept the room she remembered so well because it was somehow so like him. She did not let her interested stare linger long at the magnificent tapestry hung on the polished wood wall. She looked at the low table occupying one corner, surrounded by colorful brocaded pillows and cushions. How long could she stay hidden there in those pillows? Not long if he had more than three crew members dining with him. She passed over the old-fashioned rifles mounted on the other wall. There was the bed . . .

She could hide under the bed, which had been ingeniously placed on rollers to absorb the motion of the ship. 'Twas so large too, over seven paces long and nearly as wide. She rushed over, peered underneath, and saw a goodly space between the two rollers. Perfect!

She needed pillows.

She looked at them. Her heart pounded in anticipation as if she were a thief about to be caught.

She took two pillows, hurriedly stuffing them under the bed.

Nature's urges were undeniable. There was, needless to say, no plumbing on the ship, if one did not count the outside "head" as sailors called it—the darkest place on any ship. What could she use as a chamber pot?

There was nothing here! Spartan was an apt description of the furnishings, or lack thereof, in this room.

A number of obscenities sounded from topside, Seanessy's voice the loudest.

Hurry, hurry, hurry . . .

There was nothing but the iron welded goblet sitting innocently on top of the table. She picked it up, almost laughing when she saw it was full of water. She drained it, savoring the cool fresh water sliding down her throat. Now or never.

Blushing, she shrugged and hurriedly undid her belt.

Once finished, and after seeing there was no food to be had, she thought to take a book. Aye, the light would be poor, but if luck stayed with her, it promised to be a long, long wait. She snatched the first book she touched and raced to the bed. She shimmied under the less-than-a-foot-tall space. Settled against the wall and with a pillow at her head and shoulders, she twisted to see what book she had caught: *Frankenstein*, by Mary Shelley.

A brand-new book. Maybe not such a long wait after all. She began reading immediately.

After watching three fat fishermen bobbing in the cold winter water for the last hour and still laughing, Seanessy came through the door. Butcher and Edward followed, expletives pouring forth in a hearty torrent. Seanessy went for the maps. Butcher and Edward—dry now—sat at the table, still laughing heartily. Seanessy opened his trunk.

"What the blazes?" Over half of his books were missing. He reached for the maps, crunched as if someone had sat on them. He lifted one out, staring in stark disbelief that rapidly changed to ire. The kind that killed. He always took pains storing these precious maps after losing half a week and a hundred miles once due to the tiniest of creases.

"Someone is going to be skinned. Butcher, look at this. Just look at this." He opened the other trunk, his clothes trunk. It looked perfectly normal.

Butcher and Edward stood and moved to the trunk where they peered inside. "Sean, all your books are gone—"

Edward knelt down and lifted one up. "I saw Barker and Cherry Joe carrying it on board," Edward said with a shake of his head. "Neither one went to the science academies, but no one would be stupid enough to steal your books."

Shalyn covered her ears upon the first of Sean's expletives. Within minutes boots sounded against the wood floor, the door opened, and a man shouted. "Aye, ayes!" came back.

Seanessy said, "Good men both. I do not care how much a bookseller would give for them—" He turned to see the men step through the door. "Cherry Joe! What the devil happened to my trunks?"

"Yer trunks? Why, we carried them on board, is what. 'Tis all I know about 'em, Cap'n. Edward gave us the duty."

"This trunk is half-empty!"

Cherry Joe looked confused, taking the liberty of stepping over to the trunk and peering inside. "It sure as hell did not feel like it was half-empty! Nearly busted me weak shin, I did, as heavy as my own dear wife last time I—"

"Cherry Joe." Edward leaned over the trunk, looking inside. "Did you by chance leave the trunks for a moment as you made your merry way?"

"Well, aye. Halfway to dock one of the nags threw

a shoe. We had to rehitch with a borrowed one from Dodger's Stables. You know, off Wilkes Street."

"Sean." Edward grinned. "It looks as if we have a stowaway."

Seanessy hardly cared at this point. It would take his agent two months to replace the books and another half a year or more before he could get them to their library in Malacca. The books were gone, that's all he knew.

He began pressing out the crinkles in a map. "Well, find our merry trickster. Then toss him over the side with a barrel of slop. I want to see a few hungry sharks swimming beneath the ruddy bastard."

Shalyn almost screamed.

It took nearly an hour before she could return to the compelling story of Frankenstein. She wished she had better light. Still she kept turning the pages, her eyes widening with horror as Dr. Frankenstein forced electricity into his monster and he came alive . . .

Seanessy finally settled at the table, studying the maps. The quiet was interrupted by the pleasant sound of men's feet above on the quarterdeck, the calls and shouts that were about the sailing of the ship, the flap of sails and the waves against the sides of the ship.

Seanessy reached for his goblet of water. The movement of his arm stopped. He peered inside. His brow creased. He rose, stepping to the door.

"Hey, Butcher!" Seanessy called out.

A moment later: "Aye Sean?"

"What do you make of this?"

She heard a long pause. Finally: " 'Tis a sorry day when a cap'n asks his first mate to smell a cup of piss."

Seanessy looked into the cup curiously again before walking topside to the rail. The offending goblet was tossed unceremoniously into the deep blue sea.

Shalyn tensed with the expectancy of Seanessy's discovery, far more frightening even than Dr. Frankenstein's monster. No such thing happened. Gradually, as minutes gathered into an hour, she began to relax as nothing seemed to be happening. She returned to her book.

At last she heard the quartermaster. Edward stepped inside with Butcher and announced the conclusion of a thorough search of the ship top to bottom, starboard to port, bow to stern. "No stowaway, Sean."

"In other words," Seanessy said as he spread out the detailed map of the Gold Coast, "you're telling me someone sneaked aboard my ship in my trunk, only to change their travel plans at the last minute and leave. Again undetected?"

An uncomfortable pause followed this logic.

"Ah, Sean." Butcher often buffered Seanessy's sternness, a well-respected sternness but sternness nonetheless. "There must have been five dozen people on board the ship for departure. Seems it's possible just that thing happened, a good deal more possible than some ragtag stowaway passing through a rubdown undetected."

Seanessy's skeptical expression changed to one of irritation. "Oh, very well. I suppose if they did manage the trick, the misbegotten whoreson will turn up soon enough. Well, get Mister Slops to produce something edible, will you? Preferably supper."

"Aye, aye, Cap'n."

The men returned to their work. She returned to her book, trying to ignore her hunger and thirst. It was one of any number of things she was going to have to get used to. Like the way men talked when there were no women about. It was an education. At least she'd be losing her ability to blush soon . . .

Chapter 9

She woke with a start.

Darkness greeted her opened eyes. The air felt cool, and she was cold. Shalyn lay perfectly still, every fiber of her being intent on listening. The quiet sound of his slumber told her he was asleep just above her. She felt the gentle rise and fall of the ship at sea. In the distance, soft as a whisper, she heard someone on night duty whistling as he worked. She heard her own escalating heartbeat and the loud rumble of her stomach.

She was fully awake.

Half-starved, more thirsty than that, and desperate to relieve herself again, she would have to take a risk. He was asleep. She had fallen asleep before him, so she had no idea how long he had been asleep, but the quiet told her now was as good a time as any.

Moving soundlessly, she emerged from her hiding place. In a cloak of silence she stood up and stretched before turning to inspect her nemesis. Which was a surprise. For he was quite naked.

The faintest light filled the space, the distant light of stars above a sea mist streamed through the small portholes. He lay flat on his back, with his muscled arms cushioning his head like a pillow. A thin cotton sheet covered one leg, that was all. She stared at the slow steady rise and fall of the huge width of his chest before she found the courage necessary to look down.

The monstrous flaccid part of him made her breath catch. A tingling raced up and down her spine. She closed her eyes, washed in a hot wave of dizziness.

A memory emerged. A memory of the raw sting and scrape of ropes cutting her wrists. She rubbed her wrists, staring at them as she remembered the sick dread and the terrible helplessness. She remembered trying desperately not to move, to show any sign of life, feeling panic and fear—

She forced herself to quietly turn away.

With her heart racing, she spotted the bowl of fruit sitting on the table alongside a wood platter of after-supper bread and cheese. A huge pitcher of water sat nearby as if waiting for her. The awful memory stole her appetite. Still shaken, she forced herself to eat as much as she could, certain she would pay later if she did not. Then she wisely wrapped two thick slices of cheese in some bread and quietly pushed it under the bed. No doubt she'd not be able to come out until the next time he fell asleep.

She quietly slipped outside.

The moist sea mist engulfed the ship. It was cold. The ship appeared deserted but she knew better. She studied the darkness a long time before risking a move. It took her nearly fifteen minutes to determine the location and activity of each of three members of the night crew who sat topside. They sat in a semicircle on the far deck; she suspected they mended masts by certain words that reached her. No light shone nearby. The nearest lantern hung beneath the quarterdeck, near the ladder some paces from where she stood. It took another ten minutes to convince herself it was safe, that they could not see her in this darkness.

Then she made a silent move toward the head.

The sweet scent woke Oliver from his slumber. The dog sat up. Small animal eyes swept the deck in the direction of the smell. He rose to find the girl, coming to the head.

Shalyn greeted the dog outside. The huge furry beast wagged his tail. She smiled down, careful not to say a word but welcoming the friendly creature with vigorous strokes of kind hands.

Oliver followed the girl from dark shadow to dark shadow until she reached the side of the ship hidden by a darker shadow of the carpenter's room. Standing at the rail, she stared into the dark misty sea as she drank in the cold fresh air. The ship rose and fell over huge swells. After waiting for something to happen, the dog finally lay down at her feet with a small whine.

Shalyn closed her eyes to the darkness.

Another memory emerged: of insufferable heat, the worn wood planks of a ship deck, the loud roar of the ocean, the smaller sounds of men working to keep the ship on course.

So she had sailed before . . .

Aye. Of course she knew that. Ships were familiar to her. She knew the names of sails, the importance of rigging, masts, lines, stays, helm, all of it, even certain knots to secure the sails. She knew about sailing.

She tried to fill out the picture of this prior ship with a familiar face. Nothing and no one emerged in her mind. Desperately she tried to cling to this small piece of memory . . .

She did not know how desperately until she looked down to see her whitened knuckles as they clutched the rail. The evidence of her tension frightened her. She knew what tension cost men—their precious lives. She needed all her wits to survive this, especially when he found her out, and more when they reached Malacca where the search for the mystery of her missing memory would begin.

She knew what one did to lose fear. 'Twas a risky venture though!

After a moment's consideration she realized it was as necessary to her survival as breathing. After saying a silent farewell to her new friend, she quietly made her way back to the captain's door. She slipped back inside as quietly as she had left.

He might wake but then he might not. She suspected he slept soundly and simply because he seemed to sleep so little. As far as she had been able to tell he went to bed after everyone else, and rose before. She needed to do it; she alone knew how badly.

Seanessy never did stir that first night, nor for three nights afterward. And each night his dreams filled with hauntingly beautiful images of a young girl dancing in the dark middle of the night before him, her lithe, agile body moving gracefully through the ancient steps of the Oriental t'ai chi masters.

Love often comes only once in life, and a splendid thing it was. He was in love; as never before, he was in love. He knew it, felt it. She was unlike any other; he just wanted to get closer . . .

Oliver whined, then laid his head down.

Shalyn tensed, frantically waving her arm at the huge beast, who did not understand her problem. 'Twas no use. She lay perfectly still, careful to keep her eyes away from him. The dog was a big problem. Seanessy let him in at night when he and a few of his officers—Butcher, Edward, Taylor, and Hamilton—convened for cards or chess or backgammon.

Seeing him finally settle down, Shalyn relaxed as much as she could. She drew a deep even breath. This marked her fourth night under the bed. The ship had sailed past Gibraltar and proceeded along the Gold Coast. Yet now that she could come out, Lord, was she afraid!

Actually terror better described what she felt.

What would he do to her?

Nestled beneath the bed, she listened to the lively conversation and the conclusion of Seanessy's story, followed by the uproarious laughter of this gathering of men at his table. The crew bantered lightly, exchanging talk of politics and the decline of Dutch shipping, of all things. Their high spirits felt tangible. Apparently—from what she could gather—'twas perfect sailing weather. Not just perfect, but absolutely ideal. The ship flew at a near record pace and as a goodly north wind filled the sails, the men could barely contain their excitement at this once-in-a-lifetime situation.

Surely she could come out now. Yet ... yet she hesitated, and the reason, if she were honest, went beyond a fear of his punishment. Her existence was strange indeed: living under the bed by day and wandering a ghost ship by night. Yet for the first time not only did she feel safe, she also felt recurring moments of hope. Hope that she would be able to discover her past and then her freedom.

How she wanted that freedom! Like a great thirst it was! If her memory did return at Malacca, then she would know what she had to do to be not just safe, but free.

Seanessy and his men had spent the afternoon shifting what little cargo the ship carried to the fore and aft rafters. Seanessy wanted to demonstrate "the full power and glory of his ship's potential speed ..." Many men apparently had only heard of these prime weather conditions; Seanessy and Butcher had experienced them but three times before. She had heard them recount each time in detail for

an audience of interested men. So they all had spent
the afternoon in heavy labor, and from the unusual
peacefulness that settled over the captain's quarters,
they seemed to have exhausted their physical ener-
gies. Which did not dampen their humor.

Seanessy viewed the entire world from the lofty
tower of his considerable wit and humor, a wit as
sharp as a butcher's knife, as cunning as a gypsy
thief, and bone-ticklingly funny. It touched almost
everything he did. 'Twas the reason, she saw, so
many different men from all walks of life and corners
of the world were attracted to him. This hardened
bunch of seamen not only respected and admired
Seanessy, but loved him.

The doctor had been right. She had needed rest
and quiet to begin to recover. How unexpected to
have found it under Seanessy's bed! She slept or read
most of the day, coming awake at night to finish off
Seanessy's supper—which was thankfully not cleared
away until morning. Most of the night she practiced
the disciplined dance of the Oriental masters, a discipline that was as much a part of her as running was
to a horse, or swimming to a dolphin. She felt her
strength returning and, more important, as she
slowly moved through the ancient dance, memories
began to surface.

She remembered her training and glimpses of her
past: a picture of the encroaching jungle and an arch
of blue sky as she hung from a tree branch, hung until her arms ached and sweat poured off her frame.
She remembered how badly her arms would ache!
She would not let go until they literally shook, trembling violently. She remembered running and running on white sand beaches, running for no purpose
or rhyme or reason, past pushing her body beyond
endurance, running until her lungs burned and her
knees shook. Most of all she remembered following

the t'ai chi dance behind a man, a small older dark-skinned man who wore loose white trousers, naked to the waist. In these pictures she always stood behind him as she followed him through the t'ai chi dance. She kept waiting for him to turn around, so she could see his face and give him a name.

For she knew she had loved this man.

Yet she had no memory of his face. How she tried to find more of him in the darkened tunnels of her mind. The familiar voice that sometimes echoed in her head belonged to him; somehow he had been as a father to her. How? She was English and he an Oriental. 'Twas so odd . . .

'Twas so odd to know him, and yet she could not remember him! She did not remember his name.

She wished she could have a bath. A steaming hot perfumed bath in giant brass tub. With lavender hair soap and a hot oil rinse to help knead the knots out—

Her brow furrowed. She remembered taking these baths. Regularly!

Her heart started pounding. The picture of the tub and the room emerged from her mind. Who was with her? A dark face appeared, familiar, yet—

Who was that? Where was that?

The men settled down to a game of chess. Edward and Hamilton played against Seanessy. Twenty pounds on the game—enough for many families to live on for half a year. She hardly listened as she struggled to remember more.

She remembered the servant. She saw a picture of her in her mind and yet knew nothing else about her. They spoke only through their gazes, locked to each other in silence as if to speak was a danger. As if to smile was a danger, and yet she saw the woman's sympathy—she felt it! The servant had been young, with beautiful Negro features. She wore a formal black cotton dress. In her mind's eye Shalyn saw this woman lay out a pink silk kimono, her eyes lowered to hide the unspeakable sympathy.

Shalyn hated that kimono.

The emotion felt strong, even violent.

Shalyn almost cried out in agony as the pictures faded. No other images emerged in her mind. She tried to remember the house, another room. A large library emerged briefly, disappearing before she could remember any more.

Oliver whimpered nearby.

"Rook to white queen seven," Seanessy said, and hearing the sad cry, he looked over at the great dog. "What in blazes is wrong with him?"

The men considered the dog, then returned to the board. Except Edward. His gaze did not stray from the black-and-white-checked board. He meant to win this one. Seanessy's mind was not on the game, which meant this was a rare opportunity to beat him at it.

Despite the glory of the elements, Seanessy felt a restlessness normally associated with the very end of a journey. As if he needed a long swim or a drawn-out fight. Aye, he thought, a fight would do him good . . .

The very idea reminded him of someone. Someone with dark mysterious eyes and rich gold hair, dropping in a plait to her waist. Against his will the picture of her nudity rose in his mind; the slim, shapely curves of those long legs, the roundedness of her slender hips, the way the boy's breeches stretched across her backside, and her waist, the way his hands fitted perfectly around that unbelievably small waist, and, dear Lord, the tempting swelling of her breasts, the tease of the large peaks—

He groaned out loud, suddenly draining his cup, seized by a desire so swift and hot and strong, the girl might be in the very room. It was so much worse somehow at night. When he lay down and closed his eyes, he could taste the faintest trace of her scent in the air. That was all it took and suddenly ...

" 'Tis like the dog's pining over a lost mate or somethin'," Butcher said, but stared at Seanessy instead.

" 'Tis probably nothing more than Slops's slop," Turner said. "Makes me want to weep as well. What was that slop tonight? Rarebit stew, he said, but it tasted more like dung piles dropped in mud."

"I had a dog that started crying out like that once," Hamilton added. A sad look crossed his dark eyes, a bittersweet smile of a man remembering his faithful boyhood friend. "Didn't last the summer."

"Sean, are you going to move or—"

Edward stopped as he noticed Sean's glassy-eyed stare. He chuckled. " 'Tis going to be a long voyage if you're already missing the ripe comforts of home, Captain. I've never met a man who suffered celibacy like you. I'd swear you never learned how to abuse yourself."

Sean's eyes narrowed with irritation, and he took Edward's rook for revenge. "Abuse. Suffering. Now there are some apt descriptions." He drained his water goblet whole. "Two or three times a night, and it doesn't even touch the heat that—"

"Sean," Edward said, finally deciding on a move. "Please, my sensibilities ..."

"And here I thought you wanted details," Seanessy replied as he reached for an apple, wondering again how all the food kept disappearing from his quarters. The cheese and bread might be Oliver, but fruit? These were the last few days of fruit too. Unless they stopped at some or another wretched hovel of thieves and beggars, and women too used to even be considered.

"Cap'n." Scott burst through the door. "The stay on the square rigging just cracked. Look's like she's about to give."

Sean set down his rook. "No doubt an adjustment from that last storm she weathered."

Storms often weakened a ship structurally, sometimes causing damage that remained undetected for months, even years. Edward took a last glance at the board and rose. "I'll help Knolls put her back up." Knolls was the ship's main carpenter, but Edward had risen through Seanessy's ranks from that position and he still liked to keep a hand in the constant strengthening of the timber that kept him and all forty-five crew members afloat. "Ham?" He looked to his friend. "Would you please try to keep my king from Sean's pocket?"

"The way he's playing"—Hamilton grinned—"I might be able to pocket ten pounds."

"Ten pounds to play this game out?" Edward laughed as he left. "Between you and Butcher, 'tis little wonder I'm still a poor man."

Seanessy did not return Hamilton's smile.

Oliver continued to stare at the girl. Why was she stuck there? Why wasn't someone helping her out? He wanted to play with her!

The dog's footlong tail thumped. He lifted his head and howled softly. The howl brought gazes to him. He knew the trick. He looked steadily at the master, then turned to stare under the bed.

"What is wrong with that dog?" Sean watched with incomprehension, then moved his rook from the direct path of Ham's knight and in line with his queen. "Maybe I'll lower a boat and toss a ball for him tomorrow. Would you like that, boy?"

The dog howled softly, then fixed his head in the direction of the bed, pointing as one would with a finger. Sean had to laugh, "He's never been so restless on a voyage before. One would swear there was someone under my bed."

Oliver howled louder, thumping his tail.

Seanessy rose gracefully from his sitting position. He went to the door, opened it, and called the dog. The dog hesitated, the great tail thumping madly. Reluctantly he rose and pushed his tail between his legs. With a lingering glance at the bed, he left the quarters.

Shalyn breathed a heavy sigh of relief.

Seanessy shut the door.

Before returning to the game, Seanessy stretched long arms to the ceiling. He felt Oliver's same restlessness. He bent over, and with his famous acrobatic ease, he went up into a handstand.

Shalyn gasped in utter terror.

Yet the back of his head faced her. He couldn't see unless he turned around. Stiff with tension, she supposed 'twas hard enough to hold his weight in a handstand on a rocking ship, let alone to start turning circles. Still she lay as rigid as stone, fear pumping hard and fast through her blood as she watched this. More when he lifted onto one hand, and after a minute, switched to the other.

Of course the men in the room were very familiar with Seanessy's unusual acrobatic agility—it was famous. The only time they were compelled to watch was when he did it atop horses. This did not even rate a comment.

Strange images filled his mind as he stood upside-down. The missing books. The missing stowaway. The missing fruit. The wet tooth comb he found in the morning. The erotic dreams of Shalyn dancing in the silence of the ship. Oliver's interest in something under the bed.

Blood started pumping into his heart and it was not from his upside-down exertions. He came gracefully to his feet. He stepped over to his clothes trunk and removed his hairbrush from the velvet shelf. He pulled one mercilessly long crinkled gold hair from the bristles. He inspected it.

He waited a long moment.

Waited for a coherent thought to rise above his rage.

"Sean, 'tis your move. I believe you are doomed."

Shalyn felt her heart finally slow its pounding. She began to recover from the fright. Mercy! That was close!

Seanessy stood as still as a stone statue waiting for this precious coherency. No such civilized idea came to him as the rage felt swift, powerful, consuming.

In a sudden eruption of violence he swung his clenched fist into the hard wood wall. The thick board cracked. Pain shot up his arm, and it felt extricating.

The men all stopped and looked to where he stood. In a voice much changed for the control he placed on it, he said, "Get out!"

Shalyn gasped unseen. Who did he talk to like that? Why? The game? Why, he must have lost!

Huh! What a poor loser!

"Sean, what the devil?"

A deadly silence filled the room as the men greeted the sudden outburst as any sane man reacted to an unexpected violent madness. Butcher and Hamilton looked around the room for the source of Sean's wrath.

Yet there was nothing.

"I am warning you, Shalyn. For the love of your life, girl, do not make me lay hands on you."

'Twas as if he were mad! Butcher and Edward exchanged confused, even frightened glances as they realized Sean talked to someone who just wasn't there.

A sound came from under the bed.

A figure emerged. Butcher took one look. "Oh, Lord . . ."

With eyes downcast, Shalyn rose to her feet. Her face blanched white. She looked a hair's breadth from fainting and her knees started trembling.

Seanessy just stared at the reality of her presence: the tight thick braid of gold hair, the ashen face, the downcast eyes, the breeches and the shirt that covered a figure he was trying so hard to forget.

The girl's whole wretched scheme lay before him. Starting with her feigned theatrical indisposition the day he sailed, the empty trunk of books, the missing food, his tooth comb being wet every day, the long hairs he found in his brush, the poor dog pining under the bed, the scent at night, and the strange dreams of Shalyn moving in the darkness with the grace and beauty of an angel.

He swung away, moving swiftly to the rum bottles neatly lined on a shelf, secured from the motion of the sea by a tight cord. He took one out, ripped off the top, and put it to his lips.

Then he heard: "Seanessy, I'm . . . I'm sorry, but I—"

"No. Do not speak. Do not say a word. Butcher, you are to take care of this problem: you may do this by tossing her over the side or keeping her the hell away from me. Just do not let me see her. For God's sake, do not let me see her again."

Butcher quickly led the girl out.

The captain's door opened just as the pink light of dawn spread its long arms across the sky. Seanessy stepped out. Shrewd hazel eyes swept the clean decks, examining the position of the morning crew and the rigging of the masts. Little skipped his notice. The swift-moving clipper sailed over huge swells beneath an early morning sky, its great sails billowing in a strong north wind. A good two days past Gibraltar and fifty miles off the Gold Coast, the ship sailed at unprecedented speed.

Seanessy stood at the railing, staring at the breathtaking blue of the sea. The elements—wind and water and sun—converged to form a sailor's dream. He had logged close to fifty thousand ocean miles and of all those trips, this was the best. For many crew members it would be the first time they grasped the full glory and speed and power that belonged to the finest of oceangoing sailing ships.

He closed his eyes against the strong brisk wind. 'Twas indeed a sailor's dream as they headed south, but a nightmare if he turned around, as he fully intended to do. He had to.

He cursed Shalyn softly under his breath.

Seanessy lifted himself agilely onto the quarterdeck. He picked up the horn and called down to his men: "Step alive, mates! I need a full one-hundred-twenty-degree turn. Heading: Gibraltar."

He began calling out the rigging to individual crew members, ending at last with: "Hanson, get you up the rat line with an eye to any more cracks!"

The two dozen crew members had all turned, and now stared up at Seanessy on the quarterdeck. He stood feet apart, looking down. Showered in sunlight and with the wind blowing his long blond hair back, he looked like a mythological Nordic king standing atop the magnificent ship. Yet his eyes were still wild with rage, as if he had decided to war with God Himself. No one moved. A few men exchanged confused glances. Because they knew he couldn't mean it. 'Twas a jest . . .

Seanessy's gaze narrowed dramatically, and in a vicious whisper he said, "The day I give an order twice is the day I rig a keelhaul!"

The men stepped into action all at once.

* * *

Butcher lay still in his hammock and closed his eyes, willing his heart to a slower pace. Another hour or two of sleep would do him good. Yet he felt that rousing pace of a waking state. 'Twas no use.

'Twas a problem, this girl. He'd spent nearly two hours just trying to figure out where the lass might sleep. Needless to say the sleek lines of the ship harbored no separate passenger room for women—space was not just at a premium on board but often fought over by the crew. Almost all the crew slept in the fo'c'sle or crew's quarters, which was a small space for so many men, nothing but a chaotic array of hammocks and trunks. Shalyn could not sleep there, of course—that would bring a riot. Then there was the officers' quarters where he lay now, the same size as the fo'c'sle but for a quarter of the men. She could not sleep here either. Then there was the carpenter's room.

'Twasn't that any one crew member would risk Seanessy's wrath to hurt the lass, but the sea did strange things to a man. Add a couple of cups of rum and if truth be told, the Queen's mother could cause a problem. So after considerable deliberation and maybe a half-hour of bargaining with Knoll, he managed to settle the lass in the carpenter's room. Oliver settled down with her. That would keep her safe.

With a sigh, he gave up the pretense of trying to sleep and swung his legs over the hammock. The trouble was Sean. The trouble was that Sean's trouble was a hundred times more trouble than most men's. Sean's rage was more rare than a day without his laughter, and yet those few times it surfaced, it was enough to stop an advancing army.

He heard the distant call of Seanessy's voice shouting out the orders. His features changed with alarm. Curse it! He meant to turn the ship around!

Butcher was pushing his large feet into boots when Edward burst through the door. Fury changed the handsome features; he was livid: hands on hips, he demanded of Butcher, "A woman did this?"

"Aye. A woman."

"Seanessy's not the only man ready to rig the keel-haul for her. Half the crew's spitting mad."

"Then I'll have to make it clear that the man who so much as looks at the lass cross-eyed meets the sharp point of my revenge."

Edward did not take Butcher's threat lightly. In a subdued voice he said, "She's that special?"

"Aye. Enough to inspire Sean's own madness. A madness that is turning the ship around as we speak."

Edward wanted to see this girl, a girl he had heard so much about. "Where did you put her?"

"Carpenter's room."

"Can you talk some sense into the man?"

"Edward, you don't understand. Sean's doing the right thing. Ah, hell." He looked away, hands on knees. "I've known Sean for over ten years. I've seen the man in every condition and predicament: glad enough to buy a town full of men enough drink and women to last a week, outrageous enough to laugh as he battled ten heathens waving the sharp edge of their sabers at him; I've seen him rouse a hundred men to their feet, shaking fists and cheering, I've seen him charm the aristocracy and blind beggars alike, I've seen him fighting mad and dead drunk, I've even on occasion seen him dead serious. And I've seen him melt the hearts of a hundred ladies, and yet rarely remember a name the next day. In all this time I have never seen him as he is with Shalyn."

In frustration, Edward sighed. "Well, what is the problem?"

Butcher pushed the other boot on and stood up before answering. "The problem is she is far too young and far too fresh for Sean. The problem is the unhappy fact that she is most certainly mad; she has no memory past this idea that some band of cutthroats is chasin' her, that she has to get to Malacca." He shook his head sadly. "And I suppose the biggest problem is that Sean is madly in love with the lass. And love is one thing Seanessy doesn't know how to fight."

Shalyn tried to slow the race of her thoughts. She stared unseeing at the small space of the carpenter's room. Knives and hammers, sickles, picks, all manner of wood beams and saws cluttered the tight space around her. She curled up in the corner, struggling not to cry.

He had ordered the ship turned around. She had not expected this. He was so angry he thought to punish her by leaving her in Gibraltar. She would be returned to England and Kyler. She would never get to Malacca.

He did not know what it meant to her. She had to reach Malacca or die in the trying. Aye, she would die in the trying . . .

She had to change his mind or . . . die in the trying. Die in the trying . . .

The ancient Chinese voice in her mind said, "*The paradox of courage is that one must be a little careless with life in order to keep it . . .*"

Suddenly she knew what she had to do.

Shouts sounded from topside but neither Butcher nor Edward at first gave any mind to the sudden clamor. They were resolved to get the ship to Gibraltar as fast as possible. Butcher and Edward climbed the narrow staircase leading to the deck. "I'll have the swing shift man the rigging for the first three hours—" Edward stopped a moment. "What in blazes now?"

The two men rushed out onto the deserted deck, gazes riveting to the quarterdeck where over half the crew gathered, watching something. Oliver barked from below like the world was about to end. Edward's call joined so many others, it was lost in the roar of the men shouting at someone. Butcher went up, pushing through the crowd to Hamilton's side. He stopped in his boots; he felt the sick lurch of his heart. He couldn't speak; for his life he could not now speak.

Edward came slowly to his side, staring, seeing everything at once. Butcher still could not find his tongue. Hamilton too knew not to move, and, terrified not everyone would have the same sense, he stretched out his arms to hold everyone back.

"For the love of God, girl," Ham said, but that was all. No more words manifest from his mouth. For there were no words to express the fear felt by every man watching, desperate as they were to make the leap that would pull her to safety. Yet the courage shining in the darkened pools of her eyes proclaimed her determination.

The girl's eyes would live in their minds forever: They shone with the courage of any ten men watching, an unnatural fierceness in a man, unheard of in a woman. She stood on the rail, light as a feather and just as vulnerable to the goodly breeze blowing across the bow, bare feet apart, one arm holding the bulwark. The grasp of that slim arm was all that stood between her and a horrible death of falling a good twenty-five feet in front of a seven-hundred-ton vessel.

"Fetch Captain Seanessy—I will speak with him!" Edward snapped his fingers and whispered between gritted teeth, "Ten men to the rafts. And, my God, somebody get the cap'n!"

At least ten men jumped down to man the rafts, as futile as that would be. It was dangerous enough to drop from the side and into the ship's wake, but to do so from the bulwark left no doubt there would be little remaining of her to fish out.

Butcher stared at Shalyn, yet saw himself planning a fatal leap some ten long years ago. He remembered the months of despair so deep that no drink, much less daylight, could touch it; he remembered the morning he woke to find despair had vanished. Just like that it was gone. And in its place was . . . nothing: no feeling. A frigid numbness had settled over his heart, mind, and soul; he had been the living dead.

He remembered studying the indifferent face of his death from the top of the cathedral roof when a sudden merciless strength yanked him back from the brink, Seanessy's vicious curses singing loud as he felt the repeated strike of Seanessy's hand, over and over again until something snapped deep inside him. All the bottled rage burst like the gates of a floodwater. He had swung his fist into Sean's face. He went crazy; he had never fought as he did that day, not knowing then how much his adversary enjoyed that kind of once-in-a-lifetime fight; Seanessy broke two of his ribs, his jaw, and his nose; blackened both eyes; and busted a kneecap, and was given as good as he got and still he fought, fought until the two of them collapsed in a bloody pile on top of the cathedral roof. Through swollen eyes Butcher had turned to see his opponent and savior. With labored breath, Sean managed an introduction.

Seanessy had been laughing. The first time he had looked into Seanessy's bright eyes, Butcher had seen the wonder of Seanessy's great passion for life, like a beacon it was, leading him back from the darkness of hell and into the world again.

That very same light shone in Seanessy's eyes as he made his way through his men, stopping at last by Butcher's side, taking in the whole of the outrageous beauty poised on his bulwark and kept there by nothing more than a wonder of agility and grace. Nothing more. The wind blew her hair back and pressed the cotton shirt against her slim form. Sunlight lit her amber eyes. Never had he seen anything more beautiful than Shalyn at that moment.

Seanessy felt suspended in time; for a moment, time lost its restrained and disciplined meaning and instead became a kaleidoscope to knowledge. He realized everything, all at once: for the first time in thirty-three years he had lost his heart, lost it to this slender unlikely creature with the rich blond hair, dark eyes, and supple lithe form. He was struck as hard and painfully as the shepherd of the Irish myth, and he would pay as dearly for it. The payment would begin now and last forever, for in this moment that her life became far more precious than any other, he would now be forced to watch it slip from his grasp. The novelty and wonder of these realizations passed through him in a rush so fast that all he knew was the desperation to save her and the certainty that he could not.

The moment passed, leaving not a soft sentiment in its wake, but a tremendous murderous rage. Rage filled his chest as wind filled a sail. If she survived this, it would only be to experience a slow and painful death at his own hands. He was going to kill her for this, that was all he knew. He headed right for her.

"Not one more step, Seanessy!"

Seanessy stopped, his entire body going rigid with the lithe tension of a cat a split second from a pounce. No one moved. Though every man on board watched, the silence felt like the eerie echo resonating from a ghost ship: broken only by the whistle of the wind, the frantic flap of sails and slap of ocean water, the sliding of the rafts going down the side.

"Shalyn . . ." Their eyes locked, the key thrown away. "Shalyn, you jump down here or so help me God—"

"I have no mind to suffer the sharp bite of your tongue—" The ship gave a sudden lurch, and the girl stumbled. A sick gasp sounded almost collectively. She righted herself quickly and looked determinedly back at Seanessy. "I want only for you to decide for me." With her own anger: "I will not return to England. I must go to Malacca. Take me to Malacca with you, Seanessy, or see me dead!"

"See you dead?" Seanessy laughed, and his eyes narrowed with the pretense of irritation, for he knew this deadly game. "Don't get me excited. If you don't jump down by the count of ten, I'll give you a push!"

Shalyn stared, just stared at the challenge in the hazel eyes. He was bluffing. He had to be bluffing. He would not want her dead!

"You are bluffing!"

He never denied it. "So are you!"

"Nay," she told him in a impassioned whisper carried away in the wind. "I am not! Shall I prove it to you, Seanessy?"

What she did next would be talked about for years. Shalyn let go of the bulwark.

She stood on the rail balanced by nothing more than a miracle. A miracle that took the men nearly five seconds to realize she did not let go to jump to safety but rather to challenge Seanessy's command. Butcher wondered if he would faint like a palsied wench; his nerves were stretched taut, snapping each second she stood there. Then he realized he was trying to speak, but no sound came from his bone-dry tongue.

Softly, she said, "Take me with you, Seanessy . . ."

For a tense moment he stared at her, and in that moment he understood he never really had a chance, much less a choice. He had lost his heart and she had won it. He could only stop her from taking this precious piece of his soul with her in death.

"Very well!" he shouted as if she had reduced the emotional wealth of the treasure to little more than irritation. "But know this, Shalyn mine: I am still going to beat you within an inch of your life."

"I knew you were bluffing!"

She almost clapped her hands. She reached for the bulwark as the ship rolled down a huge swell, Shalyn balancing not by magic but by the sheer volume of thousands of hours of the Oriental dance, as if practicing for this very moment. Downside, the ship caught the oncoming swell at its side. The ship lurched. Shalyn grabbed the bulwark, her feet swung out, and more than one man screamed.

Seanessy had leaped into the air.

She stared at the incredible blue wash of the ocean swells before she felt the terrifying slip of her hands. In the same instant Seanessy's hands caught her under the arms. He swung her up and brought her feet to the safety of the deck.

A loud and long cheer went up. Neither Shalyn nor Seanessy noticed. For one magical moment he held her slender frame tight against his chest, so tight he feared he hurt her, and still it was not enough. Not enough to offset the jolt of his heart from that slip. As if life itself had tired of him, playing with her so cavalierly, and she thought to show him the awesome power of her absence. If he lived to be a hundred it would not be enough to offset that jolt.

He finally pulled away to stare down at the lovely

eyes, yet careful to keep the slim body aligned to his as he shouted out the order to turn the ship back to its original course. "You know, Shalyn mine, I still mean to beat you for this."

She smiled, happy and relieved—to say the least—and if only her knees would stop trembling, she knew she'd be fine. For she had faced death and lived to laugh again, he had granted her passage to Malacca, and she had bested him, all in one fell swoop. "I'll be sure to put it on my calendar."

Yet his face changed, the hard lines of the handsome features softened and his eyes looked different. The jolt receded, subsiding bit by bit as he stared at her, and in its wake came another jolt, almost as powerful. A jolt of lust, hard and hot lust. He wanted to lay the girl backside to the deck and fill her womanly softness with the hot stamp of his flesh.

Shalyn's face changed with her shock. "Why you are looking at me like that again!"

"Like what, Shalyn?"

"Like ... like ... you know like what." She wrenched free of his arms, forcing all the great will of her strength into steadying her wobbly knees. "Keep in mind, Seanessy: I bargained for passage, not, methinks, to audition for a sporting role as your concubine."

With that she turned away and headed to the ladder. A number of interested ears overheard the remark. Hearty laughter erupted all around, more as the words were repeated. Everyone was surprised the captain let her go. Not the least of which was Seanessy. Laughter was not the release he wanted, but then the girl had put her foot down.

Lord, she had pluck.

"Sean," Edward said, "seems you're not the only man interested in the lass. Recently a Frenchman was waving her picture down at the docks, offering a fifty-pound reward."

He had Seanessy's full attention. "What?"

Edward gave Seanessy the details of the unpleasant exchange with the Frenchman. "So what do you make of that?"

"He claimed she was insane?"

"Aye. Those were his words." Edward studied Sean's thoughtful expression and added, "Think of it, Sean: here we are chasing a Frenchman, one giving the world considerable grief, when we learn of a Frenchman waving a young woman's picture around London offering a fifty-pound reward. I would lay even odds on the proposition that these are one and the same."

"Nonsense," Sean said, dismissing this. "All Frenchmen dish up trouble, if only by forcing the rest of us to endure their malodorous stink. Besides," he added, grinning at the absurdity of it, "the man is married, you know, and probably as queer as an honest lawyer. So what could our dear duke possibly want with Shalyn?"

Tucker leaned over the spanker ledge as he attempted to secure the knot when a sudden gust of wind swept across the deck and ripped the rope from his hands. The spanker swung in a wild arc across the deck. Sean and Edward ducked just in time. Seanessy stood back up and shouted a mean epithet to Tucker.

Edward shook his head, still uncertain. "I do hope the fates weren't trying to answer the question."

"Far too preposterous, dear Edward." Then an irritated frown appeared. "Though this I know and know for sure—that girl is trouble. The moment I saw her, I knew. Here's a pretty package of trouble, I said. I was so right."

"And it's not over yet, Sean . . ."

Chapter 10

"**O**h, please ... No! No! Please—"
Upon hearing Shalyn's cry, Seanessy set his book down and rose, moving quickly to the door. He opened it and stood there, hands on hips as his gaze swept the surrounding darkness.

A high shriek sounded. "Mercy!"

Seanessy stepped quickly forward, yet stopped as his gaze found her. Beneath the light of a lamp, Shalyn stood near the carpenter's room playing tug-of-war with Oliver. In the instant he realized what had caused the scene: Shalyn had stepped out to get a cup of water. Oliver—one hundred and fifty pounds of dog—had grabbed the rope connecting the water cup with the barrel. Shalyn had valiantly tried to snatch it back.

She was no match for the dog.

Oliver loved his fun. Encouraged by the girl's shriek, he shook again, jerking it free from her hands and barking as she fell backside to the ground.

Seanessy's laughter sounded softly, but it might have been the crash of thunder for all its effect. She leaped back to her feet, startled eyes lifting to his tall form nearby. She felt a familiar queer leap of her heart, followed by the sudden need for more air in her lungs.

Oh, mercy. Mercy. Mercy.

"Shalyn." He said her name and stopped just ten feet from her.

The light shone above her head, haloing her in a circle of gold. She wore only a shirt, one of his, he realized distantly, for his mind registered the barest hint of her lovely form beneath the shirt. Registered it physically and made him forget what he was saying, even that he was saying something.

Oliver barked, excited. Seanessy played the best tug-of-war games! The dog dropped the rope, wagging his tail.

Seanessy stepped forward. Shalyn stepped back. She could see his amusement at finding her so. She smoothed a hand along her mass of gold hair—ridiculously, as if it might help.

Anxiously her gaze darted over the empty deck. They were alone. The idea made her nervous, so nervous. The entire voyage she had carefully avoided being alone with him. For even in a crowd of men, she found herself so acutely aware of him, his every word, movement, and gesture, she sometimes wondered if she was losing her mind. He was all she could think about, Seanessy this and Seanessy that, and even when he wasn't nearby, she thought of him with agonizing persistence. As if the very orbit of the sun depended on him.

"I was . . . was just getting a drink." The last word sounded in a weak whisper as she saw the way he stared at her. A way that made her remember in vivid detail his kiss the day they had said goodbye.

Seanessy tried desperately to remember every blessed reason he had for keeping his greedy hands from the girl. He tried to recall Butcher's stern lecture delivered as if Sean were a lowly mate with no rating and a dubious employment future. That very first night after what the crew laughingly referred to

as the ballsiest besting of the cap'n ever known, he
had come out on deck to find Shalyn in a semicircle
of his men, men including Ham, Edward, Butcher,
and a host of others. They were doing act one of *The
Merchant of Venice*. And so it began, this courting of
the girl by his crew. Dozens of the most hardened
seamen on earth fought nightly battles for the prize
of her laughter.

He hadn't understood how much it meant to him
until he saw it. She felt safe, for the first time since
the suspicious day she landed on his doorstep; she
felt safe surrounded by miles of sea and all of his
men. This precious happiness seemed to increase
each day, and the more it increased, the more he
knew he could not, would not snatch it from her.
"Now, Sean." Butcher had pointed his finger at him.
"This be exactly what that good doctor meant. She
gets better each day, and darn if she's not remembering more and more each day. One of these days she's
going to wake up and remember everything. Now
the last thing she needs is to find herself in that
bed—"

"Butcher! Let us save these less than scintillating
morality lectures for the day you don a vicar's cloth
and address a congregation of dry-rot spinsters, their
beardless husbands, and their mealy-mouthed brats.
If you think I care to hear of probity and virtue from
my friends—" He had stopped, realizing what he
was saying to one of his dearest friends. "I'm sorry.
Of course you are right. Find out what slop Mister
Slops dreamed up in his nightmares last night, will
you?"

Butcher had called it correctly. For Shalyn did indeed seem to blossom. After ten days of smooth
wondrous sailing, the *Wind Muse* had rounded the
cape. Then the weather had changed; the ship passed
through the violence and storms of the most danger-

ous waters on earth. The exhilaration and thrill of the constant battle against nature had taken many forms, everything from trying to keep feet planted on deck to hoisting a wind-torn sail to its masts as sheets of rain fell from a black sky. As his crew had discovered, Shalyn was as fine a sailor as any of them.

Presently he tried to recall his vow to cherish her well-being and just keep her safe. Yet the girl standing so near him in naught but a thin cotton shirt and long hair was irresistible. Far too irresistible. "Shalyn," he said, staring at the tempting press of her breasts beneath the shirt as she backed into the rail of the ship.

The hard wood offered some small support to her shaky knees and she grasped the rail with her hands, wondering wildly why her feet would not obey the edict to run. She stared at his amused gaze with the helpless fascination of a newborn bird caught in the mesmerizing stare of an interested snake, and indeed they had played a dangerous game of hunter and hunted all week, with his crew coming in firmly and thankfully on her side. If it weren't for the watchful and kind men of his crew, she might have been "long gored by the randy cap'n," as Talman gamely put it.

They were alone now . . .

"You know it has been many, many years since I last remember being titillated by a woman's dress. Or lack of such." He leaned against the ship's rail, separated from her by less than an arm's length. The intimate brush of his gaze felt like the warmest caress. She swallowed, feeling the rising rhythm of her heart and pulse—an exacting measure of his proximity and perhaps more accurately, his attention. For she had his full attention. He wore only breeches. A warm night breeze swept his long hair from the width of his shoulders.

Why, oh why was she so afraid?

"Nor have I ever wanted to kiss a bedraggled woman in the darkness of a night at sea on my ship."

"Bedraggled?" she questioned weakly as if it might be the important point.

"Shalyn, look at yourself," he said, one long arm braced against the rail. "Your hair." His free hand went to the hair falling in chaotic disarray down her back past her waist. She felt the intimate brush of his hand over the shirt and she closed her eyes a moment and forgot to breathe. "You're certainly not dressed to meet the king now, are you?"

She searched the handsome face to see his humor. "Well . . . You see, I . . . I was sleeping. I didn't think anyone would be about and—"

Why was she trying to explain?

"Shalyn." He chuckled. "I am not complaining. Why would I? Especially when this shirt allows me to see right through to the treasure beneath, a vision I've imagined maybe a thousand times or more in my dreams."

Slowly she crossed her arms over herself. "Seanessy . . ."

She said his name as a plea. For help. To let her go. The last thing he felt was mercy, and he told her so with the brazenness of his stare. She tried to meet his gaze but her eyes faltered, her lashes lowered. He reached a hand to her arms and gently brought them to her sides. Softly, but with a firmness she could not escape, one hand slipped over the small of her waist and around her back, drawing her closer, as his other hand, light as a feather, traced the contours of her slender form beneath the shirt. A rush of feathery shivers made her grasp. Her hands reached uncertainly to his arms.

"May I, Shalyn? Kiss you?"

He did not wait for a reply. He leaned over and gently touched his lips to hers. Once . . . then again.

"Say yes, Shalyn . . ." The whispered words and his warm firm lips hovering just over hers with a lover's tease fueled the pace of her heart and blood before he lightly molded his mouth to hers. The kiss, like the question, was a warm invitation to answer the dream too long denied. Her answer came in the soft pliancy of her mouth, a slight parting. His splayed fingers on her face tilted her head back so he could get a better hold on her mouth.

The warm breeze could not touch the wild ravishment of his kiss as he aligned her body against his, needing to feel, to touch all of her. He broke the kiss but for a moment. "Shalyn, put your arms around my neck. Better," he said as he lightly kissed her mouth before gently forcing her lips open and kissing her again.

A kiss without end. She didn't know she clung to his neck as if he were her lifeline, she didn't know anything except the pounding pleasure of his kiss. They might have been thrown off the deck and into the dark sea, and still she would have been clinging to him as she floated on a sea of bright colors . . .

His hands fitted around her bottom where he lifted her up onto the rail. The rail, she sat on the rail, one push separating her from a fall into the sea, and yet all she knew was the hard pressure of his male hips between her open and parted legs.

A hot gush of warmth rushed from the spot. She clung even tighter to his neck. His whole body tensed with a struggle for control as he forced her head back and moved deeper into the moist softness of her mouth. A shocking series of tremors exploded; a small cry issued from deep inside her, dying in their joined mouths.

He broke the kiss. "Oh yes and yes," he said as his lips grazed the velvety softness of her arched brows and closed lids before he gently caught her lower lip in his mouth. He watched her small surprised gasps of pleasure as his hands slide sensuously over the shirt, letting the heat of his fingertips slowly penetrate her skin like a tonic. The shirt teased him unmercifully and he reached for the buttons. "We don't need this now, do we?"

He parted the shirt from her breasts. "Oh Lord, Shalyn, you are beautiful ..." She felt the intimate brush of the warm night air before the warmth of his palms over her breasts. She gasped with a tingling pleasure and said his name in another plea.

He answered with a kiss. From the sea of shimmering colors an image formed to warn her, an image so shocking it made her pull sharply away, and with a gasp she stifled a scream. It sounded in a frightened whisper, a cry for help.

"Shalyn?"

"No, no, I can't—" She shook her head, looking as mad and tormented by it as she felt. Color drained from her face, her heart pounded alarmingly, she couldn't catch her breath as her hands reached in desperation to the sides of her head. She closed her eyes tight to shut out the image of waves washing over Seanessy's head. Just his head—

The image exploded in a burst of blinding white light ...

"Shalyn—"

He caught her in his arms and with shock and horror he stood for several long seconds staring at the limp and motionless body. His thoughts turned in frantic circles until he felt the brush of Oly's fur on his legs. And then suddenly he was racing ...

Loud snores filled the space. A dozen hammocks swung with each lift and fall of the great ship over the gentle swells. One dim lamp rocked from the ceiling. Seanessy found the right hammock.

"Wake up." Seanessy lifted his bare foot in a swift

though light kick to the sleeping man. "Wake up, old man."

Toothless woke with a start. He opened his eyes to the uncertain darkness, and when he spotted the captain holding the sleeping lass, he swung his feet to the floor. "What? What is it?"

"Shalyn fainted!"

A number of the sleeping men turned over with loud unpleasant grunts. A few came awake but only to curse. Toothless tried to rouse himself to the occasion, but he had long ago passed the age when he felt chipper upon being wakened from a dead sleep.

Dead sleep, he thought, rubbing his scratchy chin, an apt description of the state. With effort he concentrated on his captain long enough to see his worry.

"So what?" the old man said crossly. "Half the time women start drawin' enough air to float when they see you; I'm not surprised one of 'em went and fainted."

"Toothless . . ."

His name sounded in a warning. Toothless tried to put his mind to the lass. "Is she still breathin'?"

"Aye, but—"

"Well, she's doin' a sight better than I am!" He coughed as if to illustrate the comment. "What was she doing before she passed out?"

The question surprised Seanessy. "We were enjoying each other's company—"

"Oh, were we now?" Toothless interrupted, amused and irritated by this, dismissing Seanessy with a wave of his hand. "And the lass forfeits yer game by passin' out before yer ruddy jack took her sweet ace? And ye went and woke me up for that?"

"Just tell me if she's going to be all right, will you? Or are you so worthless that I'll be better served tossing you seaside and donating your pension to the Retired Maritime Officers' Foundation?"

Toothless stood up. He examined her face. He checked her pulse. He politely buttoned the top buttons of her shirt. He smiled, a smile of pure farce; his boldness owed itself less to his long friendship with Seanessy than to the fact that Sean's hands were occupied. "Would ye be wanting me to wake her so ye can—"

Seanessy rolled his eyes with a disparaging shake of his head. "I only wanted to ascertain if she was well or ill, if I should be concerned. She seems so maddeningly delicate at times, and after all the good Doctor Rush said about not letting her become excited—"

"Captain," he interrupted yet again, "I'm not the best man to instruct ye on the handlin' of a untried lass, but I'd wager she might survive long enough if ye just let her come up for air once in a while . . ."

The men listening chuckled.

After a few well-aimed barbs Seanessy swept the girl from the ribald comments that followed. He quickly brought her to his bed in the unlikely event that she woke and needed help. He carefully lifted the covers over her sleeping form. With some greater effort he squarely faced the fact that he wasn't going to have her. At least not tonight . . .

The *Wind Muse* had come up the east coast of the Dark Continent rather than sail straight across to where the duke's island sat in the mouth of the Straits of Malacca. Dawn spread in lovely colors of pink and gold, shining through low clouds. Gentle swells lifted the ship—"like being rocked in a woman's arms," Cary, one of the gunners, said as he sipped a hot cup of morning tea at the rail with Butcher.

In the captain's quarters, Seanessy was just waking from a familiar dream. In this dream Shalyn danced before him, naked, gracefully, erotically, and just as his desire reached a feverish pitch and he could take no more, he leaped up and reached out to take her into his arms. Only to watch her dance away into darkness. He felt a surge of desire as, desperate to snatch her back, he gave chase into this dark tunnel.

He wanted that girl!

Only to find himself surrounded by laughing human skulls drawn from her nightmares. Furious and enraged, he knocked first one away, then another and another. As fast as they appeared in the darkness he smashed them with all the force of his fist. The skulls rolled into the black night still laughing as Negro voices echoed eerily: "*We see her, we see her . . .*"

"*Where?*"

"*Chasin' the virgin star . . .*"

The same dream every blessed morning. Seanessy sighed, sitting upright in the hammock and planting his feet on the floor. Shalyn still slept in his bed. He stepped to the side and looked down at her sleeping face.

The morning light accented her loveliness more than usual, somehow . . .

A line from Shakespeare's *Romeo and Juliet* sounded with bitter humor in his mind: "Dreams, which are the children of an idle brain, begot of nothing but vain fantasy." How bloody true.

Except for the part when Shalyn disappeared into darkness. He thought again of Edward's recounting of the Frenchman waving her picture and promising a fifty-pound reward. Now the question was: had Kyler placed her picture in the London papers and already killed this merry Frenchman, whoever he was? Or had Kyler dismissed the whole intrigue once he discovered Shalyn missing? He wouldn't know until a message made its way to Malacca . . .

Shalyn, do you know what you do to me?

No. She hadn't a clue. The idea of her innocence, and the persistent thought of what he'd wanted to do to it, turned him away. He was thinking of a cold ocean swim as he shaved.

The third time he returned to check on her, he opened the door and saw that she was up. She sat on the edge of the bed, with her face in her hands. He quietly shut the door and approached saying her name. "Shalyn . . ."

She looked up, her amber eyes much changed.

For she remembered.

She flew into his embrace. He hesitated the briefest moment before his arms came around her slender figure to hold her there, her arms wrapping around his neck, the sweet assault on his senses far more potent than his ocean dip.

Yet she was talking. Fast. What was she saying?

"Seanessy, Seanessy, I was just lying in your bed half-asleep and suddenly I remembered the books, the beautiful books filled with enchanting watercolors. Picture after picture of fairies and forests and quaint little elf cottages, and she painted them. My Aunt Mary. I remember her!"

He had to smile as he pulled back just a bit to look at her face; he could not help it. The clear melodic English accent became pronounced whenever she became excited. Like now. Butcher was right. Every day she seemed to remember something more. "Your . . . Aunt Mary?"

"Yes." She nodded, rushing on to explain. "I remember she was plump and old and ever so much fun. I remember sitting on her lap for hours as she showed me these beautiful picture books she had made. She was so very clever! And sometimes I remember she let me play with her charm bracelet. She had a charm bracelet as thick as a ballast rope. 'Twas a lovely gold piece with charms she had taken from every place she traveled to, and I would hold up each charm to the light and she would tell me a story about it."

The handsome features changed with his own excitement upon this self-discovery. This was close. "Aye, your Aunt Mary—bless her soul. What else?"

"What else? Well, I don't know . . ."

"Your mother, Shalyn? Your mother must be in this picture?"

Her mother, her mother . . .

With his hands on her arms, Shalyn stood perfectly still, remembering this happy scene with her Aunt Mary. Then she heard the curious sound of a woman's laughter: "Mary dear, you spoil my darling so! All I hear for weeks after you visit is 'Mama, when will Aunt Mary visit us again . . .' "

The laughter echoed dizzily through her mind, resonating in some deepest part of her soul. She stiffened dramatically. "Seanessy, Seanessy . . ." Emotions shimmered in her eyes. Her heart pounded as memories rushed at her in a fast-moving stream of images, and in these memories she saw her mother. Like a beacon in the darkness of her mind, she saw her mother. She was so beautiful. With a crown of thick gold curls and smiling brown eyes, her mother was laughing as she moved toward her, the pretty teal silk gown swirling out behind.

Her beautiful mother, she remembered.

The whisper of Seanessy's voice drew Shalyn's eyes up. "You are crying . . ."

"I remember, Seanessy. I remember how beautiful she was. My mother. I remember how very much I loved her."

Seanessy pulled her into his arms as she cried so softly, remembering. He swept her off her feet and carried her two paces to the bed. She was holding her head, her eyes wide, frightened, feverish with excitement.

"I can see our house. I remember the Tudor house we lived in in England. I remember it. 'Twas in the countryside, outside of London. I remember our maids Elsie and Barbs and my strict nanny, Mrs. Rhea. I can see the nursery so clearly. It had a huge maple tree growing outside the window. There were pretty lace curtains around it. I remember staring at the sunlight through the leaves. And ivy grew so thick along the wall that I used it as a ladder to escape Mrs. Rhea. I can see my toys and dolls, and the white lace and pink comforter on my bed. There were pictures of ships on the walls . . ."

Pictures of ships on the wall . . .

Seanessy listened to the soft melodic voice and felt a relief so powerful and great he almost laughed out loud for all his joy. First that she was remembering and then that she was remembering a scene so idyllic as to have been taken from a religious manual on the proper upbringing of British children. Then his mind caught up with the last. He looked down at her, his hand stroking her hair, and gently he asked, "Your father, Shalyn. Do you remember your father?"

"Aye and . . . nay."

She closed her eyes, remembering a morning of blindingly bright sunlight. She sat primly in a carriage with her mother, excitement making her giddy. She kept clapping her small gloved hands. Her father was coming home! The carriage stopped at the docks. There was a huge ship there. Uniformed men rushed about everywhere she looked. Her mother lifted her up to watch the officers come down the plank, their arms waving frantically as her mother called, "Oh, Charles! Charles!"

"His name was Charles and . . . he was an officer."

"On a ship?"

"Aye, a huge ship. A navy ship. I don't remember anything else . . ."

Trying not to scare her, desperate not to lose this fragile first step: "Shalyn, his surname? Your surname?"

"I don't remember, I—" She stopped suddenly and said, "My mother's name was Hanna."

"Hanna?" Seanessy questioned. Why did that sound familiar? He tried to recall any Hannas he had known over the years, but drew a blank. "What about you? Do you remember your own name?"

Concentration marked her features. Oddly enough, it was strict Mrs. Rhea's shrill voice that supplied the answer: "Isabel," Shalyn said. "Isabel after my mother's mother, my grandmother whom I never knew."

Isabel? Seanessy looked away, testing the name in his mind. Only to realize it would never do, that the name mattered no more. "What happened, Shalyn? Do you remember anything else? Where are your parents?"

Tears washed her eyes; they sparkled like rare and precious gems, darting back and forth in search of the answer. Dozens of childhood memories rushed at her with dizzying speed, forming a swift-moving stream until—

It came at her suddenly.

She remembered being on a ship with her mother. They were so happy. They were going to Malacca, the Settlement Straits, to be with her father—no doubt as part of the British effort to settle the land. Memories of the voyage poured forth: the long lazy days, being told over and over not to pester the crew when they worked; she remembered they had celebrated her sixth birthday on May twelfth with a piece of sweetened brown bread with white candles stuck in it, all her mother could muster on board a ship in the middle of the sea, and how they had laughed at the absurdity of it. She remembered settling down with her picture books and games, playing cards and crocheting with her mother. She remembered curling up against her mother in bed, listening to sweet stories told to get her to sleep.

She remembered all of it.

She remembered finally reaching the aqua-blue bay of the port. This memory was vague. She could almost see it. She stood at the rail as the ship pulled closer and closer to the dark emerald-green of the land. She remembered the expression on her mother's face, 'twas filled with shock and disappointment.

"Mama, what's wrong? Is it not a pretty place?"

Her child's voice faded in her mind and only now as she recalled it through an adult's understanding could she see it was a British lady's reaction to a heathen exotic land made of thick jungles and crystal-clear blue waters, a place of wooden huts and muddied paths alongside the white stucco of a dozen British homes, dark-skinned Oriental people and coarse sailors, and all of it surrounded by jungle.

"I don't know what I was expecting!" her mother had cried. "I don't! I can't live here. I'll die. Didn't he know or couldn't he guess . . ."

"Shalyn, what are you remembering?"

"My mother. My father sent us to Malacca. 'Tis why I want to return so much. I remember the voyage, and I remember the ship sailing into port and my mother's shock at it all." Her voice changed, lowering to a frightened whisper. "She wanted to go back immediately. My father was not there though. There was only a house servant waiting to lead us to our new house. My mother was so upset, she didn't understand what was happening. It was as if she knew. She did know. I can tell. I see her face so clearly—"

"Know what, Shalyn?"

The amber eyes looked up and filled with an infinite pain. "She died there. She died, Seanessy ... I—oh, God, Seanessy, I remember ..."

They had to stay until her father joined them. Then he would make arrangements for their return to England. Everything would be as it was, she remembered her mother telling her happily. "Your father will just have to accept that this ... place is not a place I can live, let alone raise my daughter in. And honestly, Isabel, I don't know what he was thinking of, giving us this house some twenty miles away from the nearest neighbor, out in this wretched jungle. All his secrecy! And just look at you! If you get one more insect bite, I fear you'll explode."

"They do not bother me, Mama. I love our new house! 'Tis so beautiful here. And, why, Mrs. Rhea never let me go barefoot in England, or out without a proper hat."

"I promise you, darling, if bare feet is all it takes to make you happy, I shall let you march down the corridors of Westminster Abbey with them. Oh, how I'd trade the sight of this wretched jungle in an instant for one look at Westminster Abbey. Well, he'll understand, I know he will, and soon perhaps he can get another commission. My father will help, though we shan't tell him that."

She remembered these musings as they walked along the white sand beach. There was someone behind them. A manservant who never spoke and always followed them. Like a shadow he was, as he trailed them. She was trying not to think of him. She thought instead of the wonderful seashells they found. England did not have anything like them!

She remembered holding the perfect white conch in her hand, the best find. The ocean sang so loudly in it. She was begging her mother to let her keep it when they started up the cliff.

Shalyn rubbed her forehead, the cliff appearing so clearly in her mind. 'Twas so steep. Straight up almost. A narrow path had been carved into the side of the cliff, made by unknown people over hundreds of years. She loved going up, an adventure in itself. She went up much faster than her mother, as her mother's long skirts greatly encumbered her progress.

The perfect white shell fell out of her bucket as she tipped it, clinging to the rocks above her. She turned to see it roll down, stopping a few feet from her mother. She saw the strange Oriental man at the bottom. He raised his arms and shouted in the Oriental tongue to take care with her step as her mother turned to fetch it back.

Her mother's foot slipped.

Shalyn closed her eyes as a young girl's scream echoed dizzily through her mind. There came a burst of white light in her head, an unbearable pain as if it had been she falling down that treacherous slope, and from somewhere far away she heard Seanessy shouting her name ...

Seanessy caught the girl up in his arms.

He never left her side that day. She woke just past noon with tears in her eyes, immediately reaching for the comfort of his embrace. For the space of that day she relived the painful death over and over in her mind. For she and Seanessy both understood that it was her mother's death that somehow threw her into a dark future, a future that ended one cold night with a hard blow to her head and a beating, the only address in all of England where she might be safe clutched tightly in her hand.

If only she could remember more ...

The cannon fire exploded fifty paces from starboard, a futile warning. The *Wind Muse* closed, swinging around the slaver's stern, circling its victim like a hungry predator. Shalyn watched with wide-eyed fascination as Seanessy shouted quick loud orders from the quarterdeck above. He looked magnificent and frightening both, as his shouts made men run and all around them the sea exploded with cannon fire. First officers stood on deck, Butcher with the gunners and Ham with the sails, Edward, the quartermaster, stood at the bow, and every man in his place. There was little doubt that the thrilling drive of battle was a welcome diversion into dangerous waters.

Seanessy had a theory that they could make better speed by catching the West Indian current five hundred miles north of the cape. Just south of Madagascar's tip, Preston in the lookout caught sight of the slaver. Butcher explained that by the looks of the hull weighted down so in the water, the ship would be full of black bodies just snatched from that dark place, that it was always the crew's greatest pleasure to capture such ships, ride them back to the island, and let the poor sods free again.

"That is just after they set the ship ablaze."

"With the captain and crew on board?!"

Butcher had looked quite shocked. "Do you think Seanessy is a barbarian? For heaven's sake, he lets the blackguards go. Sometimes. Of course, sometimes, if we can spare a couple o' days, he sells them to this dark-skinned king who rules the land west of the big Congo. You are shocked, lass? Well, we get a rich bounty for our trouble, ye see," and he laughed. "Aye! A bunch of colorful feathers, a handful o' poisoned arrows, and if the King likes the looks of his new slaves, sometimes even these very pretty painted bowls stuffed full of dried lizard ..."

Chuckling merrily, Butcher had patted Shalyn's shoulder as he ordered her back into the carpenter's room for the duration of the battle. Which was absolutely the last place she would be, though she was smart enough not to tell him that. She wanted to see this battle.

After the shouts and thunder of the explosions reached an irresistible pitch, she slipped out again and joined an excited Oliver at the rail just outside her door. Smoke filled the blue sky, painting it gray, so thick it made her cough. Waving her hand across her face, she watched as the *Wind Muse* closed on its victim fast. Another stray cannonball exploded. Water splashed onto the deck, spilling over her.

Upon Seanessy's orders, the gunners fired back. The crest of the slaver's bow blew sky-high. Fire sprang from the spot. Another cannonball exploded straight into the lower mast, sending the great piece of timber falling with a thunderous crack to the deck. Smoke and shouts and confusion sounded.

The laughter of Seanessy and his men was a profane exclamation point. This was a game Seanessy loved and had long ago perfected. The trick was to disable the villainous ship just enough to draw alongside with impunity, just close enough for his well-trained gunners to aim, fire, and fell the mainmast. There were few casualties this way, and if he wanted the ship, it would still be intact.

"Hold your fire!" Seanessy shouted to the gunners as Edward trimmed the rigging that slowly moved the *Wind Muse* before their prize. "Easy. Steady now, mates. Steady as she goes—" He suddenly froze as the sound of her laughter echoed like a dream. His gaze found her at the rail, three dangerous feet from Harris at the guns, squealing as Oliver shook water from his coat over her.

Furious, Seanessy boomed across the deck louder than a cannon explosion, "Girl, get your feet off that deck and down below!"

A much smaller voice called up, "Oh, but—"

His voice thundered, "Move it! Preston, get that blasted dog below before he goes over the side as well!"

"Aye, aye!"

Lips pressed together, she disappeared into the carpenter's room, slamming the door behind her. He was so mean! Impossible, absolutely impossible. Like a king he was, or ruler of the world—

Or captain of the ship . . .

She looked up at the changed sound. What now? How strange! All the great clamor and noise had disappeared. The loudest sound came from the licks of sea at the side of the ship. Oliver whimpered as Preston made him retreat down below and shut and locked the latch before running back to his place at the gantline. In the distance came shouts from the other ship.

What had happened?

She had to look, she just had to!

She cracked open the door an inch. She saw Talman's backside as he bent over the gun hole. She slipped out to the side and almost screamed. They were less than three dozen paces from the slaver!

The sight of the slave ship up close felt mesmerizing; she couldn't move as the two ships slowly sided each other. Their crew scrambled amid the chaos and smoke to put out the flames. Sean's gunners waited with lit fuses at the cannons.

Seanessy's voice boomed, "Fire!"

Five seconds later three cannons blew fire at the doomed ship. Shalyn grabbed the rail, the explosion knocking her feet from under her and throwing her against the carpenter's room. She tried to rise but the wake of the explosion sent the great ship up and knocked her back against the wall.

"Butcher!"

"Aye, Cap'n, I see her!"

"You have the helm!"

"Aye, aye!"

A shadow fell over her. She looked up to see Seanessy himself standing above her. He was not smiling. He shouted out an order to a nearby deck-hand, cursed her life as he bent and picked her off the ground. She screamed as he tossed her over a shoulder unceremoniously, swung round, and shouted a quick series of parting orders before stopping outside his quarters and picking up a neat coil of rope.

Then he opened the door and disappeared inside.

Seanessy's curses sounded softly and viciously and seemed to center on the question of her sense or lack thereof, and how if she could not follow the clearest of orders to keep her safe he would simply tie her up. He dropped her on his bed and removed a dagger to cut the rope. He did not see the look in her eyes as she stared at the rope. He might have been cautioned by it, by the stark terror as she watched him cut it in halves, but he was intent on his task.

He grabbed her hands and began circling them.

She went numb as blood vacated her limbs and pumped a sick dread into her heart. The pink kimono and the ropes, the terrible ropes that tied her hands and left her helpless. She couldn't move. She could only shut her eyes as it happened to her. As the pink silk came off and—

Tears gathered thickly in her throat and she tried to shake her head, to stop this, to stop him. She managed only, "Seanessy . . . help me—"

One look at those eyes and he dropped the rope from his hands suddenly. "Dear God . . ." He drew her swiftly in his arms. Instantly she clung to his neck, his hand came to her hair, and he held her tight against his strength.

"I won't hurt you, Shalyn. Never, Shalyn, never ..."

She tried to shake her head, to tell him she knew this, but she could only cling to him more desperately as the emotions washed over her in waves. It was Seanessy, Seanessy, her mind kept repeating. Seanessy ...

The battle was brief. The slaver's captain and crew surrendered, only to be led at gunpoint onto the *Wind Muse* where they were quickly tied to a wood rail near the head with its foul air. The captain, a middle-aged ruddy man named Rand, wasted an hour alternately pleading, bribing, and bargaining for his worthless life with the stone-deaf members of the *Wind Muse*'s crew as they led over two hundred terrified and naked savages across a plank that had been laid between the two ships for the purpose, no easy task with iron chains around their feet. Once aboard the *Wind Muse*, the dark-skinned men were lined up and asked to sit.

Of course there was a language problem.

In frustration Cherry Joe attempted to push one of the terrified men down, managing because the Negro's knees were weaker than pond reeds with his fear. The slaves were certain their already dismal circumstances had just taken a dramatic shift for the worse—which meant they all thought they would soon be tossed over the side. They chose to face death standing and with as much dignity as any man could muster in the face of a drowning. So the man came back to his feet as soon as the hands left him.

Edward and a half-dozen other crew members had found these two hundred and twelve savages stacked four deep in the hull—literally piled on top of one another like sacks of potatoes or bales of cotton—for what would have been a two-month-long trip. On the more "humane" ships the savages were let topside for ten minutes once a day where they might be given a ration of water and a bowl of mush. And on these more humane slavers less than a quarter of the humanity would have survived. Less than a quarter. That quarter would have been enough to fill the captain's pocket with cold hard gold. Not long ago Sean and Edward had found themselves in a tavern with a crew that made their living in the slave trade and, curious, Edward had asked how they could stand the anguished cries of so many.

"Ah, hell, a bloke gets used to it is all."

He had flattened the man with a fist. "Get used to that, you whoreson." Every time the man came up, he put him down again and again, careful to hit him hard enough to cause damage but not enough to let him pass out. And he kept hitting him like that until the man was a blubbering mess. Seanessy had watched dispassionately until he realized, "Why, I'll be damned. One does grow accustomed to it."

The stark reality of the utter folly and stupidity of man's cruelty to his fellows always put Edward in the foulest of moods. Over the years Seanessy had attempted to show Edward the problem lay in his expectations, that he needed only to accept that "the dampness of the night is driven deep within the human soul . . ." Edward knew Sean was right, he was always right, but that didn't mean he had to muster the stoic cynicism necessary to save his fury.

Attempting to untie a rope and toss it over to the other ship, Edward abruptly realized the background noise about British naval law issued from this Captain Rand. "And what's more," the man was saying, "half these black sods are stolen property, escapees, you see, and from the very place they be goin' back to . . ."

"Butcher!" Edward wanted to kill, or at the very

least seriously maim the man. "Put a knife in the bastard's mouth and cut out his tongue, will you?"

With waving arms and enormous grins, Butcher was still trying to communicate with the savages. He had no idea how he looked to the poor Negro men: like a frightening leering demon marked by battle scars, sporting numerous queer knives for unimaginable purposes. Upon Edward's call he stopped his effort and looked over to see Rand's face go white. Whiter as Butcher removed one of his daggers and turned toward him. "Ah, look, he finally shut up. Just like that."

Seanessy sat against the wall of his quarters with his long legs stretched out in front of him and Shalyn held securely on his lap. She had finally stopped crying. His hand smoothed her long hair over and over again as he watched her fingers, light as a feather and infinitely more maddening, toy with a scar on his biceps. He was doing difficult mathematical equations in his mind.

For he knew it did not matter that he wanted her more than he ever had, and that it was a good deal more than he had ever wanted anything in his life, that his entire body was hot, aching, waiting to take her lips and lay her down on the bed as his senses filled with her scent, her softness, the promise of a time that waited for them. None of it mattered.

For 'twas too close to the memory she had just escaped, far too close. When he had her, it would not be associated with time with another. No matter what, he would not do that to her, he kept telling himself over and over.

The whole terrifying thing made perfect sense: the beast would have had to tie her up or suffer the consequences of the only woman in the world who could defend herself so well. He could not imagine the rest without his hands trembling with the need for violence. Though how this beast got her arms tied was a mystery, one he knew unwise to contemplate.

A knock sounded on the door, an intrusion on their solitude. "Aye, come in."

Butcher opened the door. His gaze found them quickly; he asked no questions. Relieved to see their clothes were still on, he came to the point: "Two hundred and twelve stacked four deep in the hull. A sorry sight."

Seanessy never looked up as he wondered why no one had ever warned him what a woman's eyes could do to a man. "Damage?"

"The masts are down. A four-foot crack in the bow is all. Sink or tow, Cap'n?"

"Tow. Casualties?"

"A few. Toothless is at 'em as we speak."

"And what was their heading?"

"I haven't started the interrogation yet. I thought you might want to do it yourself."

Sean nodded. "Very well." The door shut. In a moment he said, "I have to go."

Shalyn nodded. Seanessy brought her face up gently. "Smile, Shalyn mine, and by this treasure, I will know you are all right."

She graced him with a smile, and in that smile he saw something else he knew unwise to contemplate. In a determined swoop he lifted her off his lap and onto the bed. He never looked back; he could not leave if he looked back. She was glad for the moment's solitude.

She stood on shaky legs, then sat again, then stood. She felt so curiously on the edge of discovery. She could not see the face of the man who had tied her up; she tried but saw only a darkness she could not penetrate.

Yet she needed to remember. She felt close. So terribly close. She focused all her thoughts on the Oriental man. Was he the same man who tried to warn her mother before she fell? She tried to focus on his face, but it was a painful blur as she saw her mother falling.

She focused all her energy on the man dancing the Oriental dance. Turn around! Let me see you! For the love of God, help me remember ...

Seanessy walked out into the bright sunlight. Activity abounded as his crew worked to get a towline on the other ship, no easy feat. The decks were crammed with the two hundred standing savages as a dozen of his men attempted to rid them of their iron chains. Fear worked into almost all their faces as they watched this with incomprehension, obviously thinking only death could wait if the white men were taking off their chains. This despite the high comedy of Butcher trying desperately to explain they would be set free: in English, and as if he just said the word "free" long enough they would grasp the happy fact, never mind the terrifying grin planted ridiculously on Butcher's less than reassuring face.

Seanessy first shouted a series of sharp orders about the rigging, wanting the business over as fast as possible, before he called out to the men to stop working on the chains for a moment. "Just look at them. Set to quaking with fear. Get them some food and water first, then they'll know we aren't planning to toss them seaside. Now where is the ruddy bastard that is lord and master of this hell?"

Butcher promptly pointed out Rand, handing Seanessy a whip that had never once felt a nag's back but had been used many times nonetheless. Seanessy stepped before him, hands on hips. He looked a frightening enough sight, wearing only white breeches and a thick black belt, all of him sun-washed bronze muscle. He stood nearly a foot taller than Rand and he was barefoot. A number of prominent and rather dramatic scars showed as well, a warning when none was needed. More than anything he seemed to have a taxed, almost bored, air about him, the unconcealed disdain and contempt for the man and what he was about.

"So, Captain Rand, is it? Yes? Now where were you headed with this bit of humanity?"

It required three cracks of the whip before the man realized he could not trade the information for his life. It might have been longer but for the queer knives Butcher abruptly thought to sharpen. Through gasping breath Rand shouted, "China Seas!"

"Yes? Where?"

He spit out the bile rising in his throat with a gasping scream. Through gritted teeth: "A bloody island is where."

The whip cracked hard against his face. The man knocked his head against the wall, then doubled over with the hot stinging pain. Seanessy gave him but a moment to recover when he heard the man gasp, " 'Tis called Blue Caverns. Fifty knots from Sumatra at the mouth of Malacca Straits. Owned by French nobility, called Armanac."

A whispered rush came over the crowd of men. Everyone stopped what he was doing. Word quickly crossed the sea to the other ship where the men labored to rig a tow. Silence came over the entire proceeding. Rand's gaze frantically searched the men surrounding him for an understanding that eluded him.

"Sean . . ." Butcher said.

"Aye, I heard him. I just can't believe the piece of luck. If this doesn't sweeten the pie better than ripe blackberries," Seanessy said, and with a grin to toss like a lifeline to Rand: "My luck appears to be yours as well, Captain Rand. Butcher, the poor man can't wipe the line of blood from his face. Cut those ropes if you will?"

Rand almost screamed as Butcher stepped forward with one of his knives before he watched it slice neatly through the ropes binding his arms. Seanessy called to Prescott, "Fetch the good captain a cup of rum."

This was quickly produced. Rand looked suspiciously into the cup but knowing he would need it no matter what happened, he drained it whole. The smooth liquid went down his throat. He felt better immediately.

"Well, my good Captain Rand," Seanessy said, patting him on the back as if he were now a great admirer of the doomed captain, "let us discuss this business. You are confused, I see. Well, it amounts to this: I am very much interested in the particular island you just named. Perhaps you can provide me with some information. Perhaps too I can be so kind as to turn my back on your . . . well." His hand swept the poor savages. "This sorry life course of yours."

Rand felt a queasy uneasiness at this abrupt change of fortune. Sean held a cloth in his hand suddenly. It took Rand a moment to realize Sean was offering it to him to wipe the blood from his face. He slowly took it and set it to his face. He was no fool, though. "How do I know you're good for it?"

"Don't let your imagination work overtime," Seanessy told him, explaining, "the bargain is very simple, simply because it is no bargain. You see, if you do not provide me with what I want to know, I'll kill you. Well, not me specifically," he qualified quickly. "I rarely feel inclined to get my clothes bloody. Butcher here has no such aversion."

"You can count on that, Cap'n." Butcher grinned, nodding.

"Anyway," Seanessy continued, "the point is: once you are cut into pieces for fish bait, then we'll go to your first officer there, and so on. Until my questions are answered."

As he comprehended these dismal prospects, Rand's face went white again. Seanessy motioned to Prescott to fill the captain's cup. This was quickly drained as Rand realized this Nordic-looking captain would not likely blanch as he and his crew met the devil's own claws.

"So. The first question is: have you been to this island?"

Rand nodded as he removed the bloody cloth from his face and wished to God he had a pistole.

"Add to my picture of this place, will you? It is an island some twenty miles wide and ten long, mostly of jungle. Port is windward on the north end. The duke lives in a castle there, an absurd pretension, I'm told, the kind of thing common among members of the French aristocracy. There is a standing army of two thousand men. A slave population of? Yes? Have you an idea?"

He figured. "More than five hundred."

"How many more?"

He shrugged, the question drawing him in. "Maybe by a couple o' hundred."

"And what are they used for?"

"Sugar mostly. 'Bout the only thing that can sprout there when the monsoons hit."

He studied the man's eyes but for a moment. "Do not tax me, my merry captain. That's too many bodies by half at least; and you were bringing a hundred or so more. Furthermore, that man is not interested in sugar, I know that much. What is he using those slaves for? And don't lie again—it really annoys me."

Rand saw what everyone who knew Seanessy did: the man was as shrewd as the king's tax collector, as sharp as the executioner's ax. He quickly realized his chances here: none. "I do not know, if truth be told. Something about a treasure."

Butcher spun a dagger in his hand; Rand would not be warned again.

"I do not know—"

"A couple of us took a longshore boat around the leeward side of the island—"

Everyone turned to the crew member of the slaver who had blurted this out. The man stared at Seanessy, fearing nothing and feeling absolutely no loyalty to any member of the French nobility, even if paid gold.

"Aye," Seanessy said. "I am listening."

"The man had a couple of hundred black bodies digging on the shoreline."

"And why is he doing that?"

The man's grin answered Seanessy's demand. "Like the captain says, there be a rumor of treasure on that island. 'Tis said it be the whole reason the swarmy bloke bought the island. We reason he's digging it up looking. That's all we know."

"Imagine the novelty!" Seanessy almost swore. "An island with a rumor of treasure!" He was not the least interested in the idea, except as it indicated the duke's amusing little pastime. "Butcher—"

Yet the man continued, "Well, this one's got some bite to it, Captain. The treasure be four hundred years old, Chinese pirates, and worth more than the—"

"Crown jewels?" Seanessy gamely suggested. "Or is it—all the tea in China?"

The man apparently was not without a sense of humor and he grinned. "Something like that. Anyway, rumor says a man named Singleton, an Englishman, a surgeon or somethin' high-minded like that, got the map from a infidel, some monk or somethin' who had spent his whole bloody life chasin' it down through China. He gave it over to the English for next to nothin' 'cause no way a Chinaman's ever going to get on the island without help. Anyway, 'tis a flawed map after all. The island is not named. Still the English shows it to different mapmakers in the region. They say it took him some two years before he finally figures out 'tis buried on the duke's Isle of Blue Caverns. So he travels to the island, thinkin' to approach the duke about it. He was said to offer an even split to the duke but—"

"Let me guess," Seanessy interrupted, "he too died as hapless as a dead beggar's lice just before telling where the treasure could be uncovered!"

"I ain't sayin' 'tis true," the man said. "But the fact is no one heard of the Englishman or Chinaman again and the smarmy Frenchman be tearing up a lot of sand to find it."

"If it's true"—Butcher shook his head sadly—"the man is dumber than a box of rocks."

"Fascinating," Seanessy said, but not at all as if he meant it. "Now that we've all enjoyed our afternoon's amusement, let us return to you, Captain Rand. Here's the all-important question: did you see on this island a large house, for storage of something?"

Rand stiffened, but he shook his head.

"Nothing?"

Again he shook his head. "Nothing like that as far as I could see. We weren't allowed many paces past the dock."

After a moment's consideration, Seanessy decided he was telling the truth. The storehouse would not be out in the open anyway, and according to Ram, the duke was ever careful about letting visitors wander freely there.

"Very well. Edward?"

"Aye," he said, coming to Seanessy's side.

"See the blackguards into a lifeboat. Their lifeboats. Give them, oh, let's see: three days' worth of water and a compass."

"Aye, aye."

Fear instantly worked into Rand's face, and indeed all his crew members' faces changed with alarm. Alarm growing with their fear. "You can't do that! 'Tis nearly a hundred miles to shore. You might as well shoot us now and be done with it—"

"Oh, very well," Seanessy said. "Any man who doesn't want to work up a sweat rowing will be shot. Now." He turned to Prescott. "How are those poor beasts faring? I see they have been fed. Good. Now I believe you can begin taking their chains off—"

The chains were sawed. Butcher and Edward led the crew of the slaver up the plank to the other ship, where the lifeboats waited. "Captain!" Rand shouted with terror. "One o' me men seen a huge warehouse beneath a green pile at the far south end of the island."

"Leeward or windward?"

"Windward, looks like a patch of grassy garden from the seashore. We didn't dare a look inside. Ye can only reach it by ship—"

A very pleased smile spread across Seanessy's handsome face. "Why, thank you, Captain Rand. Edward, toss in some of Oly's chow for the captain to gnaw on as he rows."

Edward was not the only one to laugh but was unquestionably the loudest, a laughter that sounded much louder and carried much farther than Captain Rand's vicious curses. In the moment Seanessy decided on a plan. They would sail to the island, blow up this warehouse, and sail out before ever seeing the duke again.

The duke could just rot in hell . . .

Seanessy changed his mind about the tow; he had more than enough reason to make all speed to the duke's island. The slaver was set to blaze. Angry red flames leaped from the dark blue ocean. The two longshore boats drifted in the rising waves of the blue sea; Rand's crew forced to watch their ship burn. With any luck the *Wind Muse* could make Madagascar by dawn and free the poor wretches fate had consigned to his care.

Shalyn emerged from the captain's quarters. Her gaze swept the crowded decks and the sea of Negro faces: they were so frightened! Emotion filled her eyes and the Chinese voice said, "*Slavery exists everywhere; it is a weed that grows in every soil, but I have oft heard it told that the white slave master is the cruelest of all, for those slaves lose everything in their chains, even their desire to escape them . . .*"

Shalyn waited for another memory, more of this ancient voice that kept filling her mind. Seanessy stood alongside Butcher discussing the rotation of the crew when quite suddenly one of the Negroes pointed, calling out in his strange tongue.

Hazel eyes watched with incomprehension as a half-dozen dark-skinned men dropped to their knees and bowed, curled up into balls. "What the devil brought that on?"

One of the men raised his head, looking behind the place where Seanessy stood, while muttering the same word over and over. Seanessy turned around. He found himself staring at Shalyn. He looked back at the man, kneeling not just with obsequiousness, but also with fear.

"Shalyn . . ."

She came slowly to his side, her eyes wide, panicked as she tried to comprehend the men's fear at her presence. A tingling alarm shot up her spine.

"Ah, the poor sod's probably never seen such gold hair." Butcher shrugged as he dismissed it, though his brow remained furrowed as he headed to the galley to see the mess that would be supper. "She probably looks like a queen."

Seanessy stared at her hair. Sunlight lit the lovely braid, accenting a thousand different shades of gold that made it up. He smiled. "Queen Shalyn. Well now, I could get used to that." His tone changed completely. "Shalyn mine, I'm in a gamely mood. How about a wrestle to the ground to see who comes out of their clothes first?"

Seanessy had the pleasure of watching the amber eyes widen with shock and outrage. In the instant she forgot the tenderness of hours past. She forgot the queer dark-skinned men still kneeling at her side. She forgot everything except the wicked delight staring at her in hazel eyes. "I might come out of my clothes, Seanessy, but I promise I'd be holding your dismembered head in my arms!"

She looked pleased with herself; as if she had said something arch and ingenious.

"Courting our wit again, Shalyn?" Seanessy asked before laughing meanly. "Shalyn mine, haven't I warned you about these threats—that they only serve to make me want to prick the pretense with a piece of my flesh?"

She colored sharply.

"Surprise is a far superior weapon to strength . . ."

The Chinese voice sounded in her mind and before she could think better of it, her leg lifted with a swift hard kick to his midsection, knocking the wind from his chest and doubling him over. He looked up grinning, his eyes lit with excitement when—

When he saw her changed expression.

"Ti Yao," she whispered. "Ti Yao . . ."

Ti Yao. Ti Yao was the Oriental man on the beach

who waved to her mother, warning her of the slippery step that brought her death. "Ti Yao . . ."

Shalyn dropped to the hard wood deck, covered her face in her hands as at last memories formed a fast-moving kaleidoscope of the missing years of her life. "Ti Yao . . ."

Seanessy's shadow came over her bent form, kneeling as in supplication, and he knelt too, instantly subdued. "Shalyn, you remember more?"

She didn't answer, for a long moment she didn't answer, and only because instinctively she froze to protect the rush of memories as precious as life; her mind shut out the present only so she could better grab on to the past. She was hardly aware of Seanessy lifting her up in his arms and moving to his quarters.

The light changed, darkening, and she only realized it as he gently set her on the bed. A loving hand came over her forehead where he brushed back her hair. To see her remarkable eyes, feverish, filled with sudden knowledge too long denied.

"Ti Yao. He was Zinja. I remember, Seanessy. I remember . . ." Zinja was the ancient art taught to a few select men in the Orient, and Ti Yao was among them. "My father hired Ti Yao to protect us, my mother and I, and he did, Seanessy, he did. All my life . . . Because, because, you see, his promise was a sacred vow unto death he had given to my father. And because my father never did return after my mother died . . ."

She remembered that the shock and grief of her mother's death had begun to subside and was replaced by fear. A fear ignored by the strange quiet man. She remembered the days of waiting: Ti Yao carefully preparing her meals, bathing with her in the warm ocean, dressing her hair and washing her clothes, but also making her run on the hot sand with him, hang from tree limbs, stand on her head, and slowly dance the magic of t'ai chi as his intelligent dark eyes watched her follow his movements with more grace and agility than any boy he had ever taught.

"Mercy, Seanessy, I remember now . . ."

"The man . . . this Ti Yao, he is the one who taught you the Oriental dance?"

"For many years we lived in a small house along the riverbanks of the Tampin many miles north of Malacca, at the water's edge, and yet surrounded by the jungle. For two years I knew only Ti Yao and his concubine, Gschu. Gschu, dear Gschu.

"They cared for me. Like a daughter or a student. Ti Yao would not forsake me even though my father never did come back. My father left me, Seanessy. I never saw him again after my mother died."

Seanessy had knelt down to stare at her with kindness and compassion, waiting and praying she would remember everything.

"Ti Yao taught me the t'ai chi because . . ." Her voice drifted off as she remembered. "Ti Yao once said, 'You have a boy's spirit and discipline in a female body.'" She remembered pressing him for any information she could get, but he said he had no idea when her father would return, much less what fate would do with her life. "Aye, my father had paid him to protect me . . ."

"From what, Shalyn?"

She shook her head. "I don't know! I don't think I ever knew. Ti Yao had been paid to protect me, that was all I knew." It had occurred to Ti Yao that his instruction in the Oriental art fulfilled this obligation as well; her facility for learning only reinforced the idea that the fates meant her to have the abilities no other woman had. "Someday, Ti Yao always promised, my father would return."

She rubbed her forehead, memories washing over her.

"Yet Ti Yao, what if he is dead?"

"Then his soul has ascended for the reincarnation."

"I mean what of me?"

"You are not dead, little one."

"What shall become of me?"

"Whatever the fates decide."

So Ti Yao's remarkably simple mind reduced every complexity of her unusual orphan's fate. All she knew was that her mother had died and her father, an English naval officer, had left his young, refined, and very English daughter in the care and stewardship of a man he knew only as the best hired assassin money could buy, a move that spoke well of how desperate he must have been.

But why? Why?

"I remember waiting for my father's return. I was so young, eight or nine years old then. England had begun to fade into the far recesses of my mind, and all the fondness I felt toward my mother and Aunt Mary, the beauty of the English countryside and our old Tudor house became more and more like a dream or a fairy tale. I tried to keep them in my mind. I had a little black enamel box where I kept my treasures: one of Aunt Mary's books"—she looked up at him—"a book of Shakespeare's sonnets, the shell that made my mother fall, my mother's wedding ring, and a lock of her hair. I remember looking into that box and trying to remember my life in England, trying to remember my mother too but finding it all seemed like a fairy tale . . ."

She felt her heart and pulse signaling alert. Small beads of perspiration lined her lip and she bit it, a hand rubbing her forehead. More memories surfaced, like a curtain opening in her mind and light pouring in to illuminate the darkness. It was a mercy . . .

Gschu, oh, Lord, she remembered Gschu ...

"Gschu was Ti Yao's concubine. We lived in a small remote fishing village at the river's mouth. I can see it so clearly now ..."

Seanessy guided her to the soft cushion of pillows at the table where he held her on his lap. She was hardly aware of the shifting, of his strength and comfort surrounding her, for she was remembering. The village consisted of tiny one-room huts, neatly lined along the wooden levee that kept them safe during the rains and flooding. A precious junk docked in front of each wooden hut. Clothes were hung and dried on lines stretching between them. She remembered their small house situated in the middle of the village, with its red shutters and open door, and the enticing scent of Gschu's fresh shrimp and rice floating out like a lure on a fishing line.

"Ti Yao left me with Gschu for long periods of time; I don't know why. He would suddenly have to leave and I'd wake up in the morning and he would be gone. Then it was just Gschu and I. Oh, she was such a tiny woman and older than Ti Yao by at least ten years, but she was as strong as an ox. Oh, Seanessy." She buried her face against him in sudden pained horror. "How could I have forgotten Ti Yao and Gschu? I loved them, I loved them ..."

She looked at his face, tears filling her eyes as she raised her own hand. "Gschu was so small, no higher than my breast, and yet fate had given her these hands. Oh, Lord, they were so large, larger than a man's, and so strong. 'These hands are my fate,' she would say, for she would use them to heal people. We always had a line of people outside our door, waiting for her consultation. Her father was a famous physician in Canton, but she had been abandoned by her family, her husband, her class. She could not have children, you see. Ti Yao always said her hands were compensation for this sorrow, that he loved her hands more than he would ten children . . .

"It was a peaceful life. I would wake before dawn and practice t'ai chi with Ti Yao when he was there and alone when he was gone. Then after Gschu had seen all her patients, she'd give me lessons in Cantonese and Buddhism. I remember staring up the river waiting for Ti Yao's return. Until twilight, and Gschu would call me inside . . ."

She remembered the details of that part of her life. She could recall every face and name and character of each person in the village, she remembered Gschu's kimono's—the special red silk one—and her strong, large hands as they worked, their small wood dishes, the women washing and the children swimming, the rice farmers two leagues down the river, she remembered the excitement when the traveling holy men came and the New Year's Eve celebrations. She remembered the endless months of the monsoons.

Shalyn closed her eyes as she remembered staring at the steady sheet of rain falling from the sky. Endlessly falling. Rivers of mud flowing into the ocean and coloring the aqua-blue waters; she remembered the heaviness in her heart after the months and months without sunshine, until her spirits felt as if they too were drowning beneath the rain. Then one day she would wake to the strange and beautiful sound of silence and a sky made of rainbows. Ti Yao's normally dispassionate face would wear a smile of gratitude and Gschu would sing for weeks afterward. "Oh, I remember the monsoons."

"Aye. The monsoons," Seanessy agreed. "Like a bad preacher, they are an endless torment. The only thing that thrives during those rains are the insects. I always try to sail out before they start."

Seanessy had never stayed in Malacca during the

monsoons; he couldn't. He felt as if the sky was falling in on him, as if he didn't have enough space to breathe. Thankfully Malacca not only provided a convenient port for outfitting along the China trade route, but it was one of the few ports along the sheltered side of the Bay of Bengal. Unlike the eastern side of Malay, Malacca allowed a ship to sail out the Straits to the Indian Ocean during the monsoon season and still keep her rigging.

"Shalyn, what happened then? What happened to these people you loved? To Ti Yao and Gschu?"

"Gschu died of malaria," she remembered. "Nay . . . not malaria," she remembered. "Not really. She died of a broken heart. Because the last time Ti Yao left he never did return. We waited nearly half a year and then the monsoons started and Gschu fell to malaria. I cared for her until the end, always certain she would get well if only Ti Yao returned. Yet he never did. The monsoons stopped. Gschu was offered to heaven on the funeral pyre. I remember thinking I would go to the British Admiralty at Penang and appeal for passage back to England. I remember thinking they might even help me find my relations there, my Aunt Mary. I said goodbye to all the villagers and . . ."

She shook her head, her eyes filling with an unbearable agony as she tried to see through the darkness. Her uncertain memory stopped again as quickly as it started. It stopped with a young sixteen-year-old girl staring up a slow-moving river, searching one last time for Ti Yao . . .

She only saw the darkness, darkness like a waiting monster. A monster she felt drawing closer and closer. "I don't remember anything more!"

Chapter 11

Shalyn sat naked to the waist on her hammock, a small wood-framed mirror held up in one hand—she had won the glass from Edward in a card game last night. She did not notice the beauty staring back in the glass: the haloed lift of gold hair, her high cheekbones, the small pert nose and wide full mouth, or even the velvety thin brows arching with bewilderment over dark and mysterious eyes, eyes filled with feverish intensity as she lowered the glass past her slender neck and shoulders to the round fullness of her breasts.

She stared at the mark.

A diamond shape in pink. A blue point inside the diamond. An odd face—like a child's drawing. She traced a finger over the strange lines, her finger moving slowly, hesitantly, as if afraid to touch what had been done to her. She stared until the glass blurred in her mind and she saw his face: the shrewd and wise almond eyes were set in a rounded face above his flat nose and thin lips. She remembered a thin scar that traveled from the corner of his lip to his round chin. Ti Yao's was not a handsome face but strong and compelling, a face she had worshipped.

Ti Yao, Gschu . . .

She remembered everything now except what had

happened. Ti Yao had died, she knew, because he had never returned. What happened to her in the five years between sixteen and twenty-one? How did she get from the fishing village to Seanessy's doorstep in London?

"Now, lass, it will be coming back. Mind my words you remember more each day . . ."

She prayed Butcher was right.

She went to the small trunk pushed against a toolbox, where she kept her things, and opened the lid. She carefully set Edward's looking glass back inside. Her stare lingered on the ruby star.

Seanessy had showed the gem to Knolls, the ship's carpenter. Knolls's father owned a jewelry shop in London. The shop sat on Port Street and offered a young restless boy a continuous view of the proud oceangoing vessels leaving London's port, which explain why he had abandoned his jeweler's apprenticeship as a young man. Yet Knolls had learned enough about gems to offer an "educated" opinion.

"That's what's called a virgin gem." Knolls had whistled.

"A what?" Seanessy asked.

"Look at it. The untouched edges. This gem's not seen the sharp edge of a knife."

"Oh?"

"Untouched. Some lucky sod pulled this glorious bit o' rock from the cold hard earth and pinned it to a gold star."

Seanessy looked at her with a grin. "A virgin star."

"Aye." Knolls laughed, "Probably worth a hundred times as much if ye prick her proper." The bright blue eyes turned to her. "The only good be in the virgin's ruination."

The men had laughed uproariously, and she, feeling inexplicably ridiculed, snatched it back from the man and turned away. Presently she reached a hand to the jagged rough edges of the sparkling ruby. A shiver rushed magically up her spine. She withdrew her hand and slammed the lid shut.

Virgin star indeed!

Lord, it was so hot in here . . .

She thought of climbing the ratline. How she loved to be so high above the world, suspended in flight, viewing the endless blue water from every direction. 'Twas a feeling of pure sensation, a chance to escape the troubling turn of her thoughts, if only for a moment or two.

Seanessy probably would never know anyway . . .

The heat grew and grew as the sun crossed its zenith and began its grand descent, shining in a bright blaze of white light overhead. Standing at the rail and looking out to sea, Butcher swore every day seemed hotter than the last as they sailed east from Madagascar, past Ceylon, and into the Bay of Bengal. The island was no more than two days' sailing now.

He wiped the wet cloth across his forehead. The wind too had shifted, changed, blowing whisper-soft when it blew at all. Presently the barest hint of a breeze filled the sails. No one could work belowdeck before sunset—it was like a Roman sweat box. A group of men lowered buckets into the water, lifting them back to splash across the deck as the wood planks absorbed and threw back the heat. Off-duty men sat listlessly in what little shade they could find, whittling sticks, mending sails, or chalking.

Seanessy finally finished his task and stepped outside, joining Butcher at the rail. Oly lay against the side at Butcher's feet in the shade as Butcher too lowered a bucket into the water but pulled it up and dumped it on the grateful dog's coat.

Seanessy stared at the shimmering band of sunlight over the water. The light felt like a sharp assault on his vision, and he squinted with discomfort. "Another hour, maybe less, and I'll drop sails." Twice a day they dropped anchor so everyone able to swim could dive into the cool water.

"Aye, not much of a wind but it's better than nothing." Butcher nodded. "Ham still believes we will reach the bit o' rock by tomorrow, or the next night at the latest. Even with this fair virgin's breeze."

The last four days this baneful wind had blown sporadically, in fits and starts, like a capricious tease before suddenly abandoning them altogether for hours on end. "A fair virgin's breeze," the men called it, chuckling when Shalyn never did get it.

"I can't take much more of it," Seanessy said, squinting still at the brightness of the sunlight as if he had drunk too much the night before. He took the next full bucket from Butcher and dumped it over his own head. The cool moisture slid over his hot skin. He repeated the measure until he was soaked.

Butcher leveled a steady gaze on him. "Some things need time." He thought of Kenzie on their wedding night and added softly, "The best things need time."

Seanessy was in a different frame of mind. "Like I said—I can't take much more of this." The sound of a loose sail made Sean swing around, his gaze lifting as he turned. He shouted an order but stopped, his gaze focusing on the arresting sight. "I'm going to kill her!" The vow was uttered in a tight-lipped whisper as he turned back around and grabbed hold of the rail, as if needing support. "I will skin her alive!"

Butcher guessed the problem and took a casual glance skyward to confirm it: the lass hung three sheets to the wind on the ratline. "Uh, oh. Let's walk slowly back to your quarters like we never saw her up there." The last thing they wanted to see was the lass's jolt from Sean's wrath—that was until the moment her feet hit the deck. "Nice and slow now . . ."

From above, Shalyn watched the two men disappear into the captain's quarters. She released her breath all at once. That was close! She would not press her luck again! Agilely, keeping one hand to her wide-brimmed straw sun hat, she began making her way down the ratline.

Silently Seanessy came up to the bottom of the mast. Shalyn remained unaware of the extreme danger until the moment her feet landed on the deck. She turned around. She screamed. A hot wave of panic made her take a step back before she started to turn around to flee. Too late. His strong hands came to her person. The world spun in a blur as he swung her violently up in the air. Her hat tumbled to the ground, and that was the very least of her troubles, the very least. For before she could mobilize the most basic defense, Seanessy held her under the arms and over the rail of the ship.

"So we like heights, do we?"

His brows rose with his grin. Feet kicking in midair, she grabbed tight to his forearms as her stomach turned in circles and she silently cursed his great strength that let him manage the trick so effortlessly. Wide frightened eyes looked at the water twenty paces below her feet before she appealed to her captor.

"Seanessy, oh! Put me down—"

"I'll do it, child—so help me God."

Shalyn turned from the amused hazel eyes to the drop and back again, as if trying to decide which she'd choose. She'd pick the water if it weren't for all those sea terrors. "Seanessy, oh, please! You know I'm afraid—"

"Oh, aye, the sharks." He looked over the white-capped wake of ocean water. "Shalyn darling, you don't imagine I'd let a shark taste you before I had the pleasure?"

She bit her lower lip and squeezed her eyes shut, the idea making her beg, "Oh, please, Seanessy!" She kicked her legs, holding tighter to his thick forearms. "What do you want?"

"Your obedience child. I want you to mind my every word."

Instantly her unsteady gaze went cross. "Well, no! I won't! Why should I?"

"Why? I am the captain!"

She felt the warmth of his large hands under her arms; she squirmed with discomfort, more as she contemplated the choice: the promise of her will or being shark bait. Yet her eyes came back to his grin. That pleased grin made the choice.

"Captain of this ship and of these men, but not, methinks, of me!"

A low rumble of laughter sounded from the men gathering around to watch—aye, the girl had spunk and it no doubt would get her wet.

"Is that right? Hey, Slops?"

Among the dozen or so others watching this entertainment, Slops, their famous galley cook, stood nearby, arms folded across his enormous bare chest. "Aye, Captain?"

"When was the last time you dumped the rubbish?"

"Oh . . . Nearly an hour past, Captain. Must be getting closer to land—we had dozens of the sharp-toothed beasts fightin' over the measly pickin's. I managed to catch one of 'em on a hook, but, well, the others tore 'im to bits afore I could reel 'im up. What a bloody mess!" He shook his head with the horror of it. "Still, 'tis probably safe now . . ."

Shalyn swallowed, her already frantically beating heart speeding up. If it were only bushwa, but she knew better! She had watched Slops dump the rubbish from atop the lookout; with horror and fascination, she had watched this shark feast.

"Seanessy, oh, please—I am loath to swim with sharks—"

"Shalyn, you are being quite daft. If I drop you—and mind my words, Shalyn, I am going to drop you—I'll watch from up here. If—when—I see a shark, I'll send Richards for my pistoles—"

"I would be eaten by then!"

After a moment's thought he conceded, "I suppose you are right. Well." He shrugged. "I'll shoot him afterward—it's the best I can do for you. Come, child, my arms are set to shaking now," he lied. "So say goodbye, Shalyn."

"No, please—"

"Then give me your obedience, child."

"Wait! Wait!" She was not beyond begging, pleading, or bargaining. "There must be something else you want—"

"Indeed!" Seanessy's gaze lit with amusement now, as at last his luckless lass reached the point. "There is! As a matter of fact there is something I want from you, and, dear child, I do want it badly. It's a shockingly easy trade for your obedience; I don't even have to think long about it."

He laughed when it took her a minute to know what it was he wanted from her. "Well, not that! That wouldn't be fair!"

"News to you, Shalyn mine, but right now, and pretty much any and all other times, it is all I want from you."

She would not give up, not without a fight and her very best effort. One could always win if one played one's wits. "There must be something else! There must be!"

He appeared to give it some thought but finally he shook his head. "I can't think of anything!"

The men chuckled at her helplessness. Butcher, Ham, Slops, Edward, and a number others said in chorus, "Say goodbye, Shalyn!"

"Wait! Wait! I've got it!"

"Yes?"

"The sonnets. I know them all by heart too." She too lied. "I think." Seanessy loved Shakespeare, she knew, not just reciting sonnets to her but always entertaining the crew by reading parts with her, especially favoring the dramas but sometimes reading from the comedies as well. Just last night they had read from *The Taming of the Shrew* all the way to the end. Until Katharina's last speech about this very subject, obedience, which Shalyn naturally refused to say, forcing Hamilton, of all people, to finish off the part about minding your husband.

"The sonnets—"

She nodded, seizing this slim hope. "I'll sing one for you if you let me go. You do love them so, do you not?"

This surprised him—she would always surprise him—and he chuckled. "What a novel idea!" He glanced behind him. "Men? What say you? A little poetry for the girl's life?"

Slops shrugged unseen. "If it's all ye can get from the girl—"

The men laughed as Seanessy admitted, "I'm afraid it is. So far . . ."

Edwards sighed sarcastically. "Nothing caps a bloody hot day quite like a little Shakespeare sung by a lass quaking with the fear of the sharks."

She bit her lip, unable to contain her excitement. "Is it a bargain?"

"Oh, very well," Seanessy agreed reluctantly. "But I get to choose which one you sing and you must recite it word for word as the old bard wrote it or else. Agreed?"

She nodded vigorously, waiting for him to lift her safely over the rail. "Lift me back!"

"Not until you're done."

"Oh, Seanessy!" She looked at the menacing rush of water beneath her feet. "You just said your arms were tiring—"

"I lied."

"Even you are not strong enough to hold me here much longer—"

"Pray, dear child, that isn't so."

It took a full minute for her to realize he intended to hold her over the water as she recited this sonnet, another full minute to realize he now searched for the most obscure of Shakespeare's poems, hoping, no doubt, she would not know it. The truth was she only knew the sonnets numbered after one hundred and twenty-six, the ones that Shakespeare wrote to the Dark Lady, whoever that was. Truthfully she knew only the most famous of these love poems. Actually she only knew four by heart, the ones she had read a million times ...

She glanced down at the water and held tighter to the arms keeping her at his mercy. She bit her lip and squirmed. "Do hurry!"

"Ah, yes." He knew which one he would make her sing. "I know the exact one. Selected because it so poetically expresses my unambiguous feelings for you. The Dark Lady sonnet."

The amber eyes widened with shock, and she shook her head. 'Twas the very one—the Dark Lady one. The men who knew the sonnet, a surprisingly large number, laughed and laughed hard. Her already flushed cheeks colored more as her face contorted with agony. She knew that one, all the world knew that one! Dear Lord, if that expressed his feelings for her ... "Not that one again!"

"Then ..." Seanessy's brow lifted, he looked at the water, and his men joined in. "Say goodbye, Shalyn!"

She almost chose the drop—he had her nailed. If not for the sharks ... She had no choice. Silence fell over the men, broken only by a soft flap of the sails and even the rush of ocean water across the stern seemed suddenly to slow and then stop altogether to hear the girl as she began:

"My love is as a fever, longing still
For that which longer nurseth the disease;
Feeding on that which doth preserve the ill,
The uncertain sickly appetite to please.
My reason, the physician to my love,
Angry that his prescriptions are not kept,
Hath left me, and I desperate now approve
Desire is death, which physic did except.
Past cure I am, now Reason is past care,
And frantic-mad with evermore unrest;
My thoughts and my discourse as madmen's are,
At random from the truth vainly express'd;
For I have sworn thee fair, and thought thee bright—"

"Who art as black as hell, as dark as night," Seanessy finished for her to the wild applause of his men.

Shalyn bit her lip again. A pained—very!—look crossed her face as she cried, "Tell me you don't mean that, Seanessy!"

"Well, no," he conceded, grinning. "Not that last line. The rest pretty much sums up my sentiments. I would change that last line to: 'Who art as doomed as the damned, as luckless as blight. Goodbye, Shalyn."

She gasped. "But you said—"

"I lied again!"

"Why, you mean, contemptible, bullheaded—"

It was as far as she got. The scream sounded briefly as she fell through the air, her arms circling like windmills until she splashed into the cool ocean water. She emerged to hear the warm sound of his laughter joined with that of the men. Frantically she searched the water for the dark shape of what until now had been her worst fear, only to realize, fatefully, she never did have a choice. The men had had no doubt she would be in the water; they had lowered sails and dropped anchor and then stood to watch the show.

Seanessy's laughter stopped as a band of light struck his forehead. His vision blurred. He tensed dramatically and cursed softly as his hand reached to his head.

Tiny pinpoints of light danced across his vision.

He knew, of course. It had been so long, he half thought he had escaped the wretched torment. He had maybe an hour before it struck, no more. It would last until tomorrow evening . . .

Butcher listened for a moment. A brow rose with dismay. "I fear the boys have taught the lass how to curse like a longshoreman."

Butcher turned from Shalyn's impressive curses to Seanessy. He knew immediately. He had been with Sean the last time it had happened.

"Send Toothless to my quarters with his bags of tricks, will you?"

Seanessy turned away from the offending sunlight.

Butcher nodded solemnly as he stared at the wide width of Seanessy's back. Sean's tightly corded muscles on his back were already tense with an effort to brace against the oncoming pain. He hurried off to find Toothless.

*　*　*

Shalyn hadn't seen him all day since he had dropped her into the water, and it scared her. That sonnet scared her senseless. The words kept echoing through her mind: "Past cure I am, now Reason is past care,/ And frantic-mad with evermore unrest/ My thoughts and my discourse a madmen's are . . ."

Merciful heavens save me . . .

The orange ball of the sun sizzled into the darkening blue water as she sat against the lower mast with what was politely referred to as supper—a large bowl of sweetened oatmeal, a piece of dried beef, and a hard piece of bread. The spot offered a direct view of the captain's quarters. Like a theater patron awaiting the rising curtain, she kept looking toward the door to his quarters. No one went in and no one came out.

She stirred her bowl of mush absently.

Oly stared intently at her bowl.

Edward and Ham had spread out navigational star maps on the deck nearby and finally, unable to resist, Shalyn asked, "Where is Seanessy? I haven't seen him since . . . since . . ."

Edward looked over to her, surprised she hadn't heard. "Three sheets to the wind by this point, I suppose. Toothless pumped enough opium in him to topple an Indian elephant."

She set down the bowl of oatmeal. Oly took it as an invitation. She never noticed. "What?"

"He's out, lass."

Hamilton smoothed the map over a makeshift table. "He is suffering one of his headaches. It'll keep him down until tomorrow night."

Her eyes filled with concern. Seanessy's headaches were famous because anyone who knew Sean found it impossible to imagine a thing like a headache could knock him off his feet and into bed. For Seanessy's body was an exercise in masculine perfection: his unparalleled strength, a strength matched only by Mr. Slops on board, his famous fighting ability and uncommon speed, his agility, unheard of in a man his size.

How many times would he perform a circus acrobat's tricks for no reason past the fun of it? He could throw himself backward in the air, landing miraculously on his feet. Knolls and Edward swore he could do the same trick on a galloping horse! He always somersaulted three times before he stretched into a graceful dive into the water. Things she'd never believe if she hadn't seen it with her own eyes.

So the idea of a headache knocking him out gave her an idea of the terrible power of this internal demon that seized him.

She remembered what Gschu had said about headaches: most headaches were a warning of excess: an excess of spirits, tea, or emotions, and that there were as many good cures as there were kinds. Yet, by far, the worst headaches were caused by a vicious cycle: a body braces against the pain, and the tension of bracing for the pain causes a worsened headache, which causes more tension and more ... indefinitely until the body weakens and can fight no more or until hands are set in motion against the tension.

How well she knew that remedy!

She stood up and turned toward his cabin.

"Oh no, you don't," Edward said, sympathetic to her concern but knowing better. "You are about the last person he'd want to see now."

"Oh, but I can help—"

"There's no help for him but the pipe, lass. The pain pretty much knocks him out anyway, and what's left, Toothless takes care of. Just leave him be ..."

* * *

The bright light of a full moon filtered through the crack in the door, illuminating the otherwise dark space of the carpenter's room. She could not sleep. The idea of Seanessy suffering was her own agony. She wanted badly to help him. The only thing stopping her was the idea that 'twould be cruel indeed if she did rouse him from the merciful doze of an opium haze . . .

It was so hot. She wore only his long white shirt, and still it lay against her skin with a thin sheen of perspiration. She tried to settle her mind by focusing on the stream of moonlight, but it was no use. The hammock felt like an irritating web of knots on her skin; she kept twisting and turning and—

She finally gave up. Bare feet to the ground and not expecting anyone up at the hour, she rose and quietly went through the door.

Merciful heavens . . .

She stopped and stared, her hands lifting to her heart as if to contain her awe. The full moon shone brightly just above the dark water, casting a long ribbon of light on the ship. Butcher was up as well. He stood at the rail silhouetted in moonlight, staring at this moon's haunting light, a moon that somehow held all the dispassion of a disembodied soul, and something of its mystery.

This moonlight bade her to move softly toward it, as if with reverence. "The goal of Zinja, Ti Yao once told me," she whispered, "is nothing less than to be as a heavenly sphere: a light that shines with indifference above the human tragedies that played over and over on earth. I don't think I understood until now. Until I beheld this moon, so beautiful and yet utterly impervious to the march of human follies beneath its glorious light."

Butcher had not known she stood at his side until the moment the soft melodic voice sounded these words. Then he looked back to the moonlight as his mind turned the words around in his mind. "If only I could muster this magical indifference . . ."

She nodded agreement. She thought of her own mother, so newly remembered and so long ago lost, and then of Ti Yao and Gschu. Gradually she became aware of Butcher's silence and what filled it. "You are thinking of her . . . of Kenzie."

"Aye."

She studied the moonlit face, searching. The poor baby he had saved, and then all the bags of moneys he dropped on beggar's laps. "What happened, Butcher? What happened to Kenzie?"

"Shalyn, 'tis a sad story—"

"Please."

For a long moment she thought he would refuse but he grabbed hold of the rail and rocked back on his heels as a sad smile changed his bearded face, and he remembered a girl named Kenzie.

"The day I met her," he began the tale, "she was standing at a well before her small farm just outside of Dublin. I was riding past on my way to port. I stopped to beg a drink of water, and yet now I see I stopped for her: she had these beautiful brown eyes and long dark hair that fell in plaits past her knees, a smile that reached me across the distance. She was so young— only ten and four then. She said I could have as much water as I wanted but only after I put my back to the pile of wood behind the barn. There didn't seem to be a man about the place, so I obliged. Once I finished, she sent her young brother, Kenyon, and her little sister, Brenna, to invite me to supper.

" 'Twas a modest cottage and their means were poor, but there was a light in that place. It came from Kenzie, from her heart. Kenzie's laughter transformed the simplest things: the meal, the cottage, the children, changed them into something delightful and wonderful, and with nothing more than the bounty of her love. She was alone. Her father had left her when she was seven and her mother three years later after a long illness. And while they were too poor to buy shoes against the winter, Kenzie raised Kenyon and Brenna alone and raised them well: to the church, the work on the farm, and what few books she could get her hands on.

"I think I fell in love that first night though I didn't realize it, not really. Not until three weeks later when the parish priest showed up at the door and told me bluntly that either I marry Kenzie or I leave.

"He married us that very night. I knew happiness then. I came to love Kenyon and Brenna as my own, and soon Kenzie gave me a son, Christopher. I was working a small merchantman that flew from Dublin to Amsterdam during the war. I made a fair wage but I wanted more, I thought. For Kenzie. I wanted to dress Kenzie in silks and set her in a fancy parlor and give her nothing to do all day but mind the children and gossip with her neighbors. How Kenzie would laugh at my foolishness. She'd swear she never wanted anything more than the love and health of the family, that this made her happy and that she would not dare ask God for more than this happiness . . .

"Not me though. I could not get rid of my grand notions of mansions, silk dresses, jewels, my own ships. Lord, I wanted all of it. I told her it was for her too, for Kenzie, Kenzie who was happiest when barefoot, dancing in a sunlit meadow with the children. And then one day I got the opportunity I was dreaming about. There was a place on a merchantman leaving London and sailing the Orient. A risky venture but one that would start this grand fortune and give me plenty of opportunity to increase it. So I moved Kenzie and the children to London. I set them up in a nice flat and left to make this precious dream of

mine come true. And I did. I sent every penny back
to my banker in London for Kenzie and the children.
I always sent letters too, letters that spoke of how
much I missed her and little Chris, Brenna, and
Kenyon, but glad letters as I instructed Kenzie to hire
an agent and find a fine townhouse, where to do it,
what to look for and all. Then as my luck made this
fortune grow, more letters instructing Kenzie now on
how to hire servants, an exalted thing she had never
done before, where to find the best dressmakers and
whatnot. Almost a year and a half passed before we
finally set sail for home.

"The bank had closed a short month or two after I
had sailed out. There was no forwarding address. No
one had any idea of where the 'bankers' were, much
less the money I had been sending them. Of course I
raced to the flat where I had left them. The landlord
was surprised; he had forced Kenzie and the children
out December before last after tiring of her pleas for
understanding, promises of her rich husband's returning soon from sea. And he had no idea where
they had gone to.

"I cannot describe my search of months; I will not
try. I finally found Brenna. She was lying on a small
cot in a huge room of maybe fifty other sick and
dying children. She wore only the tattered rags of a
beggar. She was lice-ridden, filthy, and suffering the
last days of an influenza.

"The little girl lived long enough to tell me how
Kenzie was frantic with grief, certain, of course, that
I had died. When they were forced out of the flat and
onto the cold streets, Kenzie sold all our possessions,
hoping to get enough to buy passage back to Ireland,
to their parish. The parish would have kept them indefinitely, and I always think I—"

His pause was a struggle to continue. "She did not
have enough. The money barely got them out of Lon-

don, and then as doors shut along the way, they were forced to turn back. They had no place to go. Kenzie sold her hair but it wasn't enough. Winter set in, and, dear God, they say that winter was the worst in twenty years.

"Brenna remembered when little Christopher died. In Hyde Park. They were rushing through a bitter storm to get to a church on the other side of town. 'Twas the third church they tried that night. Brenna said she couldn't walk anymore: she was too tired and hungry and it was so cold. Kenyon tried to carry her but he started stumbling. Then Kenzie tried to carry her with little Christopher. She had to stop. They thought they would rest a moment. The little girl didn't remember anything more, until she was roused by Kenzie's screams. The baby wouldn't wake. No matter what Kenzie did, little Christopher wouldn't wake. Later, she said, Kenyon tried to take the babe from her to put in the gravediggers' cart but Kenzie couldn't let go of him. The boy finally dug a hole right there in the park.

"Kenzie stopped talking after that, Brenna said. She wouldn't eat any of the bits of bread that came their way, what little it was. Kenyon joined the poor children scouring the sewers for trinkets—the mudlarks, people call them. The little girl's eyes lit up when she told me that once Kenyon found a man's brass billfold and fetched a 'whole half-farthin' for it.' Kenyon bought her a hot potato with it. She didn't remember anything else until first Kenyon and then Kenzie got sick and someone got them into a poorhouse.

"Kenyon died first," she said. The rest was a blur in her feverish mind. The last thing she told me was how happy she thought Kenzie would be that I came back at last, that I hadn't died. She would tell Kenzie as soon as she saw her in heaven, and it would be just like Michaelmas Day to see Kenzie smile again . . ."

Shalyn stared at the moonlight filtered through tears. She closed her eyes as she felt Butcher kiss her forehead and turn away from her. The warmth of his lips lingered with the image of a young girl with soft brown eyes and long dark hair, the face, she knew, that Butcher saw in every beggar he passed. She opened her eyes and stared at the cold and dispassionate moonlight before she turned to the place she knew she'd find comfort.

Seanessy . . .

She slipped quietly inside. The moonlight followed her. A gold lamp lit the space as well. He was mercifully asleep on the bed, lying on his stomach. A sheet covered him to the waist. The discarded hookah lay on the floor, alongside a water pitcher, a wooden cup, and a whiskey bottle. She silently moved to the place.

The rich sweet scent of opium hung in the air. She drew deeply, reaching a hand to smooth tears across her cheek. The soft lamplight merged in moonlight and bathed his still and naked body. Her breath caught. A curious tingling rushed through her as her gaze traveled over the smooth and powerful muscles encasing his back with lean and sleek lines and the golden color of a Bengal tiger, all of him indeed an exercise in masculine perfection.

Seeing it, she leaned closer. She wiped her eyes as if to clear her vision, and only because she couldn't believe what she saw. An angry red knot of tension went from the back of his neck to spread out over the width of his back. Tension from pain. As if indeed all his great strength had gone into bracing against the pain, causing so much more, his own strength working against him. The impossibility of it was that the tension could seize him still, after he had smoked the pipe.

She suffered a long moment's pause. If he had sunk into an opium haze, she should not wake him. And yet her fingers trembled with her desire, her need to stop it, to ease the tension and pain from his body—

As she stood there in indecision her gaze came to rest on the pipe on the floor. The pipe. She stared without seeing as a distant memory burst on her consciousness: a man holding her down, the sweet thick choking smoke bursting in her lungs as she screamed Ti Yao's name over and over, fighting and kicking for all she was worth until the smoke worked through her veins and stole first her strength and then her will.

Who was it? The man was loud and large and smelled of the sea and whiskey and fear. She did not like him. The man was . . . was . . .

Her Father! Thoughts spun over this vital memory, her only memory of her father. Dear Lord . . .

Seanessy was not asleep, the opium had worn thin some time ago. Her shadow slipped across his face as she leaned over and he opened his eyes to see who stood there. The silence should have told him—in all his life he had never known anyone or anything that could move as silently as Shalyn.

His hand snaked around her wrist as he turned his head to see her, bracing against the rush of pain this slight move brought. She swallowed her startled scream in a gasp. The memory vanished as she stared at the handsome face. His eyes were changed, that was all. There was no sign of his pain, save for those eyes. A feverish intensity filled his gaze as he stared back at her and made him look cruel. Worse than cruel. He looked like a ravished wild animal who had caught his prey.

"Shalyn . . ."

He too stared, just stared. The light shone from behind her, casting the lovely face in shadows. She wore only a thin shirt, he saw, nothing else. Every curve silhouetted to tease, arouse, ignite his hunger. Desire shot hotly through his slowed blood and pulse, ricocheting through his pain-wracked body in the cruelest punishment. His next breath came in a groan as he braced against the brutal wave of this torture.

"What the devil are you doing here?"

His deep harshness beat the extreme fragility of her emotions and forbade, absolutely, a reply. Fear changed her eyes as she felt the inexplicably tightening grasp of his hand on her wrist. A soft bewildered cry escaped her lips as his cruel hand forced her to her knees, the better to see her face. The emotions there confused him. He wondered what caused the sadness. The fear, however, he understood. He released her wrist to keep her safe, turning away.

"Get out, Shalyn."

He tried to ease back into the merciful silence and stillness and he closed his eyes tightly against the relentless pounding in his head. Shalyn watched this struggle with alarm.

What she did next went through him in a wave of shock. He felt her small weight coming over him, straddling his back. He tensed dramatically; his breath caught. A wave of pain washed over him, so hot it sent him into blackness a moment, recovering to feel her hands on his back.

He started to turn to her in violence.

"No, Seanessy. Please. Let me."

He collapsed as the pain ricocheted through his head. He held perfectly still, waiting for it to subside, always waiting for the pain to subside, and yet it never did. Not for a day and sometimes two, not until he was beaten into an unconscious mess of muscle and bone, too weak to lift himself from the bed.

Skilled hands started at the tight knot at his neck. She knew to put all her strength and will into her hands as she kneaded his flesh in the queer tight circles that Gschu had made her practice again and again in the dirt before she ever let her touch a patient. Over and over, her breaths perfectly matched the strange rhythm of her hands until her heart felt in synchronization and the whole of her awareness was tactile, the world felt through his warm and vibrant flesh beneath his skin . . . .

He first kept bracing for a wave of pain that would not come, forgetting to breathe for long moments only to draw air into his body, and release it, mercifully, with impunity. Once his mind grasped this miracle, it changed. Slowly, like a drug, the warmth and strength of her skilled hands penetrated first his worn senses, then the hard knots of flesh. More and more he felt himself sinking into the mercy brought by her touch.

Time circled in the movement of her hands, and yet disappeared, dissipating as she eased her strength into his muscles. Over and over, harder and harder, the skilled hands slowly moved to the top of his spine and outward, over the tightly corded muscles of his shoulders, over and over, moving down his spine and back up to his neck again to start anew.

She was a sorceress and this was her magic. The sharp throbbing began to ebb, more and more as the rhythm of her hands on his flesh became the rhythm of his pulse and blood. He didn't know when it happened, only that it did. At some point the pain was gone, forced from his flesh by the miracle of her hands.

"Shalyn, sweet mercy, it's gone. The pain is gone."

She had known before he had. The muscles were

smooth now, the knots were gone, but still the movement of her hands on his back did not stop. The rhythm changed, slowing. For: "Gschu always said a man is not done until he floats away on a shimmering sea of warmth. Let me, Seanessy," she whispered. "I want to give you this . . ."

Gschu had taught her first on her own body. She remembered the pleasure well. She remembered the hot steam baths and lying naked on Gschu's mat as the old woman's strong skilled hands worked their magic and drugged her senses, the thick pleasure penetrating to touch the very core of her being . . .

She began alternating the slowed rhythm with a hard, swift pounding of the side of her palm. This felt at once arousing yet soothing, the pleasure exquisite beyond reason. He gave himself over to the erotic magic of her hands. And, dear Lord, it was erotic. His consciousness began drifting away on this shimmering sea of pleasure for long periods, then collecting anew, only to find the pleasure magnified, changing the pace of his heart and breaths as it gathered potency. Heat flowed languidly through his veins, and yet burned hotter than an exploding sun.

He knew long before she did.

Shalyn felt the power and vibrancy of his muscles beneath her fingertips, the growing heat between them. Her heart and pulse seemed to slow to a thud, then rush to start faster again. Her breaths changed and she shifted slightly, as if to ease back to the languid place of the sweet dreamscape she had so carefully constructed.

Impossible. The air between them was electrified. The dreamscape vanished, replaced by heightened senses. She felt a tingling awareness up through her legs. She shifted slightly—

A sudden warmth between her legs made her breath catch. Her hands stopped; she released her breath in the whispered rush of his name. "Seanessy . . ."

He turned over in a fluid easy movement, careful to keep her straddled over his naked male hips. Hot chills emanated from the place their bodies touched. Her hands braced against his wide shoulders, and her startled eyes shot to his face, her consciousness riveted on the hard hot part of him pressed against her parted thighs. "Seanessy . . ."

Seanessy brushed back the mass of gold hair, his touch as gentle as the kiss of a warm breeze. "Shalyn." He studied her eyes, seeing the haunting light. "What has made you so sad?"

"Butcher and Kenzie."

A strong hand came gently to her cheek with a soothing stroke of his thumb. "You know, Shalyn," he said in a heated whisper, "when Butcher first told me of Kenzie, I had so arrogantly assumed he loved Kenzie more after her precious life had been stolen from him. Because until now I had not a clue about how powerful love can be."

Emotion shimmered in her eyes. She closed them then, more frightened of the declaration than of the desire. To love and be loved, it seemed an impossible dream she had long ago parted from, only to realize now, as his words resonated through her, that it scared her. Like nothing else, it scared her.

His hands reached to the buttons of her shirt and for a moment she lost herself in the shimmering depth of his gaze. "Seanessy . . . no, I—"

"No?" he questioned, his voice husky with passion, the lingering warmth of his drugged and slowed senses. "I don't think you understand. I asked no question that needed an answer. For, Shalyn . . ." He parted the shirt as he spoke, his hands sliding over her straight slender shoulders, a caress as magical as hers, before he lifted first one hand, then the other, his movements maddeningly unhurried. "Resisting you is like touching the moon or turning back its tides. An impossibility I would not try . . ."

The shirt was thrown to the floor. Modesty burned through her and anticipation brought a tightening rush of chills. Pinpricks of pleasure erupted from every place their bodies touched. She held perfectly still, afraid to breathe, let alone move . . .

He drew a sharp breath upon seeing her beauty thus revealed: the rounded fullness of her breasts, the faint lines of her mark ignored as instead he absorbed the tempting peaks and the dramatic curve of her waist, all so seductively poised over him. He reached hands to the slender back, sliding down, watching the small gasps his touch brought. The opium had thickened his blood and slowed its pace, so that his desire, though a hot, bright fire burning in him, burned slowly . . .

"Shalyn," he said as his hands reached to cup the full softness of her breasts until he felt the coral-pink tips tighten. She moaned with pleasure, a pleasure returned twofold as he watched. His thumbs, just his thumbs, brushed over her breasts with small licks of fire. Tingling chills caught her breath, shivers gathered into a tightening knot that made her close her eyes and arch into his hands.

His name sounded with a bewildered expectation.

He answered as his large hands slid under her arms and he gently pulled her down until their lips touched. Lightly. Once, and once again, they shared the air as the shivering heat of his hard body against hers made her gasp. And then he was kissing her.

The kiss was unhurried and more sensual than any past. His hands slid over her slender form until his fingers spanned the voluptuous curve of her hips and he rocked her erotically over him. The boom in her heart dropped to her loins. Her gasp died in their joined mouths. Her untrained senses flooded with a fiery rush of warmth that melted into the alluring passion of this kiss.

He turned her unresisting form over and broke the kiss. He let his lips graze her closed eyes, her forehead, her lips again. "There were times I could almost imagine this softness beneath me," he whispered at his hand slid over the petal-soft skin, past her narrow waist to ride the curve of her hip before returning to massage the soft mounds of her breasts again, her soft pants guiding his movements. "Nights when I could almost imagine the feel of your breasts in my hands, the sound of your desire ..." He kissed her again, the kiss bursting into a voluptuous shot of heat through her. "And, dear Lord, how the brightness of those dreams pales alongside this reality ... Shalyn ..."

She melted helplessly beneath his kiss. One kiss became two. He began teasing her with his mouth, whispering love words that penetrated her like heated caresses. Tiny quivers flew over her from head to toe in a delirium of craving and need and yearning.

Hard quakes rocked her as his lips traveled down the arch of her slim throat to her breasts where he stroked softly, then harder, then soft again. He listened to her soft surprised breaths, felt the clinging of her hands sink into his shoulders. She arched into him, feeling feverish, the tightening knot making her writhe and twist against him as if he would somehow know to bring her to ease.

"Easy, Shalyn ... Here, let me show you ..."

His fingers grazed her hip, the caressing circles soothing and stirring both as he circled the sweet apex. The palm of his hand slowly stroked her belly until she cried his name. He kissed her mouth. The pounding pleasure of his kisses dragged her into a sweet thickening web of pleasure. His palm moved in slow caresses there. She broke the kiss with a bewildered kind of agony as his fingers slipped between her legs. She tensed dramatically, arching her back only to have the tension burst in a rush of warmth as he stroked her. And another and another, each crest of the wave higher and hotter until—

He felt her blossoming sex, full, ripe, ready. He withdrew his hand only to wipe the sweetness of her around her breasts and her mouth. She cried softly with the play that followed, until she wanted, needed to feel all of him and all at once. Then he was kissing her, his body coming over her as he did. She felt the stroke of his sex there, his strong muscled legs nudging hers helplessly farther apart. She tried to pull away but he kissed long and hard until she felt so curiously ready to burst down there—

He slipped inside and felt the slight tear and, dear Lord, she was so small and hot and moist. Pleasure seized the whole of him, violent and intense. He closed his eyes as it rocked him, his fists curling around the pillow. "Sweet mercy, I have died."

Her small pain-filled voice cried beneath him, "Me too! Oh . . ." Her fingernails curled into his flesh; she caught her half-scream, half-cry in her throat. She felt as if he had ripped her in two with something hot, searing, and far, far too large. "Seanessy, Seanessy!"

"Yes?"

"What are you doing?"

"Actually, I'm trying to work one of Kepler's equations."

"What?" She tried to comprehend this, but she couldn't think, she only knew: "Oh, Seanessy, it's not working!"

His ability to speak was a kind of marvel to him.

"No, it's not. I'm having a great deal of difficulty think—"

"You don't fit! I think you're killing me!"

"Do not die on me now!"

"Can you, oh, please, if you just shrink back to normal?"

His chest bounced against her. Which caused small little shock waves to resonate deep inside her. He brushed his lips lovingly across her damp forehead. "Now?" he questioned, the timbre of his voice husky. "When I'm inside you? Less likely than touching the moon. Shalyn . . ."

He kissed her mouth. The driving pleasure of the kiss sent her into a deep swoon, the searing pain melting into shimmering shivers. She twisted. A hot slap of fire rewarded the movement.

"I will be gentle, Shalyn . . ."

He moved with all the gentleness he was capable of and then some. Her breath caught, he captured her surprised "oh" in another long kiss. "Shalyn." He could only say her name. The pleasure spilled into his drugged senses. Never had he felt less control and never had he needed more. All the force of his will went into assessing her lovely face. "Oh, Shalyn. Am I still hurting you?"

Somehow she managed to shake her head. Now it was hot and shimmering and—

His hand reached down her leg to guide it over him. "Wrap your legs around me . . . That's it. Oh, Shalyn . . ."

"Seanessy . . ." She felt so feverish, so . . . "Kiss me . . ."

He did and it was heaven. She lost her consciousness on the shimmering sea as he carried her higher and higher until there was nothing but him and her and the world exploding in ecstasy . . .

An ecstasy that lasted long afterward as he held

and kissed her, lovingly washed her feverish skin and said, "Again, Shalyn, I would have you again ..." An ecstasy that lasted through their first moonlit night as lovers. Dawn crept into the sea-rocked room when he finally relinquished his claim on her, and only because he was certain he could not push her over the thin line separating her from this heaven a single time more. He gathered her small and unresisting form against his length and lovingly stroked her hair as he brushed her forehead with kisses and watched the dark eyes close. "Shalyn ..."

She nuzzled closer against his warmth, her love-soaked body sinking into a sweet saturation so deep and blissful as to be another kind of heaven.

"I love you, Shalyn."

She opened her eyes. "Madly?" she asked.

He smiled at this. "Aye ..."

The declaration was a sweet echo of her own bliss-ful rapture and she closed her eyes again. "I love you too."

"I'm afraid."

She tried to open her eyes to hear this. "Afraid?"

He gently aligned their hips, taking her limp hand in his to let her feel the part of him that was anything but. "I want you again ..."

Her sweet smile would live in his mind forever. "Yes ... Again, Seanessy. Love me again ..."

Yet she promptly fell asleep. Or almost. For he con-tinued, "That's exactly what I was afraid of ..." He kissed the soft pliancy of her lips again and sighed. "It's a big problem for me. It just doesn't go away, this desire for you. The more I have you, the more I want you." His voice changed with sudden anger. "I knew you were trouble, Shalyn, the moment I first saw you. Here's a pretty package of trouble, I thought." He swore softly. "And I was so right. So right. I knew this would happen, that you would push me right to the provincial point of utter contemptible conventionality. Me! You led me right to the place I never imagined I would trespass. Yet here I am, thinking, wanting, dear Lord, I do. I really do, Shalyn. I want to marry you."

"If you just let me sleep, I'll think about it."

"Don't think too long. We will be in Malacca before too long. I'll give this duke two weeks at most. We could make arrangements with the bishop there. I know the fellow. Unpleasant and pompous but greedy as all get out. I could promise a large pound note to the church if he's quick about it. Of course Butcher is a captain in his own right and we are at sea. I could have him do it. I could have you back in bed within an hour . . ." That thought made him smile, a smile that disappeared as he abruptly grasped what she had said. "What the devil do you mean—you'll think about it?"

Shalyn offered no answer. For she at last was very soundly asleep. Asleep with a lingering smile playing on her lips.

The sun crested the zenith when she woke. Outside the emerald-green peak of the Isle of Blue Caverns rose in the distance and Prescott called out, "Land ho" from atop the lookout. Shalyn did not hear, and wouldn't have cared if she did hear. She woke to a different sensation altogether.

She felt toasty warm encompassed in his heat. An arousing virile scent penetrated her sleepy senses like a tonic. She stiffened, feeling the brush of his breathing just beneath her ear. His chest pressed against her back and his arm crossed over her stomach, keeping her close as they slept, while that part of him cradled her buttocks. He was hard and hot—

She released her breath in a languid sigh, relaxing against the delicious feel of his huge warm body against her, and as she did, a tingling sensual awareness erupted through her. A not unpleasant soreness brought a tide of warm sensual memories flooding through her, warming her blood by degrees. Oh, Lord; oh, Seanessy . . .

He shifted slightly, his firm lips caressing her ear as his hand moved to her bare breasts. He cupped the soft swell and lightly teased the peaks until her nipples tightened. She drew a sharp breath, released in a rush of shivers. Her entire consciousness centered on the loveplay of his hand there, and she twisted seductively.

A husky chuckle sounded as he slowly caressed the sensitive peaks. Sensations stirred, heating her blood. Skilled fingers continued to stroke and tease the anxious tips. Her loins stirred with heat and she arched her back, snuggling closer to his hard shaft. A husky groan sounded. His other arm came under her so that one hand continued to massage her breast while the other drew heated shivering lines up and down her flattened stomach.

A gush of warmth rushed between her legs and she cried softly as that hand traveled lower still over the softness of her belly. Sensations grew in need and spread through her until she twisted and writhed and expelled a breath with the sound of his name.

He answered her with another husky groan. His lips came to her neck as his hand slid over her sex, gently stroking the moist recess of her most feminine part, boldly slipping in and out. Warm rushes of pleasure alternated with hot chills, leading her to the edge of a high steep cliff, keeping her there. "Oh, please—" She did not have to ask twice. He joined her to him, sending her sailing over the cliff and then up to a certain heaven . . .

Seanessy felt her heartbeat spin slowly down, and the lovely dark eyes closed again. Still he could not stop kissing her. His heart filled with strange heady sensations, so joyful and pleasant, and new to him, making him question first his sanity and then the pallor of his first thirty-three years without it.

"Shalyn . . ."

He gradually became aware of the shifting ocean beneath the ship, the pounding of his men's footsteps overhead, the frantic flap of sails as the topsails were furled. The ship had slowed. They must be approaching the island. This he wanted to see. He kissed her sleeping face again and when she didn't wake, he gently disentangled their bodies.

The sun shone brightly. Gentle waves washed the side of the ship. It was quiet. What the devil? Seanessy's gaze swept the deck and the sails. Half the men hung silently from masts, staring at something off at sea. He stepped to the rail.

They sailed through brown murky water less than a mile offshore. Fire had ravished this whole side of the island, destroying the verdant jungle. Not even the stumps of trees remained. Streams of mud ran into the water. A small mountain range made up the rest of the island, this covered in the lush green jungle spring from rich soil and four months of the steady deluge of monsoon rains. Within two months these rains would wash this whole side of the island away.

"Seanessy, what do you make of it?"

Hamilton and Butcher joined him at the rail. Butcher handed him the glass. "Edward, steady at the wheel," Sean called, his voice curiously subdued by the devastation before him. "Furl the mainsail! Lower the spanner," he called back. "Nice and easy around the point."

Butcher was but a moment confused by Seanessy's apparent well-being. "You look so—so hale—" He abruptly realized he had not seen Shalyn since the moonlit night. So Sean had taken the cure, a fortuitous move. Their game had begun and Seanessy, like all of them, would need his wits and strength to pull this one off, no doubt.

Seanessy's grin disappeared at he looked through the glass. "Not a natural disaster. The jungles around here are the thickest, most impenetrable I've ever seen. I remember when we burned to clear our property for our house—it was the hardest part. Remember—the fire kept sizzling out?"

"Aye, it had to be staked with dry kindling and even then . . ."

"You are forgetting," Ham said. "This is no doubt the man's idea of a treasure hunt."

"Aye," Seanessy said, a sly and yet somehow irritated grin lifting on the handsome face. Sly because anyone as stupid as to undertake such an endeavor for treasure would be easily thwarted, and irritated because it was so absurdly wasteful.

"As dumb as a box of rocks," Butcher repeated.

As the ship sailed slowly around the eastern tip of the island and the color of the sea returned to a sparkling blue, their game changed. Seanessy offered fifty pounds to the first man to spot the warehouse that looked like a patch of grassy green from the distance. Prescott was up the ratline with a glass to his sharp eyes, the most frequent winner of these wagers, but every man present found incentive in the reward to keep his eyes trained on the shoreline. Edward kept the ship steady at the wheel. The sails were adjusted to the light breeze blowing off starboard.

Seanessy called for the trunk of explosives to be brought up and readied. The duke was no doubt sailing the horn at the moment, perhaps not even that far. With any luck they could blow it to hell by twilight and be a thousand leagues away by the time anyone figured out what had happened.

Yet as he continued to look through the glass, he thought of Joy, and the light in her eyes. This picture was placed alongside the vision of chain gangs digging holes in sand. What would happen to the duke without the wealth represented in the opium supply? No doubt he had sufficient moneys to continue his absurd quest for treasure, at the expense of the backbreaking labor of so many black bodies . . .

A haunting loneliness and desolation covered the island as thick as its jungles, a sense of dark secrets and isolation indeed. The formidable air was inescapable and Seanessy, not usually given to fanciful notions, wondered if he only imagined it when Butcher whispered, "Somethin' about this place raises the hairs on the back of my neck. Like seeing a shrouded figure in a graveyard at night."

"Springs from its isolation," Hamilton suggested, sensing it too. "And the poor black sods put to digging up sand."

"Seanessy, what are you thinking?" Butcher asked, knowing Sean well enough to see his uncertainty.

"I was thinking of Joy, of reason enough to return after we save merry ole England."

"I don't know, Sean—a standing army of two thousand—"

Prescott spotted it first. "Ho, Cap'n! There she is!"

All gazes fixed on the island. Seanessy peered through the glass until he found it. A patch of green that did indeed appear to be a grassy spot in the jungle. The warehouse. Jungle encroached on it from all sides. An enormous black boulder marked the spot two hundred or so paces off shore in the water. Prescott noticed the boulder. "Why, 'tis almost a perfect heart shape." Seanessy and the others noticed the point at one end, with two rounded orbs at the other.

They were staring at this curiosity when Edward shouted, "Cap'n! Off the bow! We've been spotted!"

A small clipper sail at full speed toward them. Seanessy turned and saw it, swearing softly. "There goes that plan. Probably the man's henchman, this overseer I was supposed to meet who looks after the duke's business."

"Well, the man's got a lot of balls approachin' a seven-hundred tonner at that speed. For all he knows we could be the very devil come to take the place."

"Aye," Seanessy said, curiously. He ordered the explosives returned and hidden in the hold and all men to arms, just in case. The ship was naturally in a constant state of readiness for a battle: the *Wind Muse* was the last ship that would fall prey to pirates, but a number of the men rushed off to arm themselves. Except Seanessy. Not only was he glad Shalyn still slept and was safely out of trouble, if only for a time, but he would be loath to wake her. She was going to need her strength.

All gazes and looking glasses riveted onto the fast-approaching yacht. The kind of ship a gentleman might use for holidays, no doubt used by the duke to travel around his little kingdom. A number of the duke's men stood at the bow. Seanessy passed the glass to Hamilton.

"Sean!" Hamilton called as the ship came closer. "Take a look at who's waving his arms like a madman!"

The glass dropped. He stared. Surprise worked in his face. "Kyler!" His brows rose. "What the devil?" He tried to reason what had made Kyler abandon his plans and instead travel to this island, but he could not fathom it.

"And look who's standing with him," Ham said.

Seanessy put the glass back and searched the space near Kyler. A half-dozen dark-skinned heathens surrounded him, men all wearing black boots and pants, the same cut of white shirt; all of it looked hot beneath the blazing and humid tropical sun. He didn't understand at first until the glass stopped on an expensive pair of black boots, up the tailored black pants, a white silk shirt and a vest, the ridiculously hot garb of a wealthy man that announced his name before Seanessy saw his face.

"Well, if it isn't the master of ceremonies himself. They must have left just after us, chasing the eastern winds while we sat in the doldrums!"

A chill raced up Butcher's back; he could not guess what Kyler was doing here. Something warned him, though. Seanessy turned to shout a series of quick orders as the smaller yacht pulled alongside the larger ship. Sails were quickly furled. Lines were secured. A rope ladder descended.

Kyler turned to the duke and shouted something, then shook his head, motioning the duke back. The duke, however, appeared adamant about proceeding first. Too late. Kyler started up the ladder. The duke and his men followed.

"Kyler!" Seanessy shouted as he leaped down to the deck. "What the blazes—"

"Sean—" Kyler stopped and cast an anxious gaze as the duke and his men came up behind him. "We beat you by four days. Is she with you? Isabel—" He shook his head. "I mean Shalyn?"

"Shalyn? Who the devil wants to know?"

The Duke de la Armanac showed no sign of the emotion washing over him in force, except for a hand that reached for and found the sturdy rung of the ladder at his side. He seized it. His knuckles whitened as the relief, so powerfully felt, threatened his last semblance of composure.

The duke straightened, and his eyes blazed with emotion as he said, "Isabel is the Duchess de la Armanac—she is my wife!"

Hands on hips, Seanessy registered his shock.

"You!? Her husband! Why, you bloody son of a bitch!" And he threw his fist hard into the man's jaw. The resounding crack snapped the duke's head back and threw him hard against the wall, where he dropped like a puppet without stings.

The battle had begun.

Chapter 12

Seanessy did not have to think long about this bastard tying Shalyn up to make her helpless for his pathetic abuse; it took only seconds to mobilize the full force of his violence. He was going to kill him, beat the bastard to a bloody pulp and keep after the carcass like a greedy vulture long after he was dead. He viciously fought against the five men who held him back, including now Slops, Butcher, and Edward.

"I'll kill him!" He freed his elbow and shot it hard into Slops's enormous stomach. "I'm going to kill the—"

Kyler shouted to the duke's men to get the nobleman away before Seanessy managed to break free. They sprang into action. The largest among them lifted the unconscious duke over his shoulder, moving quickly to the ladder.

"Sean! Listen to me! Listen—"

Yet he wouldn't hear. Kyler swore viciously, clenched his fist, and swung hard into Seanessy's face. His blow had no effect, like the brush of a breeze.

Except it gave all his men an idea of the miracle that had passed between Sean and the girl. The idea was a kind of marvel too, for no one ever expected

345

Seanessy to be landed by a lass. Seanessy was a wild card; the force of his colorful personality, the strength of his will, the unholy passions with which he lived his randy life did not make him a probable or even likely candidate for the devotion and love known as domestication. Women, in Sean's life, satisfied physical needs, occasionally amusing him as they did, but never any more.

Until Shalyn. The wagers had been in her favor since the day she had stood on the rail and had only gone higher as the crew became familiar with her unique blend of femininity and pluck, beguiling charm, innocence, and courage. The wagers increased even more when they watched the captain's response to the package on which Butcher commented, "Enough sparks be flyin' between the two to light up Winchester Cathedral on Christmas Eve!"

The duke's yacht sailed slowly away.

Kyler had seen these signs before they had left. He was not surprised either. Not really. It made perfect sense that Sean, when he did finally fall, would fall like a ten-ton brick from the sky.

Kyler shook his head. "Throw him over the side."

It took three more men to do it, and tense moments when one of Seanessy's arms came free and he punched Slops again, then Butcher squarely in the jaw, before they managed it. Loud curses sang until the moment he hit the water. He came up cursing still.

Butcher listened to this as he watched from the rail. "Now we've got some trouble."

Concern changed Kyler's eyes too, and he rubbed his hand over the smooth surface of his head. "And it's only the beginning."

Butcher still cursed Seanessy, up one side and down the other.

The afternoon sun began its grand descent as the *Wind Muse* anchored in the aqua-blue waters of the bay. A white sand beach stretched along the leeward side of the island. The mountain range fell away at the north end here. A township made of stucco cottages cluttered the seashore—the housing for the duke's formidable army. A belltower of a church rose above the Spanish tiled roofs. Yet all gazes were drawn to the preposterous jutting towers of a stone fortress and its manned battlements, all a tribute to the duke's grandiose posturing.

Seanessy half expected a crocodile-infested moat.

One long arm reached out above the frame of his door, and Seanessy braced, trying to grasp a small measure of control. Long enough to tell her.

After an hour or more of swearing, cursing, and denting two walls, Kyler's words finally began to penetrate. Kyler had heard the duke's explanation and now Seanessy had to hear it. That was all. Just hear it. Shalyn had to learn the truth also. It was after all her life; he was after all her husband.

Her bloody husband.

"Butcher ... My God, I just want ..." He closed his eyes, steeling himself against the violence, the rage of the idea that she was married. Married to that man. He tried to see his way through this disaster. "I just want to shoot the bastard and be done with it."

Butcher lost wind all at once. His hand spanned his forehead as if to encompass all he felt. "I know, Sean, I know," he said in a whisper of regret. "But we've got to figure this thing out. And Shalyn has to at least hear what he has to say to her. It might be the only thing that brings back her memory. For Shalyn, Sean."

Seanessy nodded, looking away. With compassion and concern, Butcher patted his back and left him there. Sean's fear stretched like rain clouds over a horizon, spreading in so many different directions he couldn't make sense of it, and because he couldn't make sense of it, he just wanted to shoot the man.

He finally opened the door and stepped inside. Shalyn still slept. A bath waited for her. The man who said he was her husband had also, oh so obsequiously, sent her a trunk of clothes.

Shalyn . . .

He came and sat on the edge of the bed. "Shalyn," he whispered to the still and quiet air of the room, wishing he was many miles from this island and its master, where the whole world had turned upside-down. "I never told you the real ending to the story of the shepherd and the lady. I wanted to keep it from you. You see, after the shepherd knew the bliss of her love, they finally encountered her father and friends at a Maying party. He tried to keep the sight from her but she was entranced because her memory returned as she watched. Then came a moment in which the shepherd lost his soul: the moment when she turned to see him. In her eyes, the story goes, there was no love, no tender feeling, not even sorrow. She looked at him, her true love, with . . . revulsion. Then she turned and ran into the clearing. She never looked back." He reached down to stroke her golden hair, spread out like a glorious sunrise on the pillows of his bed.

"Can you believe that sorry end, Shalyn? Of course the family was overjoyed to find her alive and well, after those many months of thinking her dead. And when the day of her wedding feast to a neighboring noble arrived, our cowardly shepherd flung himself to his death . . .

"I told you it was not a very good story," he continued distractedly as he sat there watching her sleep. "Surely if I were to create an ending to a story I could do better. The shepherd could just shoot the baron, the lady's father, before she even sees him. I mean who really cares about the father anyway? He no doubt deserved such an untimely death. Did I mention the baron was known to steal his neighbor's cows and cheat the King's tax collector?" he mused. "So she never does remember. Then the happy shepherd and his lady get married and go on to purchase a little white cottage with a little garden surrounded by a white picket fence at the seashore. Dover or perhaps Bath, where, of course, they live happily ever after."

Instead of feeling comforted by his new tale, Seanessy felt a constriction in his chest. He saw with sudden clarity that this little white cottage was another kind of death. At least for him. Aye, he was mad in love with Shalyn. He supposed he would have to commission someone to build that cottage. For her. He might even be happy there for a while, but not in the long run. It had to do with being a man, with needing to stretch the reach of his arms; it had to do with his love for adventure.

Yet he would do anything to keep her happy. Anything. If this cottage of domestic bliss was her ticket, he would purchase it for her.

Shalyn stirred in her sleep and he saw she was dreaming. He sat on the edge of the bed, wondering at how beautiful she was, and how little that mattered now. For his desire might be directed to the package but his heart lifted with nothing more than the sound of her name. Shalyn.

Shalyn. Look what you've done to me . . .

In her dreams, Seanessy shouted for help. Someone was tying her hands. She struggled fiercely with all her strength, desperate to save him, but she couldn't get free. "Seanessy! Seanessy!" She couldn't help him. Dark shadows lifted the shovels, lifted and returned, lifted and returned, digging the hole that would be Seanessy's living grave, and he knew it. He was afraid ...

"Seanessy!"

Her eyes started moving more frantically beneath the closed lids and she tossed and turned. The thin sheet gathered at her waist and revealed her nudity. His arousal was quick and while his desire rose brighter and higher each time he had her, he began to sense the magnitude of it. The magnitude of this disaster.

The sound of his name, the anxiety marring her lovely face, told him it was a nightmare. His hands came to her, and he lifted her into his arms.

"Shalyn, Shalyn, I have you. I have you. It was just a nightmare."

"Seanessy!" Her arms reached around his neck and clung tightly.

He closed his eyes and savored the feel of her slender form against him.

"Seanessy. It was about you. I dreamed you were going to be buried alive and it was just shadows, and you couldn't fight them. Someone had tied my hands to make me watch and—"

"Shh. It's over. It's over ..."

The soft words eased her from the darkness. She closed her eyes tight. "Don't let me go."

"Never, Shalyn. Never."

The nightmare disappeared as if it never was, replaced by a rush of heady memories of their night of passion, one after another washing over her in heated waves. Oh, mercy. Oh, Seanessy. She felt suddenly dizzy as she thought of what he had done, what he had said and made her say in the heat of it, and he wouldn't stop, and she ...

The blush went from the balls of her feet to the top of her head. The force, intimacy, splendor of his passion was a thing of wonder and marvel and—

She squirmed upon feeling a soreness there, the squirm bringing a sticky moisture between her legs. She gasped in a whisper, "I am all sticky and sore! I can still feel you inside me!"

She felt the soft bounce of his chest against her. She tried to pull back to look into his face. "No, Shalyn," he said softly, with feeling, keeping her close. "Just let me hold you a moment."

She gave herself over to the comfort and feel of his arms. She felt so ... so satiated and warm. So deliciously intoxicated. Warmed from the inside out.

And also: "I am starved! Does making love make everyone so famished? I feel as if I haven't eaten in a week of Sundays, and, oh, Seanessy, the thought of one more bowl of Slops's poison—oh! How I long for a piece of fresh fruit and warm soft bread straight from the oven, smothered in strawberry jam or marmalade. Why," she said, noticing for the first time, "you're all wet."

"Aye. The mutinous bastards that make up my crew tossed me seaside three times."

She pulled back her own laughter, but sobered quickly. She stiffened, looking around the room with alarm as the stilled motion of the ship penetrated her sleep-drugged and happy senses. "Why, we have stopped!"

"Aye. We are at the Duke de la Armanac's Isle of Blue Caverns." A hand reached her face, his touch infinitely gentle as he waited for a reaction to this. She had none. She understood simply that they would be docked at this way-station for as much as a month before they sailed on to Malacca where she could begin her search for what had happened to her.

"Shalyn, I have to tell you something."

The alarmed expression on his face instantly subdued her. If she didn't know better she'd swear he was afraid. "Seanessy, you look frightened by something?"

"Aye," he said, his hand brushing her hot cheek. "I am afraid."

She searched the handsome face. His alarm told her it would be painful. Her mind produced the terrifying idea somehow that he would be saying it was a mistake, that he hadn't meant to, but the pain and the opium was . . . "No, Seanessy. You would not hurt me now."

"Nay, Shalyn. Nay. Something has happened."

"What? 'Tis bad news—"

"Aye. You see, Kyler was waiting for the ship—"

"Kyler? But—"

"Aye, they left London a full three days after us but beat us by four days. They have been waiting. You see, Shalyn . . ." His hand left her cheek to smooth back the tousled mass of hair, then lingered on the side of her head where once there had been a bump, as he searched for the right words. "Shalyn, Kyler has found your past, and, dear God, girl, it's, ah"—a telling brow rose—"difficult to believe."

The words repeated in her mind three times before she understood what he had just said. Her hands went numb, her heart skipped a beat. She swallowed. "Seanessy!" His name sounded in a frightened plea.

"You are a married lady, Shalyn."

He waited for the statement to sink in. She searched his eyes frantically. "Married . . . me?"

"Shalyn, you know him. Your name, Shalyn, is Isabel Marie de la Armanac."

It took a full minute for her dazed mind to grasp what was happening to her and then only to realize it couldn't be happening. It just couldn't! It made no sense. "The Duke de la Armanac? Married . . . to me? No!" She came off his lap, one hand holding the sheet to her nakedness, the other hand rubbing her forehead hard. "No! 'Tis not true! How can that be true? The Duke de la Armanac!"

"The man is waiting to speak to you."

"I don't believe you!" She realized it as she said it. The Duke de la Armanac! 'Twas preposterous! "How can it be? How could I be married to him? To him! Don't you think I would have remembered when I saw him? Don't you think I would have felt something ... something? I ... I ..."

He stepped to her, one hand holding her up as his other hand forced the palm away from her forehead. "I don't know, Shalyn." Then: "What did you feel when you saw him?"

"Nothing! Nothing! I felt nothing! I had never seen him before; he was a perfect stranger."

"Could he be the source of your fear?"

She searched his handsome face. Her fear. Where did it come from? It came from something she had suffered here in the China Seas ...

"I don't remember! I don't know him! He is a stranger to me. He is lying, or mistaken, somehow. I know it's not true—"

"He told Kyler that you and he had traveled together from the Isle of Blue Caverns to London. He walked into your suite and you were gone. No clothes were taken. No jewels. Nothing. He says you suffer from terrible night terrors that often take you out of your room into the dark dead of night."

He himself had witnessed them. He had seen her curled up in a ball in a closet, and more frightened than a man could know. She had not been asleep but neither had she been awake. Night terrors. Madness.

"He said he was frantic, crazed with worry. An army of men were out looking for you, and only later did he discover that two of his men had found you in the street. He says you fought them, and as they tried to subdue you, one of them hit you on the head.

They thought they had killed you. They were terrified of the consequence and disappeared, leaving you lying on the street naked like that. Well, in a chemise. His men finally found one of the two culprits, who told this tale. I asked why these men didn't snatch the ruby star. He seemed surprised to hear of it. He could only suppose they never saw it."

Her thoughts raced over this story. "If this is true then why was your name on the paper in my hand?"

"A good question. I don't know. Neither apparently does he. He was surprised to hear of it. Anyway, he says he has been searching for you all this time. He did not discover your whereabouts until after we had left. He says he has no idea what happened to you after that, or how you came to have my name and address in your hand."

Kyler had also said he had never seen a man act out more self-reproach upon learning that she had been beaten and dropped on a stranger's doorstep, but he would not tell her that. Besides, this wasn't even the best part of the story, but he'd let her assimilate this information before going into the murky cesspool of the rest. He'd let the duke explain the balance! He could hardly wait to hear it himself.

He closed his eyes, not understanding what was happening to him, all the violence he felt. He released her arm all at once and turned his back to her, fighting for and finally winning some measure of control.

"He is, Kyler says, quite desperate to see you. He sent a note requesting your compassion and mercy, which he knows is great. He wants to see you, talk with you. He is quite certain your memory will return once you are reunited, which I too hope for."

Shalyn closed her eyes and rubbed her forehead, desperate to remember something, anything, one thing that might let her believe she had been married to the Duke de la Armanac. The Duke de la Armanac! How strange. She did not know the man's Christian name, and yet a picture-perfect image of the duke rose in her mind. As clear as if he stood before her right now. Yet 'twas a stranger's face she saw.

"I do not know him, Seanessy. I do not know how he could have been my ... husband and I could not know him." She felt dizzy. Her vision blurred, and from somewhere far away she heard herself say, "Seanessy. Oh, Seanessy. Help me now ..."

He was at her side in the instant. She felt his arms sweep her off her feet and carry her back to the bed. He sat down, holding gently as she suddenly was crying. "Seanessy, what am I to do? I don't want to be married! What am I to do?"

In the end there was only one thing to do.

They had to listen to his story.

The sun sat just above the horizon over the violet waters of the calm bay. The men gathered on deck, waiting on Seanessy, talking among themselves, mostly about the battle ahead. There was no doubt there would be a battle. Sean had been forthright and blunt in the message he sent to the duke: if the duke wanted to see Shalyn, he was to come aboard the *Wind Muse* at sunset.

Seanessy would take no chances.

Seanessy called his men to gather on deck and as he waited, he looked across the waters to the last sunlight upon the jutting towers of the duke's castle. He scoffed meanly, "Don't you wish ..."

"So," he began when all his men had gathered around him. "We will not debark until the matter is settled."

Butcher wondered out loud, "And how does a

man settle the fact that he's mad in love with another man's wife?"

Seanessy cocked and readied his pistole, returning it to his shoulder harness. "Why, with murder, no less."

The men roared approval, and Oly howled at the roar, for no one had any doubt of who the villain was in this story. Seanessy's grin looked every bit as menacing as his words. His long hair fell over his shoulders and he wore the pistoles over a white washed vest, a black belt, white pants, and tall black boots.

"All right, you know what has to be done. We are going to blow up the opium stockpile. Knolls, Hanson, and Cherry Joe are in charge of the goods. You will number forty-five. Two pistoles for each of you, two shots each pistole, a hundred and eighty or so shots all together. If only half of these are well-aimed, we can take out a guard of one hundred and fifty and more if you count on my luck." He replaced the other pistole. "I would be surprised if the warehouse has a guard over twenty. Any questions?"

"Sean," Kyler said, motioning, "I want to take out the cannon fire too—they could reach us if they tried. I already have a bad case of island fever," he explained, "and I've only been here a couple of days. I'd hate to be stuck in the place."

"Aye, aye," a number of the men said.

Kyler was right, he saw. "Very well." Seanessy sighed. "That's a two-man job. Two men and a hefty bag of rocks going against a standing army of two thousand. Who's got the grit for that?"

Seanessy's gaze swept the crowd as the men exchanged glances. An argument followed on who should go. Finally Toothless's cagey voice rose above the others, "Ye should go, Edward!"

"Me?" Edward questioned.

"Aye." Toothless nodded, as if in agreement with

himself. "Why, yer nerves are as smooth as the King's breakfast cream. And I don't know a braver soul—"

"Oh, why not?" Edward said with a shrug, "I don't mind walking among two thousand armed men. Especially if I live to tell about it. And with that in mind"—his gaze turned to the old man—"I want to take the slyest, craftiest, most devious bastard on board with me."

Naturally everyone turned to stare at Toothless. The older man swore softly, viciously, before saying, "Well, I would go with ye now but me shoulder's givin' me pain, the cursed arthritis, you see, and I don't figure I could be liftin' bags of rocks very far."

"Arthritis?" Slops questioned, appearing quite concerned to hear the complaint. "Ah, ye poor sod. Now which shoulder do ye feel the pain in?"

"This one here," Toothless said.

Slops's fist slammed into the shoulder, throwing Toothless back a step with a howl of pain. "There now," the huge man said. "I'd wager the arthritis pain is a distant memory."

So the matter was decided. The men turned to the important matter of determining the odds of their success and then placing wagers. Seanessy listened to this, becoming increasingly irritated as he did, then quite put out when the odds finally settled at fifty-fifty. "Have I ever lost yet?"

The men took the important fact into consideration. The odds were adjusted. Seanessy was pleased with the outcome. He turned back to his quarters, opening the door and stepping inside. The door shut quietly behind him. He stared in silence.

Shalyn was fixing her hair, which was hard with the way her hands trembled so. She was so frightened! Frightened of what he would say to her, this man who was her husband. How would he explain

how she came to be dropped beaten and battered on
Seanessy's doorstep? How would he explain the virgin star, her dread of ropes, and her certainty of being killed if she were ever caught?

Why, dear Lord, was she so afraid?

She stuck one pin in, than another. She abruptly
became aware of his presence. She looked up and
suffered a moment of bewilderment upon meeting
his stare; her mind was so fixed on the evening
ahead.

"Do I look that changed to you, Seanessy?"

"Aye . . ."

The confirmation sounded in a husky nod. She indeed looked changed. The thick mass of gold hair
made a loose crown atop her head. She wore an old-
fashioned gown in the classical style of the French
Napoleonic court, many years out of date, and that
was odd and disconcerting. He was used to seeing
her in his own clothes. This was an empire gown of
delicate violet and green flowers on whitened China
silk, the most expensive silk, and so fine it shimmered as she moved. He had made a fortune importing shiploads of the fine cloth to England two years
ago; he knew it well. The short sleeves and neckline
were modest and he was glad for the favor—the last
thing he needed was a little more temptation from
the girl. A violet ribbon gathered tight beneath the
ample swell of her breasts to drop to the floor in a
small trail. He had never seen her in feminine attire;
he had never even imagined the scene.

Gone was the barefoot girl in breeches. Here was a
young lady who seemed at once beautiful and as delicate and fragile as a dandelion on a breeze. Her appearance of extreme fragility played a curious tune
against his masculinity, and why it bothered him he
could not say, past that it did. The startling change
registered with alarm in his mind.

She reached a hand to the virgin star on her neck, anxiously, unnerved by the way he stared. She tried to break the spell. She bent over the trunk to retrieve the long white silk gloves. " 'Tis too warm, I think, for these gloves, or a shawl. This dress too—I wonder what he will think—"

His gaze narrowed, "You wonder what he will think?"

Startled eyes shot up to him. Her own words penetrated her anxious mind and brought a pained moment of horror. She had been about to make a jest of being a duchess, the wife of a duke, hoping to relieve her tension and fear a bit. The fear only increased as Seanessy came quickly to her side. A hand snaked around her arm to lift her up. "Just who the hell did you dress for, Shalyn?"

He heard her startled gasp, her sharp intake of breath, then watched the outrage filling the lovely amber eyes. Outrage changed to red-faced fury. "How dare you!"

She slapped his face.

"Huh!" His eyes narrowed; his temper rose. "Oh, please—the banalities of a how-dare-you and a hand slap! Is that the best we can do now, child? Has our dear duke reduced us to simpering sighs, practiced faints, and a pretty silk dress—"

This was too much!

Cobra fingers shot a well-aimed and powerful blow to his esophagus, doubling him over in the instant. His arms reached to tackle her but she circled out with a lift of her knee into his groin. His painful grunt sounded much louder than the slight rip of her dress across the line of the bodice. With effort he managed to lift his head up to see her.

She sighed softly and smiled prettily. "Is that more to your liking, Seanessy?"

Softly, slowly, he said, "I'm going to kill you, Shalyn."

A very real shriek sounded as she spun around and ran for her life. Kyler was shouting at the men securing the cannons with bowline knots as he too had begun loading and cocking his pistoles. The sun had set; the duke would be here soon. Everything was readied—

A beautiful young woman, barely recognizable, raced out of the captain's quarters and dashed across the deck of the ship. The waiting men turned to see a streak of silk and heard Sean's low and vicious curses. Seanessy caught her at the galley steps, lifting her into the air as he tossed her on his shoulder to carry her back inside, swearing all the way. Oly barked at this fun, more when the girl literally flipped off his back and landed catlike on the ground, facing Seanessy.

Kyler sighed. The other men whistled with manly appreciation for the acrobatic and admirable escape. Sean wiped his chin before he looked up to see her there. She was breathing hard and fast, her eyes alive with excitement, with the determination to make him regret every word he'd said.

Desire struck as he stood there, so hard he went weak with it. His arm snaked out and grabbed hold of her skirt. She swung around but the skirt ripped more. Seanessy chuckled with the mistaken idea that she was doomed and thereby missed another turn of the girl's feet as she raised her knee and swung her leg high in the air to hit his face with the hard edge of her heel, a punishing blow that brought another round of applause.

Butcher clapped and hooted with the rest of the men.

Seanessy was chuckling, a low animallike sound

that raised the hairs on the back of her neck. "Give it up, Shalyn, I warn you now—"

"Never!"

She managed to land another blow before he threw her bodily over his shoulders and secured her there long enough to get her back to his quarters. The door shut. He crossed the space, threw her on to the bed, and pinned her there.

A wild kind of excitement shone in her eyes as she squirmed beneath his weight. The movement shot a hot rush of warmth between her legs. All the exertion of the fight changed to something else, something that warmed her blood and sweetened every breath drawn into her body.

Still it just wasn't fair. "Loose me! Loose—"

He struggled up from the onslaught of sensations coursing through him, long enough to wonder how quickly he could come out of his clothes, then he managed to respond. "Why should I?"

"Because I won the fight fair and square!"

"I believe I am the one on top!"

"Well ..." She grasped the truth of this. "Maybe, but for no more reason than brute force!"

"Which is good enough for me, Shalyn. Good?" he questioned and then chuckled, "Did I say good, Shalyn?" His darkening gaze left the curve of her mouth to travel to the swells of her breasts pushing against the silk fabric of her still intact bodice. He reached a hand to encompass the tempting peak, teasing her through the cloth. His voice changed, deepening, as she arched her back and bit her lip. He wondered again how quickly he could come out of his clothes. "Such a forceless word. I did not mean it. Not when I'm describing something so grand as to land me over this slim body of yours," he said, even as he gathered up the silk skirt to bring it to her hips, gathering her tighter against the hot waiting part of him.

Her hands quickly undid his buttons and she was pulling off his cumbersome shoulder harness. He helped the effort. This was tossed to the floor. He was kicking off his boots, then his pants, when abruptly she was struck with a sudden realization. She reached to brace against his shoulders. "Why, you provoked me on purpose! So I wouldn't be so afraid!"

"Shalyn," he said, looking up into her darkening eyes, feeling the thrilling drive of his pulse as he kissed her once, then again, "I am so glad to be of service. And I wish I were that clever and certainly that noble, but the truth is, my purpose in provoking you was far more, well, let's just say base."

"I might have guessed," she said as he ripped the remaining bodice of what moments ago had been a gown, then pulled the thin straps of the chemise from her shoulders to bare her nudity. He brushed aside the virgin star before his lips found the coral tip of the tempting peak.

"Seanessy," she said, the excitement pounding hotly through her limbs, more as his mouth drew warm circles there, and her last coherent words were, "perhaps the next time you mean to part me from my clothing, you could simply put a hand to the buttons. I'm sure it will save you a fortune in gowns . . ."

His laughter caused sparks of pleasure through her. "Shalyn, if you wanted a more conventional type you should have thought of it before you landed on my doorstep . . ."

Chapter 13

Kyler finally spotted the longshore boat moving slowly toward the ship. It appeared much like an Italian gondolier with its gold lamp swinging eerily across the darkened waters. "All right. Here he comes."

The frantic knock on the door told Seanessy his time was up. Every inch of her skin, every nerve and fiber of her being felt stroked, aroused, fanned, and finally rocked with a violent pleasure that sent her swirling into blackness, only to return to feel the pleasure seizing him.

As his sense returned and collected and he gathered her love-soaked body against his, he said, "Now as the man spins the tale he says is your life, you'll have a bit of me inside you to remind you of to whom you belong and where you'll always be. Shalyn, I love you . . ."

"Forever?"

"Aye, forever . . ."

Emotions shimmered in her eyes, and when he sealed this promise with another kiss, she met his lips with her own undying passion, passion he felt rocking his soul . . .

Seanessy slowly fitted his shoulder harness back into place before turning to help her into a pink silk dress she drew out of the duke's trunk. Like the other one, this too was many years out of fashion. The shimmering pale silk slipped over her, fitting perfectly. He started to do the buttons while she tried to work her hair back up. The virgin star still sat on her back, but he was staring at the bodice as he tied the ribbon behind her. The five inches of material barely covered the tempting lift of her breast. If one stared and he was, one could view the small mark.

It was such an odd design. Not a decorative mark . . .

He brushed the virgin star back around to her front. The heavy jewel swung around her neck to rest just above the cleavage. The heavy gold chain sliced the mark in two.

He wondered how the duke would explain that . . .

From outside he heard the duke and his men climbing aboard. He saw the beat of her pulse at the nape of her neck. He lightly brushed his lips over the spot. A delicious shiver like an aftershock raced down her spine. She turned to him.

"Are you much afraid?"

"Of what I will hear? Aye. Of what will happen to me? Nay. Not with you, Seanessy."

Grinning at this, pleased, he kissed her lips before taking her hand. "Come, my dear. Let me introduce you to your husband."

They emerged on deck hand in hand. The ship was well lit. Oly was tied up and mad about it, barking like all get out. She first saw the duke's back silhouetted against the darkened sky. The same bearing that had seemed majestic, regal in London now looked only, well . . . hot. He wore an expensive cape over formal black dress clothes, as did all the men with him. They were all formally dressed in the tropical heat.

Not so Seanessy's men. The crew wore belted cotton breeches, these cut off at the knees, and most were bare-chested, though many, like Seanessy, sported shoulder harnesses. Nearly all were barefoot or wearing those Indian moccasins his men favored.

All she could think those few moments she stared at the duke was that she did not know him. He was a stranger! How could she possibly have been married to him?

Kyler had been engaging the duke as best he could with information about the ship's outfitting, but the duke showed signs of increasing discomfort as he was made to wait and wait some more. The silence alerted him first, then Kyler motioned with his head.

The duke turned and beheld her. "Isabel!"

The nobleman rushed toward her, and before she could think of what to do, his arms came around her. She stiffened, the familiar scent of his tobacco crashing with dizzying familiarity into her mind as she started to take a step back.

Too late. Seanessy's pistole dug hard into the man's back. "The next time you touch her will be your last."

An unnerving quiet followed, the silence scaring even Oly, who crouched on his haunches and looked about with alert animal eyes. The gentle lapping of the sea alongside the ship sounded loud against the quieter cocking of pistoles. More than one pistole followed Seanessy's to the four men who had accompanied the duke.

"Shalyn."

Her name was a command. She stepped to Seanessy's side. The duke watched this with a lift of brow before, in French, he commanded his men to stand at ease. Reluctantly they lowered their pistoles. The duke turned to face Seanessy, though his eyes never left Shalyn.

Cherry Joe let Oly loose.

"We have an extraordinary situation between us Captain." The duke spoke slowly, cautiously, and yet his voice held the imperial air of authority. "If you can just imagine these last months of my worry, of my certainty that Isabel had died or worse, then perhaps you would see your—"

Oly sniffed the duke, nuzzling his crotch with a wet nose. The men chuckled as the duke backed up. "Will you get this damn dog away from me!"

Oly barked and went to stand next to Seanessy.

The duke straightened, attempting to recapture his bruised dignity. "Perhaps you would allow me this moment of unimaginable joy upon seeing her here—"

"As I said," Seanessy smoothly interrupted, granting the man no measure, "the next time you touch her will be your last." His grin did not reach his eyes. "I just want this one point perfectly clear."

The duke's face remained expressionless, though his eyes blazed with emotion. Shalyn watched as this emotion disappeared and he seemed to relax suddenly, as if accepting Seanessy's ultimatum. She breathed a sigh of relief. Until his hand reached up to smooth the fine point of his goatee and his fine dark eyes narrowed just a bit. She realized he saw it as a challenge.

Shalyn could hardly believe this man was her husband! He seemed so strange to her! The only thing familiar about him was the scent of his tobacco and the fear he inspired. The way he stared! Dear Lord, 'twas much worse than anything she had imagined. An old English nursery rhyme sounded in her mind: *I do not like thee, Doctor Fell,/ the reason why I cannot tell;/ But this I know, and know full well,/ I do not like thee, Doctor Fell* . . .

"Isabel." He beckoned to her, willfully ignoring Seanessy now. "Monsieur Kyler has told me you do not remember our life together after suffering the tragic head injury that stole your memory. I can hardly believe it! Do you remember nothing?"

"I do not know you!" She slowly shook her head. "I saw you in London that night with Seanessy. I would have sworn 'twas the first time I had ever seen you. I remember my life up until my mother and her sad death, then Ti Yao and Gschu, no more."

"Your father, Isabel? Do you remember nothing of your father?"

"Of my father, I remember ... little. I do not even remember his surname. And you, sir, are a stranger to me."

The last words were not without impact. "I can hardly believe it! Isabel, how can you have forgotten our marriage, and our subsequent life here on the island? I was so hoping that seeing me again would spark your memory."

"Ah, well." Seanessy shrugged. "Beggar's luck."

Amazingly undaunted, the duke dismissed this with nothing more than irritation, his every movement and manner composed and authoritative. He swung off his cape, causing one of his men to leap forward to take it. "I have consulted with three doctors on the subject," he told her, continuing. "The very best doctors. Each one offered only the possibility that you would remember me, our marriage, and our life again. There is a chance you never will remember." With emotion he said, "How this fear strikes at my heart!" He turned to Seanessy and said, "Just as surely as the fear that you will remember must strike at the captain's."

Seanessy groaned, "Oh, please!" He rolled his eyes as he spun the pistole around a finger with an ease and nonchalance that startled. "Spare me these theatrics, all this drama. I am not half as afraid she will remember your marriage as you might think I am. As a matter of fact . . ." He stopped the pistole, its barrel aimed straight at the duke's head, and he smiled. "I am anxious as all hell to discover the missing pieces of the puzzle made of Shalyn's life." He motioned with the pistole toward his quarters. "Shall we? Or would you care for a wider theater audience?"

The duke stared, for a long moment he stared, letting the silence stretch as he considered his nemesis. Yet he had no choice. He had to endure the captain's baiting if he were to talk to Isabel, if he had any chance with her at all.

Seanessy opened the door.

The duke passed quick orders to his men before following Butcher, Kyler, and Shalyn inside. His fine dark gaze surveyed the room with dispassion, and yet he refused to hide his disdain for the sheer size and unconventionality of what he saw. The captain's quarters on most ships of this size comprised three, sometimes even four rooms—sleeping and dressing apartment, navigation room, and dining room—all of which connected by hall to the galley and mess hall. Not so here. The room was isolated from the rest of the ship. A tapestry added color to the polished wood walls where the captain dined, dressed, and slept all in one room.

Seanessy watched as the duke's gaze came uneasily to the bed and to Shalyn's trunk near—before he turned to see Butcher guide Shalyn to the cushion of pillows set around the table. Kyler sat on Shalyn's other side.

Seanessy stood over the party, as the orchestrator of the proceeding. The duke was staring hard. Shalyn's hand nervously toyed with the virgin star. Seanessy followed his gaze. "Ah, the virgin star. One of the few things Shalyn owned before she was dropped on my doorstep."

"It was my wedding gift," he said. "Once upon a time my grandmother's."

"A grand duchess with a fondness for uncut rocks? Well, I suppose I've heard of stranger things," Seanessy said as he motioned to the low-lying table, surrounded by colorful embroidered pillows. "I am quite certain I will be hearing of stranger things."

Butcher at least was fascinated with the man's steely, lordly character. He had never before met anyone who could remain composed when being struck by the well-aimed barbs of Sean's antipathy. No one. Not even the King. Yet here he was sitting at the low table, acting as if Sean weren't standing over him waiting for the excuse to start shooting.

"Well," Butcher said, "let's get on with it. Let's hear this fabulous story."

The duke withdrew one of his cigars as Prescott entered with a tray of port. "Really, Captain," he said as he hit the tip of the cigar on the table to pack its tobacco. "I do not understand why you refused the extension of my hospitality after such a long voyage—"

"Not such a long voyage," Seanessy said, adding meaningfully as his gaze found Shalyn, "I rather enjoyed it. As to why I did not feel inclined to accept your hospitality, well"—he grinned, a smile that did not touch his eyes—"I do not trust you. Not as far as I can spit."

"So I see," the duke replied, and even offered a slight smile as he stared at the two men on either side of Shalyn. He turned to Seanessy. "You seem to think I've already lost, Captain, but you are wrong. Once Isabel's memories return she will come back. To me."

Shalyn's gaze met the duke's. She felt her already hot cheeks flush more. They way he stared at her! Penetrating, unnerving, as if ... as if he owned her.

Not at all like Seanessy's brassy stares, stares that were so boldly, unashamedly full of lust.

Butcher slipped his hand in Shalyn's, who could hardly hear, her heart pounded so loudly. Mercy—

She clutched Butcher's hand tightly, as if it were a lifeline. Prescott set crystal goblets full of a sweet port on the table. He was still smiling as he had just seen an amusing scene: Toothless, that sly devil, was speaking surprisingly silky French as he treated the duke's men to a special concoction he had worked up. Once done, Prescott left the room. Seanessy was not drinking, standing above the table, as watchful as a mother cat.

" . . . *no sluttish inebriation in my house!*"

The words echoed in Shalyn's mind as she studied the duke. 'Twas his voice! She had been in his house. The words repeated in her mind, pricking her anger. She reached her hand around her glass. She lifted it to her lips, drained it, and set it down, watching his response.

Dark brows drew together with alarm. The duke tried to hide his horror and said instead, "But I understand you, Captain. You have good reason not to trust me. In truth, I do not know how far I would go to have Isabel returned to me as she left, a loving and very much loved wife."

Shalyn drew a sharp breath and released it all at once. This whole thing was like a nightmare. There was something wrong here, something wrong with him. Her heart pounded so loud—

"So!" Seanessy said in that way he had, the way that caught everyone's attention like a clap of thunder before he directed them to his agenda. "Now let us start at the beginning. Where did you meet Shalyn?"

"I met your father first, Isabel. He was a first officer, a skilled surgeon aboard the *King Edward*. He was also long ago my friend." The duke spoke directly to her, ignoring Seanessy.

Seanessy abruptly straightened. This was not what he had been expecting. Kyler had made no mention of a liaison with Shalyn's father. One look at Kyler's face told him this was the first time Kyler had heard about it as well.

"We met during the bloodbath in Trafalgar that ended Napoleonic, and of course French, domination—the bloodiest battle the world has ever seen. I served my nation as an admiral on board the *Sovereign Prince*." With a hint of bitterness, he said, "Three British men-of-war blew the ship to hell. I and a handful of my men were sifting through the debris in a lifeboat, searching for survivors, all the while trying to row to a French camp set up on the Moroccan coast. Most of my men were suffering terrible injuries. At last we came across your father, Isabel, First Officer Henry Slakes—"

"Slakes?" The name sounded strange on her tongue; she did not remember this as her name. "My father's name was Henry Slakes?"

"Yes," the duke replied, his mind on his story, quite forgetting the cigar in his hand.

"He was drifting on a mast—it was all that was left of his ship. Because he wore the British colors, one of my men removed his pistole, meaning to shoot him. It was obvious to me that there had been enough killing, that the great war was over, the very course of history forever changed. One more death—nay, a hundred more deaths—would not change the fact, and so I stopped him. My foresight was returned twofold when at last we reached the camp. Your father saw no nationalities in the men he treated and, God knows, there were hundreds of wounded and dying at this camp. He alone was responsible for saving dozens of lives. Dozens, Isabel," he repeated with feeling. "I assisted him through these long months, months where our friendship grew. Throughout it all he never spoke of his family, or of anything personal. I suppose I thought he was a bachelor." He shook his head distractedly. "Still I came to know your father through his actions. And he was one of the noblest men it has ever been my fortune to know."

This story of her father held Shalyn spellbound. Her eyes were wide and luminous as she leaned forward, a delicate hand toying absently with the gold star around her neck. "What happened then?"

"A terrible dysentery swept through the camp. Many lives were lost. I am sorry to tell you one of them was your father."

Emotion shimmered in Shalyn's dark eyes before finally, as if too heavily laden with feeling, she lowered them.

"I held him in my arms as he died, and it was then that he told me about you, his daughter Isabel. Apparently before the war he was stationed at the British outpost at Penang, then Malacca. You remember your mother's death?"

Shalyn nodded.

"He told me how your mother died in that accident, and the worst part, how only now, as he faced the certainty of his death, could he confront his unconscionable neglect of you, his daughter. His only excuse was that after his wife died he couldn't bare the . . ." The duke sighed. "Well, he had left you in the care of a heathen—"

"Ti Yao," she supplied.

"Yes, this man Ti Yao and his mistress, a woman—"

"Gschu," she supplied.

"So you do remember them?"

"I loved them both very dearly!"

"Yes, you always thought of them so kindly. Apparently you had grown very attached to them." He conveyed his dismissal of this affection, as if Ti Yao and Gschu were the rare servant one occasionally found oneself attached to. "I never met them, of course."

"What became of Ti Yao? Do you know?"

The silence stretched with the question. Seanessy came to stand behind Shalyn, afraid for her of what he would say. Butcher too squeezed her hand to show support. The duke rose and crossed the room to the lamps where he removed the glass chimney and lit his cigar.

Smoke filled the space around him. "I am quite certain, Isabel, that some things I will tell you will be a shock. Suffice to say, I never understood what compelled these Orientals to care for a young English girl, despite all the money your father paid to them. The woman had died when we finally reached that fishing village, hoping to question her. The man Ti Yao is dead, I believe. He was known to disappear for many months; you told me this part. The last time he never came back. For you I sent a number of agents through the Canton province of China, searching for this man Ti Yao. He was never found."

Shalyn closed her eyes. Seanessy stepped behind her, his hands coming to her shoulders. She grabbed his hand tightly for support. "Somehow I knew he was among the living no more ..." she said. As if she kept the tragedy close to her heart, weeping over the secrecy of her loneliness. Aye, she had been so lonely and ... and trapped. The feelings came back to her, all the fear and dread and certainty of doom ...

"This upsets you," the duke saw. "And yet, Isabel, I have not said the worst. You have never been very strong, Isabel ..."

"I haven't?"

He shook his head. "Your feminine constitution. Indeed precious few of your sex could survive what you've been put through. You see, my agents finally found you in a house of an illustrious sultan of the Jahore province, a man named Yam Tuan something," he waved his hand in dismissal. "Munda, I believe. Something like that. Anyway, you were kept in the"—he appeared to have to force the words out—"women's quarters, with his wives and concubines. And there you suffered unconscionable abuse."

Thin dark brows arched. "I was in, in a harem?"

"I pray you never remember this part of your life. The sultan claimed he bought you from this woman Gschu you care so much for."

"She never!" Shalyn shook her head, sending an errant strand swinging down past her shoulders. "She wouldn't—"

"I don't know why he would lie about it," the duke interrupted her protest, then quickly conceded, "I suppose he could have had you snatched away from her kindness, kidnapped if you will. Or perhaps he stole you after her death. In any case, the whole sordid story illustrates the consequences of trusting the dark-skinned heathens, especially with our women."

Shalyn tried desperately to remember. Yet she couldn't. The silence gathered and grew, broken at last by Seanessy.

"So," he said, his voice curiously devoid of emotion, "then you found Isabel and shipped her off to your island. You never could find her English relations, I'm told, though you did try."

"Yes, for a number of years. My agents found no trace of them. We ... grew close as the time passed. Against conventional dictates of my nobility and station in life, I finally had to face the fact that I wanted to marry you."

"You were married," Seanessy repeated.

"Yes. We were married."

"And so how is it Shalyn was a virgin after so many years of not just marriage, but of living in this sultan's . . . harem?"

The duke stared at Seanessy for a long moment before at last he appeared to lose his phenomenal fortitude of composure. He looked away as he shut his eyes tight as if to steel himself against the previously unmentioned reality, as if he had known but had nourished the hope that perhaps it wasn't true.

His fist curled into a tight ball as he answered slowly, heatedly, "You are so irrepressibly bold, Captain Seanessy, tossing your unholy liaison with my wife in my face like that, the idea that she was in fact a virgin. If I were armed I would shoot you."

"Well! Just my luck!" Seanessy said. "Now would you answer that question. Really. I am on the edge of my seat as they say."

The silence stretched and with it the duke's obvious discomfort. He swallowed his port whole. Finally, in a voice made tight with all the control he placed on it: "As I said, Isabel had been badly used at this, ah, sultan's harem. I'm sure you have seen how she is . . . unusually qualified to defend herself—the unfortunate legacy of this other heathen, Ti Yao. After suffering more than one blow, the sultan threatened her, not with her own life, for it was quite clear she would gladly die before suffering his abuse, but rather he threatened to kill other women, even innocent children if she did not comply. Compliance meant being first tattooed, a mark that is recognized as meaning his, ah, property throughout much of the China Seas and then . . ." His pause filled with the drama of Isabel's torture. "He tied Isabel up, for he had learned to take no chances with her." In a whisper that only hinted at his rage, he finished, "He apparently suffered a number of ailments; among them drunkenness. You can imagine the awful rest.

"The effects were naturally devastating to her constitution," he continued after a thoughtful moment. "She could not suffer a man's touch; it frightened her. Any approach on my part gave her night terrors when she'd wake in the middle of the night, not knowing where she was or who was with her, more scared than you can imagine. Of course I hoped that with time, and the blessing of love, I could eventually win her affections . . .

"So there it is," the duke finished quietly, drawing on his cigar. "The whole story."

For one of the few times in Seanessy's life, he had been rendered quite hopelessly speechless. He started to speak but then turned away, changing his mind. Butcher and Kyler sat in a similar silence. Kyler stared up at the boards on the ceiling, while Butcher thoughtfully considered his hand spread over the table, then studied the duke as he drew on his cigar, finally watching Shalyn closely through a thick cloud of smoke and slightly lowered lids.

A chill raced up her spine. She swallowed, forcing herself still and unmoving, as she waited for someone to say something, anything, but it seemed, as with Seanessy, that the story of her life struck each one of the men quite hopelessly mute.

"I don't remember any of it," she said softly.

"None of it, darling?" Seanessy managed to inquire.

"Truly. None."

Finally the duke said, "There appears little left to say past that I will pray you accept an invitation to view our home—your home, Isabel. Since I have not helped to spur your memory, my only, my last hope is that moving through your rooms, the castle, and your garden will restore your past.

"Would you do that much for me at least?"

She had no idea. "Will I, Seanessy?" she asked.

"Why not?" Seanessy asked. "Needless to say, I share your own interest in sparking her memory."

"Excellent," the duke said. "I will send a boat for you in the morning."

He bowed ever so slightly before withdrawing. The door shut. Still no one moved as they listened to the duke call his men. The ladder dropped, and the duke and his party descended. A splash followed, the result of Toothless's concoction. French curses sounded as they attempted to recover the fledgling swimmer.

Chapter 14

"**S**o what do you think of my life's story?" Shalyn inquired tentatively.

Yet Seanessy could not at first reply for the sudden roar of laughter. For a long while they simply could not stop laughing. Seanessy actually leaned over with the weight of his mirth.

"Didn't I tell you it was ripe?" Kyler slapped Butcher's back. "And I swear it gets better every time he tells it!"

"Lord." Butcher laughed. "I was biting my lip so hard it bled. I haven't heard so much bull since the last Irish wake!"

Shalyn sighed as they laughed, rolled her eyes, and drummed her fingers on the tabletop, waiting for their laughter to subside. "Oh, please. Really! What do you think?"

"I'm sorry, Shalyn," Seanessy finally managed to swallow the better part of his laughter after some effort, at least long enough to answer her question. "What do I think of your life story as told by that bag of foul air? Well! I think it is remarkable. Simply remarkable! What a dazzling performance the snake gave tonight. Imagine how surprised I was to hear him cast himself as the virtuous, at last much misunderstood, hero."

"That part was simply chilling," Butcher cried, wiping at his eyes, his whole body shaking with his mirth.

"Aye!" Seanessy continued with as much drama, "I loved how our slithering hero saved your poor father, befriending the poor Brit in the enemy camp, only to—how tragic!—watch him succumb to—what was it? Dysentery?"

Butcher wiped his eyes, his chest still bouncing like a child's ball. "The sultan! That was the best part."

"That was fantastic." Seanessy's eyes were alive with amusement as he said, "How our fair and innocent maid valiantly fought the dark-skinned heathen's greedy hands until at last he had to tie you up for his repeated rapings. I was so bloody relieved to hear that our slovenly sultan knew how to belt a few drinks before bedtime. I was quaking with anxiety until he explained that part!"

"You men," Shalyn said crossly. "How would you feel if your life were reduced to the unlikely plot of a penny dreadful novel? I'd even wager Tilly herself has never read one quite so dreadful!"

"Aye," Kyler said. "All we need now is a Fleet Street publisher."

"I pray this story is never repeated!"

"Oh, I forgot," Butcher said to her, still struggling to quiet his laughter, "you've never been very strong—that lamentable feminine constitution of yours!"

This reference sent the men back with wild hoots of mirth. "But did you not see how much he hates me?" she asked. "The way he stared! It kept lifting the hairs on the back of my neck; I half thought he was going to reach out and strike me." With feeling she asked, "What have I done to him?"

Butcher wiped his eyes and finally stilled his

bouncing chest, and only with the reminder of the man's violence, a violence directed at the lass. "Aye. I can only reason you would be dead but, but—"

"He wants something from you, Shalyn," Seanessy said. "And I don't think it's that precious body of yours. It's just like Richards said—I can see it now. The man is as queer as a sweet-smelling water closet."

"What does that mean?"

Kyler swallowed his port and said, "He, ah, doesn't care for women, lass."

"Yes?"

"His, ah, amorous preference is for men."

More confused, she shifted restlessly. The pink silk gown shimmered as it settled. "What does that mean?"

"Shalyn," Kyler said gently, "*he's* the villainous sultan. Only his problem wasn't drunkenness."

"Please," Seanessy begged, "don't put the pictures in my mind."

"He was the one who ... who ..."

The men watched enlightenment dawn on the lovely face, enlightenment accompanied with relief. Relief that she didn't remember these horrid scenes. Or very much of them. This sweet and heady relief passed quickly to anger. Anger at Seanessy as she demanded, "Well, if he is that villain, then why didn't you shoot him?"

"He wanted to!" Butcher came to Seanessy's defense. "Show the lass your fingers, Sean."

Seanessy held up his hands, and she saw the tremble of his trigger fingers. "I wanted to, Shalyn. How I wanted to." He approached the place where she sat and leaned over, his hand picking the virgin star from her neck. "I can't shoot him yet. Not until we find the treasure."

"What treasure?"

"The one this virgin star belongs to. Don't be daft, Shalyn mine. Why do you think he wants you so badly?"

After a thoughtful pause: "Not my winning charm?"

Seanessy shook his head.

"Not my extraordinary grace?"

He shook his head again.

"Not my sparkling wit?"

"Afraid not. He wants you because you know where the treasure is."

"I do?"

"Well, you did."

"You see," Butcher thought to explain, "that slaver we sunk was headed here to the Isle of Blue Caverns. One of its men told us how the duke is digging up half the island looking for this treasure. Every bloody island in the world has a rumor of treasure, and at first we thought it was just a stupid reflection of the duke's ridiculous character—"

"Until we saw the whole windward side of the island devastated," Seanessy said. "Dug up and torn asunder. Then Kyler explained the more preposterous elements of the duke's story. It seems the man needs a little financial help with his plans for domination of the region, the opium and tea markets, the whole thing."

"You see, lass," Butcher explained, "it seems one of the reasons he bought this island in the first place was because of this rumor of treasure. Only he didn't know where the devil it was. Until he was approached by an Englishman, a surgeon, a man named Sinclair—"

"My father! The duke said his name was Henry Slakes, and I knew that wasn't true. It was Charles . . . Charles Sinclair!"

"Aye, and by your very own Ti Yao."

"Ti Yao? But how do you know that?"

"The rumor says it was some kind of Oriental monk. We figured it had to be Ti Yao. Anyway, they found the treasure—we know that from the pretty piece hanging on your neck. They must have found it. But apparently they needed help getting it out and off the island. The operation probably couldn't have been done without the duke's permission and aid. So they no doubt approached the duke. They probably asked for title to the island in exchange for the map telling the duke where it was—that way it would ensure their claim. They probably offered the duke a fifty-fifty split."

"Of course," Kyler said with plain masculine disgust, "that wasn't good enough for our dear duke."

"Lass, he probably tortured them to get the information."

"And they ... they, oh my—"

"Aye, they died without telling," Seanessy finished. "So our dear friend the duke backtracks over their lives, hoping to discover something that will lead to the map. And he finds a young girl who wears a curious mark on her breast. He assumed you knew where it was. You probably didn't know what he was going on about. You didn't even remember getting the mark—"

"But I do remember now," she told him. "I remembered when I saw your pipe lying on the floor. I remembered my father did come back one night. He was tall and drunk and he smelled bad! He said soon he would take me back to England and put me in a proper school for girls. The idea horrified me—I never wanted to leave Ti Yao and Gschu. We were going to be rich, he kept saying. I was so afraid he would take me away. And that night, that night he held me down and filled me with ... with opium, and I screamed for Ti Yao but then—"

"He put the mark on you, so if something went wrong you'd have the map," Butcher said. "And, Lord, did something go wrong."

"And so this mark tells where the treasure is!"

"There it is," Kyler finished. "The duke knew it. He probably thought you did too. He had to marry you in case you ever found the treasure before he did. That way it would still belong to him. You should have heard him pondering your memory loss as we sailed to his island. She truly doesn't remember me? he'd ask, and you actually saw this bump on her head? So it is true; she doesn't remember? He was going mad trying to figure out if it was a trick or not, if it could possibly be true."

"But since I don't remember—and I don't—why does he still want me?"

"In case you ever do," Kyler said. "Because he still doesn't have a clue as to where the treasure is hidden. He can't take any chances. Of course. Right now the duke is no doubt planning his attack, as soon as he gets his greedy hands on you, he'll be coming after us."

"That man will never touch her!" Sean predicted.

Shalyn's thoughts spun over this fantastic tale; she wondered if it could possibly be true. "I just wish I could remember!"

"First things first," Seanessy said. He went to his trunk and removed a large piece of parchment and one of the new French pencils. These were set before Kyler. "Draw it. We have about an hour before the men go off on their mission of mischief. A hundred pounds to the man who figures it out."

Shalyn lowered her strap just enough. Kyler carefully copied the mark. A diamond shape, a point, and a face. What could it mean? The island certainly wasn't shaped like a diamond and what could the face possibly mean?

Shaking his head, Kyler rose with Butcher. They left the room to present the case to the men. The door shut behind them. Shalyn's thoughts still spun over the wild tale of her life. She rubbed her forehead, distressed, desperate to remember. "I can't remember, Seanessy! I don't remember any of it!"

"I think I can help you."

She studied Seanessy's stare. A no-good stare. She slowly shook her head, familiar with that look of malice. A rising tide of panic pushed her to her feet. "I don't care about the treasure, you know." She shook her head adamantly. "I don't really care to remember what he did to me. Let's just shoot him and be done with it!"

He made no response.

"Seanessy, you are scaring me now . . ."

He reached behind him and picked up a coiled rope.

Her amber eyes widened like saucers. "Oh no! Oh no! You wouldn't! I know you wouldn't!"

Yet he stepped to her. She backed against the wall. A violent shudder went through her as she stared at the ropes in his hand. Her hands went clammy, her face went pale . . .

Outside Edward and Toothless had left to stuff the cannons with rocks—just in case a war broke out. Butcher and Kyler stood on crates beneath the light of a lantern, holding up the picture of Shalyn's mark. Seanessy's men always rose to the occasion of a hundred-pound note. They stared. Feet shuffled. Hardened weathered faces twisted with concentration as they stared.

"All right," Kyler said. "It's a treasure map. Think of this island we just sailed around. Two parts: the diamond and the face. Start with the diamond. What say you?"

"Could be the gems," Hamilton said. "In the treasure."

" 'Tisn't the shape of this island."

Cherry Joe called out, "Nay. This island is shaped like my wife's legs: fat end down."

The men laughed but Slops settled it. "It ain't the island, and it ain't your wife's legs. So what is it?"

No one had any idea.

"All right, let's look at the face. What does that remind you of?"

"My wife again!"

Kyler sighed, rolled his eyes. "Will you get off your wife!"

"That's the point—it's been a long time since I got on her."

"It looks like a monkey's face, don't it?"

"Like I said, my wife's—"

"Oh, shut up about your wife!"

They explored another tack. "Monkey see, monkey do—"

"There's a big help," Butcher groaned.

"Well, face, saving face," Prescott said.

"Face on cards," Knolls said.

"Poker face," Slops said, illustrating his point.

"Hey! The diamond is a suit."

"Aye, and its opposite face is a heart!"

"The heart-shaped rock! By the warehouse!" Knolls grinned. "The treasure is inside the heart-shaped rock."

Butcher laughed and as if he were an auctioneer announcing a winning bid said, "Sold to the man standing there!" A cheer went up and Knolls was lifted and thrown into the air like so much baggage. "Let's blow this place to hell and then we see if we can't get our greedy paws on the lass's treasure for her."

The men rushed to the lifeboats.

* * *

Quiet descended over the ship, interrupted only by the gentle lick of ocean on the ship's sides, Oly's occasional forlorn howl at being left alone on board, and the quickened pace of Seanessy's and Shalyn's breathing.

"Seanessy, Seanessy!"

"What?"

"I don't think it's working!"

He had tied her hands to the bedpost. He struggled up from the sweet onslaught of sensations, all of them: the rich gold curls spilling over the bedclothes, the hot sultriness in the amber eyes, the lingering taste of the sweet port in her mouth, and the heated sound of her love cries as his hands felt the swell of her breasts, soaking her softness through his fingertips and sending the sensation like a hot current through every fiber of his being. With effort he managed to register her complaint. "You don't remember anything?"

"Seanessy." His name sounded with a small delicious pant. "I can't even remember my name like this!"

"Shalyn," he told her in a husky whisper before he molded his mouth to hers. She melted helplessly beneath this kiss as she felt the caress of his spanned fingers slip along her back and lower still until they were stopped where her gown gathered loosely at her waist. He broke the kiss, only to let his lips play elsewhere along her flushed and soft form as his hands reached around the shimmering pink silk, pushing up the skirt, his fingers like his lips teasing, their movements orchestrated by her pleasure cries.

It suddenly occurred to him, "Do you think I should untie you?"

"Oh, please!" Then she gasped, feeling his fingers seek and stroke the feminine apex between her thighs. She forgot the directive as hot warmth rushed to greet him, and his lips began a molten exploration of the rest of her. The remainder of their conversation was reduced to small gasps and feverish love cries. She was swimming on the shimmering sea of warm bright colors, flushed breathless, seized with violent waves of pleasure, returning to feel him finally, mercifully join her, her consciousness filling with hot waves of pleasure.

"Oh, Lord, you are so tight, so hot . . ." He kissed her, trying to hold back for a moment longer—

"Seanessy! Someone is coming!"

"Again?" This thrilled him. He kissed her mouth, chuckling even as he was panting, "I love watching you—the surprised, almost startled look on your face . . . Like now! Oh, Shalyn . . . Oh, Lord, I don't know if I can wait—"

He felt her small body tense beneath him and she started screaming. He stared at her with amazement. The power of what seized her sent his pulse skyrocketing and that was all it took. The force of his release sent him for a moment into blackness. Only to return to see she was still screaming his name. "Good Lord, Shalyn—"

He abruptly smelled the tobacco smoke.

The duke was laughing. The men accompanying the duke chuckled too. The duke's amusement quieted a bit as he said, "An astounding performance, Captain." He smiled, his arms folded casually across his chest, the cigar dangling from well-shaped fingernails. "This surpasses my wildest hopes. I admit the ropes are a surprise. I mean considering what I put her through . . ."

Seanessy stiffened, froze. He felt the cold metal of the barrel digging into his back. The Duke de la Armanac and maybe four men. So terribly, dangerously close. His pistole lay somewhere on the floor. He didn't even have his pants on.

And Shalyn was tied to the bedpost.

He supposed if he had to die and he could see that he did, he couldn't have dreamed of a better last hour. "At least, Your Grace, I can get the job done. If you must know, I was trying to spur her memory."

"And with such flair," the duke said and chuckled again. "But come now, Captain, a man of your worldly experience would not fault a man for what he is, what he cannot change. Though I have tried, and considering Isabel's beauty and ignoring as best one can her unusual personality, I eventually came to accept it."

"This is all so fascinating," Seanessy said, "but would you mind ordering your rascal's barrel from my back?"

"Seanessy." Shalyn emerged from the heady rush of sudden and violent ideas, struggling beneath his weight, her heart pounding, urgency filling her. "You won't believe this—"

"Nonsense, darling." He watched her hands working the loosely tied ropes, his body hopefully concealing the effort. "I'll believe anything at this point."

"It did work!" she announced. "I remember!"

Outside in a small dinghy some fifty feet off the bow Toothless and Edward saw the duke's boat moored alongside the ship. Toothless swore. Edward tried to figure it out. "So who's left on board, do you think?"

"No one but the captain and the lass. Everyone else would be off blowin' up the island." Toothless's agile mind quickly figured out the rest, and his whole body began shaking with his mirth. Before they left on this mission, Butcher had said Seanessy was in there trying to help Shalyn "remember." "Five pounds says the bastard caught them doin' what they've been doin' since they started doin' it."

"Now that's a pretty picture! The captain caught with his pants down." Edward chuckled too, until an unpleasant idea occurred to him. "Hey!" he wondered, "what about Oly? You don't think they shot the big lug?"

"Ah, why should they?" Toothless dismissed this. "An idiot could take that dog out with a small side of ham. So," he said, his laughter quieted by the thought, "how are we going to do this?"

"Our guns would wake 'em up. That's useless. Looks like we'll have to start picking 'em off one by one, the old-fashioned way."

Toothless sighed as Edward broke the oar over his knee, snapping it in two before swinging it swiftly through the air. "I hate being a hero," he said. "I'm too darn old. I really am."

"Blazes, Toothless, you're such a coward. Ah, well, we can shoot once we're inside."

The whole nightmare had rushed through Shalyn's mind in violence. She remembered the French agents appearing in the village, looking for her, men of the duke's employ. They told her she was the heiress to a huge fortune, thanks to her father and Ti Yao, a treasure they had found and died for on the Isle of Blue Caverns. They would take her there where she would collect her fortune before they returned her to England. They only wanted a finder's fee, they said, which she quickly agreed to give them. The idea of being a wealthy women of independent means appealed to her free spirit immensely; she could hardly believe this good fortune.

The nightmare started when she reached the island and was brought to the duke, a nightmare she remembered in startling clarity, day after day, month after month, year after year: every moment spent trying to escape, trying to convince him she did not know where the blasted treasure was, that he could kill a thousand people and she still would not know where the treasure was.

She remembered the night she had escaped. She had worn only a chemise, for the pretense of being in the throng of a night terror—in case she was caught. And she was. She remembered clutching the ruby star and Seanessy's address tight as the lead pipe flew down on her head—then nothing.

She would not let this nightmare end with their death. At least not until she killed the duke—and she would kill him, she swore, if it was the last thing she ever did.

As Shalyn freed her hands Seanessy said, "I'm so glad for you, Shalyn!"

"If you remember," the duke said, "then you remember the years of hell you put me through, all the way up to the last wild goose chase to London looking for the elusive Mary Brackton, your aunt. She's dead, you know. Though I did manage to get a dozen of those picture books. You convinced me the secret to break the symbols was in one of her picture books, but that I might need you to get them. Huh! That performance was so convincing! I believed you had finally broken after all those years. I should have known, though—"

Shalyn was not thinking of this. She was remembering, remembering. "You kept killing people in front of me, burying them in the sand for the tides to drown, and, dear Lord, all my nightmares of skulls—"

"You make it sound so dramatic." The duke drew on his cigar, releasing his breath in a cloud of smoke. He dismissed it, for: "They all had malaria—they would have died anyway."

Shalyn absorbed this with a pained cry. "Malaria? They all had malaria?!" Her mind tore swiftly over all the dying people he had made her watch, and all the ghastly things he had made her submit to in order to avoid watching more people die. Gschu herself had died of malaria; it was the leading cause of death in the China Seas, and the island had had many cases of the dreaded disease—

"Ti Yao?" she asked in a pained whisper. "Did you kill him?"

"Ti Yao! That man! You know he killed ten of my men before we managed to subdue him? I could hardly believe the carnage—"

She cried out, "The tides? Did he die in the tides too?"

"Well!" The duke looked cross. "It was not my fault your father would not save him—your father was so greedy! Anyway ..." He paused, rolling his eyes and waving his cigar in dismissal. "Ti Yao died before he drowned. It was as if he had willed himself dead. And it was so odd watching; I always wondered how he managed the trick. Not that I wanted him to die. I did not! At the time I was considering saving him. God knows, I could have used a man like that."

"Get off me, Seanessy," she whispered through gritted teeth. "I am going to kill him!"

"He was so stubborn," the duke said angrily, "like you Isabel. I couldn't believe you wouldn't save them—"

"I couldn't," she shouted at him, and not for the first time she told him, "I never knew where that cursed treasure was! I still don't know!"

"Ah, yes," the duke said, still bemused by the irony, the impossibility of it. "You know, when Monsieur Kyler told me about this head injury business I was convinced it was just another one of your endless intrigues. I kept turning it over in my mind, trying to figure out what you were planning. Until it finally occurred to me that it really happened; that you really did lose your memory. Extraordinary, I thought! I was more than a little upset at the prospect of having to keep you on the island for God knows how long until this elusive memory of yours returned—"

"How many times do I have to tell you I don't know where the treasure is!"

"Fortunately it no longer matters, my dear. Thanks to your men, Captain, your visit has been most worthwhile after all. We were sitting out in the dark water listening. I was just hoping to get Isabel back to the island before I blew this ship sky-high when I heard them figure out what that vulgar desecration your father gave you actually meant . . ."

As he spoke, Shalyn whispered again through gritted teeth, "Will you please get off me!"

"No!" Seanessy said, his own jaw not moving. "They'll kill *you*!"

"A humiliating experience," the duke continued, his voice getting cross as he thought of it. "I listened to your cretins figure out in minutes what I've spent years trying to grasp—" He became agitated thinking about it. "Of course my men will be following them on land to the rock. I might even let your men retrieve the treasure before opening fire—"

A man called in French from outside on the deck, interrupting the duke. Shalyn translated the rapid words in her mind. The man said they were finished laying the explosives.

She exchanged an alarmed glance with Seanessy. Seanessy looked toward the door. Where the devil were Edward and Toothless? If anyone ever needed a rescue—

"Ah, we are through," the duke said. "Take them

out and tie them to the mainmast. You first, Captain." He motioned to Seanessy. "You know the rules. Two pistoles trained on Isabel the entire time. Now get up."

With fear pounding through him, Seanessy slowly stood up. Three guards with pistoles. Alarmed, he turned to Shalyn. She was so defiant, so fearless! She would do something and get killed. Oh, Lord, if she died . . .

"Shalyn," he said, forcing himself to watch. She pretended to look afraid but Seanessy knew better. "Shalyn, don't do anything! For God's sake, girl, if you do . . . if you do anything, I'll kill you myself!"

"Keep your hands on your head, Captain."

Seanessy slowly put his hands behind his head.

Shalyn's lovely features appeared torn with anxiety but this was in fact a pretense. While her heart and pulse raced and her breathing came quick and fast, she knew well how to overcome fear to act. And act she would, just as soon as someone drew close enough. With any luck she could use them as a body shield against the gunfire. It would be their only chance.

"You, Robert." The duke was motioning to a guard. "Untie Isabel. And you, Christian, keep your weapon on her."

Seanessy turned slightly to see his pistoles on the floor. He looked at them with more longing than he had ever looked at a woman, Shalyn excepted of course.

Holding the rope in both hands, Shalyn continued to look scared as Robert leaned over her. The tousled mass of gold hair spilled over the bedclothes; her nudity was only partially covered by the bedsheet.

He wiped his brow on his sleeve, trying to keep his mind on the task as he reached to untie the ropes.

Robert leaned close. Shalyn waited until she

caught the scent of rum on his breath and then moved with such speed and assurance, she might have rehearsed it a hundred times. Her hands flew up as she called out, "Now, Seanessy!" She twisted the rope around Robert's neck and sent her knee hard into his groin. A shocked howl of pain sounded. The stunned guards fired. Too late, for Robert had collapsed on top of her and took the bullets in the dead center of his back.

In the same instant Seanessy had leaped aside, swung back around with clenched fists, and knocked his guard to the floor. He kicked the pistole from the remaining guard. That man leaped back with a gasp of fear.

"No! No!" the duke cried as he crouched to retrieve the pistole himself. The duke's hand grasped the cold metal, but ever quick, Seanessy slammed his bare foot into the hand. A sickening crunch of bone sounded, then the duke's unnatural cry of pain before Seanessy threw him against the wall with enough force to knock the breath from him.

An unexpected minute of deadly calm fell over the quarters as the stunned guards looked frantically around the room, uncertain of their options. They didn't have any. Retrieving one of his pistoles, Seanessy swung the long-barreled weapon in a fast circle like a circus trick, stopping it to aim. "Out of here!" The men rushed out of the room, grateful for the captain's generosity.

Relief swept over him that he and Shalyn were both still alive—and together.

Shalyn pushed the dead man off her and struggled a moment to collect the tumult of her senses. Then she stood up, gathering the torn remnants of her gown around her neck, and surveyed the empty room with dismay. It housed only the three of them now. "Well, that wasn't too difficult," she said, regaining her composure. Then: "Seanessy, show those others outside that you hold the duke hostage and force them to remove the dynamite."

"Good idea," he managed. "Just let me catch my breath." His condition had nothing to do with any exertion and everything to do with surviving the terrible fear of losing her. That had been too bloody close . . .

A thunderous explosion sounded in the distance, then another and another. Oly howled and then barked outside.

Alarm mixed with pain as the duke gasped, "What was that?"

"The opium warehouse blown sky-high," Seanessy said, his pistole trained on the Duke de la Armanac. Oly, after a moment of self-restraint, began barking wildly. "And that must be Edward and Toothless coming to rescue us now." He supposed he should get dressed in case they needed help getting rid of the dynamite.

He just needed a moment more to recover.

Panting with his pain, the duke couldn't, wouldn't believe this. "No, no! Not my opium . . . Do you have any idea what you've done?" Each breath brought an unbearable agony, and he tightly clasped his crushed hand as he considered his much changed circumstances. "The stockpile was worth over five million pounds! My entire fortune! Why, dear God, why?"

"Why? Well," Seanessy said, finding his breeches, "Wilson promised to help repeal the hateful English law that bars Catholics from serving in Parliament for the favor, you see. So my Irish countrymen can get a seat." He grinned thinking about it. "Never mind the four years of tariff-free shipping thrown in the bargain."

"That pretty pile of money means nothing to you, does it, Seanessy?" Shalyn tossed her hair over her shoulder as she hurriedly pulled on her own pair of breeches, afraid Edward and Toothless might not find the dynamite in time to save the ship.

"Practically nothing," Seanessy said as he cinched his belt with one hand, the other holding his pistole.

"My God, five million pounds." The duke could not get past this. "Five million pounds . . ."

For a moment Shalyn wondered if the duke might cry like a child for his loss. She dipped a cloth in the water bin and as if it were no more than a splash of wine, she began washing the blood from her arm.

Sudden amusement glowed in Seanessy's eyes as he watched. That was so like her! She could finish off a roomful of nefarious villains and then calmly set about repairing her appearance. Here was a young woman like no other.

He still stared, thinking of the multitudes of other women he knew. Recently, he had heard, it had become the height of fashion among ladies to draw the stays of their corsets mercilessly tight. This allowed them to faint at whim or will. Society viewed this fainting as an admirable expression of feminine delicacy and constitution. The contrast between Shalyn and most other women was startling and powerfully felt: Shalyn's utter fearlessness and bravery set alongside some pale, simpering woman falling into a dead faint at the sight of a shirtless man or upon hearing an off-color remark.

"Shalyn, I love you . . ."

The words brought her gaze to him. All thoughts of the impending explosion disappeared as she felt her heart lift, her breath catch. The way he stared at her! With such tenderness and affection and ardor! She tried to imagine what thoughts raced through his mind as he stood there staring at her but she couldn't. "Seanessy." She said his name in a whisper of emotion.

The duke was trying to sit up. Anger trembled through him as he watched the captain and Isabel staring at each other like lovestruck adolescents. He should have killed her long ago! She was so seditious, wild, diabolical—

He stopped, spotting the pistole a scant pace from his side. He slowly reached for it.

Shots sounded from outside. "Finally!" Seanessy said, pleased. A series of seven shots fired before Edward rushed in through the doors with a pistole in each hand.

"So much for my rescue," he said, sizing up the scene. "We got them all outside, but one of the bastards set the ship to blow. We can't find the bloody fuse. Quick. Over the side—"

The duke lunged for the pistole in an agonizing movement and swung it around to aim at the girl who had frustrated his greatest plans. Edward fired his last shot in the dead center of the duke's chest.

Shalyn turned with a startled gasp to see her dead husband. "Edward! How could you! After all he had done to me, I had so wanted to get even myself—"

"There's no time." Edward realized they didn't understand. "Quick. She could go any second!"

The words resounded in the smoke-filled room. Seanessy swore as he lunged for Shalyn. His arms snaked around her waist. He swung her up in the air and over his shoulder like so much extra baggage before racing through the door, just in time to see Edward and Toothless diving over the side to safety.

Seanessy set Shalyn on the rail and said the single imperative: "Jump!"

Shalyn took one look back as if to see where the fuse and the dynamite were hidden. All she saw was: "Oly! Seanessy! Oly!"

Seanessy took one look at his doomed pet tied to the rail but instead saw the foot-long fuse rushing to a wooden water barrel some ten paces away. "No," she cried, seeing the same. "We have to save him—"

She started to swing back to rescue the dog.

Seanessy swept her up in his arms and swore, "You audacious, impetuous termagant—" and before he had finished he wisely threw her over the side into the water.

She came up in the cool ocean water, gasping for breath. Edward shouted at her to start swimming away. She dove under and swam with all her strength. She surfaced at Edward and Toothless's side a good twenty-five paces away, and turned to the ship.

The sight would live in their minds forever. Seanessy stood at the rail holding a one-hundred-and-fifty-pound dog. With a great heave, he lifted the frantic dog over the side before he jumped up on the rail and dove. Dove against a backdrop of red, gold, and orange explosions shooting twenty paces into the night sky.

"Duck under, lass!" Toothless cried.

She ducked under the water as the magnificent ship exploded, showering the darkened water with small pieces of timber. Shalyn held her breath as long as she could and more, until her lungs were bursting with a thirst for air. She popped up on the surface, took a huge gulp of air, and ducked back under.

Something struck the water just above her. 'Twas a piece of the proud oceangoing vessel Seanessy loved. She shut her eyes against the sting of salt water before surfacing again. She drew a huge gulp of air, her arms moving in smooth wide circles as she saw the worst was over. Edward and Toothless tread the water too, staring off at the ship. The mainmast had cracked, felled like a ancient oak on its side; the sails had burst into flames. She swung toward a dog's yelps and spotted Oly swimming toward them, terrified but thankfully not hurt.

"Ye be all right, lass?" Toothless called over.

"Aye, but—"

Shouts sounded from two lifeboats pulling up fast on the burning ship. Some of the crew were returning from the successful conclusion of their expedition. "There's the boys now." Edward pointed.

"Well, look at that," Toothless said, referring to the ship.

"Looks like it hit the mainmast and the carpenter's room, is all," Edward said. "If we can get the fire out quick enough. Come on."

Toothless socked the water with his fist. He was too damn old for adventures. "Lord, will this night never end!"

"But, but—" Frantically Shalyn searched the dark water, turning in a circle to see nothing but the smooth surface of the bay. The distant lanterns from the village cast long ribbons of light over the water. She looked across to see the rooftops of the stucco houses, the jutting towers of the castle, and the blackened jungle beyond. "Seanessy!" She shouted his name. "Seanessy!"

Strong hands slipped over her bare feet beneath the water, sliding up her legs even as he drew her against his huge body. Instantly her arms circled his neck as he gasped for breath, holding her so tight he was afraid he might hurt her, and still it was not enough.

"Seanessy! Seanessy, you're all right! I was so afraid—"

He drew back a bit to see her face. One strong hand clasped the wet thickness of her hair at the base of her neck, his other hand carefully tread water as he studied her face cast in the golden light of the nearby fire. A boyish grin changed the features of his face as he noticed, "So we're not totally fearless after all."

"Nay." She shook her head. "For it would have been my life too, Seanessy."

Then she clung tightly to his neck as he tread water for both of them. Her long hair floated in a semicircle around them and he twirled her happily in the dark water. "Shalyn, Shalyn." He stopped to stare down at her wet upturned face. "I love you. Kiss me, Shalyn. Kiss me now in celebration of the long rest of our lives ..."

As the men worked furiously to douse the nearby fire, as its flames sizzled and died and smoke rose, as the huge yelping dog swam in excited circles around them, she kissed him. Beneath a thousand stars and in the middle of the smooth dark waters of the ocean, she touched her lips to his. The kiss changed as he drew her against him, deepening as he gently molded his mouth to hers with all the stirring desire of a first kiss and the same hungry passion as if it were their last. A sweet prelude to the long rest of their lives indeed ...

Epilogue

Shalyn was not going to be poor.

That much was soon obvious.

During the rush of the first hours after the duke's death, his faithful army put up a spirited defense that followed the *Wind Muse* along the island's coast until she reached the heart-shaped rock. For two days the *Wind Muse* returned fire whenever any of the duke's men ventured toward them by boat.

On the third day a white flag waved. The captain of the army finally realized that with their employer's death, and no hopes of getting the treasure out when it was protected by a seven-hundred-ton, well-armed sailing ship, they would need help getting off the island; they had only one ship there. They accepted Seanessy's conditions for peace, especially as he agreed to arrange for passage back to France, just after the slave population was brought back to Madagascar. Seanessy immediately dispatched the duke's ship to Malacca with the order for all of his ships to sail at once to the island.

With Seanessy, Shalyn had walked through the stone castle only once, remembering the long days and lonely nights when she was sustained only by the dream of escaping.

"I didn't know how to do it," she told Seanessy,

sitting contentedly on the white sand beach, between his bent knees in the cradle of his arms. She stared into the dark star-filled night, remembering. "Even though I spent nearly every waking hour dreaming up farfetched and detailed plans to escape, I never knew how to do it until—"

"Until Ram and Joy arrived."

"They were so kind," she said. "They knew something was wrong, terribly wrong. Of course I couldn't appeal for their help. He and his men stood no chance against the army. I did not want them hurt; I was so afraid the duke would. I tried to be brave, to maintain the duke's pretense of, if not a loving relationship, a congenial one. Yet as you guessed, she knew. Lady Barrington knew.

"That morning they were leaving; I took my daily walk on the beach. Lord Barrington waited for me in secret. He begged me to tell him what was so amiss. He didn't know what was wrong, but he was certain there was something. 'Because my wife told me,' he said. Lady Barrington had told him I hated my husband, that I was like a trapped animal, that he was threatening me somehow. I could hardly speak, the need to relate the nightmarish world I lived in and be saved was overwhelming, yet the consequences more so. I told him I was well and fine, that his sweet wife must be mistaken. He paused for a long moment before saying, 'I know what you are thinking. You're thinking that there is no man alive who could save you from the duke. Perhaps you are right. There is no man that I know who could do the job. On this island.' Then he grabbed my arms, imploring me, 'So you must get off this island, Isabel! He will be going to London soon. Somehow you must make him take you to London with him. And once there, go directly to Nine King's Highway. Ask for . . . Seanessy.' " She smiled, remembering, "He smiled so sweetly and his last words were, 'If anyone can save you it will be Seanessy.' "

"Huh!" Seanessy said. "He did this to me on purpose. He wanted to get even with me for having arranged his marriage with Joy. He knew how much trouble you'd be. He knew it. I knew it too, the moment I saw you. I thought, Now here's a pretty package of trouble—"

He felt the gentle nudge of Shalyn's elbow against his chest, and she warned, "Don't pretend to regret it."

"Regret it? Did I say I regret it?" He chuckled lightly as he turned her lovely face around and gently kissed her lips. "When we meet my dear brother, you will see me drop to my knees and kiss his booted feet. Shalyn . . . I love you . . ."

"Yes." She turned to face him, her arms sliding around his neck. "Love me, Seanessy. Now." She kissed his lips and closed her eyes as she whispered, "On a starlit beach . . ."

Kyler and Hamilton began going through the duke's papers and soon managed to piece together all of Shalyn's various inheritances. The lass had inherited a London townhouse from her grandfather, Dr. Brackton, the famous surgeon. Her parents had left her the country estate she remembered from childhood. The duke had also discovered her dear Aunt Mary had left her a Venice townhouse. Naturally, as the duke's widow and a duchess to boot, she now owned his country estate in France, recently reinstated to his name, as well as a Parisian apartment. She owned the title to the Isle of Blue Caverns.

"You're even richer than Seanessy," Kyler summed up their findings. "And we haven't even gotten the treasure out yet."

Which turned out to be far more difficult.

The treasure was in an underwater cave in the heart shaped rock. The crew's best divers, Cherry Joe and Edward, repeatedly reached the underwater cave only to have to reemerge before they found the treasure. After a number of days spent watching these dives, and with practically everyone attempting it as well, Cherry Joe popped up and announced:

"I felt it! It's there, Shalyn!"

A roar went up from the men. She threw her arms around Seanessy, who swung her in happy circles. Encouraged, Edward dove again.

After another day it became clear that they'd have to wait for a low tide to secure a rope around the massive trunk. Seanessy's ships began arriving and the happy but arduous task of repatriating the slave population began. Most of the Frenchmen and all of the slaves had left the island when the day for retrieving the treasure finally arrived.

The sea appeared as a smooth sheet of glass, the sky a clear arc of blue overhead, and at least four more feet of the rock jutted above the water. Excitement fueled everyone's expectations as they waited. By midmorning Edward and Cherry Joe got the ropes around it and by the afternoon the massive trunk was pulled onto the deck. The strongest men went after the rusted hinges with axes and crowbars. Even though Ti Yao must have opened the chest years ago to retrieve the virgin star, it had rusted badly. Slops managed to loosen it just enough.

"Wait," Seanessy said. "I want Shalyn to open it."

She closed her eyes. Trembling hands went to the rough edges of the trunk. She lifted it up. A hushed silence descended on all the men watching. Oly howled. She opened her eyes.

The sunlight touched and blazed over the chest full to bursting with gold, rubies, emeralds, jade—a fortune like no other. After Seanessy and Toothless managed to rouse the lass from her dead faint—"So the girl can faint!" Seanessy grinned—she generously began distributing nearly half the treasure to all the men, the largest shares going to Edward, Cherry Joe, Knolls, and Toothless.

The day arrived when the *Wind Muse* set sail for England. By this point, the mainmast and the carpenter's room were fully repaired. Escorted by three of Seanessy's best ships, the *Wind Muse* sailed beneath a strong westerly wind that would soon bring the monsoons to the China Seas. Shalyn sat on the ship's rail, secured by Seanessy's arms, as they watched the Isle of Blue Caverns disappear into the oblivion that was the horizon, abandoned now to the winds, rains, and unceasing push and pull of the tides.

Seanessy managed to turn his gaze from the lovely view presented to him: she wore a fetching cotton day dress, with a print of tiny green and yellow flowers, the green bodice barely reaching to cover the mark. A matching green ribbon tied her hair back. He searched the deck until he found Butcher. "Are all the ropes secure, Butcher?"

"Aye, aye, Captain," Butcher called back. "Might be one or two loose ends here and there but nothing that could sink the ship."

Only one question remained. Seanessy's gaze returned to hers. "Shalyn," he said as his lips lightly grazed her neck and he remembered the passion and wonder of their lovemaking on the beach beneath a lovely dawn's light. "Marry me, Shalyn."

Her fingers stopped toying with his hair at the nape of his neck. She appeared to think about it. "I don't know," she said. "I've been married once. I did not care for it at all!"

"Yet you've never been married to me. I promise to make you very happy."

"You already make me happy. I hardly see that as an inducement to the altar."

"You need an inducement to the altar?!"

Her eyes sparkled beneath the sunlight. She nodded.

Why did women marry anyway? he wondered. "Well, I am very rich."

"So am I. Why, Seanessy I'd wager that I'm wealthier than you are."

"Probably true." He conceded the point, reluctantly. "Well, get rid of your fortune then. That will give the necessary motivation to marry me."

"How would I get rid of it?"

"You could . . . why, yes!" Seanessy realized. "You can give it to Butcher."

"I would not be so cruel! Why, 'twould take him years to disseminate the bulk of it. Besides," she told him, "I rather like being rich."

"Oh, aye, everyone likes the comforts." In frustration he said, "Well, there must be some reason to marry me!"

She pretended to think about it. "I can't think of any."

He thought again. "I've got it. What about dear Tilly? All the good woman's sensibilities? She would be so pleased!"

She laughed. "I'm quite certain Tilly will be even more pleased to serve a widowed duchess."

"I suppose you are right. She does love the bluebloods. Well, I just feel we ought to marry, I mean, being so madly in love and all. God, I can't keep my hands off you—"

"I know, I know! And I love that. You know how much."

He most certainly did. "That's why I always imagined we would just get a little cottage at the seashore with a white picket fence and a pretty garden and live forevermore in perfectly droll domestic bliss—"

"That's not for you, Seanessy." She laughed at his foolishness. "I know you. You wouldn't be happy. And I don't think I would be either. You see, Seanessy I've always wanted to be a woman of independent fortune, free to do what I please, when I please. Just like you. And I am! Being a widow is just the thing too. Society never minds a widow's indiscretions."

This shocked him. His gaze narrowed. "Just what indiscretions are we thinking of?"

"Why, so many wonderful ones! I can be just like you now. A celebrated patroness of the arts and theater. I do love paintings and, why, yes, I would like to start a collection—you did say you've never met a woman with such a fine eye. I also want to travel. Paris, Venice, Rome; I want to see all of them. I want to climb the Swiss mountains, watch a sunset from the very peak of an Egyptian pyramid, journey across the vast wasteland of America. A world traveler and adventurer. We could even finance expeditions to explore . . . Africa—"

"Africa?!"

"Why, last I heard they haven't yet discovered the source of the Nile. Just think of that! We could do it. Perhaps, why, yes! We could go on more treasure hunts. Ti Yao told me of one in a place called Tibet, the highest place in the world, where there are dozens of monasteries and in one of them, far, far away, there is said to be a treasure worth more than the crown jewels, and we could . . ."

As she continued the long list that was to be the rest of their lives, he thought of meeting Egyptian swindlers and American Indians, African savages and Tibetan monks, of paying outrageous sums to finance fantastic expeditions and to pay for all their worthless maps. All this was set alongside the image of domestic tranquility that took the form of a little cottage and its picket fence on the seashore. He suddenly grinned.

He always knew she'd be trouble.

He was so right . . .

Avon Romantic Treasures

*Unforgettable, enthralling love stories,
sparkling with passion and adventure
from Romance's bestselling authors*

AWAKEN MY FIRE by *Jennifer Horsman*
76701-5/$4.50 US/$5.50 Can

ONLY BY YOUR TOUCH by *Stella Cameron*
76606-X/$4.50 US/$5.50 Can

FIRE AT MIDNIGHT by *Barbara Dawson Smith*
76275-7/$4.50 US/$5.50 Can

ONLY WITH YOUR LOVE by *Lisa Kleypas*
76151-3/$4.50 US/$5.50 Can

MY WILD ROSE by *Deborah Camp*
76738-4/$4.50 US/$5.50 Can

MIDNIGHT AND MAGNOLIAS by *Rebecca Paisley*
76566-7/$4.50 US/$5.50 Can

THE MASTER'S BRIDE by *Suzannah Davis*
76821-6/$4.50 US/$5.50 Can

A ROSE AT MIDNIGHT by *Anne Stuart*
76740-6/$4.50 US/$5.50 Can